The Medical Witness

Richard Gordon

THE MEDICAL WITNESS

HEINEMANN : LONDON

William Heinemann Ltd
15 Queen St, Mayfair, London W1X 8BE

LONDON   MELBOURNE   TORONTO
JOHANNESBURG   AUCKLAND

First published 1971
© Gordon Ostlere 1971
434 30238 4

Printed in Great Britain by
Cox and Wyman Limited,
London, Fakenham and Reading

Every man at the end of the rope knew exactly what he had done. There was little or no exception.

A FORMER CHAPLAIN AT
WANDSWORTH PRISON

IT WAS COLD even for that particularly bleak April, the sun rising behind a mist like muslin over the London rooftops. In his bowler hat and his overcoat with the brown fur collar, carrying his bag as usual, Rumbelow made his way across the street from the Tube Station. He often travelled by Underground. He had never learned to drive a car, and though he could have found a taxi he was inclined to be mean, on the excuse that no career lasted for ever and it was prudent to care for the future.

It was still before seven, the other passengers in the lift all men scattering to their work. He had only a few hundred yards to walk. As he expected, a crowd of fifty or so had gathered on the pavement, many of them in black. He supposed they could hardly miss recognizing him. Ignoring their stares, he pressed the bell. The wicket gate opened at once. It was a morning they were expecting visitors.

In an office with a gas-fire roaring throatily in the corner, he uncapped his fountain-pen and with a gesture expressing familiarity signed the visitors' book on a steep desk like a lectern. The warder who had admitted him unlocked another gate in the screen of bars still separating them from the interior of the prison. The courtyard was empty, the men being kept in their cells, though Rumbelow recalled they could make an unholy racket banging on the bars with their spoons.

The sitting-room of the governor's house was invitingly comfortable, a leaping coal fire below a mantelpiece covered with framed photographs of austere-looking women, laughing children and the governor himself in Army uniform. He was scrawny and hollow-cheeked with a straggling yellow moustache, in a blue suit which looked brand-new. Rumbelow was amused to find him dressed in his best for the occasion.

'We renew our acquaintance, Doctor.'

'Yes, that's so, Major.' He offered his case. 'Cigar?'

'No, no, thank you. I don't feel like smoking this morning.'

Rumbelow cut one himself. They were among his few extravagances. Cigarettes made him cough, and a pipe he thought somewhat vulgar.

'I hate these affairs,' said the governor.

'I don't think any of us find them particularly agreeable.'

'Of course not . . . but frankly, I'm beginning to feel them quite unbearable.'

'You don't have to look you know.'

'I don't. Not when the man goes down. I turn to the chief warder and make some remark. I always keep an excuse in mind. I've one here for today.' He tapped his forehead. 'But the drop's only part of it. You see a perfectly fit human being come through the door, and you know in a second or two he'll be as dead as mutton. I shall never get used to that. It's an awesome business. It's like . . . well, like God coming into the room with you.'

He *is* rattled, thought Rumbelow. Probably been bottling it up to tell someone like me, who's in the habit of keeping secrets. 'But you must have seen men killed in the trenches?'

'There wasn't the inevitability about it. We all believed the next bullet wouldn't have our number on. God knows, that's what made the fighting possible at all.'

'You could send your deputy.'

'It's my duty.'

'Or take a stiff drink?'

'No, no, that wouldn't be right.'

Rumbelow smiled. 'Tilling gets one.'

'He refused. He said he didn't care to meet his Maker with alcohol on his lips.'

'He may change his mind.'

'I know. I've given instructions for the rum to be provided.'

The telephone rang. The governor apologized, and picking

2

an instrument from the side-table became entangled in an argument which seemed to Rumbelow to be about a burst boiler in the prison laundry.

He leant back in the chintz-covered armchair, still in his unbuttoned overcoat. He was an impressive man. Women thought him handsome, being always touched by boyish looks. He was over six feet, in his early thirties, fresh-complexioned with pale blue eyes, though his chin was overlong and his soft fair hair was having to be arranged carefully to avoid showing patches of pink scalp. He wore a stylish brown suit with a faint crimson stripe, a canary waistcoat, a carnation in his buttonhole and spats. But he was fastidious rather than dandified. His vanity was of a more cerebral and complicated sort.

He glanced absently at a copy of the *Morning Post* lying folded on the low table of Benares brass. Herr von Ribbentrop was justifying Germany's denunciation of the Locarno Treaty. The Italians in Abyssinia were advancing on Addis Ababa. The *Queen Mary*'s maiden voyage was fixed for the end of May, and there was a photograph of Miss K. Stammers already being coached for Wimbledon by Mr Dan Maskell. It was 1936, a pause between two reigns in a truce between two wars, a way-mark between two British states of mind, from God-given sovereignty to puzzled and resentful frustration.

'How's the prisoner bearing up?' he asked as the governor sat down.

'Until last night he didn't seem to realize it was actually going to happen.'

'That's often the case of course.'

'It's beyond his imagination. He's not very intelligent.'

'No murderer is. And their greatest stupidity is thinking how clever they are.'

'Doesn't that apply to all of us?' His distinguished visitor seeming to take this unkindly, the governor added, 'He might have got away with it, but for your evidence at the trial.'

'That's quite possible,' agreed Rumbelow, who never let modesty obscure plain fact. He drew from his waistcoat pocket the gold hunter watch which had belonged to his elder brother, killed on the Somme in the German push of 1918. 'My fellow

3

from the hospital should have arrived by now. Have you done anything about the mortuary?'

'I've put in an electric fire.'

'Good. I'm always complaining about mortuaries. People seem to overlook some of the occupants still having warm blood in their veins.'

The mortuary was nothing but an outhouse at the back of the prison hospital, a grey light coming through glass in the sloping roof and a high-up window with bars across it, as though the authorities feared even the dead might commit the outrage of escaping. The whitewashed walls had broken into a cold sweat, the governor's fire being a feeble single red bar plugged to the only electric light. There was a deep square sink in the corner, with a brass tap which dripped. In the middle stood a narrow zinc-topped table, a slight slope on it from head to foot, its surface scored with a herringbone of gullies converging on a hole over a white enamelled bucket. Rumbelow thought it all horribly primitive.

Still in his overcoat, he finished his cigar while making some conversation with William, a squat, grizzled man, the head mortuary porter from Blackfriars Hospital. He suddenly found himself pause. It was an instant before a clock somewhere with tinny strokes marked eight. A pair of three-inch-thick oak doors had fallen apart, caught neatly by two sprung hooks to stop the rebound. A white bag over his head, Tilling had dropped at the end of a thirteen-foot brand-new rope, three-and-a-quarter inches thick, made from five strands of fine Italian hemp, one end attached to a hook in an oak beam, the other twisted four times and threaded back on itself to form a non-slipping noose, the knot secured below his left ear. Now Tilling was rotating slowly in a narrow twelve-foot-deep brick-lined pit, always impeccably white-washed. Until the night before, he'd thought it really couldn't happen. But the perfection of the hangman's art – exercised at ten pounds a time – made it surer than anything since he had burst from his mother's womb.

'Will they wait the hour?' William's overcoat being of poorer quality, he was feeling the cold.

'They're supposed to. But they never do.'

4

Rumbelow knelt and unclasped his leather bag. The moment had stirred in him only an impulse to start work. Men died every day – in an imperfect world of murderers, accidents and wars, often enough before their time. The change from a living person to a dead one was of the highest scientific importance, but in his disciplined thinking there was no more to it than that. He began to arrange his instruments on another table of well-scrubbed wood like a butcher's block. To the right he set his long scalpel, with its black bone handle and nine-inch blade. Then smaller scalpels, forceps, a saw with a deep oblong blade, a smaller saw like one used for pruning rose-bushes, bone-cutters, scissors, a worn tape-measure, twine and needles with a cutting edge. There was room behind for two jars with screw-caps, the sort housewives bottled fruit in, with some blue-edged gummed labels. One end was free for the post-mortem report form, clipped to a board, on which he laid his fountain-pen with the cap off.

He took from his inside pocket a familiar square of paper –

I, in pursuance of section twenty-one of the Coroners' (Amendment) Act, 1926, hereby direct you to make a post-mortem examination of the body of Thomas Tilling and to report the result thereof to me in writing.
Norman Carlow, M.D., Barrister-at-Law.
H. M. Coroner.

Rumbelow slipped it behind the board. He liked to have everything exactly in place.

There was no need to roll up his sleeves. His shirts were all cut short and his suits had buttons for false cuffs complete with gold links, a time-saving invention of which he was extremely proud. He put on a bibbed apron of red rubber, tying the tapes round his waist. The pair of them waited, their breath coming in clouds.

There was a hurried noise outside. The door was thrown open. In came a green-painted new-looking handcart, of the kind costers pushed round the London streets. Tilling's body was under the canvas sheet. There were two warders pushing, both looking scared. Behind came the prison doctor – elderly, untidy, ill-paid and socially unalluring. His relations with

5

Rumbelow in the past had not been good. It was among prison doctors' duties to cut up the executed, and he had resented the Home Office pushing in some outsider. But the brilliance and explosiveness of Rumbelow's fame had somewhat mollified him, until he could now take pride in the association and imply to everyone it was closer and more equilibrious than it was.

In the restricted space there was trouble getting the body from the handcart on to the zinc table. As the warders thankfully withdrew, Rumbelow asked the prison doctor, 'Have you the weight?'

'A hundred and thirty-six pounds. He was on the slight side.'

'And the drop?'

'Six feet eight inches.'

William had begun stripping the body of grey jacket and trousers, secured with tapes – there were no buttons, through fear the condemned man might somehow forestall with them his ordained end. The shoes were missing. They always were, Rumbelow noticed. The woollen vest and underdraws were a much-laundered yellow. He wondered how many people had been hanged in them already.

The body was warm, the colour of bluish wax, as limp as a jellyfish. One eye was shut, the other half open, giving a supercilious look. The lips were apart, a smear of blood at the left angle of the mouth. Rumbelow noticed a small fresh gash on the right wrist – pinioning with the executioner's leather body-belt had not been without a struggle. Round the base of the neck, where the cut end of the rope had been removed, was a weal an inch thick. Some urine had been voided, and Rumbelow noticed with interest semen at the tip of the man's penis. Quite often, the muscular spasm of death mocked that for the furtherance of life.

'There were some heart-sounds discernible at the apex for about ten minutes afterwards,' volunteered the prison doctor.

'That isn't exceptional.'

'It makes it a little difficult to give the exact time of death.'

'Not at all. He died when his neck was broken.' Rumbelow picked up his long scalpel. 'To all intents and purposes.'

6

'I'm wondering what might happen were the point actually raised during the inquest.'

'Raised by whom?'

'Some meddlesome juryman, for instance. You know what they can be like. Especially these days.'

'You say, "A very short interval elapsed, or some general expression of opinion to the same effect". It's in Home Office instructions to prison governors, 1926. I haven't heard they'd been changed in the last ten years.'

'That's very clever of you, remembering it.'

'Some things stick in the mind.' He turned to the body. 'Death was instantaneous. The heart may be alive. But the man is dead.'

'Oh, I'm not disagreeing with you. Nor suggesting Tilling knew anything once his neck was broken.'

'Perhaps he did?' asked Rumbelow contrarily. 'Dr Gaertner of Paris has given a most illuminating paper on the behaviour of decapitated heads – the eyes opening, the mouth trying to speak and so on. The man guillotined is very obviously dead, even though the head is capable of expressing unpleasant emotions.'

'Understandable in the circumstances,' observed the prison doctor. Rumbelow gave no reply.

With his long scalpel Rumbelow made a slit starting at the point of the man's chin and ending in the pubic hair at the narrow bone bridging the front of the pelvis. A few strokes flayed the front of the neck and chest. With the cutters he snipped apart the cartilages joining ribs to breastbone, and dividing the small joints connecting this to the clavicles pulled away the entire front of the chest. Natural dexterity reinforced by experience accomplished this in a minute or two. The man was split apart, his internal organs all neatly in place arrayed under Rumbelow's eye.

To mutilate so calculatedly the dead of his own species was a uniquely human experience. When the victim had somewhat ceremoniously been killed by his own kind, it became ecologically bizarre. Rumbelow could feel this, or had once done so, acutely and nauseously. But like much else in his life, he had

7

shut it from his mind. Otherwise it would have been impossible to perform his duty to his profession, to the law, and to himself.

'I admire your thoroughness,' said the prison doctor. 'You could have left it at the neck.'

'To examine the whole patient is surely a fundamental principle of medicine?'

'Of course, of course.'

A dead man doesn't bleed. He leaks. Blood had started to run in the guttered top of the table, and drip with small distinct noises into the bucket. Rumbelow passed his knife round the inner surface of the lower jaw, separating the tongue. He pulled the whole tongue-muscle downwards with the larynx, out through the gaping neck. He severed the gullet just above the stomach, with a few more strokes of the knife freeing heart and lungs, holding them aloft by the wind-pipe like some weird freshly-plucked bird, then dropping them into an enamelled washing-bowl held out by William.

Rumbelow placed the bowl in the sink and turned the brass tap. As the water ran over the organs he examined them. He slit open the gullet and trachea for signs of vomit. He sliced into the tongue to seek internal bruising. He turned the contracted heart in his hands, opening its four chambers, washing out the blood, inspecting the valve-cusps which had opened and shut every second from Tilling's birth to some thirty minutes ago. Finally he took a pair of small pointed scissors from William and cut his way along the coronary arteries, the blood-vessels of the heart itself, twisting like worms across the shiny surface.

'All normal,' he said.

He turned back to the body. The abdominal viscera were removed and examined in the same way. As he opened the stomach the smell of rum met his nostrils. Tilling had decided to face God with a drink inside him after all.

'All normal,' he repeated.

The trunk was now eviscerated, its organs half-filling the sink. With a quick sweep of the scalpel Rumbelow cut the scalp through the hair across the top of the head, from ear to ear. Dissecting away the loose tissue beneath, he turned the scalp into a pair of flaps. The first he drew forward to cover, inside

8

out, the man's face. The other he drew back on to the neck. With the oblong-bladed saw he cut round the skull just above the level of the ears, making a high-pitched noise and trailing pinkish-tinged bone-dust on to the stone floor. He gently wiggled the bony vault, eased it up and removed it like opening a child's chocolate Easter egg. The membranes surrounding the brain glistened in the poorish light. He slit these open, and inserting his fingers under the frontal lobes of the brain, severing the nerves below as he went along, raised it whole from the base of the skull. Dividing the medulla oblongata connecting the spinal cord, he put the brain into the enamelled bowl, rinsed it under the tap, and sliced it as if cutting a new loaf.

'All normal.'

William turned the body on to its face, still masked with its own scalp. With another scalpel, Rumbelow cut down to the vertebral bones of the neck.

'Fracture-dislocation of the cervical spine, at the level of the second and third vertebrae.'

'What's the spinal cord like?' The prison doctor was looking over Rumbelow's shoulder.

'Well and truly ruptured. Across about two-thirds of its thickness.'

'The hangman will be pleased.'

'I'll take this specimen.'

To study the mechanics of judicial hanging, Rumbelow had the largest collection of broken necks in the country. Pathologists attending executions in the provinces had proved co-operative, sending him additions through the post. He freed the two circular bones with the near-severed spinal cord running inside, and dropped them into a screw-topped jar. He went back to the sink, feeling among the organs lying in pink water like butcher's offal. Asking William for a magnifying-glass from his bag, he examined again the tissues round the larynx.

'No haemorrhage from the internal jugular. I should have expected it in a man of his feminine build. It's remarkable how often the vein is ruptured in executions. And how many pathologists miss it.'

The prison doctor nodded. Rumbelow held out his hand to William for a scalpel. 'I'll have the hyoid, too. There may be a fracture on microscopical examination.'

Pulling off his rubber gloves, he wrote on a blue-edged gummed label, *Tilling, T. Judicial hanging. Cervical vertebrae 2–3 and hyoid.* Like all medical men, he had an aversion to any receptacle standing about with its contents unmarked.

He began writing his report. Though London pathologists were starting to employ secretaries, Rumbelow thought it undignified for professional notes to be typewritten, and anyway a mortuary was no place for a young woman. He asked idly, 'Did he confess before the end?'

'No.' The prison doctor paused. He was feeling hurt. Rumbelow had been contemptuous and rude to him that morning, over his doubts about the continuing heart-beat. His resentment was only partly justified. Rumbelow had an unthinking contempt for anyone who knew less than himself, but was seldom deliberately offensive. It was simply not in his nature to disguise facts, nor dress them in more agreeable garb. The prison doctor was frightened of crossing him, but he steeled himself and asked meaningfully, 'Why do you ask? Did you expect him to confirm your evidence at the trial?'

'No, but they often do confess in the last few minutes, you know.'

'You've no doubt about the correctness of the verdict, I hope?'

'Oh, no, no,' said Rumbelow hastily.

He finished writing without speaking.

Rumbelow washed his hands under the cold tap and put on his jacket. From his trouser pocket he handed William two half-crowns, the porter's cut of the post-mortem fee being traditionally paid promptly and in cash. William prepared to sew up the body with the needle and twine. The sliced-up organs in the sink would be stuffed back anyhow. So Tilling ended up like a haggis, shortly to be devoured by quicklime.

Everything that morning had to be performed with measured ceremony, from offering the condemned man his official tot of rum before eight to holding an inquest on his body at ten. Act of Parliament decreed that a coroner's jury must inquire into the deaths of all inmates of jails, and whether the event occurred at the end of a rope was immaterial. The inquest was held in the administrative block by the main gateway, in a largish, dark-panelled, ugly upstairs room, where the authorities had apparently through force of habit put more bars on the windows. There was the Royal Arms on one wall, an important-looking high-backed chair beneath, two long tables and a row of benches on which two reporters sat with notebooks staring into the middle distance. A police-constable appeared, the coroner's officer who Rumbelow knew well, and exclaimed, 'Be upstanding!' as though addressing troops across a windswept parade-ground. Dr Norman Carlow bustled in, wearing black jacket and striped trousers and polishing his monocle on a white silk handkerchief.

Carlow was a graduate of Trinity College, Dublin, a short fat Irishman with a shiny bald head ringed by small greying curls, a well-cared-for moustache, and a large pearl tie-pin. He had the appearance of a prosperous restaurateur or successful actor.

He was the only real medical friend Rumbelow had. He was an older man, but Rumbelow had a manner as well as a reputation befitting greater years, and was inclined to be impatient with his contemporaries. Unlike many coroners, who sat like little Lord Chancellors on the Woolsack of their dignity, Carlow was affable in court and breezy out of it, a mask for a shrewd and occasionally ruthless mind. They were both professionals, superb at their jobs. They both respected each other as such.

The proceedings were businesslike. The governor identified a document signed by the sheriff, an authorization to hang the prisoner. The prison doctor said death was instantaneous. Everything was put down in writing by the clerk and signed. When Rumbelow took the oath there was a stir among the jury, seven men dressed like the governor in their best and equally uneasy. He gave evidence with his usual brevity, lucidity, and authority, choosing his words as carefully as if addressing the Old Bailey. A coroner's court was still a court, whether held in a prison, a parish hall, or the upstairs parlour of a country inn, the coroner a powerful officer of the Crown begat by the Normans. Rumbelow had an awe of the law and its officers which

11

his acquaintances put among his more ridiculous peculiarities. Besides, his evidence might always be thrown in his face by some astute counsel at later, unlooked-for and more stately proceedings. He was as cautious as a cat.

Carlow screwed his monocle into his eye and addressed the jury. 'You have been privileged – I don't think that's an inappropriate word – to hear evidence of the post-mortem examination from no less an authority than Dr Rumbelow. You will perhaps be satisfied in your own minds that the execution this morning was in every way conducted properly, and that death was occasioned instantaneously and without suffering.'

The jury was satisfied. They whispered a few seconds. The foreman announced a verdict of death by judicial hanging. The inquest was closed. The only difference from any other was the coroner failing to extend sympathy to the bereaved relatives.

Rumbelow, the governor and the coroner made their way down a back staircase to a small triangular courtyard. There was the handcart again, with a coffin on it.

'I'm afraid there's been something of a disturbance outside,' the governor said nervously. 'It started when the notice was put up on the gate. But I gather the police have everything well in hand.'

'I'm not worried,' said Rumbelow.

'I often wonder if they'll ever do away with all this business.'

'What, hanging?' asked Carlow. 'That would be hard on John Rumbelow. You'd do him out of his three-guinea fee, for p.m. plus inquest.'

'They've abolished the death penalty in twenty-one countries, you know. Denmark, Norway, Sweden. . . . I can't remember them all.'

'With the notable exception of Germany,' said Rumbelow.

'Even the Nazis are talking of abolishing it for civil crimes.'

'The Germans have a headsman in evening dress with a stiff shirt and tails, like an Englishman going to the opera,' said Carlow informatively. 'I suppose it fits with their Wagnerian concept of life and death. Do you think the fellow would have a top hat about him somewhere? Perhaps one of those collapsible ones. It's all part of the uniform.'

12

'I don't see what the fuss is about,' objected Rumbelow. 'There's only some dozen executions a year. In the reign of Henry the Eighth there were seventy-two thousand of them. I suppose it's all stirred up by those socialist highbrows.'

The governor looked offended. 'You could hardly call me one.'

'If they did abolish it, there'd soon be a clamour to bring it back,' Rumbelow told him. 'Hanging's as English as roast beef.'

'I CERTAINLY SHAN'T spill any tears over the little man,' said Lady Accrington. 'The whole affair was simply squalid. But the newspapers seemed determined to turn him into a national hero. They always do these days, with all sorts of unsavoury people, as long as they're flamboyant enough. Look at that awful Rector of Stiffkey!' She held up a thin wrinkled finger with a scarlet nail the size of an almond. 'Showing himself off at a fairground in a barrel, a disgrace to humanity. Perhaps they ought to have hung him, too. Well, Dr Rumbelow, you were there this morning?'

'I didn't attend the execution. I conducted the post-mortem.'

'There were some people making a fuss outside, I hear?' asked the Member of Parliament, a fat man in a wing collar with a fatter wife in a bright green silk dress.

'I shudder to think what might happen if they abolished the death sentence,' said Lady Odgers.

'*On a diablement peur de la corde* – that's what Queen Caroline of Brunswick said about England,' added Lord Odgers. 'We still need the rope, if only to keep the lower classes from killing one another on Saturday nights.'

'People are becoming far too sensitive,' decided Lady Accrington. 'Or too fond of making exhibitions of themselves.'

'Yours is a strange privilege, Doctor.' Evan Greensmith the author was sitting across the lunch-table, a thick-set man in a plain serge suit reminding Rumbelow disappointingly of a provincial shopkeeper. He made up Lady Accrington's party of eight with a thin, gingery-haired young man introduced as his secretary.

'What is?' asked Rumbelow.

'Yesterday you could refer to a living man and say with absolute certainty, "I shall be doing an autopsy on him tomorrow morning".'

'I can't see any privilege in it. It is only part of my work. I've performed four more post-mortems since, and I have at least another half-dozen before I'm free to go home tonight.'

'But you gave evidence against him at the trial. Surely that autopsy must have been a triumph? The end of a gladiatorial battle.'

This was too fanciful for Rumbelow. 'I'm afraid I don't follow. The word, by the way, is "necropsy" not "autopsy". "Autopsy" means an examination of oneself.'

The author looked annoyed at this correction of his grammar. Even Rumbelow saw he'd been tactless. But he found it impossible to turn his eyes from any inaccuracy.

'I was in Italy during the trial.' Greensmith's irritation was submerged by an eagerness for copy. 'Would you all be bored if I persuaded Dr Rumbelow to repeat his evidence?'

A murmur indicated that no-one would be bored in the slightest. Old Lady Accrington sat back, pleased with herself. The party was proving a success. An ambitious woman born into a world of barren fields for ambition, she had nothing in which to fulfil herself except the pursuit of social fame. Though her Mayfair house was delightful, her chef had come from the Ritz and her cellar specially chosen in Paris and Coblenz, she knew her prized consequence among the savagely competitive London hostesses depended only on her guests. She had invited Rumbelow for the day she calculated Tilling would hang, and a last-minute reprieve would have distressed her immeasurably. Had he been acquitted in the first place, she might well with admirable fairness have invited him instead.

'The two men, Hutchinson and Tilling, were homosexuals, of course.' Rumbelow was pleased to see them look faintly shocked. It was a condition thought dimly only to exist among artists, public schoolboys and sailors, never to be discussed in polite society. He always enjoyed impressing an audience.

'They'd had a quarrel. These people have quite heated rows, you know, even worse than ordinary couples.'

The M.P.'s fat wife laughed, but catching Rumbelow's glance stifled it.

'Hutchinson was found in bed in their Pimlico flat, shot through the chest. He died in hospital twelve hours later without recovering consciousness. Two shots had been fired. The first went through Hutchinson's chest-wall, chipping a rib. The second went into the left lung. Tilling said it was suicide, that he'd tried to wrench the gun away – which accounted for his finger-prints. But I could tell that both shots were in fact fired from some distance away, horizontally as Hutchinson was sitting in bed.'

'How could you?' said Evan Greensmith.

'I'll explain. At first I admit I believed Tilling. I'm an impartial medical expert, you know, not a prosecutor, however the defence sometimes cares to describe me. There were no powder-marks round the entry-wounds, as you'd expect from a gun fired close to the body. But the weapon was a ·25 automatic, and the cartridges of automatic pistols contain flake powder, which is smokeless. I went so far as firing the gun at close range into a square of fresh human skin, to prove as much.'

'Skin? Where from?' The M.P. looked startled.

'I should prefer not to say. But the angles of the bullets interested me. They couldn't possibly fit in with Tilling's story. The rib fractured by the first shot was of great significance – it could have been broken in the direction I found only had the gun been fired across the room. It was the same with the second shot. As this was perhaps a theoretical point to put to a jury, I fired the gun again – this time into an anatomist's skeleton. I drew diagrams and took photographs.' He paused. 'The jury was convinced.'

The author's secretary, who had said nothing throughout the meal, observed with great sadness, 'So Tilling was hanged through geometry?'

'But surely it wasn't cold-blooded murder, punishable as such?' asked Evan Greensmith. 'You admitted they'd had a bad row.

16

Tilling was in a mental turmoil. Couldn't you regard it as a *crime passionnel*?'

'I don't recognize the term. Murder is the worst of crimes, as we all know perfectly well from childhood. Apart from those who are mentally deranged, such as schizophrenics,' Rumbelow added with his usual precision.

'But can't you distinguish between Crippen deliberately poisoning his wife, and a man who finds his wife in the arms of her lover and bludgeons her to death?'

'No.'

'I'm hardly likely to shake the great Dr Rumbelow with a cross-examination.' Everyone laughed.

'But taking your own life is a crime,' argued Lord Odgers. 'And the coroner invariably records that the balance of mind was disturbed.'

'That's a pious perjury. The Church won't afford a proper burial otherwise.'

'An improvement on the past,' said the M.P. 'They used to bury suicides in the public highway with a stake through their hearts, and confiscate all their worldly goods into the bargain.'

'I only wish I could enjoy your aloofness to the human tragedy, Doctor,' said Greensmith.

Rumbelow had turned aside much bitterer sarcasm in court. He suspected the author enjoyed the same relationship with his secretary as that between the two dead men, which accounted for his trying to knock the wickedness out of the crime. 'That's a matter of training. Inwardly, I'm as sensitive as any man.'

'May I congratulate you on your aptitude? The training of a lifetime could never remotely bring me to perform those ghoulish duties.'

'Let me tell you something. Once I nearly gave up pathology – my life's work. I was a junior at Blackfriars Hospital. I'd been working in the mortuary only a few weeks. Then I felt I couldn't go on with it. I couldn't bring myself to enter the post-mortem room, to put on the rubber gloves, to make the incision. About that time a very great friend of mine went sick – he was one of the house-physicians, we'd been through medical school together, perhaps he was the only friend I had. As too often happens with doctors, no one seemed to know what was wrong. Of course, the grand physicians came in and made their grand diagnoses. But after considerable suffering, he died.'

'You didn't do the post-mortem?' cried Lady Accrington in horror.

'I attended it. I was curious, you see. I wanted to know all about the disease which had killed him. It's a matter of science. Medical science, any science, transcends human beings.'

'I agree the astronomer measures his stars, rather than writes poems on the glory of the heavens,' said Evan Greensmith graciously.

'A doctor's duty is to study and classify disease, so as to cure or prevent it in others. If he becomes emotionally involved with a dead body, exactly as with a sick man, he's finished. After I'd watched the corpse of my friend cut to bits, I knew that nothing again in the post-mortem room could ever unsettle me.'

There was a silence.

'You mean a doctor must possess a heart of stone?' asked the author.

'A good doctor, yes.'

'You showed a singular fortitude,' observed Lord Odgers admiringly.

'Not at all. I simply got my ideas clear. There's a prison governor I know who can hardly bring himself to witness an execution. But his duty is to observe an action of the law, which is created by man to preserve civilization. The human being involved must be shut from the mind. But he doesn't see that.'

A clock in the room chimed two. Rumbelow remembered the lecture he had to give at Blackfriars. He pulled himself together, forming apologies for leaving, feeling he had been talking too freely. Perhaps the wine he had drunk was aggrandized by his abstemious habits.

The others were still eating dessert. As they had enjoyed their fill of horrors, Rumbelow left to a babble of argument about Hitler's reoccupation of the Rhineland.

'Why shouldn't he walk into his own back garden?'

'It's only the French who want us to kick him out. They're too scared to lift a finger.'

18

'Well, they were our allies during the War.'

'We can forgive them for that.'

'*I* find it a most disturbing exhibition of feebleness on the part of the Empire.'

'Don't lose any sleep over Herr Hitler, I implore you. What's Germany to gain from re-starting the War? Absolutely nothing.'

'Some of his grievances are justified.'

'He's a man of peace. Like the Prime Minister. You can take my word for it.'

The door shut. Rumbelow was surprised that Lady Accrington had disregarded etiquette to abandon her guests and accompany him across the hall. A man of even greater self-control than himself would have relished the luxury of the house, the display of glass and silver, the practised discreet attentions of the footmen, the food and wine, the atmosphere of money having no more significance than the means of obtaining anything that for the moment happened to be desired. It would have been inhuman not responding to an environment beyond his imagination as a boy or a young doctor. But he took these invitations – which could come almost every week later, during the season – much as a matter of course. It was his right to move amid the rich, powerful and clever. He was a national figure. Any errand boy stopped in the street would know his name, which was more than could be claimed by Lady Accrington, or possibly even by Evan Greensmith.

'And how's your poor wife?' asked Lady Accrington, as an afterthought.

'Still very delicate, I'm afraid.'

'She's fortunate, having a doctor for a husband.'

He picked his famous bag from the black-and-white marble floor of the hall. It was of black leather, almost square, with stout silver locks. His hostess had taken pains to have it placed in immediate view of arrivals through the front door. It still contained the section of Tilling's broken neck.

Rumbelow turned, to find her face close to his, burning with eagerness. For a moment he wondered if she were going to pay him some glowing compliment, or more wildly that she was about to kiss him. 'That skin,' she whispered. 'The piece you shot at. Where did it come from?'

'Oh! a leg – amputated by the surgeons. Its owner was run over by a brewer's dray.'

'So that's it. Well, I'm disappointed. But I suppose flaying someone alive would be a little macabre. Even for you, Dr Rumbelow?'

The footman announced a taxi, and to Rumbelow's annoyance he had to take it.

3

BLACKFRIARS HOSPITAL STOOD overlooking the Thames in
the City of London, at the angle of Blackfriars Bridge and the
Victoria Embankment. As Rumbelow took his unwanted taxi-
ride, three consultants were talking in the ground-floor committee-room. This faced on to the Embankment itself, with its
clanking, lumbering, red double-decker trams, then the chocolate-coloured river, and behind a row of cranes on the far
bank some vast grime-encrusted warehouses, cathedrals of the
Empire's commerce.

The room was like a hundred such others in the City – cheer-
less, dark-panelled, a long table down the middle, portraits of
half-forgotten past luminaries on the walls, the sour smell of
rooms which are used rather than lived in. A hospital crest
hung over the broad stone fireplace, and down one side stood
a couple of smaller tables with writing materials and reference-
books. It had turned into the consultant staff's common room,
gradually, unofficially, and more years ago than anyone cared
to remember, like many usages both social and clinical in the
ancient institution.

'But what a splendid photograph!' Sir George Smallpenny
was looking at the lunch edition of an evening paper. 'Quite the
Edgar Wallace touch.'

'It's all going a little far, surely?'

'"Dr Rumbelow leaving the prison this morning with
his murder bag".' He laughed. 'I do wish he wouldn't wear
that dreadful bowler. It makes him look like a vet, at the
races.'

'I suppose there's nothing to stop the newspapers writing

about him as they like – or as much as they like. But I don't see why he should encourage them.'

'They don't need encouragement. This nation is strongly addicted to ghouls.'

Sir George dropped the paper on the long table. He was in his usual pose, heels on the black iron fender, warming himself comfortably before the glowing coals in the basket-grate. He was a humorous, easy-going, good-looking man, grey-haired and clean-shaven, his dress of light-coloured lounge suit and spotted bow tie approaching informality. He was one of the consultant gynaecologists, believed to be the richest man on the hospital's staff. With his feet on the committee-table sat Dr Ian Bantrell. He was a physician, about the same age as Rumbelow, elected to a consultancy only some twelve months previously. Tubby, ruddy-faced, carroty-haired, he wore the professional uniform of black jacket and striped trousers, with wing collar and spats. The amiable Sir George – who eyed his colleagues more perceptively than the more inexperienced of them imagined – had decided that Bantrell's formal appearance, like his present aggressive posture, was the effect of his feeling unsure of himself.

'Rumbelow doesn't bring much credit to Blackfriars, does he? Putting himself on the level of Jack the Ripper and Sweeney Todd.'

'Isn't that a little unfair?' asked Sir George mildly. 'I don't think his ambition is ending up in the Chamber of Horrors at Tussaud's.'

'It's bad enough having one publicist on the staff already.'

'Who's that?'

'Graham Trevose.'

'Oh, Graham. But all plastic surgeons advertise themselves. They're prima donnas. It's all part of the performance.'

'Trevose is a lightweight, of course.'

'A very able lightweight.'

'I'm not denying for one moment he's clever. And he sticks to his noses and bosoms, which doesn't take private fees away from the other surgeons. I suppose that's why his antics are tolerated.'

Bantrell folded his arms pugnaciously. Sir George said nothing, reflecting what a prickly young man he was. Graham Trevose admittedly might hardly be more than a beauty specialist, but he was a colleague, and a good ten years senior to Bantrell. What might be deserved criticism delivered by a senior man in confidence became only insolence in the mouth of this new physician. But Sir George gave no rebuke. It was his way to soothe rather than ruffle, a valuable quality among the strong-minded, ambitious and often jealous men who composed the senior staff of any important hospital. He was popular, a sophisticated confessor and tolerant mediator, with great influence in the continual little discussions and arguments which eventually shaped the way their lives in the hospital were run. Because he grasped this, Bantrell was eager to talk that afternoon as they met by chance in the coming-and-going of their work.

'Trevose simply likes to get his name in the gossip-columns,' Bantrell continued. 'Well, all right. It's unethical, but I suppose it's healthy for his practice among the actresses and debutantes. But the public adulation of Rumbelow is different. He's known in every home from Land's End to John o'Groats, better than Mr Baldwin himself.'

'But not as a hangman's familiar. Rather as the infallible detective. That's another of our folk-heroes. Look at the fortunes to be made writing thrillers.'

'You're saying Rumbelow's infallible?'

'My dear Ian, all men are far from that. Though perhaps he thinks he is.'

'That is precisely my point. I don't mind him assuming an air of infallibility in court – as long as *I'm* not in the dock. But I cannot stand him adopting it towards the rest of us here. What do you think, Crampers?'

The third man in the room licked the envelope of a letter he had been finishing at one of the side-tables. The Blackfriars' consultants were as mixed a collection of individualists as might be found at the head of any large enterprise. Mr Cramphorn was the senior surgeon, short, broad-shouldered, grey-moustached, with half-moon glasses and a busily-puffing pipe, a brusque, buttoned-up man who was fond of pepper-and-salt suits, shot and fished, and operated beautifully. 'Think of Rumbelow? We've got to put up with the fellow, haven't we? We're like a club – take the rough with the smooth, or life's impossible. And it's always on the cards, *he* can't stand the rest of us.' He affixed a three-ha'penny stamp. 'No, I don't object to him. Mind, he's beastly dogmatic.'

'You may call it dogmatism. I'd call it vanity.'

'Same thing, often enough, isn't it? The Christian martyrs must have been as vain as peacocks. You have to be, if you believe in yourself to the point of going up in flames. He's certainly obstinate. Always was, even as one of my students. He'd stick to his diagnosis of a case, even if it was wrong as plain as the nose on your face. Funny thing, he sometimes turned out to be right and the rest of us had made a bloomer.'

'If he thinks rather a lot of himself,' suggested Sir George charitably, 'we're all sometimes guilty of that.'

'But I can't see what Rumbelow's done to merit such self-esteem.'

Mr Cramphorn puffed away, relighting his pipe. 'Strung up a dozen murderers.'

'Is that a lasting achievement?'

'Well, it was for the murderers.'

'But they'd have been convicted without Rumbelow so much as entering the witness-box. He cashed in because the trials were so sensational. Look at the Perryman case, the one he made his name with. You can't expect the newspapers to soft-pedal a situation where a man cuts up his mistress and sends her carriage-paid by rail to a dozen respectable and distinguished citizens.'

'Still, Rumbelow put the jig-saw together,' Sir George reminded him. 'At one time they thought the chap had carved up two mistresses, or even three.'

'I'm not denying his ability, no more than Trevose's. It's the public's fault if they imagine it's magic. Unfortunately, he gives them every opportunity to remain in that state of mind. Look at that next case, on the heels of the Perryman affair — '

24

'"The Brides at the Seaside",' smiled Sir George.

'Yes, the young fellow involved in those convenient boating accidents. What did Rumbelow do? Demonstrated the girl had been killed in a bath or a bucket or something, because there was fresh and not sea water in her lungs. What's so clever about that? We all three know our pathology, our elementary chemistry. We could have shown exactly the same.'

'Not easy holding these things up in court.' Mr Cramphorn looked over his half-moons. 'I get roped in now and then, compensation cases and the like. Those legal johnnies could tie George Washington in knots.'

'But Rumbelow's an expert – as a witness. He sticks to his facts, avoids the pitfalls and talks so even the most dimwitted juryman can understand him. *That's* what his reputation's based on. No wonder the judges love him.'

They were interrupted by the subject of their conversation appearing through a door at the far end of the room. The three fell silent, suddenly feeling embarrassed, even Bantrell. There were always letters and rolled-up journals awaiting collection at one end of the committee-table, and without saying anything, or even seeming to notice the others, Rumbelow started looking through them. Sir George Smallpenny stared through the window at a tug with a string of deep-laden barges deferentially lowering its funnel to pass under the arches of Blackfriars Bridge. Bantrell had really become quite angry, he thought. He was uncertain if it distressed or amused him. He supposed Bantrell was simply jealous of Rumbelow. They were much the same age and seniority on the staff. They were exceptionally clever. Everyone knew Bantrell was fanatically ambitious to make his name in London medicine. And the more such people wanted from life, the greater they resented the success in it of others. To break the tension he asked humorously, 'Where's the murder bag?'

Rumbelow looked up. 'My bag? It's locked in the lab.'

'The hanging went off all right, I suppose?'

'Yes.'

'Anything interesting in the p.m.?'

'No.'

'We missed you at lunch,' said Bantrell, still with his feet up. 'We were hoping to hear all the grisly details.'

'I lunched with Lady Accrington.'

'*Did* you?'

Rumbelow looked at him blankly. 'A man must eat.'

'If the condemned man enjoys a hearty breakfast, the pathologist at least deserves a decent lunch,' said Sir George.

The four then split up. Bantrell felt satisfied he had sown his seeds. If he could persuade them to germinate, they lay where the roots would run deepest.

4

IT WAS ALMOST midnight when Rumbelow reached home, by the last Southern Railway electric train from Charing Cross. Had he been later, he would have had to take a taxi all the way – a disaster.

Still carrying his bag, he trudged from Lower Sydenham station up a hill dominated by the twin towers and curved glass roofs of Prince Albert's Crystal Palace. His house was half-way along, square, brick and stucco, built fifty years previously when the railways were enticing prosperous City men to the unfashionable south-eastern suburbs. It had started to drizzle. He noticed each alternative gas-lamp wore a halo, the rest having been extinguished for the night. He felt for the latch of the wrought-iron gate leading to the constricted front garden, feeling very tired.

Despite popular notions, most of Rumbelow's work was like any medical man's – repetitive, mentally unexacting and even dull. At three that afternoon he had lectured in the steep-tiered theatre of the pathology block, its narrow much-carved benches crowded with students. They had little interest in forensic medicine, which seldom appeared in final examination papers and could therefore be safely skipped. They came to see Rumbelow. He was famous, he had his name in the papers, he was as much an object of pride as the hospital's sporting trophies. Besides, he was always likely to show with the epidiascope magnified photographs of murders, rapes, sexual aberrations and similar diversions. That afternoon he passed round the jar with the piece of Tilling's neck, and was gratified to see the impression on even such a notoriously hardened audience.

At the end of the hour he clattered down a short iron spiral staircase to the mortuary in the semi-basement. He was still annoyed at the three in the committee-room. That they were discussing him was clear from their expressions, their attitudes and their silence. He supposed Bantrell had started it. He knew how the young physician disliked him. That was something he had to tolerate, or ignore. But why should he become sarcastic over a lunch at Lady Accrington's? It was a perfectly reasonable engagement for a man in his position. Rumbelow was frankly puzzled.

He hurried into the small changing-room, already removing his jacket and false cuffs. 'How many today?' he asked Quinley, his assistant.

'Two, sir. A man with terminal bronchopneumonia following carcinimatosis —'

'Very well. Where's the primary?'

'In the left bronchus. And a woman with hepatic cirrhosis.'

'I don't want to waste time. I've six cases waiting for me at the Central Mortuary.'

He could hear the students shuffling through their own door. For some forgotten reason, the post-mortems at Blackfriars were always performed at four o'clock. Notices with the dead patients' names and particulars were posted round the medical school, all duplicated in violet copper-plate and resembling menus outside continental restaurants.

The dead man started his final journey already shrouded, a tag round his wrist with name and date like a newborn baby, on a trolley with a stiffened canvas cover to hide the load yet proclaiming it the more blatantly, Sister hurriedly rearranging screens to spare the still living the sight of a fallen comrade. He went to a new section of the mortuary, one of the many improvements Rumbelow had insisted upon in the three years since his appointment, his authority established even before by the Perryman and seaside cases. It contained a dozen drawers two foot square, refrigerated storage, in which he was left until the undertakers called or four o'clock brought him Rumbelow's attentions. Not every death meant a necropsy. Only if the doctors were interested or baffled were the bereaved relatives pressed to advance medical science, though before final examinations the dead were cut up less discriminately to give the students practice. The bereaved relatives generally agreed, in gratitude to Blackfriars, even though the patient would self-evidently have done just as well staying in his bed at home.

The post-mortem room itself was larger than the hospital's operating theatres. There were two porcelain tables with slightly raised edges, a pair of sinks, and a sloping surface like a kitchen draining-board with water trickling on to it continuously through a red rubber hose from the ceiling. At one end were half a dozen steps for the students, with metal frames to lean against, as on the terraces of football grounds.

A door led to the third room of the suite, with an abrupt change of atmosphere. The walls were of carved light oak, the lighting dim, and in the centre was a bier on which the coffin could lie beneath a cloth of tasselled velvet with a silver cross worked in it, the property of the hospital. It could be viewed by the relatives and other interested parties, strictly by appointment, though the lid could be open or shut according to preference. This transition from the impersonal to the emotional view of death, from science to sentiment, was one of the few things which always amused Rumbelow.

The row blew up suddenly.

Rumbelow did not like Quinley. He was inelegant, awkward, even clumsy, a man in his late twenties, prematurely bald with two tufts of fuzzy hair over his ears, his sallow complexion generally disfigured by an angry-looking spot or two. He had a troublesome liability to boils, for which he submitted to painful injections of staphylococcus vaccine with unnoticeable effect. Rumbelow conceded the boils were hardly Quinley's fault, but his appearance alone disturbed him. He had been more or less forced to appoint him on a memorable record of gold medals and scholarships. At least he was useful, being competent enough for the Blackfriars' post-mortems when Rumbelow was busy with the police or in court.

'I'll do the old man first,' said Rumbelow. He made the familiar sweep from point of chin to base of penis.

A house-physician stood beside him with a sheaf of the dead

man's clinical notes, it being considered good form for the consultant, or at least his underling, to be faced with organs he had known only remotely and be either vindicated, puzzled, or shamed. The old man's diagnosis had been a fell one. He had come into the hospital already shot through with cancer, one side of his chest a barrel of fluid, secondary growths in the bones of his arm and his brain. Rumbelow sliced the organs on the porcelain slab under running water, announcing to the students, 'You see, gentlemen, the primary growth was a carcinoma of the left bronchus, infiltrating the lung and pleura and giving metastases in the brain.'

Quinley was in red apron and gloves as well. He looked up from the slit-open body. 'Isn't there something down here in the prostate, sir?'

Rumbelow turned sharply. He knew that for once his thoroughness had lapsed. He had opened the bladder, but left the prostate gland below unexamined. His hurry to be away had perhaps affected him, as it had seemed clear the lethal seeds spread from the growth in the chest. He crossed to the table, asking the house-physician, 'Was there any history of dysuria? You didn't mention it.'

The houseman ruffled through the notes. 'There's some difficulty in passing urine recorded sir. But we didn't think it significant.'

Rumbelow felt into the pelvis. The prostate was enlarged. It was a small growth compared with the others, but that was usual enough. Quinley was right.

He said nothing. He didn't want Quinley to be right. Particularly in front of an audience. He had second thoughts. It might simply be old man's enlargement of the prostate, not a malignant tumour at all. It was just possible. That could be definitely determined only by cutting sections and looking down a microscope – which could be done in the seclusion of a laboratory. 'You deceive yourself, Dr Quinley.'

The assistant shifted his body awkwardly, looking put out. 'It appeared the primary to me, sir.'

'Can't you see it's a benign enlargement? Commonplace in a man of that age.'

30

'No, I can't agree, sir. I think it's a malignant adenoma.'

It was tactless and graceless, but said without hostility – he had a genuine admiration for Rumbelow. But it forced Rumbelow into his second mistake. 'You doubt my opinion?' he demanded angrily. 'That's not very respectful of you, is it? If it's my word against yours, I don't think there's much doubt which would be accepted. In a court of law, at any rate.'

There was a gasp from the students, watching fascinated and amused. It was not at all done in Blackfriars to berate assistants in front of a class. Consultants generally affected a wry pride at being tripped by juniors whose cleverness had been instilled by themselves. Rumbelow was now angry with himself for losing his temper. For years he had trained himself to control it, a necessity in the witness-box with every K.C. in London on his mettle to confuse and discredit him. Perhaps his annoyance with Bantrell that afternoon had unsettled him.

'Very well, Quinley. Remove the prostate, and we'll section it. The microscope will say which one of us is right.' To lighten the scene he added, 'Would you care to wager a five-pound note on it?'

But it fell flat. Rumbelow saw he had demeaned himself before his students. He finished both post-mortems without addressing another word to Quinley at all.

He left Blackfriars shortly after five, still carrying his bag, taking the Tube to north London. The six cases in the Central Mortuary were deaths which never reached the newspapers. The first was a suicide, a man with his face still cherry-red from the carbon monoxide of his gas oven. A woman taken from the Thames. A fat man who had collapsed in the street, the jelly of his brain suffused with the blood of a burst artery. Two road accidents. Then a nineteen-year-old girl who had died during the night, the blood and discharge caked to the inside of her thighs already telling the cause. One more woman who should have given life to another but instead brought death on herself. He handled the body gingerly. She had died from streptococcal septicaemia following an abortion. There was no effective treatment in the world, and she still harboured the living germs. From inside he cut away uterus, ovaries and vagina with the

31

connecting broad ligament. He slit the muscle of the enlarged septic womb on the porcelain slab, spreading the organ out in his gloved fingers. No foetus nor membranes. A professional job, no old woman with a knitting-needle in a back parlour. He wondered what doctor had performed the secret operation. It was the sixth he had seen in a year. He had his suspicions.

He wrote his reports, handed the mortuary porter a pound note and still with his bag took the Tube south to Piccadilly Circus. He always dined late, at his club in Pall Mall. This was a grotesque misplaced Venetian palace, a series of lofty, impersonal ill-heated rooms, its members less a fraternity than a collection of men with nowhere better to spend the evening. Everyone knew who he was, but through club convention avoided showing it – a consideration Rumbelow was not certain he appreciated. But he was new to clubland, put up by Norman Carlow, and he thought it all rather magnificent.

At his customary table in the corner he ordered a lamb chop and treated himself to his usual quarter-bottle of claret. He was half-way through when a porter called him to the telephone. It was Scotland Yard, with a message from Superintendent Sixsmith asking for him urgently at an address in Paddington. Rumbelow left his dinner unfinished, and took a taxi knowing he could claim it as expenses from the Home Office without any quibbling.

The house was in the grid of terraced streets south of Paddington Station, all small hotels, boarding-houses and bed-sitting rooms, where criminals and prostitutes drifted plentifully on the ever-flowing population. It was an area he had been called to more than once. Outside were cars, two uniformed policemen, the usual bunch of reporters giving him a cheerful greeting. If the superintendent was there himself, Rumbelow calculated, it was a major crime.

A policeman took him to a back room on the top floor. There was Sixsmith, another detective, and an inspector from the Yard's photographic department adjusting a bellows camera on a tripod. It was a cheap bed-sitting room with a sloping ceiling, a divan along one side, a washbasin half-hidden by a grubby curtain with pink flowers on it, an electric fire set in

32

the wall, and a small oil-cooker in one corner with a saucepan, which Rumbelow noticed to contain congealed baked beans. There seemed to be blood everywhere. A middle-aged man with a thick black moustache was dead in a sitting position in the opposite corner, the length of clothes-line round his neck attached to a pipe in the roof. His throat and both wrists were cut, a bloodstained open razor lying in the middle of the worn carpet. On the divan Rumbelow saw a small revolver, the cylinder swung open and three bullets on the blood-spattered cover.

'Somebody seemed intent on making a proper job of it, Doctor,' remarked Sixsmith. He was a large red-faced man with the look of a prosperous farmer with sociable habits.

Rumbelow took off his bowler, his fur-collared overcoat and his jacket with the mock cuffs. The other detective considerately held on to them. 'Know anything about him?'

'Not much. He's German or Hungarian. Been here a couple of days.'

'Who found him?'

'The old lady below saw blood coming through the ceiling as she was making her supper.'

Rumbelow crouched over the body. He lifted an eyelid and felt the slack lower jaw. 'No rigor mortis. He's been dead about three hours. Certainly not more than six.'

'The case came up to me as murder.'

'It's suicide.'

'Oh. Well, in fact I thought as much, once I'd had a look at it. What's the cause of death, Doctor?'

'Asphyxia.'

'What about the wounds?'

'The ones on the neck are superficial. They've only gone through the skin and subcutaneous tissues and the platysma muscle just beneath. A few tentative cuts are common enough, if you've the idea of cutting your throat. The ones on the wrists are deeper. The left has some of the tendons leading from the forearm muscles to the fingers severed. The right's more severe still. It's caught the radial artery, hence the blood as he staggered about after doing the deed. He was probably left-handed.'

33

Rumbelow's eyes travelled to the oil-stove. 'The position of the saucepan handle seems to confirm that.'

'He didn't seem keen on leaving anything to chance, did he?'

Rumbelow stood up, carefully dusting his knees. 'That's often the case with suicide, isn't it? If you're going to kill yourself, I suppose you must be in an unusually determined frame of mind. Two methods combined are common enough. I did a p.m. last week on a girl who'd jumped from a window. She'd already swallowed enough aspirin to kill a heavyweight boxer. This chap probably meant to use the revolver as well, once he had his head in the noose.'

'He'd got the wrong ammunition.' Sixsmith nodded towards the body. 'He didn't give himself much drop.'

'Two inches are enough, if you stick out your legs. A murderer would hoist the body to the roof.' Sixsmith nodded. 'The p.m. will show death from suffocation by the tongue forced against the back wall of the throat. Plus pressure on the arteries bringing blood to the brain. That's a factor a lot of pathologists overlook. It killed a man last year. He'd got a tracheotomy opening in his windpipe below the rope, and everyone was very puzzled until I appeared on the scene.'

Rumbelow started to put on his jacket. As usual, there were endless notes to be made and photographs to be taken. Sixsmith finally offered him a lift to Charing Cross, on his way back to the Yard. In the car Rumbelow asked, 'Is the Vickery case down for a hearing yet?'

'Soon after Easter, I gather.'

'As near as that?'

'Are you going away, Doctor?'

They had worked together, all over the country, during the past five years. They had become personal friends. Though Sixsmith perceived the relationship was improved – or only possible at all – if he steadfastly preserved the lay person's respect for the man of medicine.

'I've too much work.' They turned from Marble Arch down Park Lane, past the two newly opened luxury hotels. It prompted Rumbelow to ask, 'The Yard hasn't got any more on Dr Elgin, I suppose?'

'I could find out for you.'

'I fancy I encountered another specimen of his work today.'

'Young girl?'

'Nineteen.'

'It's difficult to trace these things. The women don't advertise who they're going to see. Often enough, they don't tell
anyone about it at all. It may be all part of the bargain.'

'One day Elgin's going to make a slip, and we'll get him.'

'You're hard on your own black sheep, Doctor.'

'We are a privileged profession, but only because we are
bound by a strict code of ethics. It is inexcusable to break it.'

Sixsmith grinned. 'It's a good job you're not a policeman.'

In the suburban train Rumbelow sat for the half-hour journey
with his bag at his feet, reading the evening paper.

But he was not glad to be home.

5

1936 WAS A good year for dance bands. He saw the light on downstairs, and the strong beat reached him even through the curtained window. As he unlocked the front door the music stopped abruptly. She knew it would only irritate him.

He set down his bag and removed his hat and coat. He took a brush from a shelf below the small oval mirror of the hall stand, and carefully removed the raindrops. Then he went into the sitting-room.

'You'd no need to stay up, you know.'

'I was listening to the wireless.'

'Anything good?'

'Some dance music. Sydney Lipton from the Grosvenor House.'

'Tune-in again, if you like.'

'It's almost twelve, anyway.' She held up the evening paper, the page folded so his photograph occupied the middle. 'Did you see it?'

'Yes. It's a little embarrassing, sometimes. I think they deliberately go out of their way to make me into some sort of monster.'

He wanted to go to bed, but felt some obligation to sit for a moment in his easy-chair beside the serenely dying fire. The room was comfortable, and furnished with neither expense nor imagination. The three-piece suite of chairs and sofa was a sort to be seen in the window of any large store in London. There were neither pictures nor photographs, and the small glass-fronted bookcase contained only textbooks and outdated copies of the *Medical Directory*. Under a standard lamp with a pink-fringed shade was a small table with the black-and-white bakelite case of their new wireless set. He saw his wife had been sewing. Her treadle-operated machine was without its cover, and on the maroon chenille tablecloth were his shirts with their cut sleeves, and a new jacket to which she had been attaching the secret buttons for his cuffs.

'I hope you weren't expecting me earlier. The Yard got hold of me at the club.'

'I only expect you when I see you, John. It's part of the job, isn't it?'

My job or her job? he wondered. She's no cause to complain about either. 'I haven't had an easy day. The inquest and so on this morning went very well, but people at Blackfriars were being extremely difficult.' He had no intention of telling her more.

'What did the Yard want?'

'Nothing very interesting.'

'What about your lunch? Did you enjoy yourself?'

'There were some quite important people there.'

She folded her hands on the library book lying in her lap. Her fingers were rough, and she never used nail-varnish. He had forgotten the times when they sat across the fire after he came home, eagerly sorting the small change of their day's activities, passing from one to another the small, familiar tokens valueless to anyone but themselves. She was the same age as himself. She was slim, almost to the dangerous point of scrawniness, with noticeable hollows at the neck of her plain green dress. She had good legs, quite arresting when she wore silk stockings. Her skin was pale, smooth and waxy, her mouth and chin small, giving her a waif-like look. Her fair hair was parted at the middle, and she curled it at home every Friday with a sixpenny Amami Wave Set from the chemist's.

'Were there any wives at the lunch?'

'Perhaps one or two. I honestly don't know. At such functions one is asked very much for oneself, you know. People in society have a different outlook from those in this part of the world.'

'Next time, say you must bring me.'

He decided she was being mischievous. 'You wouldn't be expected, Rosemary.'

37

'I'd like to meet Lady Accrington just once. I read about her in the *Bystander*.'

'She's rather formidable.' He got up and made abruptly for the kitchen.

There were two rooms at the back of the house. One he had fitted up as a laboratory, where he worked until midnight when he happened to find himself at home in the evenings. In the kitchen across the short corridor he started to prepare a milk drink, widely advertised to induce sleep of the finest quality and to overcome innumerable social and business problems. He hoped she wouldn't follow him, but she did.

'That new wireless, John. It's a wonderful tone. So much better than the last old thing.'

The feverishness of her voice put him more on his guard. 'Then I'm glad I bought it.'

'But you didn't want to, did you? How I had to talk you into it!'

'I've told you we can't be extravagant.'

'Oh, I know. We can't even have a maid.'

He turned the gas-tap. 'I thought this latest charwoman was satisfactory?'

'She's as good as any. As long as I work in the house myself. But everyone knows we haven't a maid. You can't blame them for wondering why.'

'I'm not interested in the slightest what the neighbours think of us. I've no time for such people.'

'But they don't understand. You can't deny you're famous, can you? They imagine you must be wealthy as well. The two go together in everyone's mind these days.'

'You know exactly what I earn. I've always been frank about it. Two guineas for a post-mortem, three if I give evidence at the inquest. As I'm entirely dependent on Norman Carlow for most of this, it's a good job I keep in with him. A day at the Old Bailey rewards me with the princely sum of one guinea. Plus sixpence a mile travelling expenses. For Assizes in the country I'm allowed my railway fare, third-class and at the reduced return rate. If I have to walk, I'm entitled to three-pence a mile for refreshments. In both directions. A man can

38

hardly grow rich on that. It's all in Home Office orders and the Coroners' Act. If you don't believe me, go to Dulwich public library and look it up.'

'The milk's boiling over.'

He turned off the gas.

'Couldn't you economize on your clothes?' she suggested.

'I've got to keep up a decent appearance. I can't go into the witness box in a shabby suit. It would look as if I didn't take the court seriously, or I was a second-rater. These things mean a lot. You seem to forget I've a lot of professional expenses.' He was becoming annoyed. 'I have to insure my life. I've no intention of leaving you destitute, you know. Mine's a risky trade. I could be dead in a week, if I pricked my finger tomorrow working on an infected corpse.'

'You could write articles for the newspapers. They always seem anxious enough to print your name.'

'That's a stupid idea. Apart from anything else, I'm governed by the Official Secrets Act.'

'Graham Trevose does.'

'Trevose is a slippery customer. He'll come a cropper one day.' He poured hot milk into a cup and added chocolate-coloured crystals from a tin. He was resentful of her again bringing up the business of a housemaid, when he was so tired. He supposed she had been tightly winding up the spring of her argument all evening.

'If you don't care what the local people think of you, what about Lady Accrington and that set?'

He sipped the hot drink. 'They're different. They're more intelligent. They understand the world. They're cultured.'

'Why do you keep me away from them?'

'Do I? What's this sudden enthusiasm? I thought you didn't care to mix with them.'

'You think that only because I don't create scenes and insist on going. I don't because it would only make things more difficult for you.'

'Don't I take you out often enough?'

'You're ashamed of me.'

'No, no, I'm not.' He felt he was doing badly in the argument.

39

He was much more at home in the witness-box at the Old Bailey than in his own kitchen. Then suddenly he was sorry for her. It was an uncommon emotion. However much he saw of mankind's sad inadequacies, his soul was pitifully starved of compassion. She had been the only human to draw any tenderness from him, to pierce the isolation he felt in the world, to give him a precious sense of correlation with some other being. When they married he had recognized this as love – the very essence of love, as far as it could be distilled by the inaptly scientific apparatus of his mind. That was five years ago. Now he thought her dull, small-minded, obsessed with domestic trivia, lacking in social graces, a liability. In five years he had risen in the world, by his achievement alone. She had failed to keep up with him, and that was her failure. She was a disappointment to him. But somehow all women were a disappointment to Rumbelow.

'I know it's difficult for you, Rosemary,' he said more kindly, 'if only because my life hasn't turned out the way either of us expected. I hope you're glad I'm a success. It's easy enough to miss the boat in medicine. I'd no connexions, no money, no one in the family to help me at Blackfriars, nor even in the profession. I could have ended up running a shilling surgery in the East End, making up my own medicines, running my own errands, treating no one but the working classes. A drudge without prospects. It happens, you know. Even to men who were students with me.'

'I'm not decrying everything you've done. I'd never do that. I'm proud of you, John.' He stirred uneasily. He didn't want her to be proud of him. It only emphasized her attachment. 'I talk about you a lot, every day. Even to perfect strangers, who come up in the shops and ask if I'm really your wife. It's quite thrilling, you know.'

He drained the cup of flavoured milk. 'Things might have been better had you wanted a child.'

'Why must you bring that up?' She could grow angry about this, but now she sounded only helpless. 'Haven't we been over it often enough?'

'We've been over your excuses often enough. First you

thought you'd go on with your job, teaching schoolchildren in London. Then you had the house to run. Then you didn't think you were strong enough —'

'They were reasonable excuses.'

'No excuse is reasonable for a woman to avoid having a child. It's a natural function. It's like making excuses to stop breathing.'

'Now you're making me sound inhuman.'

'I'm not. I only think you're rather pathetic. But it doesn't make your outlook any more agreeable.'

'Very well. I'll tell you the truth.' She hesitated. 'I'm scared.'

'Of childbirth! In this day and age?'

'Not of the birth itself. Of . . . of what I might produce. Some monster. A cretin, a mongol, an idiot.'

He stared at her, amazed. It was the first time she had even hinted to him of such fears. 'But that's ridiculous. They're remarkably uncommon.'

'I don't care. They can happen. I could see it happen to me.' He noticed her eyes fill with tears.

'But why *should* it happen to you? We're both healthy.'

'I don't know, I don't know. I just feel it, that's all. I've tried to conquer it, to hide it somewhere in my mind. But I can't. Won't you understand me? Won't you even try to?'

She was looking up at him imploringly, fumbling with a lace-edged handkerchief from the pocket of her dress. He was satisfied. He had dominated her, as he could dominate a jury at the Old Bailey or Lady Accrington's luncheon-table. After facing her for some seconds he said, 'I should much have liked a child, you know.'

He put out the light and made for the stairs. Partly through her aversion to motherhood and partly because there was no love left between them, they had enjoyed no sexual intercourse for some time. But they shared the same bed, Rumbelow thinking the expense of a new pair of twin ones somewhat unnecessary.

6

WHEN SIXSMITH TELEPHONED, Rumbelow imagined it was about the Vickery case. He knew by then the trial was to open at the Old Bailey after the Easter holiday, on the Wednesday, April the fifteenth.

'I've got a journey for you, I'm afraid, Doctor.'

'That's all right.' Rumbelow found himself out of London almost every month on police business.

'You said you weren't going away for Easter. I hope I was right taking you at your word?'

'Where's it to?

'Mortlock. It's a hundred-odd miles west of London. Perhaps you know the place?' Rumbelow had been through it in the train. 'It's an exhumation. At a village just outside, to be exact. I'd like it done as soon as possible. You know how these affairs have the habit of leaking out.'

'Have you obtained the Home Office order?'

'It's in front of me.' The detective sounded a little offended. 'We could do it early tomorrow, as soon as the light's good enough. I'm going back there by the evening train. I'm now at the Yard, so I could come over to Blackfriars in a car and pick you up. Say about five o'clock?'

Rumbelow pulled out his dead brother's gold watch. 'Yes, that's convenient. I've time to get a bag with some clothes sent up from home.'

'I'll give you the background when we meet.'

'I'll be in my lab.'

Rumbelow put the receiver back on its hook. He had a telephone of the old-fashioned sort in his laboratory. The room

42

was small, on the ground floor of the pathology department, just down the corridor from the committee room. The single window of frosted glass, looking inwards on to a small courtyard and the medical school library, Rumbelow had never been known to open. Under the window was a workbench with a pair of gas-taps for the Bunsen burners, a small, deep sink heavily stained with chemicals let into one end. Arranged on the bench were racks of test-tubes and a chemist's wash-bottle, his microscope with a hooded lamp, and beside it a wooden case the size of a cigar-box, notched inside to hold the glass microscope slides. One wall held racks of chemical reagents and a glass-fronted cupboard crammed with apparatus. The other was taken up with green metal filing cabinets. Everything looked as though it needed a good dusting. He always locked the door when he left, and there was only one other key, in the head-porter's lodge, in case of fire.

He had been sitting alone, on a high wooden stool, busy with the microscope. It was just after lunch on the Thursday before the Easter week-end. It suited him to be working over the next day or so. The coroners' courts wouldn't be sitting, and it was an unexpected chance to earn a fee. He picked up the telephone again and asked the hospital exchange for his home number. He told Rosemary to pack an attaché case and bring it up as soon as possible.

'How long will you be away?'

'It's impossible to say. I'm going down to the West Country. Perhaps a couple of days.'

'What about Brighton on Saturday?'

He had forgotten this promised excursion. 'We'll have to put it off. This bitterly cold weather wouldn't make it very pleasant, anyway.'

She did not seem disappointed, though he had felt she was in her small-minded way excited about the outing. Since the dispute in the kitchen they had mentioned neither maids, money nor progeny. They had continued the usual way between their fairly infrequent clashes, almost two strangers occupying the same house. What made life so difficult at home, Rumbelow thought as he replaced the telephone on the window-sill, was

43

lack of the harmless little pretences and deceptions which made life outside it possible at all. He had no barrier of reputation or professional standing to dodge behind. There were not even any rules to control an argument, as in court. He was aware that *something* must happen to them, struggling with an unstable relationship. He seldom speculated what, because it was beyond his powers even to start formulating an answer, which upset him. But he wished she wasn't so damned proud of him.

He went back to the microscope slides. He was examining sections from the abdominal skin of a woman found with her head in a gas-oven in a Soho flat. She was a prostitute, new to the district, and nobody could identify her. She had the recent scar of a hysterectomy, which would be on the records of some hospital, and the police hoped for a lead if Rumbelow could tell them exactly when the operation had been done.

This sort of puzzle had interested him for a year. He had cut pieces of the scar from patients dying in Blackfriars at various times after operations, comparing them under the microscope. An operation incision was just like any other knife-wound, uninfected and healing 'by first intention', as the surgeons said. At first the slide would be full of macrophages, large round cells, the body's scavengers, eating up the debris. Then came young fibroblasts to form the connective tissue which permeated every organ in the body, mingled with minute blood-vessels, their walls only one cell thick, to make the richly vascular 'granulation tissue'. The fibroblasts were the key, Rumbelow thought. As the macrophages and blood-vessels shrivelled away, the fibroblasts turned into different-looking flattened cells, scattered sparsely amid the fibrous mass of the scar. If this process always went at the same speed, by counting the decreasing number of fibroblasts to the square millimetre, surely the pathologist could tell exactly the time since the wound was made? He recognized it might never be a matter of great importance. But no work for Rumbelow was too trivial to escape the full impact of his ability, concentration and diligence. His task was always to systematize the processes of the body and to describe them with exactitude, because that was the basis of medicine.

44

He was busy with his slides all afternoon. There was a knock on the laboratory door. Nobody was allowed in without knocking, not even his wife.

'Rosemary?'

But it was Quinley in his white coat.

Rumbelow was embarrassed. 'Yes? I'm rather busy.'

'I'm sorry, sir. But I wondered if you had a report on that prostate. From the p.m. last week.'

'Ah, yes, Quinley . . . come in, come in.' He reached to turn off the bulb directed at the reflector of his microscope. 'I must congratulate you. You were right.'

The news did not seem to give Quinley any particular gratification. Rumbelow had taken pains to be pleasant to him since their tiff, partly because he felt ashamed of himself and partly because he conceded the damage done to his reputation and he wanted to minimize it. There was no point in encouraging Quinley to spread the story more poisonously than necessary.

'The slides are in that box in the corner. Have a look at them in your own room. I sent the report to the ward, so the houseman could issue the death certificate without any more delay.' At least the painful admission was made privately, and a week was long enough for people to start forgetting. 'How many p.m.s today?'

'Only one.'

'You'd better do it. I've been called away, so I'm a bit pushed for time.'

Quinley stood inside the closed door, wearing his usual gloomy expression. 'Could I have a word with you, sir? It's rather important.'

Rumbelow wanted to be rid of him, but suddenly fearing it was something more to do with their disputed case he indicated a hard spoke-backed chair, the only other seating in the room.

'It's about the vacant readership.'

'You weren't thinking of putting in for it?'

'I was, in fact.'

'But you're too young. A readership is quite a senior post, you know.'

Quinley ran his tongue over his thick lips. '*You*'re young, sir.'

45

'Yes, but I'm exceptional. Anyway, there are no plans to fill the post. The whole department has to be reorganized. We're all at sixes and sevens, since the last reader upped and went to the Cape.'

Because he objected to the division of our work, Rumbelow recalled. The department was shared between Rumbelow, who was consultant pathologist, and Appledore, who was the professor of morbid anatomy. The distinction between the two titles was delicate, and had anyway become meaningless as Rumbelow now did nothing but post-mortems and forensic medicine.

'I gather it's in the professor's mind to appoint someone next autumn.'

'Is it? Well, possibly. I haven't seen him for some days. Did you mention your ambition?'

'He seemed rather encouraging.'

Rumbelow sat clasping his knee. Quinley's news was a shock. He had hoped to see the back of him within a year. To be faced with the man for the remainder of his career at Blackfriars was unthinkable. 'To anyone else?'

'Dr Bantrell.'

'Bantrell!' Rumbelow almost jumped from the stool. 'Why Bantrell? What have you to do with him?'

Quinley self-consciously indicated the red lump on his cheek. 'He's treating my boils with vaccine.'

'Put in for the job by all means, if you like. It's your decision.' Bantrell! thought Rumbelow. He won't get far trying to run me in the same harness. 'What do you wish me to do?'

'I know that appointments aren't always straightforward —'

'That merit alone isn't always rewarded? Well, that's a realistic way of facing things. Oh, I'll put in a good word for you where it matters, don't worry.'

The younger man's face filled with relief as suddenly as if caught by a spotlight. He had deliberately put himself at Rumbelow's mercy before even making up his mind to apply for the job. He didn't get on with Rumbelow – neither did many others at Blackfriars – but the bitterness of Rumbelow's dislike was beyond him. Despite his academic honours, he

46

simply felt too humble to merit such hate. Now he decided that Rumbelow appreciated him, approved of his work, was prepared to be an ally, or at least not be a dangerous obstacle. He did not know that Rumbelow was for once deliberately telling a serious lie.

'I'm very grateful, sir. I know how valuable it is, having you behind me. I hope it wasn't cheek my asking?'

'Not cheek at all.' Rumbelow made an airy gesture. 'Are you still going to Dr Bantrell? I suppose that vaccine's effective? He doesn't seem to be doing you much good.'

Even as Quinley left, Rumbelow knew he had been foolish. It would have been better to have informed the fellow straight out he wouldn't raise a finger to help. It didn't matter – he was hopelessly inexperienced for the job. But Quinley might have ascribed that to ill-natured resentment over the episode in the post-mortem room. He was a surly sort, who could spread a malicious story among the students and the junior staff. It would make Rumbelow seem petty and vindictive. He turned back to his microscope, satisfied with his excuse for his duplicity. A wound to a man's vanity can bleed away his reason.

7

THE CLOCK NOT yet having been put back, at half past five on
Good Friday morning, the sun rising beyond the ridge of
Salisbury Plain, Rumbelow in his bowler and fur-collared overcoat was walking down a country lane, smoking a cigar. Beside
him was Sixsmith, behind a local policeman carrying his bag.
It was cold, even with snow in the air. Rumbelow was in a buoy-
ant mood. He always enjoyed official excursions to new places,
and it was a relief freeing himself for a while from Blackfriars
and from Rosemary. He was impressed with the tension he must
have been suffering.

'That's surprising.' He paused, peering towards a hedge. 'The
heckberry, or bird cherry. It's unusual so far south. It grows a
bitter little black fruit, which the birds are very fond of.'

'I'm not much of a gardener,' said Sixsmith.

'I was brought up in the country.'

'This part of the world?'

'In Yorkshire. Perhaps that accounts for my obstinacy,'
he added, an uncustomary self-admission. 'My father was a
clergyman, a country rector. I nearly went into the Church
myself.'

'You'd certainly have kept your flock on the path of right-
eousness,' said Sixsmith humorously.

'But I have one fundamental disadvantage. You see, I don't
believe in God. Nor the life hereafter, which is a myth based
on man's self-importance. He can't bear to think of himself
extinct for ever. We are only bodies, and the only difference
between a living and a dead one is between a machine which is
running and another which is rusting to bits.'

'So you're not worried at anyone looking from Heaven when you're cutting up his remains?'

Rumbelow laughed. 'I have critics enough, without having to contend with ghosts.'

In the strengthening light they could see the square tower of Blayford church over the hedge. They had come to the village in a police-car from Mortlock, where they had spent the night. They were taking a short cut from the local constable's house, which served as a police-station. The lane led to a small road opposite the lych-gate, where a blue van was drawn up and a young policeman in a jersey, helmetless, without collar and tie and his sleeves pushed up, was taking a pair of sharp-pointed shovels from the back.

A yew hedge separated the churchyard from the road, where two policemen in overcoats were passing the time chatting to some twenty reporters, most of whom Rumbelow recognized. Sixsmith's fear of a leak was justified. Everyone in Mortlock the night before appeared to be gossiping about 'the case'. Rumbelow's manifestation with his black bag seemed to indicate that everything was over bar the hanging.

In the lych-gate stood the vicar in his cassock.

'The parson's in a state,' said Sixsmith. 'We're ruining his Easter services.'

'I suppose we should have postponed our resurrectionist activities till Sunday?' Rumbelow threw the butt of his cigar under the yew hedge.

A hearse drew up, blinds of grey cloth down behind the glass. Two men in dark overcoats climbed out. Behind stopped a black Triumph Gloria. 'The local doctor,' said Sixsmith. 'I'll introduce you.'

He was a fat middle-aged man with sagging jowls, in a brown tweed overcoat and a broad-brimmed weather-beaten trilby. He was called Halverston. They all entered the churchyard. Nobody took any notice of the vicar.

The canvas screens had been rigged to embrace half a dozen graves, giving everyone room to move about. Two policemen and a labourer in corduroy trousers stood waiting with shovels. There was a sallow young man in a black homburg who was introduced to Rumbelow as Copley, the solicitor representing the widow's interests. On the new marble headstone he noticed,

JAMES GETHERIDGE JEAVONS
OF BLAYFORD AND SINGAPORE
WHO DEPARTED THIS LIFE
2.12.35 AGED 50.

'We can't start yet,' said Sixsmith. 'The Chief Constable hasn't turned up.'

He was a short man with a military moustache, who fussed into the churchyard from a police car a few minutes later. The labourer edged aside the headstone. The policemen started to dig.

'In popular imagination this is always done at midnight to the light of flickering oil-lamps,' Rumbelow observed to Sixsmith. 'And until quite recently it was. Quite ridiculous! You need all the light you can get. Particularly when you're liable to be closely cross-examined on the morning's activities.'

There was silence, except for the grating of the policemen's shovels against the frosty soil.

'You know we're almost in sight of his house?' said Sixsmith after some time, nodding past the church. 'You may have noticed that large red-brick place down the road.'

'The widow knows we're at work?'

'Oh, yes, I've got a man watching the house. You never know what might happen. All the blinds are drawn, like a funeral.'

'What's she like?'

'She seems a level-headed sort of woman. Scared, naturally. I've only had one interview.'

'Over twenty years younger than he was?'

Sixsmith nodded. 'She's not local, of course. She met him on the boat coming home.'

'And she gets all the money? She's been very stupid, playing fast and loose with that artist fellow.'

'It's all gossip, of course. We've still got to tread warily.' Sixsmith was in his fifties, approaching retirement, and there was nothing like the imminence of a pension to make a man cautious. 'But women *are* stupid, Doctor.'

50

'It should make your job easier.'

'It doesn't. They're so illogical it makes it twice as hard.'

A substantial pile of earth had grown to one side of the grave. Rumbelow noticed with dislike it was clayey and damp. A body could yield valuable evidence even after several years, but if it was badly putrefied too much might be left to medical detection to satisfy a jury. 'I'll have the first specimen of soil, please.'

With a wooden spoon, allowing no possibility of metallic contamination, he scooped a little and sealed it in a wide-mouthed jar from his bag. A blue-edged label affixed the night before said in his neat handwriting, *Grave Soil. Specimen* 1.

'I hate poisoners,' said Sixsmith unexpectedly.

'Why, particularly?'

'It's done at a distance. It's cowardly.'

'Murder's always murder. How it's performed is surely of interest but not of significance.' The superintendent made no reply. 'Perhaps she should have had him cremated. It's becoming sufficiently popular not to cause a stir, even in a place like this.'

Sixsmith gave a slight nod towards Dr Halverston, standing thoughtfully on the far side of the steadily deepening grave. 'Perhaps she wasn't too keen on the statutory requirement of an independent doctor to examine the body.'

'You may be right.' Rumbelow had a notorious contempt for provincial general practitioners.

'We're reaching the coffin, sir,' called out one of the policemen.

'Then I'll have another specimen,' said Rumbelow.

The policemen shovelled more carefully, until the still-polished wood with its brass plate came into view. Ropes were produced. Surprisingly easily, the coffin was pulled up and edged to one side of the grave. A plain-clothes man took photographs. When Sixsmith asked one of the undertakers from the hearse to identify it he exclaimed, 'I screwed it down myself,' clearly proud of his connection with such a notorious local affair.

'Before moving it,' said Rumbelow, 'I should like you to open the lid slightly, if Mrs Jeavons' solicitor agrees. That will be necessary to allow the escape of gases.'

51

Ten minutes later it was in the hearse on its way to Mortlock, a detective-inspector sitting in front.

By eight o'clock Rumbelow was in his shirt-sleeves and red rubber apron, starting work in the small whitewashed police mortuary behind the Shire Hall. He had with him a policeman who acted as mortuary attendant, Sixsmith and Dr Halverston. The pale-faced solicitor had decided to wait just outside. As Rumbelow set out his instruments and specimen jars, Sixsmith passed across a copy of the death certificate. Rumbelow saw that his colleague in the tweed overcoat had given the cause of death as heart-failure secondary to high blood-pressure. He nodded. In sleepy areas like Blayford, such documents were often fictional.

Rumbelow unscrewed the lid of the coffin, which was standing on trestles. With his small bone-saw he took a specimen of the wood, and dropped it with forceps into a jar. There was a surprisingly heavy growth of white mould inside, much of it hanging like a curtain from the lid. 'The shroud's adherent to the body,' said Rumbelow, taking another specimen. 'Though it's not friable. So perhaps we shall find things better preserved than I expected.'

The body on a bed of sawdust was recognizable as a burly, thick-necked man with a snub nose. 'Very strange, meeting him again,' murmured Dr Halverston.

'How long was he ill?' Rumbelow and the police were moving the corpse to the post-mortem table.

'Terminally, only a few hours. I was called at eight in the morning. I remember I was having my lunch when they phoned to say he was dead.'

'And the symptoms?'

'Complete collapse. Poor pulse. Difficulty in breathing. I prescribed sedatives. There seemed no more I could do.'

'Any vomiting and diarrhoea?'

'A little.' He added defensively, 'As might be expected.'

'Indeed,' said Rumbelow, starting work with his long scalpel.

'He was a very nice man. Quite popular in the area, you know. So is Mrs Jeavons. I really can't imagine for one moment she'd have anything to do with . . . with this.'

'Then this is all for her own good, Doctor,' said Sixsmith shortly. 'It'll clear away all those unpleasant rumours.'

'I do so hope as much.'

'Did he complain of cramp in the calves before he died?' asked Rumbelow.

'Now, that's odd. It was about the only thing he was able to say to me.'

Rumbelow had changed from conventional post-mortem technique. For once, he examined the abdomen first. He wanted to avoid disturbing the stomach when removing organs from the chest. The stomach lining seemed normal, examined under running water. The duodenum had perhaps been inflamed, though that needed the eye of faith. There *could* be yellow streaks outside the stomach walls – if his vague guess was right, due to formation of the sulphide. Everything would need careful analysis in London. The intestines were normal. He cut specimens with his scissors from each section of the gut, sealing them in separate bottles.

He went back to the body, running his knife inside the man's jaw, drawing heart and lungs through the open cage of ribs. The lungs themselves still had fluid present, to be expected whether Halverston was right or wrong. The heart was enlarged. He snipped it open, and taking his magnifying-glass inspected closely the membrane covering the left ventricle. Perhaps a trace of petechial haemorrhages? he wondered. The microscope later would tell.

'Did he have a water-hammer pulse, Dr Halverston?'

'I never detected as much.'

'But he had aortic incompetence. Look – the ascending aorta is enlarged, you can still see longitudinal rugae on the intima. They shouldn't be there. The aortic valves are thickened, though the orifices of the coronary arteries seem to have escaped.'

'Yes, yes . . . all due to high blood-pressure.'

'Not at all. He had syphilis.'

'What! But . . . but I'd certainly no inkling he suffered from it. No inkling at all.'

'Well, he probably wanted to keep it to himself.'

'No, no, not a man like James Jeavons —'

'Or perhaps he didn't know he had it? This is a very late stage, perhaps thirty years after infection. A primary chancre as a young man out East – he may have thought it a tropical sore, something else.'

'But it's impossible! Surely he would have confided in his own doctor?'

'Not necessarily. You'd better put this to the widow.'

'Certainly not. I shall say nothing, absolutely nothing, until your post-mortem diagnosis is confirmed,' said Halverston crossly.

'By whom?' Halverston looked lost. 'Call in another pathologist, if you like. There's no urgency about re-burial. It will anyway be weeks before I can complete the analysis of these specimens. My hands are full with a big case at the Old Bailey next Wednesday.'

'But surely you don't expect to find anything more?'

'I don't know. If I do, you and Mrs Jeavons' solicitor will be informed.'

'But what? What *can* you expect to find?'

'I told you, I don't know.'

'The cause of death was heart-failure, following incompetence of the aortic valve.' Halverston was now angry, his face mottled and his jowls quivering. 'If that was due to syphilis and not high blood-pressure, then I made a clinical error in signing the death certificate. Very well. What's the point of recriminations? There was no possible treatment at that stage. A correct diagnosis would not have added a minute to the man's life.'

Rumbelow had disliked Halverston from the start. He was more irritated at his arguing as though they were professionally equals. 'Perhaps it's unfortunate the condition didn't suggest itself to you earlier, when something might have been done. If you look up the notes of his blood-pressure readings, which I admit might perfectly well be raised, you may see an abnormally large pulse-pressure as well.'

'I don't have notes on everything.' Halverston tapped his head. 'I prefer to keep things in here.'

No wonder people get away with murder, thought Rumbelow.

'Surely we can get all this settled and out of the way at the inquest tomorrow?' Halverston sounded more conciliatory.

'The proceedings will be only formal, without a jury. And adjourned, of course.'

'Why need it be? Why leave everyone in suspense? What of the strain on poor Mrs Jeavons? Nobody seems to have any consideration for her feelings at all. It can surely be established right away that death was due to the effects of syphilis. I certainly should not raise any objection,' he added with the air of a man striking a bargain.

'I'm sorry for everyone concerned in the case. But a coroner's jury cannot be asked to give a verdict until they have all the facts. And that will not be so until I have analysed these specimens. Even if the analysis turns out completely negative.'

'It sounds like a lot of official fussiness to me.'

'Yes,' said Rumbelow. 'It is.'

Rumbelow and Sixsmith were staying at the Red Lion, nearly opposite the Shire Hall. As they were crossing the almost deserted main street for a late breakfast, Sixsmith said about Halverston, 'He certainly seems to stand on his dignity.'

'He's precious little else to stand on.'

'Then Jeavons died of syphilis? Hardly worth an exhumation.'

'Wait till I've completed my analysis.'

'Do you suspect anything?'

'Yes. Arsenic. Which will make matters very complicated for the Crown indeed.'

8

MRS MAVERY'S LUNCHEON parties were gayer than those of
Lady Accrington, who like many upper-class Englishwomen
instinctively deplored immorality, social inferiors, bores and
flippancy, but whose social ambitions increasingly obliged her
to put up with all four. Mrs Mavery, like other sophisticated
Americans in Europe, brought a freshness and energy to the
local customs which outshone the natives. She was unimagin-
ably wealthy – the asparagus that April Tuesday was casually
ordered from the South of France by aeroplane. She preferred
the respectable fringe of Chelsea to Mayfair. She was vivacious,
amusing and open-hearted, always ready to take people as they
were, providing they were rich and important enough. She
asked Rumbelow regularly, partly because he was always in the
news and partly because he was so often invited by Lady
Accrington, of whom she was painfully jealous.

There were a dozen guests, including a pompous actor with a
knighthood, about to play a murderer and hoping for a few
hints from Rumbelow, in which he was hurtfully disappointed.
The conversation was largely monopolized by Hugo Kirkham,
the Washington journalist. Rumbelow's experience of the Press
being restricted to crime reporters, he was surprised and at
first resentful to find a newspaperman invited. They were hardly
his social equals. But apparently journalists in America were
grand people, deferred to even by the President.

'The trouble with your Empire,' Kirkham told them genially,
'is simply and fundamentally that it's a sham. Or would it be
more complimentary to call it a brilliant confidence-trick? A
magnificent one, the most audacious the world has ever known.

All done by a huge fleet firing ceremonial salutes of blank ammunition over the heads of cleverly trained officials in plumed hats. There's no real force behind it.'

Rumbelow was shocked. To live in London was to be conscious of living in the hub of the Empire, an entity accepted as a matter of course by the newspapers and school-children's atlases, invoked continually by politicians, materialized by colourful visitors and showy exhibitions, the depository of countless younger sons, the wall of confidence at every Englishman's back, the last word to fall from the lips of the old King that blustery midnight the previous January at Sandringham.

'Surely, Hugo, all empires are only confidence-tricks?' said Mrs Mavery. 'Even Mussolini has to keep parading his soldiers all over the place to convince everyone how strong he is.'

'Or maybe to convince himself?'

'I happen to be proud of the British Empire,' said the actor.

'Well, there's *something* to be proud of. There may be no real force behind it, but there's no real oppression either.'

'I should think not! Why, the Empire exists with the deepest mutual respect between us and the Dominions. Look how we all stood together during the War.'

'Maybe the Empire didn't have much choice about that. Fifty million Africans and two hundred and fifty million Indians suddenly found themselves pitched into a war on a continent they'd never seen against an enemy they'd mostly never heard of. I don't remember their being asked nicely. King George simply signed a paper.'

'It was the responsibility of the Mother Country to organize their defence.'

Kirkham smiled. 'Isn't it perhaps time to unload the white man's burden? Those African colonies now – they're ready and waiting for self-rule.'

'I'm afraid I can't agree with you, Mr Kirkham. You must have been listening to the agitators. The African is definitely *not* ready for independence. And if we granted it, do you know what would happen in your own country? Why, your own black population would be stimulated to demand their rights. Oceans are no barrier to revolutionary ideas, as you well know. You'd have riots in your own streets, black against white, just as bad as anything that happened at Amritsar with General Dyer.'

'I'm prepared to take a chance on that.'

'Perhaps you would like us to cure our depression with your "New Deal" into the bargain?' asked the actor sarcastically.

'But Lloyd George suggested exactly that, back in 1929.' Kirkham sounded gleeful. 'It was all in something called *We Can Conquer Unemployment*. He'd almost exactly the same ideas as F.D.R. Perhaps you could do with your little Welshman back?'

The journalist was so frighteningly well-informed that Rumbelow had said nothing for fear of making a fool of himself. Now he was incited to speak up. 'There's a great feeling in the country the new King will mark a change for the better.'

'Why should he?'

'He's vigorous and comparatively young. Such things permeate the circles of government.'

'I could tell you something about your new King ... but no, it is "bad form, old boy" to mention it. Or maybe the Empire couldn't stand the shock.'

Kirkham then said he wanted to watch British justice in action, and asked Rumbelow to get him into the Old Bailey for the Vickery trial next morning. Rumbelow said he'd see what was to be done, having made up his mind to do nothing.

By the design of both themselves and their hostess, Rumbelow left the house with Diana Flavell.

'Where's the famous bag?' smiled Diana.

'I'd no need for my instruments this morning.'

'Where are you off to?'

'Back to the hospital. I was intending to take the Tube. I've plenty of time.'

'Can I give you a lift to Hyde Park Corner Station?'

'That's awfully kind.'

'I hope you don't mind a sports car?'

Her red MG was parked outside. They sped towards Sloane Street, Rumbelow keeping a tight hold on his bowler. As they turned into Sloane Square she asked, 'I wonder if you'd mind doing something for me? I've got that book they published

58

about the Perryman case – the one where the man cut up his girl-friend. We're almost going past my flat. Would you like to sign it?'

'I'd be delighted.'

They stopped outside a large red-brick block behind Harrods.

'It's only on the first floor.'

By then Rumbelow couldn't decide if he was excited or anxious. She was certainly giving him what people called 'the come hither'. They had been brought together several times at Mrs Mavery's – that winter, with the death of the King and the Court going into mourning, was not one of overfull guest-lists. He knew she had a reputation for being 'fast'. She was a blonde with large eyes and a turned-up nose, not strikingly good-looking. She must have been in her mid-twenties. She said she was divorced, though there were always people to tell you darkly she had a husband somewhere. The door was opened by a maid in a black dress and lace apron. Rumbelow felt relieved.

'Let's have some coffee. The Maverys' coffee was ghastly. Americans have just no taste for coffee, you know. Have you been over there?'

'I've never travelled abroad at all.'

The drawing-room had long windows giving on to a small balcony, a gaudy fireplace of steel and onyx, a sheepskin rug and a low marble table, an angular sofa, two vases crammed with daffodils.

'Smoke?' Diana held out a silver cigarette-box.

'Only cigars.'

'Do light one if you like.'

She lit her cigarette with a table-lighter fashioned like a mermaid. She sat on the sofa, Rumbelow taking the squarish armchair opposite, noticing how the slit in her tight-fitting black skirt extended to her knee.

'That's a nice picture.'

'It's a Picasso.' This meant nothing to Rumbelow. 'My dear Doctor, you look nervous.'

'I'm sorry. I don't often find myself alone with a pretty woman.'

'But how devastating! That *does* make me sound terrible.'

'I didn't mean anything discourteous, for one moment . . . I suppose I just wondered why you suddenly took it into your head to invite me up.'

'To be sociable.' She blew a jet of cigarette smoke. 'It's always interesting, talking to you.'

'More than to the others at lunch?'

She laughed. 'You sound as if I'm in the witness-box.' He apologized. 'Why do we never see your wife?'

'She has no interest in social life.'

'Then you must be unhappily married.'

'I wouldn't say that —'

'Yes, you must be. You go everywhere, and enjoy every moment of it. Your two outlooks are different. You're incompatible.'

'Well, possibly.' He disliked talking about Rosemary to anyone.

'Is she young? Is she pretty?'

'It would be fair to say "not particularly" to both questions.'

'A judicial pronouncement,' observed Diana.

The maid appeared for a moment with a tray containing two cups and a small, steaming brass pot. Rumbelow noticed the room had already been darkening, and now the wind threw a handful of rain against the windows.

'April is the cruellest month,' said Diana. 'Mixing memory and desire, stirring dull roots with spring rain.' He looked blank. 'That's T. S. Eliot.'

'I don't think I've heard of him. He sounds rather depressing.'

She handed him a coffee-cup. 'Don't you get depressed, spending your life cutting up dead bodies?'

'No more than a surgeon spending his cutting up live ones.' It was Turkish coffee, thick and too sweet for his taste.

'Doesn't death mean anything to you? Aren't you scared of it?'

'It's simply a nothingness, a negative factor. How can one be scared of something which doesn't exist?'

'But surely you must be sorry for the people who are hanged?'

'Why should I be? They have committed a crime, and they

60

deserve their punishment. Anyway, they're complete strangers to me. The first time I set eyes on them is in the dock. The next on the post-mortem table.'

She sipped her coffee for a moment in silence. 'After the way you hold forth at the Old Bailey, I'd no idea you could be so shy.'

'Shy? I don't think so.'

'Of course you are. We've known each other – how long? Six months, on and off. You've told me absolutely nothing about yourself. What you feel, what goes on inside.' From his expression, she took him as disinclined to remedy this omission. 'Are you fond of women?'

'I'm only human. But I don't go chasing after them, if that's what you mean. It wouldn't be at all right for a man in my position.'

She laughed. 'It's the pastime of men in all sorts of positions, believe you me. You must have had girl-friends in the past?'

'Before I married, yes.'

'The wife who is neither particularly young nor particularly pretty seems to have a powerful hold over you.' She stubbed out her cigarette. 'Come and kiss me.'

The invitation was not one of unmixed delight for Rumbelow. He disliked finding himself in an unfamiliar situation which he could not see his way to master. But he told himself that among sophisticated people a kiss meant nothing – even intercourse little more. As he crossed the sheepskin rug she thrust out her hands, pulled him down, and he felt her tongue in his mouth. It was the first time he had experienced the 'French kiss' for some years. It was not an idea which appealed to Rosemary, who if she knew of it at all took it as a habit of only the lower classes and Continentals.

'What do you think of me?' Diana spoke more tenderly than he had known her.

Rumbelow was confused. What did one say? He searched for a word . . . fascinating, bewitching, glamorous, attractive. Expressions so uncustomary in his vocabulary they might have been another language. 'I find you very charming.'

'That means nothing . . . listen, you'll have to go now, darling.

I'm expecting someone. But phone me. It's a Kensington number. I'm in the book. Promise?'

'All right.'

She drew him down and kissed him again. 'You don't seem particularly wild about the idea.'

'I . . . I'm sorry. I'm not a great ladies' man.'

She laughed again. 'Perhaps you'd feel more at home if I were a corpse?'

As he straightened up, he remembered, 'That book you wanted me to sign —'

She looked puzzled. 'Oh, that. No, I remember now, I only had it out of Harrods' library.'

Rumbelow walked down the stairs with a feeling which at least he could comfortably recognize. Relief mixed with elation. It was exactly like leaving the witness-box after a severe but triumphant cross-examination.

9

RUMBELOW WAS AT the Old Bailey early. He enjoyed being in court – of any sort, even some poky East End police-court with ink-stained desks and grimy windows, where the well-worn machinery of the law could rattle at a speed too fast for judicial purists. He relished the ceremonious courtesy of a trial, the theatricality of compressing the story into a few hours' telling within a few square feet, the contrast between a high-minded search for truth and the clever showmanship and trickery of counsel. He loved the Dickensian home of the law, the Temple itself between the Strand and the Thames. He often walked from nearby Blackfriars amid its warm brickwork and unexpected little courtyards, its twisting alleys and steep kerbs, so ill-lit at night appropriately to afford the unwary outsider an unexpected tumble. He liked barristers. They were so much more worldly than doctors.

'I say, John – that microscope we discussed last night at the conference. Could you do with one in court?'

In a grey chalk-striped suit with a red carnation in his button-hole, Rumbelow was sitting as usual on the solicitors' benches in the well of the court. Peter Ivors, K.C., who was leading for the Crown, had twisted round to speak. He was a tubby man, wigged and gowned, with large round glasses and an easy smile, wearing an air of faintly bewildered simplicity which had cost a good many wrongdoers their liberty and a few their necks. He and Rumbelow were in some half-dozen cases a year, and knew each other well.

'I don't think it necessary for me actually to produce one.'

'But it might be wise to have a microscope handy. Old Lynacre would love looking down it on the bench.'

'But if the jury did likewise, it would only confuse them.'

'Possibly.' Ivors gave a nod, turning again to a feverish study of his notes.

Rumbelow caught the eye of Sir Arthur Younghusband a couple of yards away. He was the defending K.C., a Member of Parliament, known in the Temple and the House to have ambitions in the direction of Attorney-General. A tall, hawk-nosed, bright-eyed, straight-backed man, Rumbelow knew him well also. As they exchanged smiles it warmed Rumbelow to feel the civilized lack of animosity between the two sides, the comradeship of cultured and intelligent gentlemen. They rose as Mr Justice Lynacre entered, florid-faced in short wig and red robe. Rumbelow had met him once or twice, was aware he had a large house in Northamptonshire and enjoyed fox-hunting, and felt approval of the reliability with which His Majesty chose the squirarchy to sit in judgment on his subjects. It was perhaps sad they should all be gathered that morning only to find if a young garage-mechanic from the lower middle classes had killed and burnt his bigamous wife or not.

There were three massive chairs of green-and-gold leather half-invisible behind panelling of light oak. The judge took that on the left. The grandest in the middle was reserved for the Lord Mayor of London or his Aldermen, who collectively held the Commission for the Assize, and if unrepresented about the building somewhere would invalidate the proceedings and presumably face all the prisoners with instant liberty. Everyone turned their heads. Vickery appeared with two policemen in the spacious dock, three sides screened by glass. He was thin and pale with a narrow black moustache and over-brilliantined hair, dressed in a white shirt and well-kept blue suit. Rumbelow had never set eyes on him before.

Rumbelow glanced at the crammed Press benches on his right, and the gallery sloping steeply under the huge skylight, full of inquisitive, or ghoulish, citizens who had queued all night. Vickery was being charged that on or about November the thirtieth last, in the County of Middlesex, he did murder

Eileen Bertha Durban. He replied, '*Not* guilty', as though asked an entirely ridiculous question.

Twelve men in dark suits were ushered by a police-sergeant into the jury-box on Rumbelow's left. They don't look a particularly intelligent bunch, he thought as they were sworn. But perhaps that was for the best. Scientific truth could enlighten all the more powerfully the dim and unquestioning mind.

Unexpectedly, Sir Arthur Younghusband stood up. 'My Lord, I have an application to make.'

The judge glanced over half-moon glasses, pausing in making a note. 'Is it one which can properly be made in the presence of the jury?'

'No, my Lord.'

'Very well, Sir Arthur.'

The jury were led out again, looking disappointed.

'My application, my Lord, is that Dr Rumbelow should not be allowed to remain in court. Neither during the opening speeches of my learned friend and myself, nor during the examination and cross-examination of witnesses.'

Rumbelow was astounded. He always sat in court throughout, as a matter of right. It was as ridiculous as objecting to the presence of the judge.

'I haven't known this point to be raised before, Sir Arthur,' said the judge mildly. 'Expert witnesses – particularly medical witnesses – are customarily allowed to stay in court. The only object is to make them more valuable, through their hearing all the evidence.'

'Your Lordship may think I am within my rights?'

'You may be within your rights. But what are your reasons?'

Rumbelow noticed Ivors' shoulders moving slightly, a tic when he was worried.

'I would have no objection in a general way to any expert witness for the prosecution remaining throughout. It is perfectly proper for him to hear the defence put forward on behalf of the prisoner. It would be perfectly proper in this case for my learned friend to ask Dr Rumbelow in the witness-box whether he agreed, or not, with the defence suggested for my client. As the medical evidence is likely to assume great importance – indeed, the

65

outcome may well turn on it – your Lordship will appreciate that the result of this exchange would have an effect of some weight on the jury.'

'Is this not all rather hypothetical, Sir Arthur?'

'If the prosecution has secured such a valuable witness as Dr Rumbelow, they will certainly use him to the full. There lies the point of my application. It is Dr Rumbelow's reputation. It is unnecessary for me to emphasize his outstanding skill, his wide experience in forensic medicine. Nor the lucidity and fairness of all he says in court. We must all be grateful that such a witness exists, to assist us in unravelling matters which can become highly technical. But, my Lord, Dr Rumbelow in the minds of the public – in the minds of the jury – has become an infallible expert on murder. He enjoys an affection which the British heart extends only to a few favoured detectives in fiction. In short, what Dr Rumbelow says goes. If in the present case he says that murder has been committed, the jury will be inclined to take his word for it.'

'But of course you would oblige him to give his reasons.'

'Such reasons coming from Dr Rumbelow might carry more conviction with the jury than they deserve.' Sir Arthur sat down.

Rumbelow was angry. He was no stranger to the insinuation that he was less than fair, that he put the weight of his reputation on one side rather than the other, that he was an instrument of the Crown rather than an impartial medical man. But for the first time it had been thrown in his face in open court. He could only console himself it was a trick of Sir Arthur's, who had his job to do and might be as cynical as he cared over a man's reputation.

'Well, Mr Ivors, what do you say to that?' invited the judge.

Ivors stood up. With an air of simplicity and sweet reasonableness he produced the result of some moments' anxious thought. 'My Lord, I can only leave you to decide whether the accepted practice of the court is altered or not.'

'Dr Rumbelow may stay,' said the judge. The jury returned. Rumbelow sat back on the uncomfortable bench, listening to Ivors outlining his case against Vickery, still ruffled.

Vickery had been a chauffeur, taught to drive in the Army

66

before he was invalided out. The previous summer he had met Eileen Durban on holiday at Margate. She was then thirty, admitting twenty-eight. She had a tidy sum in a building society, almost a thousand pounds. She fell for him, and in September they got married. She did not reveal having spent a couple of years in a mental asylum. Nor he of a wife already somewhere or other.

A chauffeur's job being clearly unfitting for the husband of a lady of substance, they took the lease of a garage off the Bath road on the western edge of London. The motor business had promise, Vickery told her. Cars were getting cheaper every year, and once the slump was over almost every family in the country would possess one. Rumbelow had been called to this garage just before Christmas. He had found it not much of a place, an isolated cottage against a largish shed, and a single petrol-pump in front with a broken handle. Behind was a yard surrounded by a brick wall, in which Vickery kept tyres and spare parts. Here the police found Eileen Durban's body – burnt, but not beyond recognition.

Vickery's story was of her hanging herself from one of the metal crosspieces in the shed roof – he readily pointed out the spot. He had panicked, fearing his bigamous marriage would come to light, and that her family would make trouble, particularly as she had made her money over to him. He had burnt the body with petrol and buried it. He told the neighbours his wife had been poorly and had gone on holiday. But neighbours enjoy a gossip, and as at Blayford it travelled further than any of them expected.

Rumbelow listened to this story with no particular feelings. He had no thought for the victim, her excitement and happiness at finding a husband turning to anguish and terror, whether she lost her life by her own hands or his. The feverish scheming, the panic of Vickery never occurred to Rumbelow. He never speculated on the strange dark storms of the mind which moved a human to suicide or murder. Anyway, such behaviour occurred only among a different type of person. The people he mixed with himself never did such things, being ladies and gentlemen.

When the court rose for lunch, Ivors was still speaking. He observed to Rumbelow, 'Younghusband didn't get away with it.'

'I thought it rather cheek.'

'Were you annoyed?'

'Yes.'

'Oh, I shouldn't be piqued at all. It was really a tremendous compliment, in my mind.'

'Perhaps you're right,' said Rumbelow.

When appearing at the Old Bailey he generally lunched at Blackfriars, only a few hundred yards down Ludgate Hill. His mood was not improved by running into Bantrell in the gateway.

'Hello! Are you coming to lunch in the refectory? We're all agog to hear the sordid details.'

'I was intending to send across from my lab. for something. I've a deal of work to do on some books from the library.'

'How's the trial going?'

'It's early days. There are never many surprises in the opening speeches of counsel.'

'I understand Quinley's putting up for the readership?' said Bantrell without more ado.

'So he tells me.'

'And that you're supporting him?'

'I shall do what I can.'

'I heard you two had quite a scene in the p.m. room the other week,' Bantrell laughed. 'One of my students said it was like a Bateman cartoon – you know, "The Man Who Told His Chief He'd Made a Bloomer". I wish I'd been there.' Rumbelow made no comment. 'Are you serious about helping Quinley?'

'I shouldn't have given my word otherwise.'

'But there are degrees of support. We all know that. I shouldn't like the young fellow to be living in a fool's paradise, even though I suppose it's better than no paradise at all.'

'You seem to have taken his interests to heart.'

'He's a bright fellow. I'd like to see him get on. Particularly as he's handicapped by a rather unfortunate manner. Or perhaps it's just because I'm treating his furunculosis.' They

68

started to walk towards the main courtyard of the hospital. The reason is simply that you hope somehow to get at me, Rumbelow thought. 'Of course, it's a staphylococcal infection, so even sulphanilamide would be useless. Not that I could possibly spare any for such a minor condition. Colebrook's doing the official trial in London, of course. My own supplies are painfully limited.'

'Do you think sulphanilamide has real possibilities?' Rumbelow did not object to the conversation heading away from Quinley.

'With streptococcal infections yes, I really think so. More strongly than Domagk himself, I fancy. I looked up his original paper over the week-end, in the *Deutsche Medizinische Wochenschrift*. It was rather lukewarm. And if Tréfouëls hadn't isolated sulphanilamide from the original protonsil at the Institut Pasteur, I doubt if anyone would have bothered with it at all. It seemed ludicrous to treat septicaemia with a vivid red dye.' Bantrell was fond of parading his learning.

'Of course, we've seen this sort of thing before. Intravenous thiosulphate of gold for tuberculosis, for example. The side-effects were so horrifying, most people have given it up.'

'No, I think we're on to a winner here. I just haven't met any side-effects to date, apart from some trouble with emboli.'

'If it works, your name will be linked with the new drug.'

'I suppose one must deserve some credit for pioneering.'

'It will be pioneering with a golden pick.'

'That's a little explicit, isn't it?' said Bantrell, but not unkindly.

Rumbelow left him as they reached the library. This was a showpiece amid the jumble of buildings dating from early Tudor to late Victorian, which met each other in awkward corners to make up the hospital. It was said to have been designed in the mid-eighteenth century by William Kent, and its elaborately moulded ceilings were certainly the same as Kent put into Kensington Palace. The walls of books were split into alcoves, there was a long table down the middle, a wide fireplace at one end and half a dozen comfortable armchairs in which there always seemed to be a student or two asleep.

The librarian was an old man with a long beard, immovable in a glass kiosk by the door – he was interested only in sixteenth-century herbals, and so resented being disturbed that everyone had long ago given up asking him for books. The library was run by three female assistants. Rumbelow had recently kept his own requests to the newest of these, a girl called Maria Osgood. She was about twenty, slim, pink-cheeked, brown-eyed, lively, pretty, though with a small mouth which gave her a prudish look. He saw her standing at the centre table over an open book, wearing a serge skirt and white blouse with blue dots on it. He noticed her dark hair had been newly Marcelled. She was talking to a young man in a rumpled suit, one of the students or housemen. Rumbelow suddenly felt a strong resentful feeling in his direction. He stopped, alarmed. Surely it couldn't be jealousy? That would be quite stupid. She turned and smiled. The young man seeing a consultant respectfully melted away.

'Could you get me McCarthy's *Histopathology of Skin Diseases*, please?'

'Of course, Dr Rumbelow.'

He waited as she hurried up the spiral staircase to the gallery. He wanted to refresh himself on the microscopical changes of familiar skin conditions – eczema, for instance, or even the chafing of tight clothing. The skin of the murdered woman's neck would take great importance in the case, and though he doubted Younghusband's drawing in the red herring of her suffering from a skin disease, he disliked leaving any loophole in his evidence. To quote an authority like McCarthy at him might be a useful shot in the locker.

'I thought you'd be at the Old Bailey today?'

'I am. It's the lunch adjournment.' He took the book. 'I expect it's quite improper to tell you this, but Vickery's neck is going to depend on a small piece of skin, just about six inches by three.'

She looked startled, which pleased him.

'And I wondered if you'd look out a couple of volumes of the *Lancet* for me? The second for the year 1921 and the first for 1922. There're two papers on the excretion of organic arsenical

70

compounds I wanted to look up.' She pencilled the references on a scrap of paper. He added casually, 'Do you like working among books?'

'Yes, very much. I was going to the university, you see. To study English.'

'Oh? What went wrong?'

'The usual thing these days. Financial reasons. It isn't an easy time for my father.'

'I'm sorry . . .'

'I suppose there are other girls worse off. And at least I've got a job, haven't I?'

He would have liked to have asked more about the father and his financial straits. But it would not do to appear prying. 'If you can get those two books, I'll take them across to my lab. for half an hour.'

Rumbelow settled to work feeling more cheerful. Perhaps Ivors had been right. For an experienced counsel like Young-husband to object to his skill as a pathologist was praise indeed – and from a source he should appreciate, a sophisticated fellow-professional in the law. He shouldn't take it to heart. It was all part of the rough-and-tumble of the courts. Yes, seen in retrospect it was really a splendid compliment.

But it was the first cloud of the storm which was to drown him.

10

THAT EVENING RUMBELOW took a taxi. He had locked his laboratory and was walking through the hospital gateway when one drew up, some patient's visitor jumping on to the glistening pavement with a bunch of daffodils. The weather was still bitter, with a freezing drizzle. Rumbelow grasped the open door, and asked for his club. It was an impulse, and he sat back surprised at something so uncharacteristic. He looked through the streaming window irritably as they made across Ludgate Circus and past the new black-glass-and-chromium *Daily Express* building in Fleet Street. These drivers always took you the longest way round.

He was dining with Norman Carlow. The cab had made him early, and he sat in the downstairs morning-room with the book he had bought when the court had risen for the day. As the coroner came bustling in, polishing his monocle, he greeted him, 'God, John, you look studious.'

Rumbelow held up the book. 'They're some poems.'

'Let me see . . . *The Waste Land*. Oh, T. S. Eliot. I can't understand this modern stuff. It doesn't even rhyme.'

'It certainly isn't easy going.'

'You've taken to culture in your old age, have you? Well, that's a splendid thing. A few apt quotations from your lips will impress a jury no end.'

Rumbelow was rather offended at this. 'I'm becoming aware that I'm somewhat ill-read. Not through choice, but there's never time for anything except technical literature in the struggle to keep up-to-date. It's worth an effort to remedy the deficiency. Will you have a drink?'

'As you are aware, I am the enemy of neither grape nor grain.'

Rumbelow rang the bell for a waiter. He ordered a sherry, Carlow a large whisky.

'How's it going at the Old Bailey?'

'Younghusband tried to kick me out of court.'

'*Did* he? If he's reduced to that, he can't have much of a case.'

'That's what I thought.'

'By the way, I've some news about your Dr Elgin, the fallen woman's friend, the king of the curette.' Rumbelow looked interested. 'I fancy the police have got something on him at last.'

'That's hardly before time. I've done p.m.s on half a dozen cases of septic abortion in the past year. All obviously done by a doctor, or someone with specialized knowledge. I should imagine he's responsible for at least a few of them. That's not to mention girls from the provinces, perhaps going home to die in a week or ten days. Everyone in London knows what he's up to. It's quite a scandal.'

Carlow took his whisky and water. 'But there's a dozen abortionists flourishing under our feet. It's a thriving industry for the capital of the Empire.'

'That's not the point. If Elgin's responsible for even one death, it's our duty to prosecute him.'

'Sure, sure, I can hardly disagree with you, can I? As *Custos placitorum Coronae*, charged by His Majesty to look into the unexpected deaths of his subjects, not to mention treasure trove and fires in the City of London, if alas no longer shipwrecks and the health and welfare of his royal fish, the sturgeon. But I've every sympathy with the poor girl who has a lapse just at the wrong moment in her menstrual cycle. After all, a man doesn't ring the bell every time he gets into her. I'm half-inclined to think we should make abortion legal, as they say it is in Russia. Otherwise the world will be crawling like an ant-heap.'

'That's just your anti-papism.'

'No, it's my natural fondness for the fair sex.'

73

'I've met Elgin, you know. A couple of times. At cocktail parties, in perfectly respectable houses. He seems to enjoy some social standing. He struck me as the slippery sort.'

Carlow laughed. 'Like the slippery elm he probably uses to get his results?'

'How did the police nail him?'

'A dying declaration.'

'That's interesting.'

'Yes, it's a rare bird to fly into even my window. The girl's family must have known the ropes, or her doctor was wider awake than most. You'll be doing the p.m. on her tomorrow. I'll adjourn the inquest, of course. Elgin's bound to show up with some high-powered barrister only too anxious to tell me my job.'

Rumbelow noticed his companion's glass was empty, and rang the bell.

'I thank God every day for making me a Protestant,' added Carlow reflectively. 'Two kids are enough these hard times. If I put my wife in the family way again, I honestly wouldn't object to an abortion. Not if done properly, in sterile surroundings.'

'That's a purely theoretical problem for me.'

'Oh, come, now. You and Rosemary are young enough. You never know, you might find yourselves landed with a little surprise package.'

'Rosemary doesn't want a child.'

'What, for physical reasons?'

'No, mental ones.'

'Oh. I see. Well, of course, I don't know your lady well, her being something of a recluse —'

'She's got into her head a lot of old wives' tales. I suppose they've been preying on her. She's really quite deranged about it. Are such fears common in women? I don't know. It's out of my experience. I'm not a gynaecologist.'

Carlow picked up his second whisky and stared at it quizzically. It was strange, even a little shocking, to hear such things from John Rumbelow, whom he thought a typical Englishman – stuffy, clipped of speech, prim and proper, too inhibited to discuss his wife's cooking, let alone her performance in bed. 'At least, no one ever dies from them.'

'Perhaps she should see a psychologist? I've often thought of the idea. She's very . . . well, she's rather cold, you know.'

So she's frigid, thought Carlow, shutting her vagina like a trap-door with old John outside using his prick as a knocker. Or perhaps it's really his fault, not getting a proper stand on? It's a wonder these Englishmen in their bowler hats ever get an erection at all, it's all so frightfully vulgar, don't you know, perhaps they stuff their umbrellas up . . .

'What are you grinning at? It isn't amusing to me, I assure you.'

'I'm sorry. It was only the idea of psychologists. I wouldn't touch them with a barge-pole.' Carlow knew more of sexual psychology than he was inclined to admit, having studied it in depth, for his own satisfaction, in books brought specially by friends from France and Germany. 'Now listen to me, John. I'll tell you what to do. Take Rosemary out for a nice dinner. Spread yourself, a bottle of champagne, all the trimmings. Talk to her like you did in your courting days. That'll put her in a better frame of mind. Women are terribly sentimental. If you play on it, you can do anything with them.'

Rumbelow looked doubtful. But before he could comment a voice behind him exclaimed, 'There's the great pundit himself!' The lean, bald figure of Dr Urrick leant over his armchair.

'Hello, Urrick. You're just down from Edinburgh?'

'This very moment.' The Scot had the habit of puckering his eyes and smiling over the most commonplace remarks, as though they were delicious specimens of wit. It always irritated Rumbelow greatly.

'You know Carlow, of course?'

'Oh, yes. A very good thing for men in our humble position to keep in with the coroners. Eh, Rumbelow?'

'Are you staying here during the trial?'

'I am. It's very convenient, the arrangement for reciprocal hospitality between your splendid club and mine in Edinburgh. You should take advantage of it yourself, in the other direction.'

75

'I seem very comfortable in that little hotel off Princes Street.' He did not relish anywhere likely to bring more of Urrick's company.

'Ah, I can't afford hotels. We're not all rolling in it like you, Rumbelow.' Urrick looked down with the same twinkling expression. He was a pathologist at Edinburgh, an expert in the Scottish courts, who had been called in to the Vickery case for the defence. He and Rumbelow had been on different sides of a courtroom before. 'I suppose I shouldn't be seen talking to you? You're great sticklers for convention in the legal world down here.'

'I couldn't tell you anything about the trial which isn't in the evening papers.'

Urrick clasped him firmly on the shoulder, another item of behaviour to which Rumbelow objected. 'I'll get a bite to eat. Perhaps we can meet for a social talk later? Though we'll be seeing quite enough of each other over the next few days.'

As his spindly figure disappeared, Rumbelow said, 'That was slack of him, travelling down today. He should have been in court from the start.'

'He can read the transcript of the opening speeches.'

'It's not the same thing. You miss how counsel looked, what he emphasized, any weak spot he hurried over. *I* always make a point of being there from the first.'

'You're not expecting Urrick to put a spoke in your wheel?'

'Not for one moment. I've a shrewd idea of the line he's going to take. It'll all come down to those two slides of the woman's neck-tissues. But I'm confident the jury's going to believe me rather than him.'

'Because you're Dr Rumbelow?'

'No, because I'm simply the better pathologist. Urrick is second-rate. He can hardly be otherwise, can he? In Scotland they simply don't get the volume of work we see down here. It's the cases which create the experts.'

'You don't care much for him, do you?'

'Frankly, no.' Rumbelow considered for a moment. 'He's far too much of a prima donna.'

76

'I think I'll have another whisky before dinner. It's your turn to foot the bill, I believe.'

'Is it? I'd forgotten.'

At dinner Carlow wanted oysters, but Rumbelow persuaded him they were poor at the end of the season. He was still remembering what he had paid for the taxi.

11

'HOW WOULD YOU define a pathologist?' asked Peter Ivors, in a tone suggesting such terms were beyond his own simple understanding.

It was the Friday morning, two days later, and Rumbelow had just started to give evidence.

'A pathologist is a person learned in that branch of medicine concerned with the essential nature of disease. And with all changes in the body caused by disease.'

'"Disease" would include injuries?'

'Yes.'

'And how would you define forensic medicine?'

'Medicine applied to such problems as might arise in the administration of justice.'

'Are all students of medicine instructed in both these subjects?'

'Yes. That is required by law.'

'So every doctor in the land possesses some knowledge of them?'

'Yes.'

'There is nothing mysterious or magical about either?'

'Nothing whatsoever. These subjects are exactly like any other specialized branch of medical practice.'

The tactic had been rehearsed at a conference in Ivors' chambers earlier that morning. Ivors now saw Sir Arthur Younghusband's objection to Rumbelow's remaining in court as a blunder – he had needlessly shown his hand. If the defence was going to rely on discrediting Rumbelow, presenting him as a witness who somehow mesmerized juries, then the Crown would have to show him as a perfectly ordinary medical man who happened to specialize in a perfectly ordinary branch of the profession. Rumbelow's skill at his job – particularly compared with that of the opposition's medical expert – could be hammered into the jury's heads far more effectively later in the trial. Rumbelow agreed. It was all part of an intellectual game, which he delighted in.

'In an average day's work, how many post-mortem examinations would you perform?'

'Twelve to fifteen.'

'Not all those cases would have met their end through criminal acts?'

'Very few of them.'

'Much the same proportion holds over Great Britain as a whole?'

'No. Statistics show criminality to be involved more often in the Greater London area.'

Peter Ivors then took Rumbelow through his main evidence.

Rumbelow described how he had arrived at Vickery's garage in the dark of a mid-December morning. Once it was light, he had examined Miss Durban's body in a shallow grave against the brick wall which surrounded the back-yard. It had been compressed into a fairly narrow hole, the legs bent, the head against the knees, its back towards him. There were signs of burning. It still wore the tatters of a pink winceyette vest. The wrists were tied behind the back with electrician's flex. He added that from examination of the skin this would have been done after death.

'How long had Miss Durban been dead?'

'Three weeks. Putrefaction was present. There was a generalized green discolouration, particularly where the surfaces were touching in the bundled-up position. The body as a whole was somewhat bloated, with blebs on the surface. The hair and nails were loose. There was a general softening of the tissues.'

'All this is consistent with death three weeks previously?'

'In the cold weather of the period. Had it been summer, I should have put it at two weeks.'

'How was the body affected by fire?'

'It had been badly burnt, but selectively. The back and left side were mainly intact. The right half of the trunk was severely charred, the skin and underlying tissues having been burnt away, and even parts of the right lung and abdominal organs.'

'Could these burns have been caused by petrol?'

'They could only have been caused by petrol.'

'Did they bring about Miss Durban's death?'

'No.'

'Then did they occur before or after her death?'

'They had the typical appearance of burns inflicted after death.'

'Would they be consistent with the prisoner having started to burn Miss Durban's body, perhaps with the idea of destroying it completely as evidence? And then having panicked, or appreciating the difficulty of his task, or even overcome by the sheer horror of it, abandoning the idea and burying what was left?'

'Yes.' Rumbelow was no spendthrift with words.

'Dr Rumbelow, you heard the evidence of the police. The accused in his first statement to Superintendent Sixsmith said he had discovered his "wife" hanging dead from the roof of his garage. In his concern over the repercussions to himself, the following night he buried the body after having set it alight with petrol. Well, you are agreed with the prisoner's statement as far as the burning and the burying go. Do you agree with the hanging?'

'No.'

'Why not?'

Rumbelow always knew the point to become more expansive. 'There were simply no signs of hanging. In my examination of the lungs, the left of which was completely intact, I found no evidence of death being due to suffocation. I found no small bruises on the thighs, as I would expect from breakages of the minor blood-vessels in a suspended body. The neck as a whole, particularly on the left side, was sufficiently unburnt for adequate examination. I found no bruising nor tearing nor any damage whatsoever to its structures. The skin, the underlying tissues, the muscles, the windpipe, the large arteries and veins passing from the chest to the head were all intact. There was no breakage of the small delicate bones round the voice-box. Above all there was no mark round the neck.'

'What sort of mark?'

'One circling the neck, showing the pattern of the ligature used. This would assume a brownish appearance after death – possibly some hours after death.'

'Does this mark always appear?'

'Invariably.'

'However smooth the ligature?'

'I would exclude only a silk or woollen scarf.'

'You have seen produced in court, as an exhibit, the rope of half an inch diameter with which the prisoner says Miss Durban killed herself?'

'Yes.'

'This would not fit with the medical facts?'

'No. The only marks to be seen on the neck were those of some burning.'

'To be seen by the naked eye?'

'By the naked eye and the microscope. I made sections of the skin and examined them. The slides are contained in the wooden box, Exhibit K.'

'Then what was death due to?'

'Shock, following blows to the head. There were probably three, of moderate severity. There was sufficient flesh intact for me to find evidence of bruising and splitting of the skin.'

'There was no other cause for you to attribute her death?'

'None whatever.'

'You think such injuries themselves sufficient?'

'In the case of Miss Durban. She was thin, small-boned, of poor physique – what is described as the "asthenic type".' He looked apologetic for introducing a technical term. 'Death is not uncommon in such persons from injuries which might leave a well-built man comparatively unscathed.'

'Had the whole of the surface of the neck been burnt away, you would then not have been able to exclude hanging?'

'Not to exclude it definitely.'

Peter Ivors sat down. The judge's half-moon glasses were still directed on his notebook, his hand still went steadily across the page. Rumbelow noticed two reporters slip away, he knew to catch the lunchtime editions. He stood as usual with the tips of his fingers resting on the witness-box, his shoulders a little back, in his brown suit with the stripe, a pink carnation in the buttonhole. He had often read in the papers of his 'fine presence in the witness-box'. It amused him, though he knew it was right.

Sir Arthur Younghusband rose for the cross-examination.

'Dr Rumbelow, did you undertake the post-mortem examination of Miss Durban's body with an open mind?'

'I undertake my examination in every case with an open mind.'

'You ascribed Miss Durban's death to shock following three blows to the head. Did you find any fractures of the skull bones in these regions?'

'No.'

'Would you not have expected them?'

'Not in a woman of Miss Durban's frailty,' Rumbelow repeated. 'She would succumb to a blow of less force than needed actually to break a bone.'

'But suppose she had been a woman of normal physique. You might have expected a fracture then?'

'It would have been more likely.'

'So there exists some ill-defined point between rude health and frailty, when it is no longer necessary to break a bone to kill someone with a blow to the head?'

'That would be the case,' Rumbelow admitted.

'But you never saw Miss Durban alive. You concluded she was frail only from her appearance when dead?'

'That is true.'

'Some small, apparently fragile, people may be surprisingly robust?'

'That is true.'

Sir Arthur picked up another sheet of foolscap. He's getting somewhere, Rumbelow thought.

'Let us turn to the question of the hanging. You say that a rope was never round Miss Durban's neck. You base this assertion on the absence of damage to the structures forming the neck, and in particular to the absence of a characteristic mark on the skin. You found no evidence of this, even on examination by the microscope?'

'No evidence at all.'

'Did you cut the sections of skin for your microscope slides before or after the second post-mortem examination? I refer to the examination conducted after your own by Dr Urrick, before the remains were finally interred.'

'After.'

'You knew then that my client had made a full explanation to the police, of finding Miss Durban's body hanging in the garage?'

'Yes.'

'But you did not know this when you made your original examination of the body, Superintendent Sixsmith not then having interviewed my client?'

'That is right.'

'I suggest that you did not make your original examination of the neck with particular care?'

'That is incorrect. I took sections for the microscope later, purely as a confirmatory measure.'

'Why should your attention be directed to the neck, when you still had no notion this portion of the body would assume such importance in the case?'

'My attention is directed to all parts of the body in every case. That is a fundamental principle in medicine.' He was fond of repeating this.

'I suggest that once hanging was postulated as the cause of death – which would have exculpated my client – you returned to the body with the express intention of demonstrating somehow or other this could not be so?'

Rumbelow's expression stayed unchanged. In the witness-box he had the professional self-control of a champion boxer in the ring. 'Whatever is postulated as the cause of death, in whatever case, I set it from my mind in reaching my own conclusions.'

'Is this the practice of all pathologists?'

'I cannot answer for my colleagues.'

'It all comes down to a matter of bruises, does it not? You

say there were no bruises on the skin of the neck. But that there were bruises and splitting of the skin of the head?'

'Yes.'

'I noticed you did not preface your replies to my learned friend with, "In my opinion", or some such formula. That is what it comes down to, yet again, does it not? All this is purely a matter of opinions. Yours against any other medical man's?'

'My opinion is correct.'

'Is that not overweening vanity, Dr Rumbelow?'

'No. It is assurance based on my professional ability and experience.'

The judge looked up. 'Sir Arthur, it is your client who is on trial, not Dr Rumbelow.'

'I apologize, my Lord, if I have given the contrary impression.' He reached for another sheet of paper. 'Well, Dr Rumbelow. You heard the evidence of Miss Durban's father. How she spent some time in a mental institution, undergoing treatment of neurasthenia and melancholia?'

Rumbelow wondered what questions the judge's interruption had obliged Sir Arthur to leave unasked. 'I did.'

'He described her as "neurotic". Would a neurotic person be more likely to commit suicide than a mentally robust one?'

'Yes.'

'And might not life in an isolated house, in the dark unpleasant days of winter, increase the tendency of a comparatively young woman towards suicide?'

'No. Suicide is committed most frequently in crowded cities. And among females at the age of fifty. The latest Registrar-General's report gives 243 cases of that age against 112 at thirty, which Miss Durban was. The commonest month for suicide is May. I quote from the same source.' This answer so satisfied Rumbelow, he became unusually expansive. 'Suicide has certainly some connexion with marriage, which Miss Durban at least believed she had contracted. Recent marriage is cited in point-three per cent of cases, as against six-point eight where the cause is given as mental conditions, and two-point-four per cent due to financial worry.'

I couldn't be fairer than that, he thought.

84

'But a person intending to commit suicide would hardly study the Registrar-General's tables beforehand, to find if the act were statistically feasible?'

Rumbelow did not condescend to answer.

'Thank you, Dr Rumbelow,' said Sir Arthur with great courtesy.

The court wanted its lunch.

'A bit below the belt, that, wasn't it?' Ivors observed mildly to Rumbelow as they pushed their way out. He had no reply.

Descending the front steps of the Old Bailey, Rumbelow's eye caught the newsvendor's placard opposite saying, RUMBELOW IN THE BOX. He crossed the street to get a paper. Sometimes he went to the expense of buying several, from different pitches all over the City. It always distressed him a little that the paper-sellers never seemed to recognize him.

12

HE WAS AWARE of being followed.

April of 1936 was one of the coldest in memory. Rumbelow turned up the fur collar of his overcoat as he walked down the Old Bailey southwards towards Ludgate Hill, with his usual intention of lunching in the refectory at Blackfriars. The case was making such a splash in the papers, the other consultants would be burning to quizz him about it, which would be agreeable. He stood on the pavement of Ludgate Hill itself, waiting for a gap in the traffic before crossing. Turning idly to his left, glancing towards the west front of St Paul's up the hill, he noticed someone standing in the doorway of a men's outfitters on the opposite corner. She was a slim woman with fair hair, eyeing him intently. She was smartly dressed in an overcoat of small black-and-white check, a fox-fur round her neck, on the top of her head a small hat with a large bow. She was quite young, under thirty. And pretty. He had already noticed her waiting to one side of the steps as he left the courts, the corner of his eye catching her following on the far side of the street after he had crossed for his paper. It was strange. Though perhaps only imagination, he told himself. Or she was from a newspaper office. They got up to all sorts of tricks these days.

He crossed the road, turning away from the cathedral towards Ludgate Circus. Stealing a glance behind, he saw her in his footsteps. He began to feel uneasy. He paused, while the policeman in his little wooden box changed the lights to stop the traffic. She crossed the Circus beside him, taking no notice of him but staring fixedly ahead. Rumbelow smiled to himself. He was really being unnecessarily anxious. Some men would have given a lot to be followed across the City of London by an attractive strange woman.

He turned towards the river. She kept close, just behind his right elbow. Really! thought Rumbelow. This is too much. In sight of Blackfriars Bridge, as he reached the walls of the hospital itself, he stopped. 'What is it? Why are you following me?'

She gave a gasp, a hand to her mouth.

'What do you want?'

He thought for a moment she was going to vanish in the lunchtime crowds, but she made an effort to speak. 'You're Dr Rumbelow, aren't you?'

She had a cultured voice, he noticed. 'What's your game?'

'I couldn't bring myself to stop you . . . I've got to speak to you.'

'Is it about the Vickery case? You know you may be committing an offence, approaching a witness like this? A serious offence.' She shook her head vigorously. 'You're from Fleet Street?'

'I'm nothing to do with the papers, nothing at all.' She looked round desperately. 'Can't we go somewhere to talk?'

'That's out of the question. I don't know who you are, or what your business is. But I must ask you to leave me alone.'

He turned away, though politely raising his bowler hat.

'Listen —' She hurried after him. 'Please, *please* listen to me. I'm Mrs Jeavons.' The name for a moment meant nothing to Rumbelow. Then he remembered it as the label on some of his specimens. 'You know. From Blayford. You were down with the police.'

'You mustn't talk to me about that. It is improper. This sort of behaviour won't do you any good at all, you know.'

She grabbed the sleeve of his coat. 'I saw in the papers you were at the Old Bailey. I had to come to London, just on the chance of meeting you. They think I murdered my husband. The police think so. They've taken away my passport. They've been searching my house. They've got a man opposite, nearly always, watching my movements —'

'Please take your hand off my coat.'

'But I'm innocent. I did nothing. Oh, its a horrible notion,

87

just put about by people because they're jealous of me, or they hate me, or they want to make trouble for me. It's wrong, it's ridiculous. I couldn't ever do a thing like that. Not in a million years. I couldn't take a human life. Particularly my husband's. It was impossible, impossible! We had rows, I'm not denying that. I've been foolish, I know I've been foolish, but I never knew where my stupidity would lead me. I could never do anything so terrible —'

'Stop it!'

'I know what you think. That I poisoned him. I know you're doing all sorts of tests, just to prove I did. I know you've only to say so, and they'll arrest me. But it's wrong, all quite wrong. Can't I appeal to you? Do I look like a murderess?'

'This is nothing whatever to do with me.' Rumbelow was angry. 'I'm not a police officer. If you've anything to say, go to Scotland Yard and tell them there.'

He noticed she was crying. 'Oh God, what a mess I'm in! Oh God. I know you'll say I killed him —'

'Go away. Go away at once. If you don't, I'll call a policeman and get him to take you off.'

'Haven't you got a heart?'

His anger suddenly turned to exasperation. 'This is really most unwise of you. Stopping me in the street like this. Do you understand that? I shall have to report it to Scotland Yard.'

'Why must you do that?'

'It's my duty, as an ordinary citizen. I advise you to make your position no worse.'

'Won't you listen to me? Won't you let me explain? About all the things that happened, about the circumstances of my husband and myself, even about my own weakness? It was bad enough with the shock of his death —'

Rumbelow abruptly walked on. She started to follow, but after a few steps she stopped, and as he turned the corner towards the hospital entrance on the Embankment he saw her standing still staring after him. What a stupid woman! he thought. Why on earth should she come up to London and attack *me*? If she wants to protest her innocence, she should go to Sixsmith. If she *is* innocent. He had seen how frightened she was, and sup-

88

posed it was because she had something to hide – an innocent suspect would have stayed calmly at home. Well, we shall see better when I have completed my analysis, he decided. He intended to telephone Scotland Yard about the incident at once, and turned into the corridor towards his laboratory, feeling in his pocket for the key.

Standing outside the door was a fat grey-haired woman in a khaki overall, with a bucket and mop.

'This ain't good enough, sir. It ain't good enough at all.' She seemed deeply offended at something.

Rumbelow stared at her blankly. He could not recall setting eyes on her in his life. 'I beg your pardon?'

'It's your room, sir. How do you expect a body to clean it? I've got my job to do, you know.'

He still felt lost. 'It's ... it's quite clean I think, thank you.'

'It *ain't*. It must be six whole weeks since I got in there. Always locked, it is.'

'Please don't bother yourself about it. I'm quite content as it is.'

'But I *must* bother myself, sir. I've had the House Governor after me. "When did you last clean Dr Rumbelow's room?" he said. "I was in there talking to him yesterday, and it was a proper disgrace," he said. I don't want to get myself into no trouble —'

'Very well, very well, I'll leave it open for you,' he said hastily. He wanted only to get rid of her. 'But please leave me in peace for now. Come back later.'

She stood with her hands clasping the top of her mop, not satisfied. 'I can't do my work properly, sir, if the door's always shut in my face —'

'Oh, just as you please. It'll be unlocked in the future, if that's what you want. But you must be very careful not to touch anything, or look into any drawers or cupboards.'

'I've been working in the medical school for ten years, sir. I don't need to be told —'

'Yes, yes, I'm sure you don't.'

He closed the door behind him, frowning. What amazing things people got up to in this day and age.

13

DURING THE MONDAY morning, Dr Urrick was called to give evidence in Vickery's defence.

Rumbelow folded his arms on the uncomfortable seat he had occupied throughout the trial. He wore his light grey striped suit, not quite so smart as the brown one, spats, and his usual buttonhole. A carnation was kept for him every morning by an old lady with a basket outside the hospital gate, who did a fair trade selling flowers to visitors.

He listened while Sir Arthur Younghusband led Urrick through his qualifications and appointments – doctor of medicine in the University of Edinburgh, fellow of the Royal College of Physicians of Edinburgh, Pathologist to the McCurdy Institute in the same city.

'Taking the country as a whole,' suggested Sir Arthur, 'would you put your professional standing on the same par as Dr Rumbelow's?'

Urrick puckered his eyes. He had the habit of carrying his pawky manner into the witness-box, striking Rumbelow as a man telling diverting after-dinner anecdotes rather than giving evidence in a trial for murder. 'I should say that. Yes, definitely.'

Rumbelow grunted. Everyone knew – or they should – that the McCurdy Institute was mainly an institution which specialized in cramming hundreds of students through their examinations. And that Urrick was an uninspired, even a careless, pathologist. And that he owed his position largely to having failed at everything else. Still, Rumbelow thought hopefully, the man's evidence might shortly make all that apparent.

Most of Urrick's testimony was unexciting, uncontroversial,

and long-winded. He described how he had been telephoned in Edinburgh by Vickery's solicitors. How he had left at once his urgent and weighty duties, had taken the very first express from Edinburgh, only to find that Rumbelow had already performed a post-mortem on Eileen Durban's remains. He recounted in intense detail his own examination of the body, made the next day in the Central Mortuary in the presence of a detective-inspector and the solicitor. He recited his post-mortem findings from a thick folder of notes on the edge of the witness-box, at which he peered through a pair of pince-nez. He was perfectly entitled to an *aide-mémoire*, Rumbelow knew, though he himself took pains to memorize everything thoroughly, having decided this looked more authoritative, and thus more impressive to the jury. He stared along the rows of reporters scribbling painstakingly in the Press benches, even for a few minutes allowing his attention to wander.

'To what opinion did your examination lead, Dr Urrick, on the cause of Miss Durban's death?' asked Sir Arthur.

Urrick tilted his head and screwed up his eyes. 'The young lady died by her own hand. From hanging.'

Having an ear for such things, Rumbelow caught a stirring among the pressmen. There could not have been a flatter contradiction to himself.

'Will you tell the court exactly why you reached that conclusion?'

'From examination of the deceased woman's neck. Even by the naked eye, there was undoubted evidence of a ligature.'

'What evidence, precisely?'

'A brownish mark circling the neck.'

'Will you indicate it on this photograph of the body, Exhibit G?'

Urrick adjusted the pince-nez on a black ribbon attached to his lapel. He took a propelling pencil from his pocket and carefully made a mark. The photograph was passed to the judge, who looked at it impassively, and then round the jury, who did their best to stare penetratingly.

'Did you take further steps to confirm that a ligature had been round the neck?'

'I did that.' Urrick swung the pince-nez on its cord. 'I made a dissection of the underlying neck-tissues. I was able to detect definite extravasation of blood, and certain trauma to the trachea.'

'You made this dissection, despite Dr Rumbelow having examined the same area previously?'

'Such interference is no hindrance to the trained patholo-gist,' said Urrick airily.

'Did you make any further investigations?'

'I took sections of the skin and subcutaneous tissues for micro-scopical examination. The black cardboard box you are holding up is that containing the relevant microscope slides, Exhibit M. My views were amply confirmed.'

'You have heard Dr Rumbelow. He put the cause of death as three blows to the head. Did you find any evidence which might support his theory?'

'Not a jot.' The pince-nez swung jauntily. 'I found contusions in the cephalic region. But from my examination of the neck, both macroscopical and microscopical, I have no doubt what-ever the poor woman met her end through the agency of the rope produced in court.'

'Contusions?' The judge looked up.

'Bruises, my Lord.' Urrick sounded condescending. 'That is the lay term.'

'But you did find some bruising of the head,' the judge con-tinued. 'You agree with Dr Rumbelow on that point?'

'I found some bruising.'

'Were these bruises trivial? Or were they severe?'

'I'd say . . . quite severe. Yes, quite severe.'

'Then how do you suppose they were caused?'

'They could have happened through the young woman striking some structure during the process of hanging herself.'

'While she was still living?'

'Oh, yes. They were not post-mortem bruises.'

The judge nodded towards Sir Arthur.

'I have no more questions, my Lord.'

Peter Ivors rose, immediately in front of Rumbelow. 'Dr Urrick, would you assist the court a little more about this mark

92

on the neck? I should like to take you through it from the out-side inwards, so to speak. Let us start with the photograph.'
Ivors handed him the picture. 'The line you indicated with your pencil is somewhat faint, is it not?'

'But it is undoubtedly the mark of a ligature.'

'Might it not be one of the normal skin-creases of the neck? As one would expect to find in a woman of Miss Durban's age?'

Urrick screwed up his eyes. 'A skin-crease might be possible. Yes, just possible. But that is not at one with my dissection of the cervical tissues.'

'Let us move deeper, then. You say you found extravasation of blood and certain trauma to the trachea – that is the windpipe, is it not?'

'In the language of the laity.'

'You can see from the photograph the extent of burning on the body. Might not your findings be due to this?'

'They would not.'

'Or to Dr Rumbelow's already having dissected the region?'

'They would not.'

'Let us delve more. These microscope slides of yours, Exhibit M.' Ivors held up the small cardboard box. He opened it, and added in a tone of faint wonderment, 'But the glass slides have no labels on them. Unlike Dr Rumbelow's, they have no identifying mark at all. They might have come from anywhere, surely? From anyone? Is this your normal practice?'

Urrick looked offended. 'I can keep track of my own materials.'

'In a case with a man's life depending on it, would you not be more particular?'

'We are all open to criticism.'

'But not to a charge of gross carelessness?'

Urrick said nothing.

'Let us go deeper still, into the lungs. You agree with Dr Rumbelow there was no sign of suffocation? Or asphyxia, if you would prefer the medical term.'

'It is the only point on which I fully agree with him.'

'So what was the immediate cause of Miss Durban's death?'

'Shock.'

'Again, as Dr Rumbelow says.'

'Yes. But shock caused by suicidal hanging. Such an effect is far from uncommon.'

'Yet hanging itself is not common, among deaths due to criminal acts? You will appreciate, Dr Urrick, that suicide in England is a criminal act, though by one of our subtle differences of law not so in Scotland.'

'I will agree. Hanging is not so common.'

'You heard what Dr Rumbelow had to say. That among the cases a pathologist examines in his daily work, those meeting their ends through criminal acts are few? Do you agree with that?'

The pince-nez were now poked into a waistcoat pocket. 'I would agree with that, too.'

'Dr Urrick, how many post-mortems, on an average, do you conduct in a day?'

'One or two.'

'You also heard Dr Rumbelow say he conducts twelve to fifteen. Let us allow that criminal cases form a small proportion of these. Let us further allow that deaths from hanging form a smaller proportion still. Yet as a matter of simple arithmetic, Dr Rumbelow's experience of the signs of hanging – such as the presence or absence of ligature marks on the neck – must be very considerably greater than your own?'

'They see more of such things down in London,' said Urrick uncomfortably.

'The shock which killed Miss Durban could have resulted from blows to her head?'

'The blows were not very severe.'

'But allowing for her frailness, could they have killed her?'

'I suppose that would be possible.'

'You ascribe these blows to Miss Durban striking herself in some way while committing suicide. Have you seen such injuries in a case of hanging?'

Urrick hesitated. 'I cannot say.'

'Have you? Even in your limited experience of such cases?'

'No, I . . . no, I must say. I have not.'

94

'It never occurred to you that the blows might have been inflicted by the prisoner?'

Urrick made no reply. Peter Ivors sat down. He turned with a look Rumbelow had learnt to interpret. It meant, 'With a bit of luck, we've won.'

14

TOWARDS THE MIDDLE of that afternoon, Vickery himself went into the witness-box.

The prisoner's evidence was awaited by the Press even more eagerly than Rumbelow's had been. But Rumbelow himself was not in court. He had no more to contribute to the trial. He would certainly be there for the summing-up, to see how the judge treated his evidence – a valuable lesson for the future. But now he could release himself, having work to do.

In his laboratory at Blackfriars, he lit a Bunsen burner and placed a glass beaker on the tripod over the flame. The beaker contained a mixture, half of distilled water and half of concentrated hydrochloric acid. He then took a small piece of copper foil from a jar, burnished it with emery paper, and boiled it in the fluid for fifteen minutes. The copper strip remained bright. The chemicals and apparatus were free from any contamination with arsenic.

Rumbelow unlocked a cupboard under the workbench, and produced one of his wide-mouthed jars, the blue-edged label marked *Jeavons. Filtrate of Liver*. He added a few drops to the beaker, letting it all simmer for a further quarter of an hour. The copper foil was still bright. He picked it out with forceps, examining it through his magnifying-glass. No trace of any deposit. He turned off the Bunsen, making a note. *Reinsch Test – Negative, no arsenic present.*

He took more apparatus from the glass cupboard on the wall. He should already have completed the analysis, but the Vickery case was taking so much of his time, with the sessions in court and repeated conferences in Peter Ivors' chambers. The chemistry would be difficult, because he suspected only a small amount of arsenic had been given, and it would have to be thorough to stand up in court. But he supposed there was no particular urgency. Sixsmith still had a good many inquiries to make, with lines to follow in Singapore, and seemed confident that Mrs Jeavons wouldn't give him the slip. That the widow was frightened, ostracized, persecuted by malicious tongues, and living in horrible suspense was not a matter which occurred to Rumbelow at all.

He arranged on the bench a jar like the water-carafe on the platforms of public meetings. It had a glass stopper – a cork was a possible contaminant with arsenic. Through one hole in the stopper ran a funnel shaped like a thistle, with a glass tap. From another came a short bent glass tube. This tube entered a thicker one, running horizontally, filled with calcium chloride to dry out gases passing through it. At the end was a finer tube of the same length, made of transparent silica to withstand the Bunsen flame.

Rumbelow took the glass cover from a chemist's balance in the corner of the bench. He weighed out a few grams of zinc and tipped them into the flask. With a pipette, he added to the zinc some dilute sulphuric acid. He replaced the stopper with its funnel and tube, and watched the mixture bubbling as it evolved hydrogen gas. Then he poured through the thistle-funnel a little of the fluid from James Jeavons' liver. He lit the Bunsen burner under the fine end of the tube, watching the silica glow to redness. He would have half an hour to wait.

He sat on the wooden stool, writing up his notes of the case in a manilla folder. He placed on the bench the gold watch which had belonged to his brother. He waited the full thirty minutes before peering at the silica tube just beyond the edge of the flame. There was no deposit. He moved away the Bunsen burner. With a match, he ignited the gases escaping from the end of the tube. He took a small square of porcelain and held it in the jet. Now there was some discoloration, a greyish deposit.

'Very interesting,' murmured Rumbelow with satisfaction.

He added a drop of nitric acid to the stain, let it dry and touched it with silver nitrate. A brick-red colour formed at once. He reached for his fountain-pen, and wrote on his notes, *Marsh Test – Positive. Arsenic present in liver.*

He dismantled the apparatus, rinsed it out with distilled water, and reassembling it repeated the experiment. The same result.

'Good, good,' he said to himself. He wondered whether to telephone Sixsmith, but set the idea aside as too sensational. The proper method was to submit a written report. Anyway, time was getting on. At seven he would have to go. He wrote the report and carefully put everything away, locking the drawers and cupboards. He would leave the laboratory door unfastened, if it pleased the charwoman. He took his brown leather attaché case, the famous black bag staying behind on the floor. He supposed she would be curious about it, but it was securely locked.

He went by Tube to his club, where he asked the porter for the key of a changing room. He put on his dinner-jacket, and being a little early sat in the morning-room with a cigar, reading about the trial in the evening papers. He had left his book of poems at the club and considered dipping into them for a few moments. But he decided against it. Eliot's casual momentousness was rather beyond him.

In his coat and hat he walked across Trafalgar Square to Charing Cross Station. His wife was just coming through the barrier from a suburban electric train.

She smiled at him. 'You weren't late after all.'

'I was working in the lab. I had more time than I expected, as a matter of fact. Peter Ivors finished off Urrick pretty promptly this morning.'

'How's the trial going?'

'Very well for us, I think.'

'Yes, I thought so when I read about it in the train.'

'Urrick is a fool,' said Rumbelow, as though making a simple statement of fact.

They walked towards the station entrance. She was in a long gown of green shot-silk, tight to the knees and flaring over her feet. On top she had a grey cape of dyed squirrel, a wedding-present from her father. She clutched tightly a small handbag done in petit-point. Her lipstick was vivid red, her fair hair newly set – by a hairdresser – and drawn into a bunch of curls at the back of the head. He noticed she wore the pair of jade earrings he had given her on their first anniversary. She had met him from the train with an expression of admiration and tenderness heightened by excitement, which would have moved another man to take her into his arms.

'This is an unexpected treat, John.'

'I haven't been particularly attentive recently.'

'Let's just forget our worries and enjoy ourselves.' They reached the pavement. 'How are we getting to the theatre?'

'We'll take a taxi,' he told her impressively.

They had tickets for the Phoenix in Charing Cross Road to see Noel Coward's *Tonight at 8.30*. Rumbelow had half-decided on James Bridie's *Storm in a Teacup* at the Haymarket, solely because the author was also a doctor, but people at Blackfriars had told him the Coward show was awfully good. He knew nothing about such matters himself. He was careful over not hinting to Rosemary that the real begetter of her evening's entertainment was Norman Carlow.

They sat in the second row of the stalls. Rosemary put her fur in her lap, revealing her spiky shoulders. Rumbelow looked round, smoothing his bow against the points of his wing-collar, noticing people staring at him. He had figured in a good many newspaper photographs over the past few days. It was very pleasant. Though he was disconcerted to find the perfor-mance not one play, instead three short ones. But Coward himself was very clever, and he liked the red-headed girl who appeared in her brassière for the theatrical sketch. He looked at his programme, read 'Gertrude Lawrence', and felt he had heard the name before. He wished he could meet more actresses, but Lady Accrington thought stage people common and Mrs Mavery was jealous of them. He turned his head to glance at Rosemary. Her eyes were wide and her lips apart, like a child at the pantomime.

They went for supper afterwards at a nearby restaurant where, Rumbelow had gathered, actors and actresses themselves ate after their performances. This part of the evening had cost him the most thought. Unless the play finished remarkably early, they would not have time to catch their last train to Lower Sydenham. But he remembered some trains ran later from the station opposite Blackfriars Hospital for the convenience of late workers on Fleet Street. It would land them at Penge East, with a fair walk afterwards, but that was nothing compared to the expense of a taxi half across London, particularly as a meal for the pair of them could hardly cost less than thirty shillings, even if they had the carafe wine.

He asked the head-waiter for a table, glancing round for actors and actresses. A woman near him said loudly, 'But how devastating! Look – it's Dr Rumbelow,' and her companion added admiringly, 'I say, so it jolly well is.' It took him an effort not to turn and bow.

For much of the meal they talked harmlessly, mostly about the show.

'That scene where she takes the overdose of sleeping-pills,' Rosemary said. 'How would *you* have treated her?'

'Much less romantically, if more effectively. I'd have given her a mixture of mustard and water, and made her vomit.'

Rosemary laughed. 'That doesn't sound at all pleasant. I'd better not try it on myself, then?'

'Oh, you wouldn't.'

'Wouldn't I? Why are you so sure?'

He suddenly felt uneasy. He thought she was perhaps teasing him, one of her habits he found irritating. But he was unable to let the remark go by. 'You wouldn't contemplate suicide, would you? Not in any circumstances?'

'How you're looking at me! Have I frightened you?'

'No, of course not . . . but you *wouldn't* surely? You'd not even think of it.'

'How can I tell?' She still spoke lightly. 'Do you imagine some poor woman who has committed suicide today would even remotely have been able to answer the same question six months ago? Or six weeks, or six days? Perhaps even six hours before she put her head in a gas-oven.'

'I wish you wouldn't talk like this.'

'Why shouldn't I?'

'Because it's wrong. Suicide is against the law. Even attempted suicide is a crime. I hope you realize that.'

'That's how you see everything, isn't it, John? Legal or illegal. All inside the law shining pure, all outside wicked black.'

'You're speaking as though it was a lot of arbitrary rules. It isn't. The law is the essence of our civilization.'

'I'm not sure if I always agree with our civilization.'

'My brother was killed defending it.'

'A lot of things people do inside the law are horrible. Look at the way we treat the unemployed, for instance. We give them a few shillings a week, hardly enough to feed them decently, but it lets us all sleep with an easy conscience. Nothing constructive is done at all. Nothing to provide them with some sort of work. So that they'll feel useful, wanted in the community. Without that, a man might as well be dead.'

'I thought you'd grown out of your socialism?'

'It isn't socialism. It's simple compassion. And a lot of things which happen outside the law deserve that, not punishment.'

'What things?' he demanded.

'Well . . . look at some poor miserable unmarried girl, procuring herself an abortion. She's a criminal, because she doesn't want to give the world an unwanted life. But the law doesn't think twice about taking one, to justify itself.' He grunted. She took a sip from her wine-glass. 'Don't worry, John. I can assure you I've no immediate plans for doing away with myself.'

'Then I'm delighted to hear it.'

'It's only because you'd be afraid of the scandal, isn't it? How it would look in the newspapers. How you might be discredited in court. How a clever barrister might somehow use it—'

'Stop it!'

She fell silent, rebuking herself for going too far. She had told herself desperately she must do everything that evening to avoid upsetting him. But like every couple who strive hopefully to change old attitudes with fresh surroundings, they found the familiar shadow of their bitter home-life fallen across the restaurant table.

'You know I'm concerned only with your welfare, Rosemary.'

She made no reply, carving the roast duck on her plate. 'I've been wondering lately if you should consult a psychologist.'

She looked up, startled. 'Why should I need that?'

'For those fears of yours. About giving birth to monsters, and so on. They're abnormal emotions in any woman.'

'Why must you bring all that up now?'

'It must be brought up sometime.'

'Forget it . . . just forget I said it.'

'I find that impossible.'

'I told you, it's stupid, all irrational. I'm ashamed of it.'

'Or is it an excuse?'

'An excuse for what?'

'To avoid me touching you. It must be ages since —'

'It's not always my fault. Often you're late, you're tired —'

'Excuses, excuses, more excuses. I don't believe you've these peculiar phobias at all. You're just using them as a convenience.'

'Very well. I don't like this sex business. The whole thing is repugnant to me. You must know that already, surely? Why do you force me to tell you in so many words?'

'Perhaps you *don't* care for it. But a wife has a duty towards her husband.'

She abruptly started to cry. Now it was Rumbelow telling himself he had been stupid, pushing her too far. But his main concern was their being in public. He wondered anxiously if people had noticed, perhaps even the woman who had spotted him at the entrance. 'Please control yourself. Get on with your dinner.'

She shook her head, groping for a handkerchief in the petit-point bag. 'I was so enjoying this evening —'

'Come along! Behave like an adult.'

She stood up. 'I want to go.'

Before he could stop her, she was making towards the door. He beckoned to a surprised-looking waiter for the bill. He glanced at the other diners in panic, but they were chattering away, apparently unaware of the 'scene'. He collected his over-coat and her fur. Outside the restaurant he took her elbow firmly, as they started to walk aimlessly along the pavement.

'That was very stupid of you, Rosemary.'

'Why are you so unkind to me?'

'I'm not unkind. Is it unkind to mention the very fault which is ruining our marriage?'

She turned to him angrily. 'All right. If you don't like me, if I don't give you the service you want, go off and leave me. Get it elsewhere.'

He gripped her the tighter. 'Why should I leave you? You're my wife. Your duty is to provide an outlet for my normal emotions. Why should I put myself out to look for another woman?'

'What a terrible way to talk!'

'How did you expect me to reply? To break into song about love?'

'You don't know anything about love.' He saw her lip trembling in the light of the street-lamps. 'Perhaps neither of us do.'

'What's it matter? A measure of affection, tolerance and habit – there's the average marriage for you. I nose into plenty of them in my work.'

'I'm not going home tonight.'

'Yes, you are.' She tore away her arm. He knew he would dominate her in the end, though sometimes it took longer than others. Then he was aware of a passer-by, a man of the lower classes in a cap, who had stopped and was staring at them with amusement. This so embarrassed Rumbelow, he said more gently, 'Perhaps we've had enough hysterics for one night.'

She hurried away from him, half tripping over her skirt. He caught up with her.

'If you're not coming home, where are you going instead? Back to your parents? You wouldn't be very welcome. Not at a poverty-stricken farm, with another mouth to feed these days. Or back to schoolmistressing? You wouldn't get a job. There are teachers on the dole already. You're stuck with me, you see. You'd better make the most of it.' She still said nothing, walking on, staring straight ahead. 'Or perhaps you've ideas of going off and finding another man to keep you? That certainly wouldn't work. You wouldn't be any use to him. Not all men are quite so patient in these matters as I am.'

103

She stopped. 'My God, I wish I'd never met you,' she said quietly.

'Are you coming home?'

She shrugged her shoulders. 'Where else can I go?'

'There you are. You're seeing reason.'

Rumbelow took her arm again. They started down the street. There would be just time if they stepped out, he calculated, to catch the last train from Charing Cross. She was now wholly subdued, and he even assumed a feverish jauntiness. In the train he remembered his attaché case with the grey suit which he had meant to collect from the club. He was most annoyed. His brown suit was at the cleaners, and he was anxious to appear particularly smart the following day for the verdict and sentence.

15

THE NEXT MORNING the British public had more on its mind than the outcome of the Vickery trial. It was Budget Day.

'How was Vickery in the box?' Rumbelow asked Peter Ivors, when they met in the Old Bailey during the lunch adjournment.

'Absolutely splendid. He gave the impression of a respectful and reliable chauffeur, whom anyone could entrust themselves to from London to Glasgow. You almost expected a blue peaked cap perched on the edge of the box. There's a wonderful bit I must tell you – when I took him up on the bigamy, he asserted he knew several people who'd done the same thing. I asked, "You're used to the company of men who commit crime?" and he said, "Such persons, sir, were among my employers and their friends, whose names I should prefer not to mention to save embarrassment". Of course I looked shocked, and said, "Do you mean bigamy is rife in the motor-car-owning classes?" to which he answered, "Very rife, sir, you can tell that from the society papers".'

Ivors laughed heartily. 'But that's not the end of it. Old Lynacre looked down his nose and asked, "Aren't you confusing bigamy with divorce, Vickery?" He replied, "It always strikes me as the same thing, my lord, there's only technical legal matters in between." Not bad, eh? So I asked if his employers took him into their confidence over such matters. He replied that a chauffeur gets to know a lot, and I'd be surprised. Oh, he was very quick-witted. I really couldn't do much with him.'

'Do you think it'll make any difference to the result?'

'Not a scrap. It's all out of Vickery's hands. It's between you and Urrick.'

Counsel's closing speeches had occupied much of the morning. The judge's charge to the jury ran well into the afternoon. Rumbelow thought he summed-up well – he was becoming something of a connoisseur of judges. The medical evidence was, as expected, prominent in his address. He struck squarely the point already hammered by prosecution and defence alike – was Eileen Durban hanged, or was she not? Were the jury to take the opinion of Dr Urrick or Dr Rumbelow?

'Much has been made of the reputations of these two distinguished medical men, members of the jury,' the judge told them. 'Well, that is to some extent relevant. Dr Rumbelow is certainly not infallible. He would never claim to be, I am sure, no more than any other doctor, nor any member of the bar, nor of the bench. But his opinion is undoubtedly backed with great experience. You heard that he is in the habit of performing as many as fifteen post-mortems every day of his working life. Though only a few of these would be the result of hanging – either suicidal, or murderous, or judicial – that still leaves him with greater experience of such cases, and of their post-mortem appearances, than many other pathologists. At the same time you must, of course, take into account the qualifications and experience of Dr Urrick.'

An agreeably perfunctory reference to them, thought Rumbelow.

'These doctors were called solely to assist you, members of the jury, to decide some highly technical matters. You may feel their reputations outside this court are of less importance than what you saw and heard with your own eyes and ears. You have observed both in the witness-box. You have heard both give their opinions on the cause of death in this young woman. You have heard from both their reasons for these opinions. And you have heard the methods they employed to establish these reasons. You have all the facts. You must choose which set you prefer to believe, either Dr Rumbelow's or Dr Urrick's.'

The judge's pause emphasized this was the hub round which the whole case revolved. 'It is perhaps a strange position for you, as ordinary men. If you are attended by your own doctor, you accept his word on your illness without question. If he calls in a second opinion to assist him, and this is a contrary one, you rely on your doctor's view of that. You are not obliged to make up your mind which opinion is correct, or more nearly correct. Now you find yourselves, members of the jury, exactly in that position. It is your decision alone.'

The jury went out at ten past five.

'God!' said Peter Ivors in the corridor outside. He had tipped back his wig and lit a cigarette, and was holding an evening paper. On the front was a photograph of Mr Neville Chamberlain, Chancellor of the Exchequer, the traditional battered dispatch-box aloft, a smile on his droopy-moustached face, about to make his short trip from the Treasury across Parliament Square to dip ceremoniously into the electorate's pockets. 'Threepence on the income-tax! The Government's gone mad.'

Rumbelow was reading over his shoulder. 'Tuppence a pound more on tea, I see. And a pound a barrel on imported beer.'

'I don't touch either. I'm a coffee and scotch man. Thank heavens they haven't gone for those. Twelve-and-six a bottle is bad enough as it is.'

'How long do you suppose the jury will take?'

'About an hour.' He was a shrewd forecaster of such things.

'So short? With so much technical evidence?'

'The more technical the evidence the quicker they are. Everyone falls over backwards to make it simple. They can't look beyond what we tell them. They're too ignorant, anyway.'

'Do you still think he'll go down?'

'Yes. Though of course you can never be sure. It's like the races.' He looked back at his newspaper. 'Threepence in the pound! Really, this country is becoming far too expensive to live in.'

'Excuse me, sir.' A policeman was at Rumbelow's side. 'There's a telephone message just come for you, sir.'

Rumbelow took the scrap of paper. It asked him to telephone a Kensington number, which meant nothing to him. He wondered if it were Sixsmith, who would have had his report that morning on the Jeavons' specimens. He went to a public callbox, found two pennies, and dialled. 'Dr Rumbelow here.'

'You *do* sound official.'

'Who's that?'

'Diana. Diana Flavell. Where on earth have you been hiding?'

She should never have telephoned me at the Old Bailey, he thought irritably. 'I'm afraid I've been very busy.'

'I can see that. It's ever so thrilling reading about you every morning. And knowing you're not just some sort of figure invented by the reporters, but real flesh and blood.'

'The papers exaggerate everything, of course.'

'Why didn't you telephone me?'

The answer was simple – really, he was frightened of her.

'I was intending to.'

'I was utterly disappointed, not hearing a thing,' she added gaily. 'Listen, dear – I've got an invitation for you. To a party.' Rumbelow said nothing. 'Do tell me you'll come.'

'When is it?'

'Tomorrow night. Some friends of mine are throwing it.'

'It's rather short notice,' he said evasively.

'But you *must* come, dear. I've promised to produce you. I'll be absolutely devastated if you let me down.'

'May I think it over?'

'Oh, come on! Be a sport. I promise you won't be bored.'

'I'll ring you in the morning.'

She laughed. 'You sound as if I was going to eat you. Do make the effort, dear. It's only in Chelsea. You could pick me up at the flat about nine-ish.'

Rumbelow left the telephone box both undecided on his actions and uncertain of himself. A party . . . that would be a more relaxed affair than even Mrs Mavery's luncheons. And after their last encounter, it was on the cards Diana would invite him into her flat afterwards. But would he really want her to? He stood with his hands in his pockets, in the middle of the hall of the Old Bailey, running his tongue over his lips trying to settle this delicate self-inquisition. Diana could bring unlooked-for and embarrassing complications. A man in his position must keep a sharp eye for spiders' webs. On the other hand, Rosemary herself had suggested he look elsewhere. It was all very difficult for a person of propriety.

At six-thirty they went back to court. The judge entered through his door under the Royal Arms. Behind came a chaplain. The prisoner reappeared in the dock. Everyone stared at him. Then the jury filed in, and they looked towards them instead.

The clerk of the court rose below the bench. 'Members of the jury, you are all agreed on your verdict?'

The foreman was a fat man in a brown tweed suit, with all three buttons done up. 'Yes.'

'Do you find the prisoner at the bar, Thomas Vickery, guilty or not guilty?'

'Guilty.'

'You find him guilty of murder, and that is the verdict of you all?'

'Yes.'

'Thomas Vickery, you stand convicted of murder. Have you anything to say why the court should not give you judgment of death according to law?'

Vickery said nothing. Now no one was looking at him.

They all stood. The judge's clerk fussed round the green-and-gold chair, placing a square of black flannel, point-forwards, on the judge's wig. The clerk wore a swallow-tailed coat, which Rumbelow knew to be specially bought for such occasions, and allowable from income-tax.

'Thomas Vickery, the sentence of the court upon you is that you be taken from hence to a lawful prison, and thence . . .' Even the fox-hunter faltered over his instrumentality in sending a man to oblivion. 'And thence to a place of execution and that you be hanged by the neck until you are dead, and that your body be buried within the precincts of the prison within which you shall last have been confined before your execution, and may the Lord have mercy upon your soul.'

'Amen,' said the chaplain.

Rumbelow turned. Vickery was being led out of sight like a sleepwalker. The judge departed very quickly. Everyone started to leave the court, suddenly making a lot of noise.

'That fellow was very foolish,' observed Peter Ivors, walking with Rumbelow down the corridor. 'He should never have made up the story that she hanged herself in the first place. I suppose he had to think of something on the spur of the moment. He should have said they'd had a fight, that he hit her and found he'd killed her. Then he'd have got off with fifteen years for manslaughter. Murderers should take counsel's opinion before talking to the police.'

'Or before doing the murder?' Rumbelow was in a good mood.

Ivors took off his large round glasses, rubbing his eyes with the back of his hand. Rumbelow noticed how exhausted he looked.

'Perhaps Vickery was right, sticking to his tale. It doesn't look too good to change it. Or perhaps he was just vain, and thought he could fool us all?' He put the glasses on again. 'Murderers are really very stupid. And murder is really such a simple crime. It takes much more in the way of brains to do a decent robbery.'

As Rumbelow left the court, several pressmen took his photograph. He was suddenly elated. The result of any trial was in his own mind never cut and dried. As Ivors had said, it was as uncertain as the races. But they had won. The judge had been fair, even complimentary in his summing-up. He had beaten Urrick – discredited him, crushed him completely. It all added up. It would be remembered by the jury at their next encounter. His own reputation stood higher than ever. Life was really very pleasant.

He strode rapidly towards the Embankment and into Blackfriars. As he came down the corridor he noticed with shock his laboratory door ajar. Then he remembered his concession to the charwoman. He pushed it open and found Quinley inside.

'What the devil are you doing here?'

The young man was leaning over the workbench. He spun round. 'Oh! I . . . I'm sorry, sir. I found the door open, so I came in.'

'What business have you to?'

Quinley held out a white foolscap envelope. 'I'd a letter for you, sir. It's a copy of my application for the new job. I was going to slip it under the door.'

'You know perfectly well how I dislike people nosing about.'

'I only looked in for a moment.' Quinley looked agonizedly apologetic. 'Perhaps I was prompted by curiosity.'

'Curiosity? You've been in here often enough.'

'I suppose I was fascinated to find myself in the holy of holies alone.' Rumbelow said nothing. 'Honestly, sir, I wasn't prying.'

'You wouldn't get far.' He produced a bunch of keys. 'Every drawer and cabinet is locked.'

'I'm awfully sorry, sir.'

Rumbelow took off his overcoat, and laid it carefully on the spoke-backed chair. 'Give me that letter.'

'Perhaps you'd rather not be troubled —'

'No, give it to me. I promised I'd help. Help I shall.'

'I'd be tremendously grateful if you'd look through it.' Quinley sounded a little encouraged. 'I don't know if I've said the right thing.' He handed over the envelope. 'I'm really most grateful.'

Rumbelow grunted. Quinley left, carefully closing the door behind him. Rumbelow unlocked a drawer under his workbench, threw in the letter, and locked it up again.

From his jacket he took his pocket diary. Vickery was officially given three weeks to compose his soul, but there would be an appeal, which would delay matters. It would certainly be dismissed – the man had been convicted on indisputable facts, there was no misdirection in law. The appeal would be heard towards the end of May. The most likely day after that was Tuesday, the second of June. Rumbelow made a note under the date: ?*Vickery, post-mortem.* Another addition to his superb collection of broken necks.

16

THE ATTACK STARTED the next morning.

Rumbelow always kept his daily paper for the train from Lower Sydenham to Charing Cross. That day's leading article was expectedly a dissection of Mr Chamberlain's budget, but he was flattered to notice a shorter editorial headed *The Vickery Case*, his own name prominent in the first paragraph. It said,

'Vickery has been found guilty and condemned to death. His fate lay in the answer to a simple question – did his bigamous wife, Eileen Durban, hang herself or not? The jury obviously could not make up their own minds on the delicate points of forensic medicine by which this answer might be determined. They had to take the experts' word for it. Dr Rumbelow said she did not hang herself. Dr Urrick said she did.

'That Dr Rumbelow's word was accepted with little question – the jury were absent for barely an hour – is a disturbing inference from this distinguished expert's regular appearance in the courts. However little Dr Rumbelow would seek it, or desire it, the fact remains that he enjoys something of a reputation for infallibility. Jurymen read newspapers like everyone else. They remember Dr Rumbelow's evidence in former trials. They remember it is generally accepted as the truth. The remarks about Dr Rumbelow in the judge's summing-up, which stopped hardly short of the eulogistic, must have confirmed their belief that his version of the tragedy was to be preferred to that of the expert for the defence.

'This is surely a dangerous state of affairs. In important cases of this nature the Crown always has the big battalions. That Dr Rumbelow has a better-known name than Dr Urrick from Edinburgh is indisputable. That it should possibly cost a man his life is unthinkable. There may be a case for the establishment of a medical commission to decide on controversial evidence of this sort. Indeed, the Criminal Appeal Act gave the Appeal Court power to take this step. It will be of interest to see if such a plea is advanced on behalf of the condemned man when his appeal is heard.'

Rumbelow's immediate feeling was of amazement, of outrage at the ingratitude. His evidence had achieved the conviction of a murderer, and now he was being pilloried for it. It was ridiculous! The skill, the work, the experience he had brought to the case deserved instead the heartfelt appreciation of the public, who enjoyed unthinkingly the protection of the law. It was arrogant to question the opinion of judge and jury. He would never have expected it from such a responsible newspaper. Then he wondered if the anonymous journalist bore some grudge against him, was blackening his reputation to make one for himself. It was pompous, it was unnecessary, but of course everyone at Blackfriars would have read it with relish, and he must prepare to have his leg pulled.

He walked into the hospital, carrying his attaché case with his dress clothes in it, deciding for once not to look into the committee-room for his letters. But as he was passing, the door opened and Bantrell came out.

'Well, John Rumbelow! You're hitting the headlines this morning.'

Rumbelow noticed a newspaper under his arm. 'They must have been very short of something to write about,' he said with exceptional modesty.

'You've seen it?' Bantrell opened the paper, which Rumbelow saw to his horror was not his own, but a cheap popular one he had hardly read in his life. 'Quite a spread they've given you. Almost a whole page.'

Rumbelow saw a photograph of himself. Next to it was one of Evan Greensmith. A headline above asked, IS HE DR GOD? He started to read the first paragraph, set in bold type.

'At the beginning of George Gissing's strangely neglected novel *New Grub Street*, a family are sitting down to breakfast in the country when the parish clock strikes eight. Someone says cheerfully over his boiled egg, 'There's a man being hanged in London at this moment . . .'

Rumbelow's eye ran more quickly down the columns. It was the same argument as the editorial's – was it right for a man's life to depend on Rumbelow's reputation? But it was more pungent, more flamboyant in language. What irritated Rumbelow most was the author's sly impression of knowing him intimately, of their meeting constantly in the houses of fashionable London hostesses, of Rumbelow's relish for a social reputation gained from other men's necks. It even suggested he was something of an uncouth stranger in the elegant, civilized world decorated by Evan Greensmith himself. Rumbelow finished reading with a gasp, as though he had been struck. Bantrell was standing in silence, grinning at him.

'All this is . . . is most uncalled for,' said Rumbelow savagely.

'I didn't know you were a pal of Evan Greensmith's?'

'But I hardly know the man. I only met him once. God knows why he took it into his head to write this rubbish.'

'It's almost libellous, isn't it? Perhaps you can sue him, and get vast damages?'

'Oh, these newspapers have every word carefully read by a barrister,' replied Rumbelow seriously. 'I can only suppose Greensmith was paid for it handsomely.'

'With his name on the top, a lot of people will read it.'

'But it's all so puerile! It will amuse the students, at least. I can't believe anyone else would take it at its face value.'

He thrust the paper at Bantrell, and strode down the corridor to the security of his laboratory. Bantrell himself hurried out and across the main courtyard. It was just on ten o'clock, when he should catch Cramphorn going into the surgical block to start his ward-round. Sure enough, the surgeon was as usual stepping briskly towards the entrance, a white coat over his tweed suit, his houseman at his side. Bantrell caught them up.

'I say, Crampers, can you spare a second?' Cramphorn stopped, not looking particularly pleased. 'I thought you'd care to glance at this article in the morning's paper. It's about Rumbelow.'

'Eh? What?' Cramphorn inspected it through his half-moon glasses. The houseman moved away discreetly. He grunted as he finished reading, handing it back. 'A bit much, isn't it?'

'It's strong, admittedly. Though there's more than a germ of truth in it. I'm sure you'll agree with that?'

'No smoke without fire, I suppose,' Cramphorn admitted.

'I'm afraid Rumbelow imagines he's got some sort of Divine right in the witness-box,' Bantrell observed sorrowfully. 'We all know that. And I'm afraid he's a terrible snob. We all know that as well.'

'What do you expect me to do about it?'

'I don't see what any of us can do about it. I only thought I should bring it to your notice. It isn't very good for Blackfriars, these sort of things appearing in the papers. If the public's persuaded to lose faith in Rumbelow, they may lose faith in us all.'

'Shouldn't imagine so.'

'The hospital's mentioned by name. A lot of patients, and potential patients, will have read it.' Bantrell hesitated. 'I *did* wonder if you wanted to bring it officially to the notice of the committee? A letter might be written to the editor, deploring it.'

'What's the point? By then, people will have forgotten it.'

'But it's there in black and white —'

'It's only a newspaper, Bantrell. Tomorrow morning, everyone will have wiped their arses on it.' Cramphorn strode off.

Bantrell stood staring irritably after him. It really was frustrating. Rumbelow had clearly been responsible for the throwing of discredit and doubt on the hospital. But the senior surgeon himself couldn't see it. 'Crampers is an oaf,' murmured Bantrell. It was not the first time he had regretfully doubted his senior's intelligence.

Rumbelow meanwhile sat alone on the high stool in his laboratory, unable to start work. He kept telling himself it was childish to become angry over such personal attacks. He was still puzzled by both articles. His mind went back to Sir Arthur Younghusband's objections to his remaining in court on the first morning of the trial. Perhaps Younghusband was behind it, somehow trying to salvage political advantage from his defeat? Everyone knew his ambitions to join the Government. Bantrell was of course simply jealous of himself, Rumbelow decided. Yet he had not *sought* to become a public figure. He certainly made less money than Bantrell, much less than surgeons like Cramphorn or Graham Trevose. It was all so mysterious and so unfair.

He unhooked the receiver from his old-fashioned telephone and asked for Lady Accrington's number.

There was a long delay in reaching her. It occurred to him that she might well still be in bed. When she finally came on the line he realized he really had no idea what he intended to say.

'Did you see that article about me this morning? By Evan Greensmith.'

'In the newspapers? I hardly ever read them these days. They're so unreliable.'

'It wasn't very pleasant. It upset me very much.'

'How unfortunate.'

There was a pause. 'I wondered if you might possibly have some notion of what impelled him to write it.'

'I? But why should I?'

'Greensmith and I met only once. That was at luncheon in your house.'

'My dear Dr Rumbelow, I can't concern myself with all the little quarrels of my guests. I should never have a moment's peace if I did. Literary people can be quite savagely contentious, you know.'

'I'm sorry I troubled you, Lady Accrington.'

'Never upset yourself over what the newspapers say. They have to sell their copies, that's all. Sometimes they print the most awful things about *me*. But I assure you I never lose any sleep over it.'

He hung up the telephone. It had been an unsatisfactory conversation. Then he knew he had wanted reassurance, to learn they were all on his side – the right side – against Evan Greensmith. But he did not seem as important to Lady Accrington that morning as he had imagined. He picked up the telephone again.

'You're lucky to catch me,' said Diana Flavell. 'I was just going shopping.'

'I should very much like to accompany you this evening.'

'Oh, I'm thrilled. See you about nine.'

She made a noise which he interpreted as throwing him a kiss. He took off his jacket with the false cuffs, to begin work again on the Jeavons' entrails. He decided that perhaps Greensmith was only nettled by his saying 'autopsy' was bad English.

17

RUMBELOW'S DEEPEST CONCERN as he rang the bell of Diana's flat promptly at nine that evening was whether she had dined or not. Was he expected to take her to dinner before the party? He had no experience whatever in the social conventions of such occasions. He could hardly invite a woman of her tastes elsewhere than the Savoy or the Ritz Grill. The bill would be two pounds – perhaps three! She might want champagne, oysters, things out of season, though he would certainly order frugally for himself, even plead indigestion. As the maid showed him into the drawing-room, he was relieved at her greeting, 'I hope you haven't eaten? There'll be oodles there, I'm sure.'

He stood smoothing the black bow against his wing collar. It was warmer, and he had left his overcoat behind. 'I don't even know where the party is.'

'Didn't I tell you? It's at Archie Trexley-Blake's.' She seemed to imagine this a complete answer.

'Is that far?'

'Oh, no. Just off the King's Road. Hardly five minutes in a taxi.'

A taxi? Well, I must take such extravagances in my stride, he thought.

Diana stubbed out a half-smoked cigarette. She wore a plain black dress, tight-fitting, its shoulder-straps no thicker than shoe-laces showing off her shoulders and the tops of her breasts. The skirt was in overlaps of fringed material, and reached hardly below her knee. She wore heavier make-up than at their daytime meetings, Rumbelow noticed, and a perfume that made a new experience for his nostrils. He was most uneasy. He was starting an adventure so strange to him it was almost unbelievable. He had no idea exactly how it would end, which disturbed him with any new happening. He had the greatest difficulty picturing himself alone with Diana afterwards. The prospect of access to her willing body was less exciting than alarming. But he deserved a gay evening, he told himself. The day which should have warmed him with triumph had turned out sullen. He saw less clearly his need for the comfort of acceptance by society, the respect of people he himself respected, who would see those newspaper attacks for what they were, simply shafts of well-paid malevolence.

The maid appeared with a full-length mink coat.

'You were certainly all over the papers this morning, weren't you?'

'Was I? I never pay much attention to them.'

'*Don't* you? I thought you read avidly every word they printed about you?'

'What on earth gave you that impression?'

They left the flat, Rumbelow taking her arm. He hailed a taxi outside in Basil Street, and sat back holding her hand.

She laughed. 'Does your wife know you're out?'

He knew she was teasing, but it offended him. 'My wife never questions where I go.'

'She probably imagines you're digging up some corpse or other.'

'She might.'

'Well! *That's* not a very flattering alibi from my point of view.'

'I'm sorry, Diana. As a matter of fact, she thinks I'm at an official dinner,' he admitted with unusual frankness. 'I'm not going home tonight. I've taken a room at the club.' He wondered if she would make some encouraging comment on this. She said nothing. 'One can be quite comfortable there,' he went on. She was still looking through the window. He made to kiss her. After all, she was a woman of easygoing virtue who would think nothing of it. And he had to start somewhere. She pushed him away. 'You'll ruin my lipstick.' She added quietly, 'Later, later.'

The taxi turned off the King's Road and stopped in one of the dingy Chelsea streets which were being steadily eliminated by the huge newly rising blocks of service flats. It was a terrace house, narrow, of four storeys, the first-floor windows open and emitting a good deal of noise. The front door was ajar. He followed Diana up a steep boxed-in stairway with a tasselled rope for a handrail, his eyes on the level of her silk-covered ankles. The room upstairs ran the depth of the house, ending under a broad skylight suggesting a studio, though there was no sign of painting equipment. The furnishing was modern, the chairs scarlet leather across chromium-plated tubing. The place was crowded. There seemed to be opened bottles everywhere. He couldn't see anything to eat at all.

Diana threw her mink unconcernedly over one of the chairs, waving and calling out names and blowing kisses all round the room. A radiogram in the corner was playing a comic tune even Rumbelow could recognize, *The Music Goes Round and Round*. He noticed with a shock nobody else wore evening dress. The men were in their street clothes, one to his horror in a tweed sports-jacket. The women were dressed sloppily, mostly in brightly-coloured skirts and loose blouses, some with vivid chiffon scarves round their necks or festooned with beads and bangles. He supposed they were all the arty kind. Misgivings stirred in him. They were not at all the sort of people he cared to mix with. It was not at all the sort of place he wished to be. Then he saw on the far side of the room that a figure he'd taken for a small boy was in fact an adult, a dwarf, alone and looking unhappy.

'Why, there's an achondroplastic,' he couldn't prevent himself exclaiming. But Diana was tugging him by the sleeve towards a thin, fair, effeminate young man in a white tunic buttoned high round the neck like a Russian peasant's.

'John darling, you must meet Archie Trexley-Blake.'

The young man cringed in mock horror. 'The great Rumbelow! Where've you hidden the body?'

Rumbelow managed a faint smile. He supposed he had a duty to indulge his host. All of them anyway appeared pathetically childish, worse than the students at Blackfriars.

'And where's the murder bag?' asked the young man querulously. 'Don't say you haven't brought the murder bag? Oh, no. We were all hoping you'd show what's inside.'

'I hardly need my instruments on a social occasion. I hope not, at least.'

'But you *must* cut somebody up for me. I absolutely insist. There's lots of people I'm longing to know what's inside. I'm sure when my father died they found he was stuffed with cigar-butts and the ends from sticks of sealing-wax. Some of my friends must be nothing but masses of tiny compressed coiled springs, and would simply explode all over the floor once you slit them apart.' He caught a girl hurrying past with a glass of champagne in her hand. 'Or hundreds and hundreds of Coty's pink powder-puffs. Janet darling, this is Dr Rumbelow. He's come to cut you open.'

She gave a theatrical show of alarm.

'I hope there'll be no occasion for that for many years.' The chivalry sounded elephantine even to Rumbelow himself.

'Tell us all about a hanging,' she asked brightly. 'What happens?'

'Can you actually hear something when the neck breaks? Like a muffled pistol-shot?'

'I don't attend the execution.'

'Yes, but you must know what goes on,' she insisted. 'Do they have chaplains intoning the burial service as they all walk along?'

'With a bell tolling like mad in the background?'

'Is the condemned man really allowed to have exactly what he likes for breakfast?'

'And one last wish?'

'Do they always play draughts with the warders?'

'I do hope the warders let them win.'

'Do they actually have to walk up thirteen steps?'

'Or is the whole thing bogus? They simply fill the chap up with drugs, don't they, so he hasn't the slightest idea what's happening to him?'

'I'm afraid I'm not at liberty to disclose official secrets.'

'You *are* a fuss-pot,' said the girl.

'It's a serious matter, you know. If I did, I could face a criminal charge.'

'*We* won't tell on you. Will we, Janet?'

'Be a sport. Do give us the grisly details.'

'We're absolutely *aching* to hear.'

'I should prefer not to discuss my work at all,' said Rumbelow firmly.

The girl laughed. 'I think he's utterly bogus, don't you?'

'You've been invented by Sax Rohmer, like Dr Fu-Manchu,' said the young man. 'Come on, confess it.'

Two others came up and dragged the pair away, to Rumbelow's deep relief. What a ridiculous conversation! he thought. It was really most irritating, people having no idea how he deserved to be treated seriously. But he supposed such young things had little respect for anybody. Anyway, strangers often reacted oddly when he was introduced. He looked round for Diana, but she had disappeared. The radiogram had an automatic device for changing the records, and was now playing *Cheek to Cheek*. He wished she had suggested dinner *tête-à-tête* instead, and blow the expense. On a chromium-legged table beside him was a bottle of scotch and some glasses. He poured himself a whisky-and-soda, though usually he never touched spirits.

Another girl came up and asked if he knew Boris Karloff. He replied he had no acquaintances in the world of films. 'He was coming tonight, you know,' she told him. 'Though he's not a monster at all. He's just like a colonel from India who plays cricket.'

Rumbelow eased himself away from the noisy crowd, flattening himself against the wall, hoping no more of these peculiar persons would notice him. After some time another man and two girls came up to ask him about the Vickery case, but drifted away apparently finding him dull. He discovered himself next to a small man with brilliantined hair and horn-rimmed glasses, in a badly-fitting blue suit and holding a glass of beer. Rumbelow would have put him down as a clerk. He was saying to Trexley-Blake in a flat, matter-of-fact voice, 'Yes, we use gas.'

'What, like in the cooker?'

'Same principle.'

'I suppose it is.'

'Mind, we don't do them all at once. The service takes twenty minutes, and it's the best part of a couple of hours to incinerate a human body. We've only one furnace, though they're talking of expanding.'

'I hope you haven't much backlog of work?'

'They're all done the same day. We've an unwritten rule about that.'

'What's left at the end?'

'Coffin ash. Handles, and that. Bones. The skull, often. We break it up with a hammer.'

'That's the official ashes?'

'Not quite. We grind it up. It ends the consistency of castor sugar.'

'Ah, but what about the gold teeth?'

'Sold off, and a cheque goes to charity.'

'I hope I shan't need your services for a while, but such shining honesty I find reassuring.'

'Have to be honest. Short-sighted policy otherwise, isn't it?'

'I thought you just bundled three or four stiffs in your crematorium together, and sold the coffins back to the undertakers?'

'You've been reading stories.'

Rumbelow felt himself nudged. It was the man in the green sports-jacket, fat and red-faced, in his hand a glass with some bright red liqueur. 'What's your line?'

'I am a doctor.' Rumbelow decided to let it go at that.

'Go on? I'm a slaughterman.'

'A slaughterman!'

'Yes, at the abattoir up in Islington. We do the killing for Smithfield Market.'

Rumbelow moved quickly away. An idea was forming in his mind, a suspicion so ridiculous, so terrible that he couldn't bring himself to delineate it with logical thought. He searched for Diana, but she was talking animatedly to someone and only waved at him. Some couples in the middle started to dance, he noticed, holding each other very close. Then he was comforted to see another man in evening dress. He was almost at his elbow, also abandoned by the others, pale, grey-eyed, with fair hair cut very short. Rumbelow struck up a conversation, to discover he was a foreigner.

'You speak very good English.'

'Thank you. All of us at the Embassy do our best with your formidable tongue.'

'Which Embassy?'

'Of the German Reich.'

'Oh.' Rumbelow could not remember having spoken before to one of the nation which had killed his brother. He added by the way of making conversation, 'Your ambassador has just died, hasn't he? I believe I saw it in the papers.'

'Yes, that was a sadness for us all. But perhaps it has opened the way for something important.' Rumbelow made no comment, but the diplomat was eager to be impressive. 'I can tell you that the Führer is shortly to appoint Herr von Ribbentrop to the Court of St James's.'

'What, your Foreign Minister?'

'It shows how valuable the Führer sees the links between our two countries. We shall never fight again. That is out of the question. Together, we can be the greatest force in the entire world.'

'Possibly.'

'Are you an artist?'

'No, I'm a pathologist. Dr Rumbelow.'

A smile lit the German's face. 'You are an important man. I know about you from the newspapers. I am most honoured to meet you.' He clicked his heels. 'I was talking of you only yesterday. To a Dr Bantrell. You know him?'

'Very well. He's a physician on the staff of my own hospital.' What's Bantrell up to with the Germans? Rumbelow wondered.

'It was at a reception in the Embassy. You know perhaps that he has a German mother?'

'I don't think I was aware of it.'

'She was the Countess of . . . the name is from my mind for the moment. I shall look it up the second I get back.' Rumbelow had the impression he meant that exactly. 'Of course, she is now as English as Queen Mary. Though she had something of a bad time during the War. In the days when the Battenburgs had to turn into the Mountbattens, you know, old chap.' He raised his glass. 'I give you a toast. To the amity of our two countries.'

Rumbelow matched his gesture hesitantly. 'I'm no apologist for the British Empire, please understand that.'

'Why should you be, Doctor? It is magnificent! The Führer has great respect for your Empire. He offers it only peace, as he does to all nations.' At least this fellow's more complimentary than the American journalist at Mrs Mavery's, Rumbelow thought. He saw the German looking at him appraisingly, and wondered for a moment if he were about to be entrusted with secret information, or even invited to perform some minor act of treason. 'If you would like to see the Olympics at Berlin in August, Doctor, I might be able to arrange something for you.'

'That is very kind,' said Rumbelow politely.

They drifted away. The room was becoming noisier. Now all the young people were dancing in the middle. Rumbelow found himself next to an old man with a pointed beard, gazing on the scene with an expression of bottomless sorrow. Then he saw it wasn't a man, but a bearded lady, the sort you paid to stare at in freak shows.

'Darling, you look terrifically bored.' Diana was at last beside him. 'Of course, you can't know a soul, can you?'

'I've certainly little in common with anyone.'

'Who's the other man in the stiff shirt?'

'A German. From their Embassy.'

She laughed. 'I suppose he's one of the horrors.' She put her arms round his neck and made kissing motions, her lips an inch from his. 'Are you cross that I asked you?'

'Why should I be?'

'Come on. Let's go home.'

'I'm not very good at parties, I'm afraid.'

'We'll see what you are good at.'

She took his hand, and snatching up her mink hurried down the steep staircase. It occurred to Rumbelow he had not taken leave of his hostess, nor was he aware who his hostess was, but he supposed it didn't matter.

18

THEY TOOK ANOTHER TAXI. When Diana let herself into the flat there was no sign of the maid. Rumbelow wondered absently if the girl slept somewhere about the place. Diana went straight into the bedroom, throwing her coat over another chair. He followed automatically.

'Perhaps it was all a bore, that party.'

'Not entirely. Some of the people looked quite interesting.'

'No, they were all bores, crashing bores.'

She stuck a cigarette in her mouth. He saw a petrol-lighter on a dressing-table skirted with folds of pink satin. He flicked it and she leant towards the flame. 'Are you musical?'

'Why do you say that?'

'Your hands. You use them with such lightness, such precision, such economy of movement, like a concert pianist.'

'No, I'm not musical at all.'

She turned her back. 'Unzip me, darling.'

She slipped off the black dress, throwing it on top of her fur coat. Underneath she was wearing camiknickers. Rumbelow had noticed the thin pink shoulder-straps slipping from careful hiding under those of her dress. She sat on the bed and started detaching her silk stockings from their pink suspenders. She looked at him mockingly. 'Aren't you taking anything off?'

He removed his jacket and laid it carefully on a stool in front of the dressing-table. As he undid his dress-waistcoat she stepped out of her underclothes. 'No *soutien-gorge*.' She grasped her breasts with both hands and directed the nipples at him. 'Nice eh?'

Rumbelow was beginning to feel alarmed. This was not the

woman he had met at Mrs Mavery's lunch-table. She was wearing only a pink suspender-belt, which she unhooked and threw on the rest of her clothes. He noticed her pubic hair was jet-black. That on her head must be bleached, which hadn't occurred to him. She picked up her cigarette again and lay on the bed. She started to sing *The Isle of Capri*, a tune which had had always struck him as vulgar.

'What's the matter?' She laughed. 'You must have seen millions of bodies.'

'I'm not much of a ladies' man.'

'Of course you are. All men are.' She patted the bed reassuringly. 'Why are you so nervous?'

He would by then have liked to rush from the flat, but he decided that would in some way be cowardly. 'I'm just a little out of my depth, that's all.'

'Come and sit down. We must have a little chat.'

As she put her arm round him he saw the bristles where she had shaved her armpit, and thought it odd to notice such details.

'But must you be so shy?'

'I told you, I'm not used to women.'

'You can't be shy with your wife.' Rumbelow gave no reply.

'Tell me about her.'

'Is this quite the time and place?'

'Oh, yes. It seems to be, for most men.'

'There's not much to say about her.'

'Is she good between the sheets?'

It was the casual intimacy of her questioning which snapped one of his strongest inhibitions. 'She's useless to me. Like a marble statue lying at my side. She isn't a wife. Only in name. She's my housekeeper, that's all.'

He had made this revelation to no other living soul, but Diana seemed unmoved by it. 'You picked a loser, darling.'

'It's hardly my fault. One can't tell these things beforehand.'

'Surely you slept together before you married?'

'I never touched her. My father was a clergyman. I was brought up strictly. Not that I regret that. The life any man builds for himself can be a rickety affair. It's best to have firm foundations.'

She leant over to stub out the cigarette. It struck him that she never seemed to smoke more than half of one.

'I didn't know much of the world when we married. Nothing of women at all. Only what I'd learnt in hospital. And that's all distorted. You're only handling people who are in trouble or in pain, sick or dying. You begin to imagine the whole world's the same. You get in the habit of keeping yourself aloof, detached from other people's problems. People imagine doctors are kindly. But we're not. In our hearts, we're utterly contemptuous of humanity, I think.'

'So it's a success story? Parson's son makes good? There's a joke somewhere in my mind. About "over my dead body".'

'I wish everyone wouldn't keep coming back to that,' Rumbelow said irritably.

But she was finding the conversation tedious, and started unbuttoning his flies. 'Well, darling, at least you're in the mood, I see.'

There are some things beyond any man's inhibitions, Rumbelow thought a little gloomily. He was averse to exposing himself before Diana. After all, she was a woman he really knew so little. As her fingers eased out his penis, he consoled himself that such directness was probably commonplace in her set. As he looked at her, his expression was of pathetic helplessness.

'Before we go on, darling, there's one little thing. What present had you in mind?'

'Present?'

'I'm a businesswoman. You have to be, these days.'

'I don't think I understand . . . of course, if there's anything you fancy in the shops —'

She took her hand away, and made a gesture rubbing thumb and forefinger. 'Cash.'

He was astounded. 'I . . . I thought you want . . . you wanted me.'

'I do, darling. I can assure you that you wouldn't be here otherwise. But I've got to live.'

It was almost too difficult for him to grasp. 'So you're . . . you're a prostitute?'

'That's putting it rather ungenerously, isn't it?' Her voice had an edge to it.

'But you quote poetry!'

'I don't exactly walk the pavements of Shaftesbury Avenue in high heels and an imitation fox-fur, you know. I choose my friends extremely carefully. You don't know how privileged you are.'

'I can't believe it! I just can't believe it. We met at Mrs Mavery's. I could never imagine for one moment she'd allow your sort of person under her roof.'

Diana sat up abruptly. 'Get out.'

He sat staring at her. To find himself with a prostitute – one of those whose worn-out bodies came so regularly under his knife in the mortuary – was an unbelievably sudden and terrifying degeneration. He had been thrown headlong amid the mass of human beings whom he handled dead, and despised. She grabbed a pink chiffon dressing-gown with a feathery collar. 'Go on. Get out.'

'You should have made your profession clear to me,' he said severely.

'God! What a stuck-up swine you are.'

'I have my name to think about. Which is more than you have.'

For a second she looked at him calmly. Then she spat in his face. 'Name? What name? Listen, you fool. Do you know why we ask you through our front doors? Because you're a clown. A ghoul or a clown. It's the same thing. You amuse us. You're a stupid and boring little piece of insignificance. But we listen to you because we like revelling in the gory details. It's a little more exciting than reading them in the Sunday papers, like the cook. You're a fad, that's all. Like a boxer or a crooner. And we kill ourselves laughing behind your back.'

He sat with his face set, wiping her spittle slowly with his handkerchief.

'Do you know why I took you to that party?' She was almost screaming at him. 'Do you know? Not for your blue eyes. But because I had to. It was a Chamber of Horrors party. But of course you were far too fond of yourself to notice it, weren't you? We wanted to get Pierpoint the executioner, warders from the condemned cell, maybe some Chicago gangster with his machine-gun. *That's* your place. You're a curiosity, a freak, a monster.'

He silently put on his waistcoat and dinner-jacket. She came and stood close to him – as close as an hour before at the party.

'You despise me, don't you? You damn well despise me. My God, that's funny! Because I think you're contemptible, utterly contemptible. You enjoy making people's flesh creep, don't you? You revel in all the flattery. You love us playing up to you, pretending you're something in society. You're a hypocrite. You're disgusting.'

Rumbelow strode from the room. He slammed the flat door and hurried down the stairs. There was a taxi passing with its flag up. He stopped it and asked for his club. He noticed the driver looking downwards, and realized his trousers were still unbuttoned.

The evening had been a crescendo of humiliation. He sat staring through the taxi window with the strange, almost unremembered sensation of tears coming to his eyes. He realized – he forced himself to realize – every word that woman had said was right. He only wondered how long he had really known as much, in his heart.

'I have not been true to myself,' he murmured. 'I have not been true . . . that is my evil, my one evil. It could be the end of me.'

For a man who had no pity for others, at least he kept none to lavish on himself.

THE TRAIN HAD left Paddington just after seven in the morning, and was puffing with increasing briskness through the threadbare western fringes of London. Rumbelow sat facing the engine, in his striped grey flannel with a carnation in the buttonhole. Sixsmith opposite had his usual blue suit – Rumbelow seriously wondered if he possessed another. Scotland Yard had produced first-class tickets, so they had the compartment to themselves. It was almost a fortnight later, Tuesday May the fifth, and they were travelling to Mortlock for the adjourned inquest on James Jeavons.

'Vickery's garage must be somewhere in this area,' Sixsmith observed.

'When's his appeal?'

'It's not down for hearing yet.'

'It won't get him very far.'

'Mind, he might still end up with life instead.'

'Why should he?'

'There's quite a movement getting up to influence the Home Secretary.'

'Oh, I know that. Though I can't see why the Home Secretary should take the slightest notice. I can't even see the reason for it. Apart from misplaced sentiment, muddled thinking, or plain hysteria.'

'You know what people are, Doctor.'

'Only too well, I assure you.' Rumbelow opened his attaché case on the seat beside him and drew out a thick manilla folder. He was beginning to recover his enthusiasm for work and for life itself. His detractors in the Press had faded away. Even something of a counter-attack had been mounted by the intellectual weeklies, praising him as the world's first truly scientific forensic expert, a pathologist of international fame whom the country should cherish in an age of perilously rising crime. Rumbelow felt these writers were admirably clear-headed men, performing a duty in dispelling public prejudice, and probably paid only meagrely for it.

The wound he had suffered in Diana Flavell's bedroom was more reluctant to heal. He could only take comfort from his own unworldliness. There was no image in his mind of a prostitute who read T. S. Eliot and hung paintings by Picasso on her walls, much less one accepted by even the laxer fringe of London society. He supposed there were degrees of prostitution, like of most unsavoury activities. He remembered reading in some magazine about the grand courtesans of pre-Revolutionary France, who were most important ladies indeed. He even began to worry less about his moral contamination than at the horrific sum she certainly would have expected from him.

But the hurt ran far deeper. His self-esteem had been badly dented – in a man less sure of himself and his abilities it would have been shattered. He had enjoyed the self-delusion of moving in London society as a right, when he was only some kind of macabre entertainment. He would cut away that part of his life for good, however painful the stroke. When the next few days produced an invitation to lunch at Lady Accrington's, he wrote a courteous refusal, then tore the card into tiny pieces and burnt them in the flame of his Bunsen, an unusual act of symbolism. Henceforward he would lose himself in his work.

Rumbelow opened the manilla folder. 'Shall we run through the case now? It'll save us a last-minute rush before the inquest.' Sixsmith nodded. 'As you know, I've reached my opinion. I believe Jeavons died from the effect of arsenious oxide. That's white arsenic, the usual choice for the poisoner. You can buy it anywhere – in weed-killers, rat-poisons, even fly-papers. I extracted almost ten grains of arsenic from one brand. Enough to kill five adults. And God knows how many flies.'

This was a broad joke for Rumbelow. Sixsmith was glad to

find him in a good mood for the expedition. Over the past couple of weeks the doctor had been uncommonly snappish.

'Now for my reasons.' Rumbelow produced a silver propelling-pencil and started checking a foolscap page of numbered handwritten paragraphs. 'It's simply a matter of approaching the case systematically. Like every other in medicine, whether the subject is living or dead.' To Sixsmith, these were familiar footsteps in which he had often plodded. 'We start with the signs and symptoms of the man's last illness. I admit, here we're on weak ground. The weakest in the case. We have to take Halverston's word for everything. He said he found Jeavons collapsed, his pulse thready, his breathing bad. That was at eight in the morning, and he died about five hours later. Halverston put it down to heart-failure consequent to high blood-pressure. Some of these country doctors are the best accomplices any murderer could wish.'

'The symptoms are typical of arsenic poisoning, are they?'

'Not entirely. In medicine, few things follow a rigid pattern – there'd be no need of our being particularly clever if they did. It's the small variations which mislead you so dangerously. In "typical" acute arsenic poisoning, one would expect severe gastroenteritis – uncontrollable vomiting and torrential diarrhoea. Plus burning of the eyes and mouth and cramp in the calves – Jeavons complained of cramps. I at least got that out of Halverston, you remember. Plus restlessness, sometimes even convulsions. And what's important to this case, the signs of heart failure. Now – in arsenic poisoning irritation of the gut with diarrhoea and vomiting may never happen at all. This is when the dose is so large the patient succumbs rapidly from heart failure. You follow, Sixsmith? The "typical" signs and symptoms may have *no time* to appear before death supervenes.'

'And a large dose was given in this case?'

'It was not in fact very large. But the man's heart was already severely damaged. It needed little more to push it into failure. It would have been exactly the same with other toxic drugs in quite moderate doses.'

Rumbelow moved his pencil down the paper. 'Point two. The post-mortem appearances. Here we can take a firmer

133

stand. It's unfortunate I had to examine the body so long after burial. If that fool Halverston had reported the death to the coroner we should all have been spared a good deal of trouble. Though a fair amount of decomposition had occurred, there were two signs which immediately aroused my suspicion. One was the presence of tiny bleeding points under the lining of the left ventricle of the heart. They're very common in arsenic poisoning, even with no irritation to be found in the stomach or intestines. Two, yellow streaking outside the duodenum, the highest part of the intestine, just below the stomach. These streaks were likely to be yellow arsenic. That's the sulphate form of the drug, to which white arsenic is converted by putrefaction.'

'But it still remains arsenic?'

'Yes. Arsenic can come in many forms. That's another matter of considerable importance in this particular case, as I shall explain in a minute. Now to our third step, chemical analysis. Here we are unassailable. Arsenic was definitely present in the body. I applied two tests, Reinsch's and Marsh's. They're both well established in toxicology. The results from the Reinsch test were inconclusive, but Marsh's was positive. Absolutely positive.'

'So we can at least take that as definite, Doctor? Death was caused by arsenic.'

Rumbelow leant back, his head against a white antimacassar embroidered G.W.R. 'This case has a very odd complication. One which affects it in two distinct ways. As I said at the p.m., Jeavons suffered from syphilis.'

'Dr Halverston disagreed with that.'

Rumbelow made a dismissive gesture. 'The aorta showed all the changes of syphilis, so did the valve leading to it from the heart. That is quite definite. The defence at the trial – if it comes to a trial – will anyway accept it. It could be their strongest card. You see, Jeavons might well have been undergoing injections of arsenic for this condition. In secret, either in the district or more likely up in London. You should be able to lay hands on the doctor who was giving them, if he exists.'

Sixsmith had his own note-book out. 'You mean, these injections killed him?'

'Not at all. *That* arsenic would be in an entirely different form. Organic arsenic, an arsphenamide, quite unlike the simple arsenical salts used to kill weeds, or rats – or humans. That organic sort of arsenic reacts to neither the Reinsch test nor the Marsh test. There is a special test for it, the Fresenius method, which of course I applied. It was negative. So if Jeavons were having injections containing arsenic, he certainly hadn't received one for several days. That's the time taken for an injection to be completely eliminated from the body. He might well not have had any for months, or even years, or even at all. The disease had done its damage and was quiescent. He was a 'burnt-out case', as the physicians say. But even had I found traces of organic arsenic, they would be totally irrelevant to the simple arsenic I found as well. So if the defence do decide to play that card, you see how easily I can trump it.'

Rumbelow closed the folder, looking pleased with himself.

'It seems an odd coincidence, Doctor?'

'A chance in several thousand. But far from an impossibility.'

'Have there been any other cases with this sort of complication?'

'I've combed the Blackfriars' library, but could find nothing. Of course, the possibility's been mooted often enough. But only as an exercise in theoretical toxicology.'

'Mrs Jeavons might have read something about it in a medical book. It would have given her the idea.'

'I fancy that's putting too fine a point on it. Though keep it in mind. You never know when counsel might find himself in need of more ammunition.'

'We've nothing yet to prove she gave the arsenic with her own hands. And I'm still not happy on a motive which will stand up in court. But she's an impulsive and foolish woman – she must be, coming up and tackling you in the street like that. I'll let her stew for a bit. There's a chance she'll give something away. That's why I don't want a coroner's verdict of murder against her this morning.'

'I shouldn't think that's likely. It's only a couple of months since the Wright report came down on "trial by inquest". How much do you want me to say, or not to say?'

'As little as possible. I'd prefer nothing definite to come out of the inquest. An adjournment *sine die* would suit me very well.'

Rumbelow locked his attaché case. The detective stared at the fleeting, neatly-edged fields of the Thames valley, coloured by spring late that year. The day had started bright but was turning thundery, with heavy drops of rain running almost horizontally across the carriage windows. Sixsmith remembered a joke someone had told him at Scotland Yard, about a man who wanted to kill his wife so 'took his razor and gave her arse a nick'. He wondered whether to tell Rumbelow, but decided the doctor would not be amused.

'I've finished with the newspaper, if you'd like it.'

Sixsmith took the *Morning Post*. 'What's happened about the Budget leak?'

'Parliament's setting up a tribunal.'

'That J. H. Thomas is a bit of a card, isn't he?' There was a photograph of the new King of Egypt, a slim youngster of seventeen called Farouk. Sixsmith wondered if the boy would be half as popular as the new King of England. Opposite was a map of the war in Abyssinia. 'You have to learn too many names of faraway places to keep up with things these days,' he complained.

'You soldiered out in Mesopotamia yourself, didn't you?'

'Yes. Perhaps I never really settled back into the world after the war. When I retire I'm getting right away from it all, I'm buying a bungalow in Jersey.'

'Jersey! That's certainly outlandish. When do you go?'

'I leave the force at the beginning of September, 1939. I'm looking forward to the peace.'

They steamed into Mortlock Station in good time for the inquest. It was held at ten-thirty in the Shire Hall, in a large, oblong, high-ceilinged room rather knocked about. Drawing out his chair, Rumbelow was startled to find several feet of red paper streamer twined round the legs. He supposed the place was hired for dances, and up on the dais with the coroner's desk the band played.

The coroner himself was thin and anxious-looking, in black with a wing collar, a local solicitor. This was the first point against him for Rumbelow, who believed all coroners should be medical men. The second was his opening the proceedings by warning the jury against ascribing to any doctor, however eminent, the gift of infallibility. Words which were galling enough from Sir Arthur Younghusband became in Rumbelow's ears plain insults from such a lowly functionary. He caught Dr Halverston's eye across the room, and fancied the fellow was grinning at him. His third objection was the widow's absence. It was Jeavons' solicitor who gave evidence of identifying the body. There seemed some agreement – or perhaps he should call it conspiracy – to save the woman the publicity of appearing in court. He supposed it was misplaced sympathy, or simply resentment of interfering people coming down from London. But there was nothing Rumbelow could do about it. A coroner alone had the right to call what witnesses he pleased, and in his own court was above correction by anyone.

Dr Halverston gave evidence that the cause of death was heart failure secondary to high blood-pressure. Rumbelow followed him into the witness-box, a portable structure like a low-church pulpit under a wooden umbrella. He said simply that the cause of death was poisoning by arsenic. He imagined almost everybody in court gave a gasp, and looked at each other as though they had just witnessed some horrific sight, like a child knocked down by a motor-car.

'Then you disagree completely with Dr Halverston's opinion of the cause of death?'

'Completely.'

'You found no evidence of heart disease?'

'I did. Of heart disease caused by syphilis.'

This brought another gasp. The coroner seemed unsure how to go on. He folded his hands on the desk, and Rumbelow noticed they were shaking. He's frightened of me! Rumbelow thought. Frightened of my reputation. Or frightened of seeming overawed by it. He felt less enmity towards the man.

'I see. But this – er, form of heart disease was not the cause of death, Dr Rumbelow?'

137

'No.'

'Not even a contributory cause?'

'That might be possible. Contributory to arsenic poisoning as the immediate cause.'

'Did you find any signs suggesting high blood-pressure?'

'No.'

The coroner asked no more. Perhaps through his agitated state of mind, perhaps preferring to guard his local reputation by appearing to know of syphilis only faintly by hearsay, Rumbelow thought. And Rumbelow was certainly not in the habit of volunteering evidence unasked. He signed his deposition. The coroner adjourned the inquest for three months, seeming glad to push everything from his hands into those of the police.

'More or less what we wanted,' said Sixsmith, as they left the court.

'Quite satisfactory. There's a train at twelve-fifty-five, I saw. I can get a sandwich in the station buffet and catch it.'

'I expect I'll be here for the rest of the week. Could you get down again if necessary, Doctor?'

'Yes, of course.'

Rumbelow made down the main corridor towards a lobby leading on to the front steps. It had a glass roof, the rain of a thunderstorm falling on it loudly. He became aware of someone walking close beside him, and turned to face Halverston.

'You were rather hard on me, weren't you?' The local doctor was plainly struggling to keep his temper. 'Disagreeing so flatly with my opinion. In open court, like that. It'll all get in the newspapers.'

'Aren't you being oversensitive?' Rumbelow stopped impatiently. 'Any clinician's liable to have his diagnosis upset by a pathologist. It happens often enough at Blackfriars. I don't remember any of the consultants objecting.'

'This isn't the same thing.'

'Isn't it? It strikes me as exactly the same principle.'

'Listen, Rumbelow. Jeavons was my patient at Blayford ever since he returned from the East. Now you're saying in public that I misdiagnosed him, that I treated him for the wrong

138

condition. That I even got the cause of his death wrong. You're accusing me of professional negligence, in fact.'

'I'm not at all.'

'Yes you are. You're simply being insulting.'

'You take it as an insult, do you, anyone holding a different opinion from your own? No worthwhile general practitioner would feel insulted at being corrected by a consultant. That's what consultants are for.'

'I take a second opinion readily enough, I assure you. I know my own limitations. But I take them only from consultants I respect.'

The twin plate-glass doors leading to the street were suddenly illuminated by a lightning-flash. 'So you don't respect me?'

'Frankly, I don't. Not after what I've read recently in the newspapers.'

'If you believe all that, you're an even bigger fool than I took you for.'

'How dare you speak to me in that arrogant way! Have you no idea of the proper relationship between one doctor and another? Were you never taught the rudiments of medical etiquette? Or even of ordinary good manners?'

'You are a fool, Halverston, a fool. And I shall show you up.' Rumbelow abruptly opened the glass door, and turning up the collar of his trench-coat hurried down the steps. A policeman in a streaming cape asked if he wanted a taxi.

'No, no, it's only a few minutes, I'll walk.'

He was furious with Halverston. To do one's duty in court, and then to be attacked for it by the very man whose gross mistakes lay at the bottom of the whole case . . . oh, it was stupid, ridiculous, exasperating! If Halverston hadn't liked his evidence, that was Halverston's affair. But he had no right to come up afterwards and berate him for it. The man was an uncouth simpleton. So was the coroner. Perhaps they all were in that part of the country. He was eager to be back in the more civilized atmosphere of London. He paced the rainswept platform angrily. Then he saw a man put a fresh newsvendor's placard outside the bookstall saying RUMBELOW SENSATION and felt better.

20

RUMBELOW WAS BACK in London in time for the daily post-mortems at Blackfriars. Then he had his accumulated work in the Central Mortuary. He dined as usual at his club. It was after ten when he trudged up the hill towards his house, still carrying his bag. As there was no light downstairs, Rosemary had gone to bed. Perhaps she was growing tired of dance music.

He let himself in and switched on the hall lamp. He had a sudden feeling of uneasiness. Not being a man to let any irrational sensation pass unanalysed, he hung up his trench-coat and stood trying to account for it. The house was cold. Unusually cold, even for such a chilly evening. Rosemary must have let the kitchen stove go out.

He went to the kitchen and tipped some coke on the dull embers. Returning to the sitting-room, he found a few letters which had arrived after his departure for Mortlock that morning, and glanced through them quickly. There was also a new copy of the *British Medical Journal*, which he unwrapped and stuck under his arm before switching off the lights and making upstairs.

The bedroom was dark, though for once Rosemary had left the curtains undrawn, the yellow glow of the street-lamp out-lining the familiar curves and angles. He switched on the read-ing-lamp and saw the bed was empty.

He stood frowning for a second. He threw open the bedroom door. 'Rosemary!'

He hurried through the house, opening more doors, switching on all the lights.

'Rosemary! Rosemary!'

He found a flashlight in the kitchen and searched the garden, peering under all the bushes and in the dark corners of the fencing. Nothing. He went back into the hall, carefully switched off the torch and laid it on the table. He stood still for almost a minute. He was frightened, an almost unknown sensation for him. Their quarrel in the restaurant came back. Had she killed herself? Was she already dead in the river, or beside some railway track? He had talked of suicide then in a detached, almost intellectual way, but to imagine the act really being accomplished was appalling. Then he wondered if she had been kidnapped, for ransom or out of revenge. There was no sign of a struggle, though he supposed she could easily have been tricked away. He reached for the telephone, about to dial Scotland Yard, but hesitated. She might have been taken ill. Or simply gone out for the evening. Though he felt either event was unlikely to have occurred without his knowledge.

He hurried from the house, leaving the front door wide open. Their neighbour was a middle-aged tea-broker, with a business in Mincing Lane. Rumbelow had exchanged barely a dozen snatches of conversation with him in his life. The house was exactly like his own. As he unlatched the front gate he saw a light behind the sitting-room curtains and heard the familiar rhythm of a dance band. He rang the bell. The tea-broker himself opened the door, immediately looking uneasy.

'May I come in?'

'Of course, of course, Doctor.' The broker was a little bald man with a thick grey moustache and large round glasses, in his shirtsleeves. He fussed Rumbelow into the sitting-room, quickly and stealthily putting on his jacket, as though trying to pretend he was wearing it all the time. Rumbelow noticed the room was much better furnished than his own, with brocade armchairs and deep matching pelmets over the curtains. The broker's wife, fat and in a flowered dress, hastily switched off the radiogram. They both stared as though he had called professionally to dig up the floorboards for bodies.

Rumbelow stood in the middle of the flowered carpet, rather at a loss. 'I called concerning my wife.'

'Not ill, I hope?' asked the broker quickly.

'Oh, no. At least, I sincerely hope not. You see, she's not at home.' This seemed to Rumbelow a scarcely adequate explanation of his presence. 'For various reasons, it's a little worrying. I wondered if you'd seen anything of her, that's all.'

The couple exchanged glances.

'We haven't set eyes on your good lady for some time, Doctor.' The tea-broker shifted from one foot to the other. 'Not for quite some time. Have we, my dear?'

The wife made no reply. Rumbelow stared hard at them in turn. Something made him suspect a conspiracy. 'I only ask your help because I'm concerned with my wife's safety. As you can imagine, I have plenty of enemies in the criminal classes.' Two red spots appeared on the woman's cheeks. 'Unless I've some positive idea where she's got to, I can assure you the police will be here in five minutes.'

This decided the woman to speak. 'Your wife's gone away, Doctor.'

'What do you mean, "gone away"?'

'She's left. Left her home. I saw her go this morning with her suitcase. She had a taxi.'

'But that's impossible!' They offered no comment. 'I think I'm entitled to ask why you didn't tell me as much in the first place?'

The woman stared at the carpet, slowly rubbing her hands.

'We don't care to meddle in other folk's private affairs.'

'But where's she gone? Didn't she say? Did she leave a message?'

The wife shook her head. The tea-broker cleared his throat loudly and began, 'You see, we were in something of the horns of a dilemma, Doctor. It being somebody famous like yourself—'

'Why should she do a thing like that? She never even hinted as much. Certainly never to me. Did she say anything to you?'

As the woman looked up, Rumbelow noticed her dull-looking features wore an expression of bitter reproach. She knows more about me than I imagined, he told himself. Rosemary must have been gossiping, in the hideously intimate way that women did. This tea-merchant's wife has decided I'm to blame for it all. For the second time that day he felt angry. These inconsequential people had no right to form judgments on him. They were nothing compared with him, nothing at all. They only knew him through the sheer accident of his living in the next house. He wanted them out of his sight. 'I wish you were more forthcoming. You might save me a good deal of trouble and anxiety.' He turned and strode from the house, the tea-broker following him to the door, looking aghast and still babbling about the horns of his dilemma.

In his own sitting-room, Rumbelow started searching in case she had left a letter. It was propped on the wireless-set, almost invisible with the pink-fringed standard-lamp unlit. It was written in her clear schoolmistress' hand, on stiff blue paper with a scalloped edge.

Dear John,

You may be surprised that I have left you. But perhaps only because you could not have thought me capable of such resolute action.

I have been near to doing as much several times. More recently, it has come into my head every time you've had to be away. Nothing in particular has made up my mind for me now.

I have always been unhappy with you. I was not happy even before we married, but I hoped that things would get better between us. I know what I am doing is wrong, because I know my responsibilities as a wife. God knows, they have been tested enough.

I am sorry for you, John. But at least you have your work, which is always your first interest. Please don't follow me. I'll be all right. When things become clearer to me, I shall get in touch with you through a third party.

Your wife,
Rosemary.

He crumpled the letter and threw it savagely into a corner. He sat in his easy-chair, chin cupped in hand. It was humiliating. It was also genuinely puzzling. Their life together admittedly hadn't been blissful – not in the nonsensical way portrayed by advertisements for instalment-plan furniture and suchlike. But Rosemary had more reason for contentment than most women. In hard times he had given her security, a home – and a reflected glory to warm even her corner of the suburbs. It was most ungrateful of her to leave. Particularly so theatrically. He thought nervously of it getting into the newspapers, making him look ridiculous, drawing irritating sympathy from his friends in the hospital and the courts, and God knows what in the way of jokes behind his back. Then he wondered exactly where she had gone. He assumed back to her parents in Yorkshire. They wouldn't be overjoyed to see her. They might even throw her out again. Well, she was able to look after herself, he supposed. After all, she was basically a sensible woman. He began to calm down.

He returned to the kitchen to make his usual milk drink. It occurred to him she might be back the next morning. Even the most level-headed females did such hysterical things, as they so often ineffectively attempted suicide, simply to call attention on themselves. He decided he would leave matters for the night, that he would write the next day to the address of her parents' farm. He would be careful what he said, because in her absence they would certainly open it. A wire sent immediately might alarm them, and he knew they had no telephone. He went round the house again, locking the doors and carefully switching off the lights. He climbed upstairs and got into bed. He slept soundly, in the knowledge that if you intend to commit suicide you don't take your luggage with you.

21

WHIT MONDAY IN 1936 was on June the first, cold and wet like most of the preceding month. Rumbelow rose early, leaving his bed unmade with the depressing knowledge it would be in exactly the same state on his return. He was managing his house with the charwoman – whom he suspected stole his groceries – and she enjoyed the bank holiday off.

He prepared himself two boiled eggs and a pot of tea, eating in the kitchen. In his attaché case he packed some medical journals and a sheaf of post-mortem reports on which he had work to do. Shortly before seven o'clock he made his way in bowler hat and trench-coat down the hill to Lower Sydenham Station. He took the Underground from his suburban train to King's Cross, which was already crowded with day-trippers. The bookstall was open, and he bought a copy of *The Strand Magazine* with a guilty feeling of extravagance. As he was travelling at his own expense, he went third-class.

He hoped for a compartment to himself, but at the last minute a young couple got in and started talking animatedly about King Edward's Coronation, officially proclaimed that Thursday for May the twelfth the following year. An experienced railway traveller, Rumbelow knew that once the excitement of the journey had dwindled they would lapse into tolerable silence. With the magazine on his knees, he stared through the window as the express jerked its way amid the tenements, the compressed terraces of houses and engrimed factories of Islington, then under the wall of the prison he would be visiting the following morning. Since his wife had gone away, he reflected, his professional career had certainly offered that satisfaction which her blue, scalloped-edged letter recommended as a substitute for herself.

Mrs Jeavons had been arrested by Superintendent Sixsmith a week after the adjourned inquest. While she was appearing briefly the next morning in the magistrates' court at Mortlock, a detective-inspector from Scotland Yard arrived at Blackfriars with an empty tin, rusty and unlabelled, found in the garden shed by the police. The detective told Rumbelow the tin was the kind used by a local manufacturer, to contain insecticide for spraying fruit-trees. There were traces of powder still inside, which simple analysis showed Rumbelow to be a mixture of white arsenic and barium carbonate. He supposed she had poured the rest of it down the lavatory, and either innocently imagined the traces too sparse to identify, or had been too frightened to throw the tin out or drop it into some river with a detective's eye always on the door. Anyway, that's cooked *her* goose, Rumbelow thought. Though right from his own first appearance in Blayford, the public at large had imagined Mrs Jeavons already arrested, tried, convicted and hanged.

Vickery's appeal had been even more gratifying. A Member of Parliament – a Labour man, Rumbelow noted – had several million signatures on a petition for the new King to exercise his prerogative of mercy, and was making speeches about it up and down the country. Attacks on Rumbelow were published again in the papers, with letters signed by collections of academics of impeccable conscience, the same bunch it seemed to him who protested regularly against everything from Italian atrocities in Abyssinia to the addiction of the working class to greyhound-racing. It all left him unmoved. He was even becoming used to such treatment by the public, if he could never be reconciled to it.

Rumbelow attended the appeal himself. It was held towards the end of May, as customary in the Law Courts in the Strand, before three judges in surroundings of elaborately carved light-oak, like the choir-stalls in a Victorian church of a prosperous parish. Vickery sat half-screened by the green curtain of the dock, between two warders and looking as dapper as ever.

There were no witnesses. At that stage, his life was obliged to balance only on points of law.

Sir Arthur Younghusband had only one argument. That the judge in his charge had unduly influenced the jury to accept the evidence of Dr Rumbelow in preference to that of Dr Urrick. But he spoke at length, one of the appeal judges seeming to Rumbelow to show plain signs of boredom. As he finally sat down, the judges got into a huddle, whispering fiercely. Thus a man's fate was decided. Rumbelow wondered if they would want to hear from the Crown. But the senior judge in the middle said, 'We need not trouble you, Mr Ivors,' and Ivors rose to bow silently. The senior judge started to deliver the court's decision, painstakingly going over the medical evidence at the trial yet once again. Rumbelow saw the bored judge yawn widely, and felt confident.

'Counsel for the applicant has argued today that the learned judge during the trial was wrong in law – indeed, he put it more strongly than that, was quite improper – in praising the qualifications, experience and methods of Dr Rumbelow to the detriment of those of Dr Urrick. Sir Arthur maintained, in fact, that these two medical gentlemen were of equal worth in the witness-box, and should have been treated as such by the jury. And that it was quite outside the province of the judge to indicate which of them should be believed, or believed to a greater extent than the other.'

The appeal judge paused. 'The court does not accept that argument. Clearly, in any case both sides will call as experienced and skilful medical witnesses as are available to them. But there is nothing whatever to prevent either calling a doctor with little experience in matters of forensic medicine, or with no practical experience in the subject at all. It is not inconceivable that some medical man whose name is a household word – a surgeon, or a heart specialist – might be invited to give his opinion. That might well impress the jury. But the witness' knowledge of forensic evidence could be sketchy, or much like any other busy doctor's. Nothing said by the learned trial judge invaded the jury's province and right of deciding between the two medical experts. His observations about the relative weight of their evidence did not go beyond the limits of permissible comment. Both were distinguished medical men. They gave not only their opinions, but in some considerable detail their reasons for reaching those opinions. From a consideration of this, and from all he had learned in evidence of their comparative experience in similar cases, if the learned judge thought Dr Rumbelow was to be preferred to Dr Urrick, then it was only right he should say so.'

Rumbelow's movement, just easing up the sharp crease of his grey trousers, expressed an infinity of satisfaction.

'Sir Arthur made a further point. It is specific to a case of this nature, depending so largely on the medical evidence. He submitted that his evidence should be referred to arbitration by an independent medical commissioner, to be appointed by this court. Such a procedure is certainly authorized by the Criminal Appeal Act. But the Act makes clear that it is a special and exceptional power for the court to invoke. In this case, the court does not feel what it has heard today justifies such invocation. The medical evidence was correctly summed-up by the learned judge and acted upon by the jury. The court finds no ground to interfere. The appeal is dismissed.'

Vickery disappeared from the public view, for the last time.

As Rumbelow left the building he took out his diary. He had heard from Sixsmith on the telephone that the execution was fixed for June the first, but that must have been a slip of the tongue. He changed the date. It would not be at all proper to hang a man on a bank holiday.

As Rumbelow expected, the couple on the train soon fell silent, and sat staring across the compartment at each other rather sullenly. They got out at Grantham. He went on to Leeds, where he ate a sandwich and caught another train to Harrogate. There he knew he would be obliged to take a taxi. As they motored into the countryside, Rumbelow encountered an unusual sight. Not one aeroplane of the R.A.F. but two of them were making their separate ways across the rainy sky. An uneasy reminder of mankind's new power to destroy itself.

It was early afternoon when he reached the farm. He remembered it perfectly though he had hardly set eyes on the place since his marriage. It was neither large nor elegant, the out-buildings now appearing even more tumbledown and the ugly red-brick farmhouse even more in need of a coat of paint. He saw Rosemary in the front door as the taxi drew up. Rumbelow told the driver he had a train at six, and asked whether he cared to wait. But it was cheaper for the man to go and come back.

'You've had a long journey, John.' She didn't smile at him.

'It's a public holiday. I've not much else to do.'

There was no sign of her parents, to his relief. She took him into the small, neat, musty front room which he knew to be reserved for formal visitors. It was chilly, the well-blacked grate containing a fan of folded shiny white paper spattered with soot. The mantelpiece was covered with tasselled crimson cloth, and bore pictures of the family in silver frames. As he anticipated, his own had been removed. They sat opposite one another in a pair of high-backed chairs stuffed with horsehair, which were very uncomfortable.

'Why did you have to come?'

'I wanted to see you again.'

'I imagined you wouldn't be particularly sorry at getting rid of me.'

'You can't just switch a marriage off like the electric light, you know.'

He took out a cigar and cut it. He was surprised how at home he felt in the bleak little room, where he hadn't been alone with her since his days as a suitor.

'I'm only prepared to discuss strictly practical things, John.'

'So you said in your letter. I only wondered which ones.'

'Well . . . whether you wanted a divorce. Things like that.'

'A divorce is somewhat chillingly final.'

'You can't persuade me to come back to you. I hope you realize that?' She sounded a little hysterical.

'Oh, I shan't get down on my knees or throw myself at your feet, don't worry.' He lit the cigar. 'I thought you meant about money.'

She shook her head vigorously.

'You've got a job?'

'I'm helping on the farm.'

He suspected it was a superfluous assistance. 'You might find a teaching post if you searched hard enough in the newspapers, you know. People say times are beginning to look up. Though I'm quite prepared to make you a reasonable allowance. That's only right.'

'I don't want a penny.'

'Why did you leave?' She said nothing. 'And in that manner? It was most embarrassing.'

'I'm sorry.'

'Did it occur to you, the same end could have been achieved with considerably less drama had you told me of your intentions?'

'How could I speak to you about it? I never spoke to you about anything I really felt.'

'Whose fault was that?'

She rubbed the palms of her hands together uncomfortably. 'Mine, I suppose.'

'Yes, it was. I had the right to know at least something of what went on in your head.'

'The right!'

'Marriage has its duties. But you always took a rather selfish view of ours.' She refused to be drawn. 'It's not very pleasant, you know, living alone.'

For the first time in the room her eyes met his. 'I told you, there's no chance of my coming back.'

'That's your emotions speaking. As they spoke when they told you to leave home so suddenly. But listen, Rosemary. We're intelligent persons. We're mature. We've no need to behave like the children who get married today as soon as they're twenty-one. We can sit down and talk things over. All this . . .' He gave the room a depreciating glance. 'It's only an incident. We can forget about it. We need never mention it again. Hundreds of couples go through a similar sort of crisis every month of the year. I'm certain of that. No one gets to hear about it. They even begin to convince each other it never really happened. The most successful marriages are conspiracies of silence.'

'I know why you're asking this. Only because my absence might be an embarrassment to your career.'

'That's not the case at all.' He looked uncomfortable. She was only partly correct. He was genuinely lonely, and wondered how far he should go in admitting he missed her.

'You know it wouldn't work, John. It's not just my getting emotional, bottling it up till the cork blows off. There's that other business.'

'Your failure in the sexual department? I don't see that as a fundamental difficulty. In time we could overcome it. I'm sure there's some treatment.'

'I don't want any treatment.' She looked at him bitterly. 'You seem to imagine my body's yours, to do as you please with. But it isn't. It's mine, mine alone. It couldn't belong to you or to any man alive. I think all that part is loathsome – horrible, filthy, disgusting.' She turned her eyes away, and added in a helpless voice, 'I'm not made for marriage. That's all there is to it.'

He sat gently puffing his cigar. He perceived her feelings only dimly. He had learnt gynaecology at Blackfriars, but it was only a study of the machine for reproduction, with such airy peculiarities never mentioned. He decided he wouldn't press her, and for once wouldn't dominate her. Though that was the sensation he missed most from her absence. 'Very well. If that's final, I suppose a divorce can be obtained.'

'I don't want a divorce. Not if it will embarrass you.'

'It's a matter of law, isn't it? The law sees the attachment of man and wife as a singularly powerful bond. In many things they become simply one person. For them to live apart, never even to set eyes on one another, makes a nonsense of it.' He flicked his cigar-ash on to the sooty paper in the grate. 'I shall allow you to sue me. It's the gentlemanly thing to do, it appears. I shall go with some professional woman to Brighton. It will be in the papers, but some annoyances can't be helped. I'll get a firm of solicitors to write to you. One which specializes in the shadier side of practice. After all, I'm acquainted with plenty of them.' He took out his watch. 'I'm afraid I must continue to embarrass you with my presence. My train for

Leeds isn't until six. Then I have a wait for the slow train at midnight. It'll be five in the morning before I reach London.'

'Poor John! You've had such a long trip, and all for nothing.' For the first time she looked tenderly at him. She felt guilty and ashamed, and sorry for him. But she dared to show it only over irrelevant details. 'Are you hungry?'

'I've no appetite today.'

'How about a cup of tea?'

He nodded. As she left him he stood up, and still smoking his cigar examined carefully the photographs, the china ornaments and other uninspiring objects in the room. When the door opened he did not for the moment look round, then he saw to his disconcertion it was not Rosemary but her father.

'Well! The famous Dr Rumbelow. I suppose we should feel ourselves honoured, having you here?'

He was a thick-set, grey-haired Yorkshireman in his fifties. Rumbelow had always despised him, even more than his neighbours in London. He wondered how pressingly Rosemary had tried to keep him out of the way. 'Feel how you wish. I only took the trouble of coming here to discuss a matter which concerns Rosemary and myself.'

'Aren't you ashamed? Of the way you've treated her?'

'I am not. And you have no reason to suggest as much. You don't know the full story.'

'Oh, yes, I do. Or as much as I need to. You married my daughter when you were an ordinary doctor, struggling to get on. There's half a dozen of them I could name in this area, killing themselves to keep up appearances without a couple of ha'pence to their name. Now you find yourself famous, you've no time for her. That's it, isn't it?'

'You can accuse me of what you like. Anyone can, if they're not particular about the truth.'

'You don't seem to care that you've ruined her life. All that money and effort it took for her to train as a teacher! It was a great achievement. A great achievement. And she gave it up. Gave up her job, everything. Just for you.'

Rumbelow regarded becoming a school-teacher as an achievement hardly worth mentioning, and as for the job he had seen himself as her saviour in releasing her from it. 'The facts speak for themselves, if only you'd open your eyes and look at them. Rosemary left our home of her own free will. She didn't even favour me with a warning, a hint. It was a great shock to me. I came here today inviting her to return. She refuses. You have no argument. You have nothing to reproach me with at all.'

Rumbelow staggered back in alarm as his father-in-law grabbed the lapels of his suit. 'If I were a few years younger, I'd thrash you.'

'Take your hands off me! This is completely uncivilized.' The farmer started shaking him. 'If you're not careful, you'll be facing a summons for assault.'

'You're not in bloody court now. Hiding behind the law, that's your game, isn't it? It's time you faced the world like a man.'

Rumbelow was afraid the man would lose his temper and hit him. But Rosemary appeared in the door with a tray of tea-things. He released his hold, giving a look of disgust. 'I've no time for you. Get out of my house, just as soon as you've done your business. Don't try to come back. Leave my daughter in peace. She's had enough of you.'

He gave Rosemary a sullen glance, but he left them alone together. They drank the tea almost in silence. The rain had stopped, so afterwards they went for a walk in the country. They talked about the Jeavons case and other impersonal things. When the time came for Rumbelow to leave, they were quite good friends.

22

RUMBELOW HAD LEFT a clean collar and a razor in the laboratory at Blackfriars. By seven the next morning he was sprucing himself in the consultants' lavatory behind the committee-room, when Graham Trevose walked in.

'You're up early, John.' The slim, gnome-like plastic surgeon was as usual dressed even more stylishly than Rumbelow.

'I've just got off a train from the north.'

'Poor fellow. I hope you had a decent week-end. The weather's so miserable.'

'It was something of a duty call.'

'I got back last night from Paris.'

Trust Trevose, Rumbelow thought, to spend his holiday somewhere glamorous. 'Was it a rough crossing?'

'Oh, I went by plane.'

'By plane? That's very daring of you.'

'Safe as houses, Imperial Airways. So much more comfortable than the boat. And so much longer to enjoy yourself the other end.'

'I suppose you've been called in this morning for a case?'

'Not really. I rout my houseman out early, I'm afraid. I've so much private work piled up, I'd never see a hospital patient at all unless I missed my breakfast.'

Trevose did up his flies and strolled out. He hasn't expressed the slightest interest in my own activities this morning, Rumbelow thought. Irritating, but typical of Trevose. He moved in a self-centred little world of his own. As he knotted his tie, Rumbelow remembered rumours of Trevose's own wife, how she was neurotic, or even downright mad, locked away in an asylum.

He wondered fleetingly if he dare approach the surgeon with his own problems. But he doubted if his advice would be more constructive than to find some pretty girl and sleep with her.

He still had good time to travel by Tube. He had expected a crowd outside the prison, but as he approached with his bag he was surprised to find it several times larger than on the last occasion. As he was about to cross the street someone shouted excitedly, 'That's him! That's Rumbelow!' The cry was taken up. There were jeers and boos, people started running across the roadway, one man even shook a fist in his face. The crowd was fortunately strongly laced with policemen, who under the orders of a flurried inspector hurried to form a bodyguard, pushing their way with Rumbelow in the middle to the prison gate. It was an unsettling incident, worse for being unexpected, but Rumbelow's only feelings were disgust at such unruly and hysterical behaviour in a London street. He had not been frightened. He represented the law, he was entering a citadel of the law, and the law was never attacked with impunity. But it left him in a bad temper.

The governor seemed jumpier than ever. The man really should pull himself together or find another job, Rumbelow thought impatiently. William was waiting in the mortuary. At least it was warmer there in June. Rumbelow remarked as he started laying out his instruments, 'The police will have to seal off the streets all round, if these disturbances go on much longer.'

'People have been getting over-excited, if you ask me, sir.'

'There'll always be trouble-makers. Insignificant men, eager to take up any cause, as long as it makes them seem more important than they really are. These people outside are blind to the protection they enjoy from the law. We'd be murdered in our beds if they had their way. Or perhaps it's just the fashionable thing to do. I wouldn't know.'

Eight o'clock struck. A noise rose outside, half a moan, half a shout of anger. Rumbelow waited silently. But instead of the body the governor appeared, white and shaking.

'Something went wrong. Oh, God! It was a terrible business.'

'Is he dead?'

'Yes, but it was bungled. Not the hangman's fault, not mine, not anyone's. Vickery seemed to know something of the procedure. I don't know where he got it from. You know the two chalk-lines? The ones the prisoner has to stand between.' Rumbelow gave a nod. 'At the last moment . . . when the hood was on and the hangman about to throw the lever, he managed to kick his feet away, trying to scramble on to the platform beside the trap.'

'Weren't there two warders supporting him?'

'They must have been taken by surprise. His legs were strapped below the knee, exactly as usual. Everything was in order. I took care to see as much myself.'

'It all sounds very unfortunate.'

'He went down, of course, But the base of his spine caught on the edge of the trap. There was a loud thump – perhaps not a violent one, but you can imagine how it affected us at the time. If he hadn't fallen cleanly, the result for the poor man could have been terrible.'

'The result for the Home Office wouldn't have been too pleasant, either.' Rumbelow was not in a mood to be sympathetic, particularly to the governor. 'Could the doctor pronounce him dead at once?'

'The pulse was still beating, but I understand that's not unusual. It's been one of the most awful experiences of my life.'

Rumbelow picked up his long scalpel, tapping it idly on the edge of the zinc-topped table with its fishbone of gullies. 'You might have expected a smart Alec like Vickery to discover such things. A pity he wasn't so cautious over his wife's death. He might still have been breathing at this moment.'

'He refused the rum, you know. I suppose he wanted to keep his head clear. I only hope your examination will show nothing untoward, Doctor.'

'We can only wait and see, can't we?'

'I really can't stand any more of these affairs. Next time I'll ask the deputy to take my place.'

'With desperate men you should always be prepared for anything,' Rumbelow told him primly.

Half an hour later the handcart appeared.

Rumbelow and the elderly prison doctor turned over the

body on the post-mortem table. At the base of the spine the skin had been split horizontally, the top lip forced up as though by the blade of a large chisel. There was no bleeding. Rumbelow picked up the flap with forceps. 'Would that be a post-mortem wound or an ante-mortem wound? Perhaps the right term would be a "syn-mortem" wound. Though I shouldn't care to be accused of coining phrases.'

The neck bones were broken. The white spinal cord, running into the body from the base of the brain like the tail of a tadpole, was torn in two.

'The fellow's antics seem to have made the execution more efficient than usual,' Rumbelow observed. 'Perhaps it should be recommended practice on future occasions?'

The inquest went off commendably. The governor gave evidence the hanging was expeditious and efficient, and that death was instantaneous. Rumbelow gave evidence supporting him. They were in the same large upstairs room near the gate, and people were making a lot of noise outside.

'The police want us to slip away round the back somewhere,' said Norman Carlow to Rumbelow as they went down the staircase. 'It seems they've laid on a car. Would we appear like a couple of funks, do you suppose?'

'If the police recommend it for our safety, we have no alternative but to accept.'

'There's my conscience saved again. You're a useful fellow to know, John. Nothing like logic, when it agrees precisely with the unpleasant fluttering feeling in the pit of your stomach.'

As they drove away in the back of a police-car, unnoticed by anyone, Carlow said, 'John, you're looking dead beat. If I didn't know you, I'd have said you were out all last night on a jag.'

'It was less amusing, I'm afraid. I slept on a train. Or I tried to. I'd been up to see Rosemary.'

'Any luck?' Carlow was the only man in Rumbelow's circle to know of her disappearance.

'It depends which way you look at it. She certainly refused point-blank to come back. I'm beginning to think that's really for the best.'

'I see. So you're reconciled to your fate. Now you can make a fresh start. That's often a good thing, in the life of any man.'

'I'm not going to do exactly the same with a different person, if that's what you mean. I've learnt my lesson.'

'Oh, you're just down in the dumps for the moment.'

'I'm depressed, certainly. I could hardly avoid it. But I don't think it's prevented my mind from working clearly.'

'You need taking out of yourself. Listen, John. You know what day it is tomorrow?' Rumbelow looked lost. 'Derby Day. The greatest pagan festival in the land since they slaughtered virgins at Stonehenge, as I'm sure they did. The English in their full Hogarthian magnificence. The lower classes tight on beer and the upper on champagne, as ordained by Nature. We get up a party every year. Why don't you join us?'

'But it's a Wednesday. I've work to do.'

'My deputy sweats it out for me. You must have a registrar.'

'I don't think it's my style, Norman. I've never even been to a horse-race.'

'Come on, it'll do you good. A fellow like you needs to let his hair down now and then. Surely there's some pretty little thing you can take along, a secretary or something? You're a free man now, John, to all intents and purposes. I only wish to God I was.'

'That certainly isn't my style.'

'I'm counting you in for two seats. I'll be bitterly hurt if you let me down. Ah, here we are at my court. I wonder if that mob we left behind has brought down the prison walls? I hope the poor major doesn't suffer the same fate as the governor of the Bastille. I shouldn't much care to meet his head on a pikestaff when I'm walking along Pall Mall this evening.'

The police-car took Rumbelow on to Blackfriars. He sat thinking seriously about the invitation. It would be a day in the open air, and a spectacle a man deserved to see at least once in his life. It was quite respectable even for Carlow, his late Majesty had attended it often. He drummed his fingers on the leather of the seat. Perhaps he would accept. Quinley could do the work. Though of course he would avoid anything so foolish as betting on the horses.

23

WHEN HE SAW her his heart fluttered, an uncontrollable response which alarmed him greatly.

They had arranged to meet on the pavement outside Blackfriars. She was wearing a dress of yellow muslin in the latest fashion, short-sleeved, its square neckline edged with white lace, the hem to the middle of her calf. Her hat was wide-brimmed, decorated with a cluster of large imitation daisies. She wore white gloves reaching above the wrist, and though the day promised fine she carried an umbrella out of respect for the summer's poor weather – her usual one, in severe black.

'We'll take a taxi,' said Rumbelow.

'I'm ever so excited. I've never been to the Derby before, though I've listened to it on the wireless.'

'I hope you won't be disappointed.'

'I'm sure I won't. It's so kind to have asked me.'

'Not at all. It's a way of showing my appreciation. You've done an enormous amount of work for me. All that stuff I had to go through for the Jeavons case. You've been acting almost as my part-time assistant.'

'I was glad to help. Honestly.'

'Was there any trouble about the note I sent the librarian?'

'Oh, he looked a bit grumpy, but in the end he said I could have the day off.'

'I should think so, too! Though I hope you didn't say exactly where you were going.'

Maria Osgood laughed.

The taxi took them to an address Carlow had given Rumbelow in Soho Square. He hadn't thought how they would be travelling to Epsom, and was surprised to find an open-topped bus drawn up, the kind which had disappeared from the London streets but still plied between the Sussex coast resorts. About two dozen couples stood chattering animatedly on the pavement, the men in magenta jackets and waistcoats with silver buttons, some wearing old-fashioned straw hats with ribbons to match. Carlow greeted the pair effusively. It was apparently the outing of some dining club he belonged to, and to which the members looked forward throughout the year.

The rain kept off. They drove through the streets of London in high spirits, all on the top of the bus, passers-by grinning and waving good-humouredly. It was pleasant, Rumbelow thought, to steal a mid-week holiday which seemed to enjoy the traditional blessing of the entire country. He sat on the rearmost seat, Maria beside him. She kept her hands clasped tightly and smiled at everyone. Rumbelow was glad to see her so enjoying the reward for extra work.

The racecourse startled him. There were far more people than he imagined, a ragtaggle army encamped on the Downs as far as he could see. He had somehow expected horseboxes and stable-lads everywhere, but the middle was occupied by a fun-fair, the hurdy-gurdies grinding out music and emitting puffs of steam. Their bus joined a line of others in a roped-off field beyond the grandstand. Rumbelow stood with Maria on the grass, looking blankly while fat gypsy-women with shawl-wrapped babies offered him sprigs of white heather or a glimpse into the future, and a man with a greasy tweed cap and a handful of race-cards promised for trivial sums priceless information from the stables. Rumbelow looked at his watch, buttoning his jacket again securely, wondering how they could manage to pass the time till the races began. He noticed the coroner busily supervising the extraction of trestle tables from the lower deck of the bus. These were quickly set up under awnings in the club's colours, then two men in green-baize aprons appeared with a pair of new-looking galvanized dust-bins, which puzzled Rumbelow until they disgorged bottles of champagne from among lumps of ice. The club certainly knew how to do themselves well, he thought. Carlow popped a cork with an expression of deep satisfaction, and approached with three glasses.

'A little early, isn't it?' Rumbelow protested.

'Oh, I just regard this stuff as a sort of mineral water. A nice astringent mouthwash for the mucous membranes. We'll have lunch by-and-by, and a drop of brandy to keep the cold out. John, you're a deep one. You never told me you were hiding such a pretty girl in the mortuary.'

'Not the mortuary. Miss Osgood's one of the Blackfriars' librarians.'

'Indeed? Brains as well as beauty?'

Maria continued to smile, but looked embarrassed. Rumbelow thought severely that Carlow's ebullience could make him somewhat brash. But he was glad to see he approved of her.

'Brains? She should by rights be a student at the university. That's so, isn't it?'

Maria made a wry face, and Rumbelow saw he had fumbled on a sore point. 'Perhaps I may still, one day. There's time enough yet.'

'You're not telling us you're a bluestocking? I just won't believe it. You're far too attractive. You're the right girl for handling John here. He's so clever he frightens me in court. I fancy he frightens the judges, too. I daren't think how scared stiff the prisoners must be.'

One of the men in baize aprons came up with a deep, square, leather-covered box. Rumbelow said humorously, 'Norman, you haven't brought a set of instruments? I'm not going to perform a post-mortem on a horse in any circumstances.'

'It's a portable wireless-set. Latest model,' he said proudly. 'We'll be able to hear the commentary as the race is actually going on. Providing of course I've remembered to get the accumulator charged. Now I must see the others aren't dying of thirst.' He poured a little more champagne into the glass in Maria's white-gloved hand. 'It's a fine hat you're wearing. This year all the hats seem to be either as big as umbrellas or as tiny as pillboxes. I much prefer that sort.'

'Do you really?' Maria sounded delighted, taking the

161

compliment as heartfelt. She confessed, 'I put the flowers on myself.'

'You *are* a clever girl,' said Carlow.

Rumbelow had only a hazy idea of what would happen on the racecourse. The pair of them stood talking for some time. He saw she drank hardly any champagne. She was unused to it and perhaps frightened of it. Well, that suited him. He preferred people of sober tastes. But their conversation became stilted and difficult. It was inevitable when they had no idea what to say to please one another. Their relationshp had seemed easygoing amid the leather bindings and mahogany shelves at Blackfriars, but it shrivelled in the noisy open-air crowds of Epsom Downs. Then she mentioned Carlow and said, 'Oh, I should *die* if I went into a mortuary,' an unconscious little joke at which they laughed uproariously. But it started them on an easier track.

'I don't even know where you live.'

'In Muswell Hill.' A good middle-class area of north London, Rumbelow thought with satisfaction. 'It's my parents' house.'

'Have you brothers and sisters?'

She shook her head. 'Have you?'

'I had a brother killed in the war. And a sister who died shortly afterwards of that terrible Spanish 'flu. I always think of her as a war-casualty, too. If it hadn't been for the privations we suffered, the epidemic would never have taken a grip. You can understand that I've no love left for the Germans.'

'Perhaps it's a good job I'm an only child. These days, my parents couldn't afford any more.'

'What's your father do?'

'He's an engineer. He had a business, but the Depression finished it off.'

'I'm sorry.'

'It's the times we live in.'

'It's nice to find someone being philosophical about their misfortunes. In my experience, nearly everyone makes the most of them.'

'This is hardly the day to be miserable, is it, Dr Rumbelow?'

'As we're so obviously off duty, why don't you call me

John?' The invitation made her look flustered, whether through the suggestion of intimacy or his own enormous importance he was unable to decide. Before she could reply, Carlow appeared balancing two plates of cold salmon and cucumber. Rumbelow noticed Maria had used his Christian name deliberately three or four times before they finished eating.

It seemed to him the races were very short and the intervals between them very long. Carlow insisted Rumbelow put a shilling on the Derby, with advice on the right horse. Finding himself handing money to a bookmaker with chalked board and battered leather satchel, pressed all round by strangers holding out half-crowns and even ten-shilling notes, pocketing some strange gaudy ticket, Rumbelow had a feeling of unreality. Even the day before he couldn't have imagined himself in this setting. They all climbed to the top of the bus, which made a passable grandstand. Carlow lent Maria his binoculars and went back to manipulating his wireless-set, which emitted nothing but shrieks and whistles. Rumbelow pointed out the moving colours on the far side of the course, the horses assembling for the start. Maria was already jumping up and down with excitement. Suddenly he exclaimed, 'I say, this is fun!' He couldn't recall using the word 'fun' before in his life.

The crowd shouted, 'They're off!' Everything seemed to Rumbelow to be happening too quickly. In a few seconds the horses were thundering downhill towards Tattenham Corner. A few more, and they were slowing up past the winning-post. 'Who won?' he asked confusedly.

'Mahmoud. Smirke up.' Carlow had abandoned the wireless-set and was peering past Rumbelow, having lifted himself during the race on his shoulders. 'That's a double for the Aga Khan. He won it with Bahram last year.' He took the glasses from Maria. 'Gordon Richards on Taj Akbar second. Same stable, by God! Can't see who's third.'

'What about the horse you told me to back?'

'Didn't finish, I'm afraid.'

'Don't I get even part of my shilling back?'

'I'm afraid you don't, old bean.'

After the last race the bus started for London. The day seemed to Rumbelow to end suddenly and sombrely. As the club had some sort of ceremonial dinner, Rumbelow and Maria got off in Trafalgar Square. They stood looking at each other on the pavement, the protective wrapping of their companions' good fellowship disconcertingly torn away. It started to look like rain again.

'Well, that's that,' said Rumbelow.

'It was a lovely day. I'll always remember it.'

'Your parents don't mind your coming with me?'

'Why should they?'

'Some people think I'm a kind of Frankenstein, you know.'

'Oh, no! Those people couldn't know you.'

'It's what the newspapers say, I suppose.'

'I think you're very nice. And very kind.' She hesitated. 'And very misunderstood.'

'You mean all that criticism I had to stand? About the Vickery case.'

'I didn't believe that for one moment, John. I've seen you at work. I admire you.' She stopped again. 'I'm so glad you asked me today. I'd been . . . well, I suppose I'd been hoping something like this would happen.'

Rumbelow gave a grunt. 'You knew that I had a wife?'

'Yes, I did.'

'Though we're separated.'

'That's something I didn't know.'

'Perhaps it couldn't be helped. Our marriage was a mistake in the first place.'

'I'm sorry if it made you unhappy.'

'I don't think it did, really. It just brought me no happiness, which is a different thing.'

They fell silent. Rumbelow wondered if he should ask her somewhere, perhaps to a meal. He couldn't decide whether to feel relieved or disappointed when she announced, 'I'd better be getting along. My parents are expecting me. It was one of the nicest times I've had in my whole life.'

'I enjoyed it. I don't lead a very gay life, you know.'

Very delicately she held out a white-gloved hand. He

164

took the tips of her fingers firmly. 'May I see you again?'
She said nothing, but ran her tongue quickly over her lips.
'Nobody would know. Nobody in the hospital, I mean. I'd see
to that.'

'Yes, I'd love that.'

She took her hand away, and she was gone down the Underground.

24

OVER THE NEXT six weeks Rumbelow saw Maria two or three evenings out of every seven. He took her to the pictures, or to a small French restaurant Norman Carlow had recommended in Soho, where you could get a tasty meal with wine thrown in at five shillings a head. His sexual advances ventured no further than holding her hand, kissing, and pressing her breasts through her dress in the back of cinema stalls and occasionally in taxis. He felt no obsession to be alone with her. He would hardly invite her to Sydenham, under the eyes of the tea-broker and his wife. He had anyway decided to shut up his house and instruct a local estate agent to sell it. A bedroom had unexpectedly become free at his club, through one of its few permanent residents dying suddenly over his soup, and Rumbelow appropriately enough was chosen to move in.

They were walking after dinner on one of those evenings in St James's Park, enjoying the long twilight of mid-June, when she asked, 'Have you any more news of your wife, John?'

She seldom mentioned Rosemary, he wondered whether through delicacy, through shyness, or to further the illusion that she did not really exist. 'Our solicitors are in correspondence. I'm perfectly glad to leave it at that.'

'Would you still have her back?'

'That's a very mature question for one of your age, isn't it?'

'I don't think so. Lots of girls my age are wives these days. I'm quite old enough to think sensibly about marriage.'

Even the distant implications of this remark disturbed him. 'I certainly can't think sensibly about it – not remarriage, that is. Even if I got a divorce from Rosemary, it could take a year, even two. I'm afraid speed is not among the law's virtues.'

'Oh, I know that.'

They stood on the edge of the lake watching the ducks, some of them already tucking their beaks under their wings for the night. Rumbelow wondered absently how they managed to get enough oxygen. 'Do your parents yet know I'm seeing you so regularly?'

'They don't know at all. They just think I've got a new boy-friend. I can make him sound wonderfully mysterious.'

'Don't you suppose the time's come for them to know?'

'Of course, I'd love to tell them, to tell everybody. But I haven't breathed a word, because I knew you didn't want me to.'

'There's so much malicious gossip in the hospital. It would be silly, going out of our way to attract a share of it.'

They started to move away. 'Why should you have picked on me? There're so many other girls in the world. In *your* world, John. Sometimes I don't think you realize how important and famous you are.'

He laughed. 'That's certainly an unfamiliar accusation.'

'But it's true. You talk about people – the other consultants at the hospital, for instance – just as a matter of course. To me, they're gods.'

'I'm really a very simple man.'

'What do you want of me?'

'I don't want anything of you. Just your company. No, that's inadequate, isn't it? And awfully unflattering. But there're some things in the world on which it's impossible to be specific.'

'Do you want to go on seeing me?'

'Of course I do. Very much.'

She looked up at him. 'Are you fond of me?'

'I hope that's a rhetorical question?'

'But why are you?'

'Perhaps because you don't frighten me.'

'*That* doesn't sound very flattering.'

'It is. It's perfectly true I've never felt so completely at ease with any other woman in the world. And that includes my wife.'

They parted as usual at the Underground. He walked towards his club in Pall Mall with an ill-defined feeling of something unpleasant behind their conversation. Of course he was fond of her. It was quite thrilling, as they said, to enjoy the company of a girl much younger than himself. That was a privilege he had believed confined to international financiers on the Riviera, though Norman Carlow had a succession of secretaries who Rumbelow imagined did more than type his letters. There was – there *must* be – no question of letting the affair go too far. But wherever was 'too far'? And what *did* he want of her? He didn't know.

Then something happened to him which was outlandish, even ludicrous, but in the end perhaps did more damage than all the outcry over the Vickery case.

It was a morning which had started badly. Quinley had come into his laboratory at Blackfriars, and announced with his usual expression of gloom and surliness, 'I've withdrawn my application for the readership.'

'You have? Well, quite honestly I think you're wise. You'd only have been courting disappointment, which is unpleasant for any of us. I don't truthfully believe you'd stand much chance for the job.'

'I was aware of that, sir, from the start. I saw you weren't keen on pushing me.'

Rumbelow took this as an affront. 'That's not a very pleasant accusation, is it? I told you I'd do all I could to help. Are you now trying to say I was deceitful?'

'I didn't mean it that way at all. I just thought you didn't consider my work good enough.'

'I'd let you know pretty soon if it wasn't.' Rumbelow noticed the boils on Quinley's cheeks were worse than ever. 'Have you been discussing my view – my possible view – of you and your work with anyone else on the staff?' Quinley remained silent. 'With Dr Bantrell, for instance?'

'I've talked about the job to him, yes.'

'You must take care that a man like Bantrell doesn't mislead

168

you, Quinley. He's a busy grinder of axes. Let me tell you I was prepared to do everything I could to help. Had you got the job, I'd have been as delighted as anyone. Now you've withdrawn all this becomes irrelevant, doesn't it?'

Rumbelow turned on the high stool back to his workbench, but Quinley stayed in the room. 'Might I have my draft application back, please?'

Rumbelow had forgotten about it. He took out his keys, unlocked the drawer and handed over the envelope.

'You haven't looked at it, I see, sir.'

Rumbelow gave him a glance of annoyance. 'I intended to. There's time yet before the applications must be in, and I'm a busy man.'

'Had you looked at it, that would have at least afforded me some encouragement. You need it at my stage. Though perhaps you've forgotten that, sir.'

This was such a surprisingly insubordinate remark that Rumbelow was about to order Quinley angrily from the room. But he checked himself, and said only, 'You really must learn to develop a sense of tact. It's necessary even for a pathologist. Were you a physician, half your practice would depend on it.'

'Would you be happier if I resigned, sir?'

'What on earth put that idea in your head? Though of course you can leave tomorrow morning if you want to.'

'I don't want to at all, sir. I admire your work very much.'

Returning to his usual state of submission Quinley left the laboratory, carefully shutting the door behind him. Rumbelow went back to his microscope, still irritated. Quinley really was a strange young fellow, he thought. Still, he had only a few months left, thank God, in which to put up with him.

A few minutes later the laboratory telephone rang. It was the crime reporter on a popular daily, whom Rumbelow knew fairly well. He was never reluctant to chat with newspapermen, whom he knew to have a reliable professionalism over what to publish and what to suppress.

'I wondered if you'd any comment on this Gretna Green affair, Doctor?'

'What affair? I've been mixed with a variety of cases, but never yet called in to trace an eloping couple.'

The reporter laughed. 'It's enjoying some extra notoriety. There was a body found there this morning.'

'Oh? It's the first I've heard of it.'

'It was in a trunk, sent unaccompanied luggage by goods train from Euston to Glasgow. It got as far as Gretna Junction about two o'clock this morning, when the train stopped to unload some stuff. One of the railwaymen noticed a smell, and thought something had gone bad inside. Well, he was right. The railway police decided to open up. Our man up there says it was cut into little bits, and had been dead for a long, long while.'

'I expect the Yard will be on to me. Obviously, I can't comment when I still don't even know officially about the case.'

'Very well, Doctor. I'll ring you back later on.'

Rumbelow sat lightly drumming his fingers on the bench. That was strange. It was clearly a case of first-class importance, yet the newspapers had heard the news before himself. He picked up the receiver and asked for Scotland Yard. Sixsmith was on holiday – at that very moment on the boat from Weymouth to his bungalow on Jersey. Rumbelow got on to a detective inspector he knew well instead.

'Yes, we've had Glasgow on to us,' the detective told him cheerfully. 'Quite a jamboree they're having up there.'

'Do you want me to go to Gretna? Or are you bringing the body back here?'

'I'm afraid it's out of our hands, Doctor.'

'What do you mean?'

'It's the Scottish police's pigeon. The trunk was consigned to an address in Glasgow. Which they've checked and found not to exist.'

'What's that got to do with it? It was dispatched from London.'

'Oh, yes. But it was discovered north of the border. So it's not our headache.'

'I don't agree with that at all,' Rumbelow said sharply. 'It's quite immaterial where the body happened to be found. It was put on a train from London, so presumably in London the crime was committed. It's absolutely ridiculous to say the Scottish police have any jurisdiction in the matter. You might just as well maintain that a sailor knifing someone aboard a British ship should be tried in Valparaiso, or wherever it happened to be going to.'

'I wouldn't know about that, Doctor. But the powers-that-be seem quite happy.'

'Oh, very well, very well. It's one of those administrative muddles, I suppose. I'll have a word with the Home Office. I expect it can be easily sorted out.'

'I'm sorry if you're disappointed, Doctor. Not getting your hands on it.'

'I'm quite indifferent to whoever investigates the case, Inspector. I want to know where I stand, that's all.'

Rumbelow hooked up the telephone. The man to examine the remains would be Urrick. Urrick! Why, the murderer was as free as air already. Urrick would be useless at a case of such intricacy. And I made my name with exactly the same sort of murder, Rumbelow thought crossly. Putting together the bits of Perryman's mistress, and in the end bringing him to the gallows. But he did not telephone the Home Office. He feared in some way it might make him look ridiculous.

Bodies in trunks consigned by rail have a powerful attraction for the British people. The 'Gretna Green Murder' was for the next few days on the front of all the newspapers. The Scottish police seemed unable to say whether it was one body, or two, or even more, and whether they were male or female. So much for Urrick! Rumbelow thought. The investigation is pathetic. Such things are really perfectly straightforward to sort out, if only you approach them systematically. His fingers tingled almost physically to turn over the chopped-up human remains. One evening when he was not meeting Maria, he could stand it no longer. He made a trunk call from his laboratory to Urrick's home in Edinburgh. At least it would be charged at the cheaper rates.

'I hope this isn't an inconvenient time to telephone?'

'No, no, I've just finished my tea.'

Tea? Rumbelow reflected that the Scots did not dine, like civilized people. 'I've been reading about the Gretna Green case, naturally.'

'We're having some fun up here, Rumbelow, I don't mind telling you.' Urrick seemed to twinkle even over the telephone.

'I hope the newspapers are exaggerating your difficulties, like they exaggerate everything?'

'It's a tricky business, to be sure.'

'I wondered if I might offer my help?'

There was silence. 'Help?'

'You might care to draw on my experience of the Perryman murder?'

'That's very good of you, Rumbelow, very good of you indeed. But it won't be necessary.'

'I could catch the Flying Scotsman tomorrow morning, if you wish.'

'No, no, it won't be necessary. Not necessary at all. I am doing all that is possible up here, absolutely all that a man could do. And we're making progress. We're certainly making progress. We shall get there in the end. I was reminded of the line by Robbie Burns—'

'Three minutes,' cut in the operator. Rumbelow hung up the telephone.

If it hadn't rung again almost immediately, Rumbelow might have saved himself getting into deeper trouble. It was the reporter who had first telephoned with the news of the body's recovery.

'Any comments yet, Doctor?'

'Yes, I have a comment. Do you realize this case illustrates one of the most peculiar quirks in the administration of British justice? If that train had stopped just a mile up the line, Scotland Yard would have been in charge of the investigations and I myself would now be examining the body. The fact that the trunk was discovered a few hundred yards north of the Scottish border means all the forensic work's in the hands of Dr Urrick of Edinburgh.'

The reporter was interested. 'Dr Urrick, who was against you in the Vickery case?'

'Yes. And I don't need emphasize which of us came out best.'

'Oh, you trounced him, I remember. So you think you'd do a better job on this case, do you, Doctor?'

'Of course I would. Urrick's making a terrible hash of it. He doesn't seem to know if it's one body or an entire family. Today he announced there were two heads, yesterday there were three. He can't decide whether they were cut up by a surgeon or a slaughterman. He doesn't even say how long they've been dead. How he expects the police to identify them, I've no idea. He's a rotten pathologist, and that's all there is to it. They haven't a chance of catching the murderer.'

'Perhaps he sent the trunk to Scotland deliberately, Doctor? To get out of your clutches.'

'That's a flattering suggestion. But anyone who thought as intelligently as that would never commit a murder in the first place.'

Rumbelow did not usually read that popular newspaper. But the next day he idly looked into the morning-room before his club breakfast to see the result of his conversation. He picked it from the paper-rack in horror. Across the front page in heavy type was the headline, DOCTORS ROW OVER TRUNK TORSOS. He agitatedly read below. The reporter had clearly telephoned Urrick at once. It had all been turned into a laughable and undignified squabble between the pair of them, over who should get his hands on the remains. It made Rumbelow look ludicrous. It made Urrick look silly, too, but that was no consolation. He brought himself to open the paper and saw the political cartoon, Hitler and Mussolini with long aprons and scalpels, squabbling over a sheeted corpse marked AFRICAN COLONIES. Rumbelow stuck it back in the slot savagely. He had no doubt someone would draw his attention to it again as soon as he set foot in Blackfriars.

It was worse than that. The notion of two pathologists wrangling over a chopped-up body seemed to tickle popular fancy hugely. *Punch* next week had something to say in Chari-vari. A facetious fourth leader in *The Times* almost had Rumbe-low making a bigger fool of himself by writing to the editor.

173

Late one night he sat with a few men in the club waiting for the news on the wireless, when a variety performer broke into a comic song about it. Rumbelow rose and left, his face stony. He noticed the others laughing outrageously. It was a regrettable failing of the British public to take serious matters frivolously, he told himself bitterly.

25

'I SAY, this is rich,' said Bantrell one morning about the middle of July. 'Look what one of my students presented me with.'

He handed Sir George Smallpenny a sheet of cartridge-paper. By luck, he found himself alone in the committee-room in the right company. Cramphorn was reading *The Times*. Sir George stood as usual with his heels on the fender before the empty grate.

'I thought you might be amused, George.'

It was a crayoned drawing showing a corpse on the post-mortem table, an open book propped against its feet. Reading it were Rumbelow and a girl, his arm round her. Underneath was written in large letters, DR RUMBELOW IS INFECTED WITH THE DEADLY BOOKWORM (ANKYLOSTOMA OSGOODII).

'It's rather well done,' observed Sir George. 'The fellow's quite an artist.'

'He's the firm's humorist. You always get one of them.'

'The corpse is extremely realistic. Rather more than Rumbelow. But it *is* somewhat libellous, don't you think?'

'Not at all. Unless you go on the dictum, "the greater the truth the greater the libel".'

Sir George looked startled. 'Not Rumbelow, surely?' He glanced again at the cartoon. 'Who's the lady?'

'Miss Osgood. She works in the library.'

'Oh, yes! I recognize her now. It really is a good resemblance. That young man might have quite a future, illustrating ana-tomical textbooks, or drawing Mickey Mouse cartoons, or some-thing.'

Bantrell thrust the drawing towards Cramphorn, who studied it for some seconds, grunted, and went on with his newspaper.

'But surely you knew he'd been carrying on with this girl?' Bantrell asked Sir George.

'I certainly did not. It surprises me. Indeed, it frightens me. We shall have pigs flying at any moment.'

'I heard about it weeks ago, from one of the students. It's all round the medical school.'

'Well, she's very pretty. Perhaps we ought to congratulate him?'

Bantrell began to despair of piercing this air of good-humoured tolerance. 'It's hardly the thing for a consultant, is it?'

'But, surely, Ian, you don't take students' gossip seriously? We'd be all struck off and in jail long ago if anyone did.'

'I'm *sure* there's something in this. The boys are pretty shrewd, you know. They're always about the hospital with time on their hands, far better placed to notice such things than we are.'

'But if Rumbelow's up to any tricks – which I really can't believe for one moment – it's his wife's job to put him back on the straight and narrow, not ours.'

'She's left him. Didn't you know? Some time ago now.'

'Really? Well, I suppose that's not an uncommon misfortune these days. If misfortune it is.'

'It's obvious she only did it because he's playing around with this girl.'

'I hardly knew her. Rumbelow never seemed to produce her in public. Perhaps he thought exposing her to the temptations of the world might involve him in more expense.'

'I don't know what you feel, George. But personally I think it's wrong on any count – completely wrong – for a Blackfriars' consultant to entangle himself with a working girl.'

'My dear Ian, aren't you being terribly old-fashioned? In this day and age social barriers are crashing down everywhere. I've a number of highly respectable friends with sons marrying girls who've never even been presented.'

'You don't believe the story, do you?' Bantrell asked bluntly.

'Frankly, I don't. Not with Rumbelow. He may have many faults, but he's as strait-laced as Queen Victoria.'

'What about you, Crampers? Do you think it's true?'

'No. I can't see any lass in her right mind taking up with Rumbelow. He's a typical pathologist – a fellow who sits all day on a stool examining other people's.'

Bantrell decided to illustrate another facet of his subject. 'We may not be perfectly sure he's making a fool of himself over a girl. But he was certainly a prize ass over that Gretna Green affair.'

'Oh, there's no love lost between Rumbelow and Urrick,' said Sir George.

'Like a couple of actresses, if you ask me.' Cramphorn looked over his half-moons. 'Get hysterics when the deadly rival lands the juicy part.'

'I think Urrick's a perfectly sound pathologist,' Bantrell said. 'He never gets a fair crack of the whip against someone so obstinate and plausible as Rumbelow.'

Sir George demurred. 'That's not the opinion of the general public.'

'I have the deepest suspicion of the opinion of the general public on anything, from household remedies to household names.'

'Well, perhaps the episode did Rumbelow some good.'

'It didn't do the hospital any good.'

'You're always on about that, Ian. But I doubt if the world at large connects him with Blackfriars. Or has even heard of us at all. The public doesn't *want* to hear of hospitals. They're only places where people do unpleasant things to you, and you have to go to die.'

'Be that as it may. But I'm growing a little tired of the amount of leg-pulling I have to stand from others inside the profession.'

'Aren't you being a little over-sensitive about Rumbelow?'

It was a mild rebuke, but Bantrell was discomfited to find the complaint recoil on him. He switched his line of attack. 'Crampers is right. He's a quite desperately jealous man. He did nothing to help Quinley towards that reader's job.'

'Quinley would never have got it.'

'That's beside the point. Rumbelow was outraged because Quinley dared to question his opinion about something in a p.m. The fact that Quinley was right makes it even worse.'

'Oh, come! You can't say Rumbelow's actually jealous of his own registrar. That simply doesn't make sense.'

'I think he's capable of being jealous of his own students.' Sir George was tiring of the conversation, and started to leave the room. 'And of course he's a snob,' Bantrell added, determined to make his final point.

Cramphorn folded his newspaper and rose. 'Snobbery? In this country, you're always liable to find that in anyone, even bishops. Like the pox.'

Bantrell was left alone, exasperated and disappointed. It seemed impossible to rouse a healthy feeling of hostility in the hospital. Another idea struck him. He went down the corridor and tapped on the door of Rumbelow's laboratory. There was no reply. He had intended confronting Rumbelow with the drawing, but instead propped it on the workbench. He walked away rubbing his hands and grinning. 'One must be allowed occasional indulgence in *schadenfreude*,' he told himself.

Rumbelow was in Norman Carlow's court, and appeared at Blackfriars about an hour later. He gave the picture one glance, tore it to shreds and threw it in the wastepaper basket. It was a terrible blow. The life which in his mind was separate and secret stood unexpectedly in the broad daylight of normal existence. This must be how a criminal feels, he thought distractedly, when he's confronted by the police. Or was it simply a typical student joke, a shot in the dark, because Maria did so much for him in the library? He panicked at a vision of the drawing in the hospital magazine, whose pages had seen worse lampoons of the staff. He started to pace the little room, asking himself who was behind it. Quinley, perhaps? But it was something you couldn't tax a man with. He took off his overcoat, sat on the high stool and wondered what to do. He decided he must not on any account approach the library. But after trying to work for half an hour he abruptly got up, went outside and crossed the small courtyard.

178

There was no sign of her. He opened a bound volume of the *British Medical Journal*, looking slyly round, wondering where she had got to. After a few minutes he shut the book impatiently, went to the librarian's cubicle, and tapped on the closed window through which he was supposed to dispense bibliographical information.

'Does Miss Osgood happen to be about?'

'Miss Osgood, sir?' The old man never seemed to have heard the name in his life. 'Oh, she's left.'

Rumbelow stared at him aghast. 'That's unexpected, isn't it?'

The librarian looked uneasy. Though Rumbelow had seen him almost every week since entering Blackfriars years ago as a student, it struck him they had exchanged hardly a dozen words before. 'I had to ask her to leave.'

'Why should you do that?'

The librarian fixed him with a hooded, bleary eye. Suddenly Rumbelow was a little scared of him. 'Her work was unsatisfactory, sir.'

'That's ridiculous. It always seemed perfectly satisfactory to me.'

The old man replied with a mutter. '*I* thought her unsatisfactory.'

'I suppose you know your own staff best,' Rumbelow told him shortly.

'She couldn't keep her mind on her work.' The librarian hesitated. 'It's not easy for me, sir, if I have to keep discipline among the students, when others take liberties . . .'

Rumbelow turned and strode from the building. He sat in his laboratory with a feeling of appalling disgrace. The librarian had noticed them. The students had noticed them. It would be all round his colleagues, all round London, that he was mixed up with a working girl – even one who should by rights have been at university, he thought in a faint attempt at consolation. He must never see her again. Never. He had been incredibly foolish. He had anyway no exact idea where she lived, and her parents would hardly rise to the telephone-book. Though of course she might pester him – that was very likely now she had a grievance to air. She might return to the hospital, make a nuisance of herself. He wished he could have vanished on a holiday, but that was impossible. He had too much work, he always had too much work. He blamed her for enticing him, quite mischievously in view of their different social standings. He blamed Norman Carlow for encouraging him to take her to the races. He blamed his wife for leaving him at a loose end. As usual, he blamed everyone but himself.

26

REX *v* ELGIN OPENED at the Old Bailey on Wednesday, July the twenty-second.

The courtroom was the one which served Vickery and a good many others as an anteroom to the condemned cell. Peter Ivors led for the Crown. Dr Elgin had entrusted his defence to a K.C. named Brabner, a short square-faced Welshman with grey hair flowing in the style of Lloyd George, on whom he was reputed to model his oratory. On the bench sat the vinegary-voiced Mr Justice Easterbrook, who was as well known to the public as Rumbelow himself. The Press described him with unimaginative repetition as 'waspish', and with his sharp-chinned face, spiky eyebrows and puny body there was certainly some suggestion of a wasp about him.

Elgin himself was among the most elegant characters ever to be paraded in the glass-screened dock. Tall, handsome, in his sixties, with brilliantined white hair, superbly tailored, he sat with his hands folded in his lap, perfectly relaxed, his large dark eyes expressing faintly amused disbelief he could possibly be involved in such sordid proceedings at all. The public gallery was crowded with women in fashionable hats, causing Rumbelow to reflect that a woman's devotion to her gynae-cologist was indeed a bond of poetic intensity. He wondered idly how many of them had sought Elgin's attentions, when suffering unlooked-for complications of Ascot week and the like.

The case made a welcome diversion for Rumbelow. For a week, he had hardly dared to show himself in the hospital outside his laboratory. To his relief, Maria had neither appeared nor even telephoned. No-one had mentioned the student's drawing – he preferred to imagine through ignorance rather than tact – though he fancied Bantrell had given some odd looks. Quinley plainly knew nothing of the episode whatever. He was beginning to hope that it would all die down, that he would remember Maria simply as some pretty girl who helped him in the library, and whom he had condescendingly taken to the races as a treat. When Norman Carlow asked after her Rumbelow tried to impress the coroner he barely remembered the girl's name, with no success whatever.

Elgin faced two charges. The first was manslaughter of Julia Mary Kendall, the twenty-one-year-old girl whose body Rumbelow had examined. On the second, of performing an illegal operation on her, Ivors intended to offer no evidence. A verdict of guilty on the other already exposed the prisoner to imprisonment for life. Rumbelow himself had suggested a charge of murder, pointing out this was possible for death after an abortion under the Offences Against the Person Act, 1861. But this struck Ivors as too much of a good thing, and likely to scare the jury away from a conviction at all.

Rumbelow already felt gratified by something which had *not* happened. It was his first appearance in an important trial since the Vickery case, and Brabner had made no application for his exclusion from the court. Of course, there was no reason why the Welshman should have taken Sir Arthur Young-husband's tactics. It might even have been foolish, trying a move which had already failed before a more easygoing judge. But Rumbelow had come into court with a nagging worry. That it was unfounded, he simply accepted as a further vindication of himself.

'The evidence I shall put before you concerns only the last fortnight of Miss Julia Kendall's life,' began Peter Ivors, with his usual air of an ordinary man thrust unexpectedly into complicated and important affairs and doing his best to explain things as simply as possible. 'Though it is necessary for me to go a little further back to make the actions of her final days, and of her final hours – those will assume great importance in this case – more readily understandable to you.'

He looked towards the two women jurors, sitting together in

garden-party hats. 'You are going to hear of most unpleasant things. Of abortion – the taking of life from a human being yet unborn, indeed yet hardly formed, but still the taking of life. Of those parts of a woman's body we do not customarily mention in public, or across the barrier of the sexes. Of unmarried sexual relationships, which these days may hardly shock you, but may somewhat disgust you. Yet I must warn you now, as my duty, that in reaching your verdict you must not be influenced in the slightest by your feelings towards such things. Nor towards the prisoner, or any party in the case, but solely on facts proved to you beyond all reasonable doubt. This is not a court of morals.'

How unfailingly counsel say that, Rumbelow meditated, when they want to rouse the moral indignation of the jury on their behalf.

'Miss Kendall was what is known as a "bachelor girl". She worked in a flower shop in the West End of London, and shared a flat in the area of Earl's Court with a Miss Fuller, a secretary. She was an attractive girl, with the normal number of masculine admirers. But only one concerns this court, a Mr Edward Taylor, who hails from Cape Town in the Union of South Africa.

'Mr Taylor is a young man of substance, who made the acquaintance of Miss Kendall quite simply by walking into her flower shop. He invited her to various entertainments in London, and affection sprang up between the pair of them. We know that early this year intercourse occurred. That is not denied by Mr Taylor. And we know that some three or four weeks later Miss Kendall suspected she was pregnant. She confided her anxieties to Miss Fuller, then she confronted Mr Taylor with the situation. He responded that her condition was not his fault, that some other man must be responsible. This may strike you, members of the jury, as somewhat on the harsh side.

'Mr Taylor said it was merely a ruse on her part, to trap him into an immediate marriage. He claimed it was one used on him before in various parts of the world. This was a great shock to Miss Kendall. She was a young woman in love. As we shall hear from Miss Fuller, she looked on marriage to Mr Taylor as a serious possibility. Even he admits they discussed the prospect, if only in a distant way. Well, members of the jury, you may feel that marriage is not a topic which can be debated between two young persons at all distantly. She appealed to him for help. He gave her some money, a hundred pounds. Perhaps that was the instinctive gesture of a man wanting to get rid of her, and brought up to believe that anything could be achieved by the dissipation of banknotes. To a very tragic extent in the present case, achieved it was.'

Ivors paused for the judge's writing to catch him up. 'We do not know how Miss Kendall obtained the name of the prisoner. Mr Taylor says he had never heard of Dr Elgin in his life. Miss Kendall did not mention to anyone her intention of obtaining an abortion. She was perhaps deeply ashamed and frightened of what she was about to do. Miss Fuller will tell you that one day she returned from her employment to find her flat-mate in bed, looking unwell. Miss Kendall did not confess that she had been that day to Dr Elgin's consulting-room, where he had passed an instrument into her. Miss Fuller assumed the disability was the effect of her pregnancy, and the nervous strain of her treatment by Mr Taylor. For the next few days Miss Kendall stayed in the flat, most of the time alone. During this period, as you will hear from a medical expert, the abortion would have been proceeding.'

'Was she attended during that time by another medical man?' asked the judge.

'No, my Lord. In fact, she dissuaded Miss Fuller from calling one. Then she announced she felt better, and returned to work in the flower shop. But after the Easter week-end she suddenly decided to return to her parents' home.

'Miss Kendall's parents lived in Wimbledon. She appeared on the doorstep with the announcement that she was ill – very ill, those were her exact words. To her mother's inquiries about the exact nature of her illness she gave evasive replies. Her mother being naturally alarmed at this unexpected return put her daughter to bed and sent for their local practitioner, a Dr Carus.

'All this happened on the morning of April the fourteenth last. Unfortunately, there was some delay before Dr Carus appeared, and about eleven o'clock Miss Kendall announced that she must see Mr Taylor, giving her mother the telephone number of his flat in Mayfair. This was the first her mother had heard of the gentleman. He came to Wimbledon straight away in his motor-car, perhaps a commendable change in his attitude towards the unfortunate girl. Meanwhile, Miss Kendall's condition was causing her mother increasing concern.

'About three in the afternoon, she suddenly deteriorated. She suffered a profuse haemorrhage from the region of the womb – a haemorrhage which you will hear from medical experts had already been proceeding internally. It was the direct result of a secondary infection, itself occasioned by the surgical interference of Dr Elgin. The mother telephoned a second time for Dr Carus, who now realizing the extreme gravity of the case arrived within a few minutes. By then Miss Kendall was *in extremis*. And so we come to that part of the sad day's events on which the case against the prisoner stands.'

Peter Ivors picked up another sheaf of papers. Rumbelow was interested how he would illuminate for the jury the remote points of law now rising before them. 'Miss Kendall, in the presence of both Dr Carus and her mother, asked if she were going to die. Dr Carus at first made a soothing reply, but Miss Kendall, who despite her desperate state remained perfectly lucid, insisted she know the truth. Then she stated she had something to say concerning her plight. And Dr Carus realized that he was about to hear a dying declaration. I should explain that a "dying declaration" is to some extent a technical term of the law. It is a statement hedged by certain strict, well-defined conditions, which I have no doubt his Lordship will at the proper time make clear to you.'

'Do not let that inhibit your own explanations, Mr Ivors.'

'I am obliged to your Lordship for the encouragement,' said Ivors equally dryly. 'The statement itself, which will be read to you in due course, is only hearsay evidence – that is, evidence of what another person has said, not ordinarily accepted by a court. But the law admits such a declaration, subject to five conditions.

'The first is that the person must in fact die. If she recovers, the declaration is invalidated. Secondly, she must know she is dying, lost beyond hope of recovery. And she must be *compos mentis*, fully understanding what she is saying. On those two points Dr Carus was entirely satisfied. As a fourth condition, the statement must concern those circumstances causing the patient's death, and the trial must be for the infliction of that death – for murder or, as in this case, for manslaughter. Lastly, the declaration must be voluntary and unprompted. All these conditions, I submit, you will find completely fulfilled.

'Miss Kendall's declaration was taken down by Dr Carus in the presence of her mother, and her father who had been summoned from his office in the City. Mr Taylor remained outside the room. That all happened before four o'clock in the afternoon. Miss Kendall died just before eight that same evening.

'In her statement, Miss Kendall named Dr Elgin as the man who had performed her abortion, giving certain details of the event. When the next morning Dr Elgin was interviewed by a detective-inspector of the Metropolitan Police, he denied any knowledge of Miss Kendall. He denied he was in any way connected with the practice of abortion. But that is not a defence, members of the jury. A dying declaration, that solemn document, perhaps the most solemn ever to be admitted to a court of law, cannot be contradicted. The law assumes as a fact that a dying person tells the truth. You may perhaps have thought now and then that the law and commonsense sometimes part company. But how would you feel were you to know – to be fully assured – that you were about to meet your Maker? Would you not tell the truth? At such an awe-inspiring moment, would there be any room in your mind for duplicity? For animus, for wanting to get your own back? Or to damage someone you did not even know, except through ill-repute? Honestly, members of the jury! We have only to imagine ourselves in such terrible circumstances to realize that the petty animosities of the world would mean nothing to us, absolutely nothing at all.'

After this unusually florid peroration Peter Ivors announced he would call his first witness, but the judge looked at the clock and said they would have lunch instead.

27

THAT AFTERNOON, DURING cross-examination of the dead
girl's mother, Rumbelow was puzzled to notice Peter Ivors'
shoulders twitching. The case seemed cast-iron. The only
defence witness was Elgin himself, who would do nothing
except stand in the box and deny the charges as plausibly as he
could. Miss Kendall's dying declaration was an enormously
powerful document in the hands of the Crown, the rest of the
evidence simply painting the picture of her last days and hours
in which to fit it. But if Ivors was worried, so was Rumbelow.
He knew the barrister had a sixth sense for the way things were
going in a courtroom.

They had already heard from Miss Fuller, a young lady
whom Rumbelow marked in his mind as a 'dizzy blonde'. She
was certain her flat-mate had never once mentioned the name
of Dr Elgin. The mother was a forthright woman dressed
unrelievedly in black, the sort Rumbelow occasionally encountered on committees concerned with prostitution, drunkenness,
hooliganism and similar human frailties. When Ivors had
finished the examination-in-chief, Brabner started by asking,
'Mrs Kendall, before your daughter arrived on your doorstep
that ill-fated morning last April, when had you last set eyes on
her?'

'Several months before. She wanted to lead an independent
life. So many girls do these days.'

'She led her independent life remarkably close at hand, did
she not? To see her parents was barely a five miles' journey
across London?' There was no reply. 'Were you not concerned

at the moral implications of a young woman setting up in her own flat, albeit with a young female companion?'

'I knew I could trust my daughter.'

'Mrs Kendall, do you know a Mr Thomas Hunter?'

There was another pause. 'Yes. He was a friend of my daughter's.'

'Was he the cause of her leaving your home?'

'You are not being very kind to my daughter's memory, dragging all this up.'

'I agree that I am not, but dragged up it must be. Did the relationship of your daughter to Mr Hunter result in her invoking the services of an abortionist?'

'No. That isn't right.'

'But did it result in an abortion?'

'Well . . . she took some drugs. Something a friend gave her.'

'Very well. When did you first meet the South African gentleman, Mr Taylor?'

'The day my daughter died.'

'Did you not suggest to him that he marry your daughter, were she to survive?'

'That would have been the right and proper thing for him to do.'

'Do you not think she bestowed her favours on him simply in return for the entertainment and the presents he bestowed upon her?'

'I certainly do not. She was in love with him.'

'As she was in love with Mr Hunter previously?'

'Girls fall in love many times.'

'Did you like Mr Taylor?'

'How can I say? I hardly knew him.'

'Your daughter was in something of the habit of procuring herself abortions?'

'Mr Brabner, will you kindly frame your questions in less extravagant language,' said the judge.

'I apologize to your Lordship. I shall in fact withdraw the question. Thank you, Mrs Kendall.'

Rumbelow was next. He felt satisfaction at being able to advance the case with evidence more solid than of vagaries of the female heart. He replied to Peter Ivors that he had examined the body of Julia Kendall in the Central Mortuary. That he found the cause of death to be shock associated with haemorrhage, which was both internal and external. That the haemorrhage followed secondary infection of the uterus, Fallopian tubes, and related anatomical structures. And that the infection itself resulted from surgical interference to procure an abortion.

'How long before death, in your opinion, would the illegal operation have been performed?'

'About ten days.'

'And at that time, at what stage of pregnancy would Miss Kendall have been?'

'Not more than two months.'

'Will you tell the court, Dr Rumbelow, exactly how the operation would have been performed?'

He explained how a sharp instrument had passed through the girl's vagina and then the neck of her womb to damage and kill the embryo. And how the dead embryo with its nutritive attachments would be partly expelled by contractions of the womb muscles over the next few days, like the foreign body it had become.

'Did you in this case confirm your findings with examination of the relevant tissues under the microscope?'

'I do so in every case.'

Brabner rose to cross-examine. 'Dr Rumbelow, do you hold strong views on abortions and those who perform them?'

Rumbelow had expected something like this. The evidence of his post-mortem findings was unshakable, and defending counsel had to ask something to justify himself. 'I hold the views of every other citizen who respects the law.'

'Did you on Thursday, September the twenty-sixth, 1935, give an interview to several newspapers – I have a cutting from one here – in which you said, "The vile practice of abortion is performed not only by ignorant women using knitting-needles. I am ashamed that it is also done by members of my profession. This should be stamped out. Were I not so busy, I should be happy to hound these gentlemen down."'

'That is the gist of what I said.'

189

'Have you mentioned to your colleagues the name of Dr Elgin as one of the gentlemen to be hounded?'

'It was perfectly proper for me to do so among other medical men.'

'Have you any personal animosity towards Dr Elgin?'

'No more than to any doctor suspected of procuring abortions.'

'You would not be distressed at the prospect of his going to prison for a very long time?'

'Not if he were an abortionist.'

'Thank you, Dr Rumbelow.'

The court adjourned for the day. 'Brabner was on pretty thin ground with me, wasn't he?' Rumbelow said to Peter Ivors.

But the barrister had his mind elsewhere. 'So our snow-white chick had a few black feathers. It's disturbing. I wish the mother had been as frank when she first spoke to the police.'

'The colour of the girl's morals can't make any difference.'

'No, but you wonder what else the mother's kept locked in that ample bosom.'

'You and I together haven't lost a major case yet,' Rumbelow reminded him cheerfully.

'Possibly. But even Don Bradman will get bowled for a duck one day.'

The next morning was to start with the evidence of Taylor himself. But he was not to be found. The usher dispatched officially to proclaim his name three times in the corridors might have been calling to the wind. Peter Ivors looked angry. There were feverish conversations in whispers. Finally he apologized to the judge, 'I can only suggest my witness has been unexpectedly taken ill, your Lordship, or met with some mishap.'

'Or returned to South Africa?'

'I am reliably informed he is still in London.'

'Then you had better find him, hadn't you? If he does not appear by midday, I shall have him brought here.'

Dr Carus went into the box instead. He was short, bald, with large horn-rimmed glasses, agitated at finding himself in such painful surroundings. For over an hour Ivors questioned him about the desperate afternoon in Wimbledon. Then the essential document, the dying declaration, was officially produced for the doctor to read out. It was on sheets of thick, pinkish writing paper, as might bear the correspondence of any middle-class suburban home, in Dr Carus' barely legible handwriting. The dying girl had managed to sign at the bottom. Underneath was his own signature, and those of the mother and father as witnesses.

Brabner began his cross-examination by asking, 'Dr Carus, what were your feelings that afternoon, when you realized you would have to write down a dying declaration?'

'I saw it as my duty.'

'You knew it would be a statement of solemn importance?'

'Of course I did.'

'Did you know that a magistrate should have been called? To undertake both the task of recording it, and the responsibility for seeing the strict conditions – already fully enumerated by my learned friend – were each and every one of them complied with?'

'I know as much now. I admit I didn't then. I believe I was perfectly competent to take such a statement, none the less.'

'Was there time to fetch a magistrate?' the judge interrupted. 'We know Miss Kendall had only another four hours to live. You may have thought, Dr Carus, she was likely to die even sooner?'

'That was the case.' Dr Carus looked grateful.

'Though you may be perfectly competent in law to take a dying declaration,' Brabner continued, 'how much experience had you of so doing in your entire professional career?'

'This is the only one.'

'How did you come to learn of the procedure?'

'I learnt in medical school. All students have instruction in forensic medicine.'

'When did you leave medical school, Doctor?'

'I qualified in 1899.'

'Thank you.'

Dr Carus was released. By then, Edward Taylor had appeared. He was thin, ferret-faced, fair-haired, in his mid-twenties, stylishly dressed with a double-breasted waistcoat and a monocle. Rumbelow immediately put him down as 'a cad' or even 'a rotter'. He stood in the witness-box looking as if he expected to to be dispatched forthwith to the gallows.

'Why were you not in court earlier?' the judge asked bleakly.

'Afraid my car broke down.'

'Have you not heard of a taxi? Or an omnibus?'

If he had, he was too frightened to say so. Rumbelow despised him more than ever. Peter Ivors' first questions were almost irrelevant, giving the young man a chance to collect himself. There was anyway not much he cared to ask. Taylor admitted giving the dead girl money. He denied having heard of Dr Elgin.

Again it was Brabner's turn.

'Mr Taylor, you are the only son of a family enjoying considerable social standing in the city of Cape Town, in the Union of South Africa, are you not?'

'I'd say that was right.'

'As this case has already received prominence in the Cape Town newspapers, you may think your position at this moment in the eyes of your family and friends somewhat unenviable?'

'I am not too happy about it, certainly.'

'You may also think the unfavourable way in which you have been presented not entirely fair?'

'No, I don't think it's fair at all.'

'You had real affection for Miss Kendall?'

'Yes.'

'But when she came and declared you were the father of her unborn child, you not only rebuffed her but added a grave insult?'

'I panicked. That's all it was. It was a situation I'd never been caught in before.'

'But when you went to her home in Wimbledon, when she was critically ill, you told her mother that you would marry Miss Kendall?'

'Yes. I meant it.'

'Your state of mind had changed?'

'Everything had changed.'

The man's trying to whitewash himself, thought Rumbelow.

He can say what he likes, now there's no danger whatever of being obliged to keep his word.

'When did you last see Julia Kendall alive?'

'I was with her when she died.'

'That was after she had made the declaration to Dr Carus? Some four hours afterwards?'

'That's right. She seemed to rally.'

'During that late afternoon, in the period between her making the dying declaration and death itself, did you make a telephone call from the house in Wimbledon?'

'I may have done. I can't say.'

'About five o'clock did you telephone the passenger office of the Union Castle Steamship Company?'

'Yes. I remember now. I did. About a passage home to South Africa.'

'Two passages to South Africa?'

'That's right. I'd told Julie I wanted to marry her, that we'd go to South Africa as soon as she was better.'

Rumbelow noticed Peter Ivors tear a piece of paper with an angry gesture.

'She agreed to this course?' Brabner continued.

'Yes.'

'So you booked the passages there and then?'

'To cheer her up, mostly.'

'Doubtless it did. But the fact that Julia Kendall agreed to marry you, and to go to South Africa with you, plainly indicates that she really believed she was going to recover?'

The young man looked nonplussed. 'I suppose it does. I hadn't thought of that.'

Brabner turned towards the judge. 'With respect, my Lord, I submit that my client has no case to answer.'

'Well, Mr Ivors? What have you to say to this development?'

Peter Ivors was already on his feet.

'I do not accept, my Lord, that a subterfuge with the sole object of making the girl's dying moments more tolerable has any bearing whatever on the case.'

'But it may not have been a subterfuge, Mr Ivors. Mr Taylor might well have been perfectly sincere. The fact is,

Miss Kendall did not believe that she was going to die. She had not resigned herself to enjoying no hope whatever of recovery. That must have been her state of mind when she made her declaration to Dr Carus. Even were it not – we heard from Mr Taylor she rallied before death overtook her – that would be immaterial. The belief of imminent dissolution is the foundation of a dying declaration, and the dying declaration was the foundation of your case. It need not have been, but it was, so there you are. If the first foundation is undermined the whole edifice collapses. You cannot make a valid declaration believing yourself to be dying one minute and not the next.' The judge squared up some papers before him. 'In short, Mr Ivors, if you really believe yourself to be on your deathbed, you do not make preparations to go on your honeymoon. The court rules the declaration inadmissible. There is plainly no case for the prisoner to answer.'

A few minutes later Elgin was free.

Rumbelow strode from the court without even glancing at Peter Ivors. He had been made to look a fool – and so soon after that ridiculous business of Gretna Green. He had been tricked, he thought angrily, out-smarted on a trifling point of law. He blamed Ivors for letting him down. It was intolerable, particularly after the difficulty in bringing Elgin to book. The barrister should have been more on his toes. The judge had said so, almost in as many words. As he strode across the hall of the Old Bailey to the main entrance, he suddenly found himself face-to-face with Elgin. The man who a few minutes before had stood in the dock greeted him with a pleasant smile.

'Well, Rumbelow, your little vendetta got nowhere.'

'I don't know what you're talking about.'

'You can't pull the wool over *my* eyes, you know, however skilfully you can festoon those of a British jury. I'm perfectly aware you've got your knife into me. Perhaps now you've been shown up in public as a self-righteous ass, you'll leave me in peace.'

'You've no right speaking to me like this.'

'I've a perfect right. I'm a free man, like yourself. Acquitted by a British court.'

'By a stroke of extreme good fortune.'

'That's a little carping of you, isn't it? Well, perhaps we were a trifle lucky. We only looked into those steamship bookings at the last moment, in case Mr Taylor had ideas of skipping the country. Listen, Rumbelow —' Elgin's manner changed. 'I have been acquitted, and so I can never again be charged with that dreadful business. I will tell you – and you alone – that I did perform an abortion on that girl. I suffer no qualms about it. I'm a realist, not a hypocrite like you. When she came to me in trouble, I saw it as my duty to help her.'

'Your duty as a doctor, I suppose?'

'I am far too humane to abide by our bigoted professional ethics.' Rumbelow tried to escape, but Elgin held his sleeve with a well-manicured hand. 'Where do you suppose such girls would go otherwise? To Sarah Gamp. You know how dangerous that is. Or they start messing about with themselves, which is often worse. You don't give me credit for the social service I perform, do you, Rumbelow?'

'You caused that girl's death. I'm sorry it doesn't trouble your conscience.'

'Some patients die. It's an inescapable fact of medicine.'

'Will you let me go at once?' Elgin released his hand. 'I don't wish to speak another word to you in my life.'

'And I hope that you will have no occasion to.'

Rumbelow strode from the court building. He walked halfway to Blackfriars Hospital, then changed his mind. He couldn't face any of his colleagues. He turned towards the Embankment and spent the next two or three hours walking aimlessly up and down, staring at the oily waters of the Thames, dreading the moment when the evening papers would start to appear on the streets.

28

AUGUST WAS THE month when London, the flywheel of the
Empire, dropped to idling speed. Rumbelow became miserable.
The weather stayed bad – the July had been one of the wettest
ever recorded. Norman Carlow and Peter Ivors were away, and
he had no other friends in London. Most consultants at Blackfriars
had chosen to holiday at the same time as their paying patients,
often in the same places, but idleness did not appeal to him.
He was in fact more heavily worked than usual, with so many
other London pathologists away. People still met sudden death,
holiday season or not, and he knew well enough the suicide rate
always showed an August peak in its regular fall from May to
November. He even had to give Quinley the post-mortem work
at Blackfriars, the young man seeming to have settled into a
taciturn respectfulness since the abandonment of his ambitions.
Rumbelow's only cheer was public reaction to the Elgin case.
He had expected another outburst from the Press, but there was
no criticism of him at all. The acquittal had come by means too
rarefied for the grasp of newspaper readers. Even at Blackfriars,
the doctors were inclined only to gloat over the lawyers having
made a hash of things. But the trial was undeniably another hit
on the dreadnought of his self-confidence. As for Elgin himself,
Rumbelow tried not to imagine his practice quadrupling over-
night through the publicity.

It was the month when Rumbelow became homeless. His
club in Pall Mall being shut annually, he took a room across
Hyde Park in Bayswater, at a small private hotel where everyone stopped eating to stare whenever he entered the dining-
room. He avoided his fellow-guests and became painfully

lonely. He began to think more often of Rosemary. He had received through the post – anonymously, which disturbed him – a cutting from a Yorkshire paper reporting that the wife of the famous Dr Rumbelow had taken a teaching post in a Harrogate school. Thankfully, the London gossip columns seemed to have overlooked this titbit. He had heard no more from her solicitors. She seemed in no hurry for a divorce. As a matter of conscience he sent her a cheque for five pounds every month, which she never acknowledged.

One evening towards the end of the month the manageress appeared at his table in the dining-room, a little agitated. 'There's a gentleman to see you, sir. A Major Standring.'

For once Rumbelow's memory let him down. 'I don't know a Standring. What's he want?'

'He said it's official, sir. And very important and secret. I showed him into the office.'

'Oh, very well.' Rumbelow got up, under his arm the illustrated society paper he had been reading over his meal. It contained a picture of Lady Accrington in a tweed costume standing with a gun amid a carpet of dead grouse. In the manageress's tiny office beside the front door he found the prison governor, sucking his teeth and looking as jumpy as ever.

'Ah! Doctor.' He shook hands. 'Forgive my coming unannounced. But it's best to be discreet, as I'll explain. You heard I'd changed my job?'

'No, I don't think I did.' So the fellow's nerve has completely given way over the executions, Rumbelow thought.

'It's not been announced officially yet. In fact, it may never be actually announced at all. Very hush-hush, you know. But it's much more congenial than my last appointment. And I believe more important.' He looked round, as though spies might be crouching behind the roll-top desk. 'I'm still with the Home Office. But they've transferred me from the Prison Service to a team working with the Royal Air Force. We're studying the effect of blast from bomb explosions on civilians.'

'I hope it will turn out to be an unnecessary study.'

'So do I, with all my heart. But things in Europe look a little disturbing, and we can't close our eyes to it.'

'Aren't the Germans becoming more civilized? The Olympics were a great success.'

'I hope you're right. With von Ribbentrop himself in London, there might well be some understanding in sight. We'll see, when Hitler makes his speech next month at Nuremburg. And now there's the war in Spain, which could lead to more trouble. The Government is prepared for the worst, you can take my word for it. The Air Raid Precautions Department intends to see there's a gas-proof room in every house in London.'

'Gas! A lot of London houses are incapable of keeping out the rain, let alone phosgene.'

'We must protect our civilians as best we can. Though I must say, some of the local councils are being very difficult about it, putting up the rates. We've innumerable plans – the London streets might well be in complete darkness, you know, there'd be so much less warning than in the last dust-up, barely ten minutes perhaps. It's for one of these schemes we need your assistance, Doctor.'

'This is hardly my line, you know.'

'Let me explain. The Home Office is very anxious to find exactly the sort of injuries inflicted on human beings of various ages by aerial bombs. We're to conduct an experiment at one of the R.A.F. target areas on the East Coast, and we'd greatly value your assistance in performing the post-mortems. Indeed you are the only man in the country we can turn to with real confidence.'

'That presupposes a supply of particularly patriotic volunteers, doesn't it? Or are you offering it as an alternative for condemned prisoners?'

'Oh, the persons will be already dead. That's no worry. There're always plenty of people dying with no relatives or friends, paupers and the like. They're consigned regularly to the anatomy departments of medical schools, as you know.'

'I see.' Rumbelow thought the idea fantastic. 'And the R.A.F. are going to drop bombs on corpses? That indicates great confidence in their marksmanship.'

'They won't actually drop the bombs from aeroplanes. They will be detonated on the ground, the subjects occupying various structures considered by the Home Office to afford protection.'

'Well, I'm always ready to help my countrymen.' The proposed excursion could in its way be amusing, he supposed, and would give him some fresh air. There would anyway be a fee, perhaps a substantial one. Though he would have preferred a different companion on a bombing range to the jumpy major. 'And I've reason enough to detest the Germans and all their works.'

'Then you accept? Splendid! It will be within the next week or two. Of course transport will be provided. Though I must ask you, Doctor, to keep it a close secret.'

'You should know by now, Major, you can trust me in that respect!'

The major fussed on his way. Rumbelow finished his dinner, put the conversation from his mind and sat over post-mortem reports up in his bedroom. He had the habit before going to bed of walking as far as Piccadilly, to look at the lights in the Circus and watch the passers-by. It did something to lessen his sense of isolation. That evening he stood on the corner of Regent Street gazing across the traffic at the statue of Eros and thinking unpleasantly of bombs raining down on the Empire's capital. It seemed unreal, quite impossible, for high explosives to blast the plate-glass windows, to make craters among such everyday objects as pillar-boxes and telephone kiosks, to turn the familiar solid buildings into rubble, to kill the Londoners strolling peaceably all round him. But he had the fatalistic feeling that wars must come to all nations as death came to all men. Then the corner of his eye caught a figure, instantly recognizable, hurrying towards the steps of the Underground. Hardly knowing what he did, he ran after her, seizing her by the arm. She turned round, looking alarmed, only after some moments her startled stare melting into an uncertain smile. They stood looking at each other in silence. 'Maria, my darling, how I've missed you,' said Rumbelow.

29

THERE IS A MOMENT as a man wakes when he is filled with nothing but a pleasant sense of self-awareness, of rediscovery after sleep. Then there came to Rumbelow, before memory flooded the empty caverns of his mind, a feeling that something was wrong, that something strange had happened to him. He opened his eyes, for a second wondering where he was. He had never slept in such a room in his life. It was an Elizabethan bedchamber, walls and sloping ceiling of white plasterwork and oak beams. It looked an even bigger fake in the daylight. The door had a latch instead of a handle, the window through a gap in the flowered curtains was of blue- and green-tinted lozenges, on the walls hung a framed Victorian sampler depicting the alphabet and a coloured print of a grossly overloaded stage-coach. Rumbelow turned his head. Maria was still asleep, her dark hair spread over the pillow, her full lips apart. He noticed for the first time how long her eyelashes were.

He got carefully from the four-poster. Their window looked over a garden containing some bedraggled late-summer roses and an asphalt forecourt with a dozen cars – mostly open sports models and one new-looking Rolls-Royce limousine. Beyond was the main road and the amiable green slopes of the Sussex Downs. It was a sunny morning, a Sunday, almost a fortnight later. The establishment was a roadhouse, brand-new and fashionable, a place he had never contemplated visiting before.

He dropped back the curtain. His eye caught her underwear, thrown on a high-backed rush-bottomed chair in the corner. A pair of beige lisle stockings and a worn-looking pink suspender-belt with its dangling shiny buckles. A brassière, also not particularly new. A mauve petticoat on which he noticed a pair of careful darns in white cotton. How different from the stylish, immaculate undergarments of Diana Flavell, he reflected. How much more homely. How much less frightening.

Maria sat up suddenly, fully awake instantly, like a child. 'What's the time?'

'Almost eight.'

'You've got your pyjamas on.'

Rumbelow looked a little abashed. 'I prefer not to sleep without them.'

'Funny. I don't even remember you having any.' She smiled, pushing back her hair, her full breasts with their salmon-pink nipples the size of five-shilling pieces exposed above the bed-clothes. He felt a return of the awkwardness which had afflicted him the night before.

'Wouldn't you like some breakfast, Maria? We can have it up here, if you want. Or we could go down to the dining-room.'

'I must look a mess. Do I?'

'No, of course you don't. You look lovely – so gay, so innocent.'

She gave a laugh. 'I've never been so happy. Honestly, John. Never in my life.'

'Last night – was it all right?'

'Why should you sound so worried?'

'It's such a paradoxical business. Receiving yet giving. Both of us, at the same time. I'd the feeling of taking more than I'd granted.'

'Don't be silly. Anyway, the giving is as nice as the having.'

'That's a womanly view.'

'Was *I* all right?'

'Oh yes.' He had no other words to express it.

She stretched, smiling and yawning together. 'Have you been to bed with lots of girls?'

'Not with any. Only my wife.'

'You fibber.'

'It's the truth. Quite honestly. I've had lady friends, of course I have. Before I was married, even afterwards. Even quite recently. I'd sometimes gone quite far, but never to the end. There's a whole world of difference between that and just kissing and cuddling, you know. It's the generative act. It has a purpose beyond itself, beyond the feelings, often beyond the intentions, of the couple concerned. People always seem to forget that.'

'But you were strictly brought up.'

'Well, I certainly didn't enjoy the bohemian existence the students have today. It wasn't so much my father being in the Church. He was extremely poor. And poverty forces a man to learn either self-control or the elements of crime.'

Another flowered curtain in the corner concealed the washbasin. Pulling it back, he started to unbutton the jacket of his brown-and-white striped flannel pyjamas. 'I'm not complaining. In many ways it's an advantage to be brought up with few possessions and few pleasures. It gives you a correct sense of values. And that's the only object of any education.' He turned on the tap and started brushing his teeth.

'Are your parents still alive, John?'

He shook his head. 'My mother died only last winter.'

'What a shame.'

'It meant very little to me. She was a peculiar woman. She never got over my brother being killed. He was an infantry subaltern, so he hadn't really much of a chance, I suppose. But she hated the Germans for it, even more than I do.' He flicked the drops from his tooth-brush. 'She was even stricter than my father, you know. She brought me up to believe that sex – what we've been doing, you and I – was something nasty, unclean, horrible. It must have had its effect on me. I think it even led me to choose my own wife. *She* was sexless. Completely sexless. She'd no taste for it, though to give her credit she tried for a while. I knew all that well enough before marriage, though afterwards I did my best to pretend that I hadn't.' He filled a tooth-glass with water and rinsed his mouth.

'But why did you marry her at all?'

'I can tell you exactly. She gave me a sense of security. I felt she wouldn't make any sexual demands on me. I felt . . . not frightened of it, but that it was something of an unpleasant necessity. Something I didn't want the responsibility of providing night after night.'

Maria seemed amused. 'I hope you don't still think so?'

'With you it's all so different.' He said this solemnly. 'But with my wife . . . oh, I tried to pretend after we married that I hadn't thought all this, either. I still try to pretend it.'

'You poor darling. You poor darling.'

It occurred to him that he had told the girl more about himself than any other person in the world. She had suddenly become in a way the most intimate of human beings to him – in a physical way, in a narrow mental way. Otherwise, they were almost strangers. And all divulged in the inappropriate surroundings of a roadhouse. He was amazed at himself.' What about your own parents, Maria?'

'They're not very interesting.'

'They'll find out about this, won't they?'

She laughed. 'Why should they? They think I'm staying with my friend at Brighton. I often do at week-ends, you know. When I get home, my mother will say how much healthier I look.'

He had laid his shaving things out neatly the night before on the glass shelf over the basin. He let the hot tap run and started to lather the brush. 'Were they upset at your losing the library job?'

'A little.'

'It was my fault.'

'Let's not talk about it.'

'But it makes me feel so guilty. That a girl of your intelligence, a girl who should be at university, is now reduced to serving in a department store.'

'Jobs are difficult to get. Everyone has to take what they can these days, don't they? Anyway, it's enormous fun sometimes, with all the peculiar old ladies we get as customers. I'd hate to grow up like that.'

Half his face soaped, he turned and looked at her. 'Please don't grow up, Maria. I love you as you are.'

She was now sitting up in the four-poster, smoothing the edge of the sheet across her thighs. 'Shall we see each other again?' she asked timidly.

'Why shouldn't we? As often as we care to? Listen, I had an idea – I'm rootless. I'm selling my house, and living in a club is awfully depressing, seeing the same old faces day after day. Why shouldn't I rent a small flat? They seem to be building them everywhere these days. Then you could come whenever you liked, with no one any the wiser.'

'Perhaps you'd like to marry me?' She saw him look flustered, and added with a laugh, 'It's leap year, John. At least I'm entitled to ask.'

'I'm still married.'

'You won't be for ever.'

'No, that's true.' Their future was so complex, so fruitful with delights yet so spiked with dangers, so unpredictable and even uncontrollable, he found it painful to think of.

'If I thought I'd never see you again, John darling, I'd be wretched. Utterly wretched. I know I should, don't I? It happened before.'

'But you never tried to see me after that business of the librarian.'

'I was frightened, I think, of what I'd done. Just by going out with you.'

'Yet then we were miles distant from each other, compared with now.'

'Did you always want to make love to me?'

'Yes, I did.' He turned on more hot water. 'Did you always want me to?'

'I was awfully disappointed I wasn't making a hit.'

She said this lightly, but he took the teasing seriously. 'I had to hold myself in. To exercise self-control. I always have to. So's to keep myself worthy of . . . that part of me the public knows.'

'But that's a very small part of you.'

'The face is a very small part of the body, but it's what you're recognized by.'

'You *must* let yourself go now and then. Have a good time. Like other men.'

'Some other men have too good a time, I fancy. If a man murders his principles he murders his self-esteem, then life becomes pointless. And the principles which control his inner life – his secret life – are the important ones. He can betray them with absolutely nobody knowing except himself.'

Her response was to hold out her arms. 'John, darling – come to me now.'

He felt frightened. Making love to her he thought a highly inappropriate act in broad daylight, at breakfast-time, too. It was to his mind something done only at night, with the curtains drawn, in pitch darkness. 'Someone might come in.' His voice dropped to a guilty whisper.

'No, they won't. The door's locked.' He hesitated. 'Come on. Come on!'

He wiped the lather from his half-shaved face. She pulled the cord of his pyjama trousers as he lay against her, the skin of his body smooth, almost hairless, with a few clusters of caramel-coloured moles. The physical contact with her, as the night before, burst something in his mind. It was an immensely more powerful trigger than when he had first seen her naked. The steel bands of his inhibitions sprung apart, there was nothing left in his world but a simple desire for her. She kicked aside the bedclothes, falling on her back, drawing his penis avidly towards her. But he pulled away. 'We must be careful . . . '

'I want to feel you . . . this time I want to feel you.'

Rumbelow's was a caution which could never abandon him, however strong the emotional tempest. He fumbled on the bedside table with the packet of condoms he had bought in an obscure chemist's off Shaftesbury Avenue. She leant on her elbow, pouting a little, watching as he drew one on. His fingers moved with the same controlled care as they manipulated the internal organs of the dead.

Afterwards, before he had left her, his inhibitions returned. That again had been exactly the same the night before. There was almost a physical sensation of something being tightened inside his skull. He was Rumbelow again.

They left shortly after breakfast. They would take the train to Brighton, they decided, and spend the day there, with a trip in the open bus along the coast. He paid the bill standing self-consciously next to a curly-haired young man with a ten-foot woollen scarf looped round his neck, his wife in a Maggy Rouff coat. He was surprised at the matter-of-fact way the manager took his money. He was almost prepared for a violent denunciation in the hall of his deceit and wickedness. He had intended immediately to tear up the receipted bill, to destroy the evidence. But instead he folded it and put it carefully in his pocket. If Rosemary still wanted a divorce, that bill would be first-class evidence. And it would save him a good deal of expense, undertaking a sham of the same expedition with a lady who charged for it as her profession.

30

IT WAS TO BE A LONG DAY.

At six-thirty Rumbelow stood on the pavement outside his club, in bowler and trench-coat though the September morning promised fine. It was still growing light, the grey-sided, broad gorge of Pall Mall almost empty. A taxi crawled past with its driver eyeing him hopefully, the milkman's pony-cart clattered from St James's Square, three official functionaries were at work – the policeman, the postman, and a man in a wide-awake hat sweeping the gutter. After a couple of minutes a black limousine appeared from the direction of Whitehall. 'I hope this isn't all dashed inconvenient?' said Major Standring through the window.

'I'm used to irregular hours.'

A chauffeur in peaked cap and leather leggings opened the car door and started strapping Rumbelow's black bag to the luggage-rack at the rear.

'Had any breakfast?' asked the Major, as Rumbelow settled beside him. 'Too bad. But I've brought a few things.' He indicated a wicker picnic basket at this feet. 'A thermos of coffee, some hard-boiled eggs, chocolate biscuits and the like. We'll stop once we're in the country. One must always look after the inner man, don't you agree? They'll be giving us lunch out there, of course.'

Like many ageing military men, he had developed an old-maidish fussiness towards his personal comfort. He wore a heavy tweed coat with leather gauntlets, and obligingly shared a tartan rug over his knees with Rumbelow. He declined a cigar. 'At this unearthly hour I'd prefer a fag. These De Reszke

Minors aren't bad at two bob for sixty. Quite enough to pay, these are hard times.' Rumbelow surmised that the major's transfer had brought a cut in salary. Well, he shouldn't have been so squeamish, he thought. 'We look like being in for an interesting day.'

'I hope so.'

'If the balloon *does* go up, at least this time we'll be ready for the Hun. Our Army may be small but it's damned efficient, you can take that from me. Mind, I'd like to see it attract more recruits. I'm a bit of a reformer, you know, I'm not against a few changes.'

'Such as?'

'Well . . . letting the Tommies get married before they're twenty-six, that sort of thing. At the same time, I'm not against conscription.'

'The country wouldn't stand for it.'

'I don't agree. Only the communists, socialists and persons of that ilk wouldn't stand for it. They're always ready to make nuisances of themselves. Take this Left Book Club thing. Have you come across any of its effusions?' Rumbelow shook his head. 'It's for those Bolshie school-teachers and journalists and the like, who make such an infernal clamour about arms for Spain. To my mind, they're just as bad as Mosley's blackshirts.'

Rumbelow lit a cigar, leaning back and enjoying the luxury of the car. It must have cost the taxpayers at least four hundred pounds, he calculated. To the last minute he was prepared for the journey to be called off, the idea pigeon-holed like so many freakish products of official imagination. They drove eastwards through the awakening streets of London, filled with tradesmen's vans and early buses taking people to work. In the countryside north of the Thames at Tilbury they made a stop for their coffee, hard-boiled eggs and chocolate buscuits. The major produced also some slices of cold ham and tongue and a flask of brandy.

Beyond Southend they turned off the main road, and found themselves driving beside a fence of concrete posts and barbed wire which seemed to run across the flat scenery as far as the horizon. They stopped at a gate flanked by large notices. An

R.A.F. sentry inspected some sort of pass the major thrust through the car window. Inside, they followed a straight narrow tarmac road towards a huddle of buildings, some brick, some wooden sheds, some the corrugated-iron half-cylinders of Nissen huts. The car stopped and the major got out. No one appeared. 'They don't seem to be expecting us,' said the major crossly. 'Just like the R.A.F.'

They sat in the car for ten minutes, the major increasingly impatient. Rumbelow lit another cigar, rather enjoying finding himself in some secret military establishment. Another car appeared down the narrow road. Two officers got out, one with pilot's wings and the rings of a wing commander, the other a squadron leader, twined gold snakes on his lapels denoting he was a doctor.

'Sorry to keep you waiting.' The wing commander was red-faced and in a bad temper. 'But I've a job to do, you know.'

Both cars drove beyond the buildings, until the road abruptly stopped. The ground was level and marshy, the mouth of the Thames estuary sparkling in the distance. They continued on foot beyond a board saying, FORBIDDEN TO PASS THIS NOTICE WHEN RED FLAG IS FLYING. A red flag fluttered from a pole beside it. Rumbelow supposed it was all right.

They halted at some concrete steps leading to a dugout, a sergeant and an airman outside vibrating at the salute. Rumbelow noticed wires running from it along the ground to a canvas screen in the distance. The wing commander disappeared briefly, then all four set off towards the screen, which was further away than it appeared. Behind it stood a military ambulance and two small structures, one of brick and one of concrete, recalling to Rumbelow photographs of Eskimoes' igloos. Upright between them on a metal tripod, connected to the wires from the dugout, was an aeroplane bomb about three feet high. It was one of the few things ever to induce a sickening feeling in him.

'I designed those two shelters myself.' The major's eyes were starting to glisten with excitement.

'That's very clever.'

'Right, Dr Rumbelow, now it's up to you,' said the wing commander.

The ambulance doors were already open. The stretchers were folded back, a pair of coffins occupying the floor. Rumbelow climbed in, glancing at the brass plates on the lids. One said,

JEREMIAH HACKTHORPE

BORN AUGUST 1, 1860. DIED SEPTEMBER 10, 1936.

The other,

MARY ALICE SMITH

BORN 1856. DIED SEPTEMBER 14, 1936.

'Anyone got a screwdriver?'

The R.A.F. doctor looked mystified.

'To take the lid, off.'

'I rather thought we could leave the stiffs in the coffins.'

'Oh, no. That might invalidate the whole experiment. Besides, how do you imagine we'd squeeze them into those shelters? We'll have to get on all fours to crawl in ourselves.'

The ambulance driver produced a screwdriver from his tool-kit. Rumbelow got to work, noticing the wing commander and the major kept their distance. 'We'd better have the shrouds off, too.'

The R.A.F. doctor began to look uneasy. 'Is that really necessary?'

'I wouldn't suggest it otherwise. We'll have to get one of these stretchers out of the ambulance and lift the bodies on it in turn. There really should be a table of some sort. Your preparations are most inadequate.'

'We thought it would simply be a matter of popping the coffins back in the ambulance and sending them down to Blackfriars, as arranged.'

'The whole business is going to be much more difficult than that. Have none of you heard of rigor mortis?'

The body of the old man was so wizened he must have resembled a mummy during life, Rumbelow thought. They carried him on a stretcher to the brick shelter, then he took the shoulders, the R.A.F. doctor the feet. Rumbelow crawled inside. It was some eight feet square with a concrete floor and smelt damp. There was no lighting and no ventilation apart from the constricted entrance. He would not have cared to find himself inside during an air-raid. He pulled the body in, then crawled out carefully, dusting the knees of his trousers.

'This is becoming more trouble than it's worth,' complained the R.A.F. doctor. 'After all, we're only interested in the effects of blast. There may not be any. It's a subject nobody knows anything about.'

'I hope you're right.'

The body of the old lady was more difficult. She was extremely fat, and from her elephantine legs Rumbelow concluded she had died of congestive heart failure. 'At least they're helping to defend their country,' he remarked. 'Precious few can claim as much when they've been dead the best part of a week.'

The driver and an airman rolled up the canvas screen. They all got in with the empty coffins and drove over the bumpy ground back to the dug-out. The ambulance disappeared towards the safety of the main buildings. The four of them descended the concrete steps.

'We should be through in time for a drink before lunch.' The prospect seemed to put the wing commander in a better mood. 'I take it there's not much you'll want to do in the way of cutting up, Doctor?'

'I imagine that can be kept for my mortuary at Blackfriars.'

'I've great faith in those shelters,' said the major enthusiastically. 'I even volunteered to stay inside myself. But the Home Office wouldn't hear of it.'

Rumbelow was now enjoying his morning thoroughly. It was agreeable to watch the Armed Forces at work, to feel part of some military operation, to be doing something towards the country's security. The wing commander went up with a pair of field-glasses to satisfy himself nobody was left on the scene of the imminent explosion. In the dugout was a box with a handle, which Rumbelow had seen in countless illustrations for boys' adventure stories. They all put their fingers in their ears. The wing commander gave an order. The sergeant depressed the handle. The explosion seemed much nearer than Rumbelow expected, shaking the walls of the dugout. 'Well, let's have a look-see,' said the wing commander.

They walked over the ground again. There was a hole with smoke coming from it. There was no sign of the tripod holding the bomb, nor of the igloos.

The major fell silent.

They peered over the edge of the crater. Among crumbled bricks and concrete Rumbelow noticed the head of a human femur sticking up, glistening in the sunshine. His eyes ran round, identifying fragments of skin and muscle, the old man's head, an arm, a hand which could have belonged to either unknowing volunteer. Under a slab of concrete was the top of the fat woman's torso, torn across as though bitten by an enormous animal. 'Someone had better pick up the bits. If they can be put in a suitable container, you can send them down to me in London. I'll sort them out when they get there. I suppose there's arrangements to give them a decent burial?'

The major spent most of the journey back in silence. 'I was sure, so terribly sure, about those shelters. I had a lot of experience of that sort of thing in the Army, you know.'

'Many useful inventions have seemed unsuccessful at their first demonstration.'

'I just can't understand it. I just can't. It really is disheartening. I shall have to redesign them, going right back to basic principles.'

'Well, the war is hardly likely to break out tomorrow,' Rumbelow told him consolingly.

When Rumbelow got out in Pall Mall, the major thanked him effusively if sadly. 'We must keep in touch. I've reports to write, no end of details. I'm sure next time will go much better.'

Rumbelow scribbled on one of his visiting-cards. 'You'd better have my new address. I'm leaving here and moving to a service flat. I shall have to fend for myself, but I fancy I can manage that.'

'You're a bachelor?'

'In effect,' said Rumbelow.

31

THE NEXT FEW weeks were the happiest of Rumbelow's life. The flat was new, still smelling of fresh paint, in a block the size of an ocean liner, risen on foundations of demolished workmen's cottages round the back of Chelsea Square. He had one smallish room with a divan bed in an alcove, a single armchair, a bathroom and a 'kitchenette' the size of a telephone kiosk. Everything was provided, down to the teaspoons. The tenants were assumed to work the week in London, or to come up for a few days' shopping and theatres, before returning to more socially acceptable accommodation in the country. But from the unfashionable look of most of them, Rumbelow suspected the rooms to be their only homes in the world. It was cramped but it was easy to keep himself tidy. And the rent was remarkably modest.

Maria came to him almost every evening. This caused severe reorganization of his work – he had to let some of it go to other pathologists, even to Quinley, and however delightful the reason this always caused him a pang. Maria insisted on cleaning the flat and cooking a meal. Often they just sat listening to the wireless, which was provided at the turn of a knob, like the bathwater. One weekend, she invoked the excuse which had served for the Sussex roadhouse and spent the Saturday night with him.

'Your people *must* be getting suspicious,' he decided. They were lying on top of the divan on the Sunday morning, the flats having excellent modern central heating. 'Either they're remarkably trusting – which would upset me. Or they know very well and don't let on. Perhaps not even to themselves. That's a convenient little human failing.'

'I don't think so. Honestly. They're terribly curious about you. They keep asking when I'm going to bring my young man home to tea.'

'I'll have to meet them *some* day.'

'You've never suggested that before. Never so positively.'

'Haven't I? Well, there's no point in keeping everything such a dead secret, is there? We've no longer the hospital to worry about.'

'They'll be thrilled meeting you.'

'They'll get an awful shock.'

'Why?'

'I'm hardly your "young man". I'm a good ten years older than you.'

'Does that worry you, darling?'

'It must be of some significance. Now and then I even think it's rather abnormal.'

'But I *love* older men,' she said playfully.

'That raises a terrible vision. Fat, heavy-jowled financiers with chorus-girls.'

'Oh, dear! Perhaps it's fairer to say I'm not mad about young ones? A lot of them just bore me. Do you suppose I should write to Dorothy Dix about it in the *Mirror*?'

'Have there been many others?'

'That's asking.'

He decided not to pursue it. 'Not that I set great store by a man's looks. Or a woman's, if it comes to that.'

'Now you're trying to tell me I'm plain, but you'll put up with it.'

As usual, he took her seriously. 'I didn't mean that for one moment. A man's intellect and character are what I see, not the set of his eyes or the shape of his chin. A philosopher can be as ugly as the devil, but the whole world admires him. I've met actresses who can hold an audience spellbound, but they're not pretty. Sometimes they're downright ugly under the paint. And I've seen criminals, even murderers, who've the looks of film stars. It's of no consequence, you see.'

'Oh, you're a good-looking chap.' She ran her fingers lightly down the ribs of his long chest, as though she were playing the piano.

'Why do I attract you, Maria? Why me, particularly?'

'You're kind, sweet and gentle. And clever. I like clever people. That's why I enjoyed working in the library.'

'And I'm famous. I suppose that's a consideration? I'm hardly Ronald Colman, but people have heard of me.'

'It *is* something. I can't deny it, can I?'

'I missed you awfully when you left Blackfriars.'

'So did I. Terribly.'

'Yet I didn't quite realize it. It's strange – I suppose I submerged it in my mind. It's easy enough, my days are so full. I've always relied on my work to help me forget anything that's jarring and unpleasant. Work's my drug. But I knew it at once, the moment I set eyes on you that night. I suppose the same thing happens to other people. Though it frightens me sometimes, how difficult it is to control our emotions.'

'Why should we try to?'

'They're dangerous things. I've seen too often the tragic results, when a man lets them dominate him.'

'Tell me you love me, John darling.'

He had no reply for the moment. She asked often, he supposed like any girl in love. She would only be after reassurance or harmless flattery. But whatever he said, he had been clear-sighted enough to know his was only an infatuation. He had heard of many men, responsible level-headed men like himself, who had thrown themselves overboard from society for the same reason. It accounted for his desperation to keep her a secret. He hadn't the sophistication and brazenness of Graham Trevose, who wore a scandalous life lightly, and even saw it add to his private patients and his popularity at Blackfriars as 'a card'. Any assumptions otherwise had been finally demolished by his fumbling humiliation in the hands of Diana Flavell.

But Rumbelow's mind was beginning to change. When he had made a stupid mistake in court and Norman Carlow accused him half-humorously afterwards of being in love, he had been terrified that the affair was slipping from his control. Now he wasn't so alarmed that the shrewd Carlow might be right. He was starting to ask himself – cautiously, being Rumbelow – exactly what his feelings were towards Maria. Over the past few weeks, the excitement of being alone with her in the flat – in his own home, where they could do exactly as they pleased – had turned to an acceptance of the situation as perfectly natural, which he found far more deeply satisfying. He was experiencing a domesticity quickened with love and tenderness which was never part of his marriage. The idea of making her his second wife had stolen upon him. After all, a man could not live alone for ever, it wasn't biologically normal. But he had not cared to put the feeling into words. He spent his life locked in a cell with himself his own jailer, only rarely the urge to escape becoming overpowering.

He asked abruptly, 'Maria, would you like to marry me?'

She looked solemn for a moment, still running her finger down his chest. 'You know how I would.'

'But you understand how it might take some time – the divorce, all that business?'

'I don't mind how long I wait.'

He smiled. 'There's the difference in our ages again. At yours, life is limitless. At mine, you're starting to see your days are numbered.'

She pressed closer to him. 'I wish you wouldn't keep thinking of that.'

'But it colours your thoughts, your actions. It's the young people who want to change everything – look at the Nazis, shouting youths with banners. When you get a little older you appreciate the world, you want nothing but to enjoy it. Do you suppose we could reconcile those two outlooks?'

'You think too much, John,' she told him gently. 'Why don't you trust your own nature?'

'Perhaps I should. A woman would, without question, wouldn't she?' He thought for a moment. 'If you'd like me to, I'll write to my wife.'

'I should like you to.'

'And see your parents.'

'I should love that, very much.'

'Then I shall.'

The rendezvous with the parents was left vague, but the following week he gave much thought to the letter. He finally composed it on the Friday afternoon, sitting in his laboratory. At the top, he put the address of his new flat.

Dear Rosemary,

I have not communicated before because there seemed no reason to. I understood that you had a job, and you seemed to wish nothing from me. For my part, my life and work continue in London more or less as usual.

But now I have become involved in a relationship which you, who are still legally my wife, are entitled to know about. I have met a lady who was at first a solace for my loneliness, and has since become very dear to me. I will not say that we wish to marry in the immediate future, but obviously such an outcome must always be in the minds of us both. In the event, I should have to invite you to divorce me.

You may not see your way to doing as much, of course. But I felt it only right to place the facts before you as early as possible.

I hope that you are continuing to receive my monthly cheques safely.

Yours sincerely,
John

He read it through several times. An admirable letter, he thought, which might have been composed by an able solicitor. It was guarded, told her little and committed him to nothing. It threw at least some of the guilt on herself, for abandoning him to loneliness. Though he had to recognize that he was, if only technically, committing the sin of adultery. But after all, there was no law against that. He put the paper in an envelope and addressed it. It was a little before four o'clock. He posted it, and went down to the mortuary for the afternoon's post-mortems.

32

THERE WERE THREE post-mortems that afternoon. The first was one of Mr Cramphorn's patients, a meat-porter from Smithfield Market, who had died a few hours after surgery for perforated duodenal ulcer. Rumbelow's sweeping incision contemptuously reopened the neatly-stitched operation wound, then he demonstrated to the students, craning over each other's shoulders from their football-stand steps, the internal stitches closing the hole in the gut. The pelvis was full of bad-smelling greenish-yellow pus, with fragments of carrot still identifiable in it, too much to drain through the stiff, red rubber tube hopefully stuck through a second incision above the bladder. Rumbelow slipped his gloved hand over the domed upper surface of the liver. 'There's a subprenic abscess as well,' he told Quinley, who was assisting him. 'That ulcer must have been leaking for some time. Anything about it in the clinical notes?'

'No, sir.'

'Then Crampers must have missed it.' He looked round for the house-surgeon, but supposed he was engaged in the operating theatre. 'What's the clinician's cause of death?'

'Peritonitis.'

'I suppose we can let it go at that. The abscess is all part of the same picture. Though I've a feeling that surgical shock had a good deal to do with it – they ought to warm these perforations up in bed, on morphine and rectal saline before they go into the abdomen. It would give them a chance to recover. Do you know, I once did a p.m. on a man who perforated in the street, right outside the hospital. They had him on the operating table in an hour, and killed him. Crampers is far too impatient. Though I suppose he wouldn't take very kindly to it, if I told him as much.'

'No, sir.'

They left William to sew up the body. On the other table was an old woman who had died after breaking her hip. Rumbelow sliced into lungs like wet sponges, demonstrating the pus and fluid which had filled the air-spaces to extinguish her life. 'Hypostatic bronchopneumonia. Nearly always fatal, at this age inevitably so. A disease which lives up to its reputation as "the old person's friend". There's no treatment.' He turned to Quinley. 'What's the next one?'

'A child, sir. Female. A patient of Dr Bantrell's. He particularly wants to see the p.m.'

'Why wasn't she in the pediatric ward?'

'It was a duty case, when his firm was on take-in.'

'I see. What's the diagnosis?'

'Epilepsy.'

'I suppose the immediate cause of death was asphyxia, or injury during a fit?'

'It's given as post-epileptic shock.'

'That's unusual. There won't be much for us to see, anyway. What was her age?'

'Six.'

William and his assistant busied themselves with a trolley. The meat-porter's body was replaced with that of the child. At the same moment the red-headed physician bustled in, in his long white coat and accompanied by his houseman. Rumbelow thought Bantrell greeted him with rather too emphatic cordiality.

'I see she died as long ago as last Monday.'

'Yes, we'd some difficulty getting permission for a p.m.,' Bantrell told him. 'The parents aren't very intelligent, I'm afraid. Do you mind if I have a word to the students? It's a case with some interesting features.'

'I don't mind in the least.'

'This girl was admitted early on Monday morning, with a story of fits during the night. She was in bed, apparently sleeping normally.' Bantrell enjoyed a first-rate reputation in the medical school as a teacher, of which he was fully aware. 'Her father works as a van-driver, and there are four older brothers and a sister, all alive and well. She had a history of fits and dizziness over the past two years, though it may have been longer – the mother was a somewhat unreliable witness. The fits lasted about half an hour, occurred about once a month, and were becoming more frequent. She had been seen by her local g.p., who prescribed bromides. Well, Doctor, have you already reached a diagnosis?' he asked a front-row student genially.

'I'd say epilepsy, sir.'

'Quite brilliant, Doctor. And the form? *Grand mal*, or *petit mal*?'

'*Grand mal*, sir.'

'Correct. She was unconscious when admitted, and in fact did not recover consciousness before she died. The blood pressure was low, so low that at first we couldn't get a reading. There was tachycardia. The pupil was dilated. The limbs were flaccid. There were no more convulsions. On examination, we found no further abnormality. There was nothing suggestive of congenital defects in the history, Mr Carten?' House-physicians at Blackfriars, like subalterns in the Army, were never awarded in speech their entitled rank.

'The mother described her as a normal healthy child, sir, though not very lively.'

'We will accept that for what it's worth. Dr Rumbelow may well demonstrate some congenital intracranial abnormality which could have caused these fits. In the absence of such evidence, we must of course put them down to idiopathic epilepsy.'

He turned aside, leaving the stage to Rumbelow.

'The body's very thin,' Rumbelow observed. 'At a glance, she might have died from starvation.'

'Some of the working class have odd ideas on diet for their young.'

Rumbelow pointed with the tip of his long scalpel. 'Note these scars, gentlemen. She had injured or burnt herself during previous attacks.'

'As we should expect.'

Rumbelow's incision split the front of the child's body in two. The knife cut cleanly through the soft breastbone, the ribs falling open like the carcass of a carved chicken. The heart, the lungs, the stomach and intestines, the kidneys, the minuscule uterus and ovaries, Rumbelow extracted together. He dropped them in a bowl, then crossed to the porcelain slab to dissect them under running water. Nothing abnormal, he thought. But behind the stomach, in the loop formed by the upper gut, lay the fish-shaped pancreas. As soon as Rumbelow felt it between his gloved fingers, he knew that something was wrong.

'This pancreas is rather thick.'

Bantrell frowned, looking over Rumbelow's shoulder. 'There's not much of it.'

'It's thicker than normal for a child of this size.'

'She may have suffered in the past from sub-acute pancreatitis. Any history of that, Mr Carten?' The houseman shook his head. 'It may be a minor congenital abnormality, as I suggested. Or it may be an artefact. Perhaps we can have a look inside the skull?'

'As you wish.' Rumbelow carefully put the scrap of pancreatic tissue to one side of the slab.

The child's hair was long and fair, matted from the refrigerator. Rumbelow made his usual incision from ear to ear across the dome of her head, pulling half the scalp forward over her face. Only a touch of his knife was needed to free the tissues from the bone. The other half he pulled back on the child's neck, which he supported on a wooden block before starting his circular saw-cut through the bone. He lifted the top half of the skull away. Bantrell and himself peered in together.

'No spurs or bony abnormalities. No injuries,' said Rumbelow. 'Quite normal.'

'Let's take a look under the membranes.'

Rumbelow dissected away the thicker dura mater, with its blood sinuses. Below was the fragile arachnoid mater, then the convoluted white surface of the brain crossed by wriggling blood-vessels. 'Normal,' said Rumbelow.

He lifted out the brain, cutting the nerves underneath, took it to the porcelain slab and sliced it. 'Normal.'

'Then the epilepsy was idiopathic, as we suspected.'

'Unusual to cause death, isn't it?'

'But not unknown.'

Rumbelow reached for the fragment of pancreas.

'There's no history of diabetes, you know.' Bantrell sounded a little sharp. 'We found no sugar or ketones in the urine.'

Rumbelow said nothing. He took his magnifying glass, turning the scrap of tissue over in his gloved fingers. The students started to yawn, mutter and shuffle their feet. Bored easily, they were wondering if there would be anything more worth seeing before they could escape for their tea.

Rumbelow handed the glass to Bantrell.

'Well, there's some thickening of the body of the organ,' Bantrell agreed. 'Any history of mumps, Mr Carten?'

'No, sir. Only the other childhood infections.'

Bantrell turned to the students again. 'As I suggested to Dr Rumbelow, this thickening might be the legacy of an attack of pancreatitis. That itself can be the somewhat rare complication of mumps. Can you offer any other cause?'

'Gallstones,' said the front-row student.

'Oh, very common in a child aged six, eh, Doctor?' The young man looked abashed. 'Trauma might be a cause, or duodenitis. But mumps is the most likely. The diagnosis must have been missed at the time. As I said, the mother was of poor intelligence.'

'This pancreas was never infected at all, at any time,' said Rumbelow.

Bantrell did not take to having his diagnosis questioned, certainly not before his houseman and the students. And most certainly not by Rumbelow. But to preserve his dignity he decided to swallow his resentment and treat the correction lightly. 'Perhaps Dr Rumbelow will enlighten us? We'll be privileged to observe his skill at nosing out clues.'

'The thickening is due to a tumour. A benign adenoma of the islets of Langerhans.'

Bantrell's ginger eyebrows shot up. 'That's a canary, isn't

it? Don't you think it more useful to look for the common-or-garden sparrows?'

'I've seen two cases. Neither diagnosed during life.'

'It's an entertaining notion, at least. Gentlemen, you are aware that the pancreas has two functions, the production of digestive enzymes and —'

'Insulin,' several students interrupted at once.

'Malfunction of the islets of Langerhans cells usually causes diabetes. But Dr Rumbelow suggests we have here a growth of these same cells – a benign growth, one remaining *in situ*, not a carcinoma spreading through the body – causing an *overproduction* of insulin. We would have the unusual condition of natural hyperinsulinism, the exact replica of a diabetic patient inadvertently receiving an excess of insulin by injection.'

'Which I believe to be the cause of death,' said Rumbelow.

Bantrell gave a hostile glance. 'Surely you're not serious? My diagnosis was epilepsy.'

'In my opinion, that was incorrect.'

The students had fallen silent. The afternoon's diversion was, after all, far from over.

'The child's fits, her coma, were due to excess insulin in the blood,' Rumbelow went on steadily.

'I disagree.'

Rumbelow nodded towards the eviscerated body on the table. 'The emaciation confirms the condition.'

'I disagree.'

The ill-feeling which both had been suppressing burst to the surface. 'Had the diagnosis been made, had sugar been administered to the child, she would be alive today.'

Bantrell went white. 'As a man of your forensic experience should know, that's a slanderous statement.'

'I hardly think so. I am merely expressing an opinion. We all of us make mistakes.'

'There is *no* adenoma in that pancreas.'

'You cannot say that with any certainty until the organ has been sectioned. You are quite at liberty to inspect the microscope slides.'

'Slides! What do you expect them to show? Precious little!

The pancreas degenerates extremely rapidly after death. I should have imagined you'd know that.'

'On the contrary, I should expect the slides to be conclusive.'

Bantrell thrust his hands into the pockets of his white coat, struggling to control himself. 'Very well. Make your slides. Tell my house-physician when they're ready. I'm perfectly confident they'll show nothing, nothing whatever.'

'If you like, a blood-sugar estimation would confirm it, one way or another.'

'Four days after death? Completely useless! Autolysis will have pushed the sugar-level in the blood right down. I should have imagined you'd know that, too.'

The pair of them suddenly looked self-conscious. They had forgotten the audience. It even occurred to Rumbelow that he could restore their dignity with some half-hearted apology, some sort of concession that he might not be completely right. He knew that Bantrell would have seized it, to save his face. But the depth of his obstinacy, and his dislike, were against it. He did manage a more matter-of-fact tone to say, 'Preparing the slides will be simple enough. You'd need a set anyway, before signing the death certificate.'

Bantrell said briefly, 'Thank you for performing the post-mortem, Dr Rumbelow,' and strode from the mortuary followed by his houseman. Rumbelow slowly stripped off his gloves. The students, always impressionable, were staring wide-eyed, embarrassed, fascinated, amused, but above all shocked at an explosion to them so incomprehensible.

'That will be all for today, gentlemen,' Rumbelow told them calmly.

33

THE TRIAL OF MRS JEAVONS was to open at Mortlock Assizes on Monday, October the eighteenth, 1936. Rumbelow went down on a train which left Paddington at seven-thirty on the Sunday evening. There was a dining-car, but he had some sandwiches and a glass of beer in the buffet beforehand – railway meals always struck him as ridiculously expensive. He travelled third-class, sharing the compartment with a fat, red-faced man with the air of a commercial traveller, silent and busy pencilling order books. Rumbelow sat watching the lights of western London flickering past with increasing speed, dimming and brightening in the steam from the engine, wondering exactly what to do about Bantrell.

On that Saturday morning, the day after the row, he had taken the pancreas of the dead child in a jar from a small refrigerator in the mortuary used for keeping specimens. In his laboratory he cut sections of it with a microtome, transferring the almost invisible wafers of tissue to half a dozen oblong glass microscope slides, spreading them out with a needle, then fixing them in pure alcohol. Three of the slides he stained with haematoxylin and eosin dye, the one employed for most specimens in his day's work. For the other three, he used a special stain which brought out the granular cells composing the islets of Langerhans, and even differentiated them into the alpha and beta types. He switched on the lamp and slipped one of these under his microscope.

'Ah,' he said at once, with great satisfaction.

There was undoubtedly an abnormal growth of the islet cells, the beta type predominating – as he would have expected, those being the producers of insulin. As he moved the slide his eye caught some clear patches – hyaline areas, which too might have been expected with an adenoma. Despite the time since death, despite the inevitable degeneration of enzyme-rich pancreatic tissue, his own diagnosis was confirmed. He was right. Bantrell was wrong. The question remained, exactly what should he do about it?

Rumbelow sat for a moment on the high stool, hands clasped on the bench. Well, the first move was to prepare a report. He took a tinted pathology form from the rack, uncapped his fountain-pen, and started to write:

Patient in the care of Dr Bantrell.

Monica Jane Evans. Aet 6. Died 12.10.36. Post-mortem 16.10.36.

Specimen: Pancreas.

Naked-eye appearance: Pancreas somewhat thickened with numerous discrete raised nodules occupying the body and tail of the organ. Head, pancreatic duct and ampulla normal.

Microscopical appearance: Nesidiocytoma. Adenoma of the islets of Langerhans occupying the greater part of the body, largely arranged in trabeculae. Alpha and beta cells present, beta cells predominating. I would expect these latter cells to be insulin-producing, but estimation of the insulin-content would not be possible so long after death. Some hyalinization, no fibrosis, no calcification. No evidence of malignancy.

Opinion: This adenoma would have caused hyperinsulinism to a degree accounting for the patient's symptoms and death.

The adenoma was of the localized type, not a diffuse hypertrophy of islet tissue throughout the pancreas, and would in my opinion have been amenable to surgery.

Cause of death: Hyperinsulinism due to adenoma of the islets of Langerhans.

> Signed,
> John Rumbelow, M.D.

Just along the corridor, outside the door of the main clinical pathology laboratory, was a wire basket into which the report forms were dropped. They were distributed to the wards twice daily by one of the porters, who collected in return another batch of specimens in variously-shaped bottles. But the basket was empty, and looking at his watch Rumbelow realized there would be no further collection until the Monday. He set off with his slip of paper to find Bantrell's houseman.

The resident medical staff occupied an ugly six-storey red-brick building to the far side of the library, approached down a narrow alley from the main square. As Rumbelow turned into it he saw the young man himself approaching, in tweed jacket and grey flannels, a long scarf in hospital colours round his neck.

'Mr Carten, I have the report on that pancreas.' The house-man stopped, politeness and deference just managing to mask his impatience. Rumbelow supposed he was off to some football match or other. 'I was right, you know. It *was* an adenoma of the islet cells. You'd better take the report in your pocket. When you get back, you can sign the death certificate.'

'Oh, the death certificate, sir . . . as a matter of fact, I've already signed it. It's gone to the registrar's office.'

Rumbelow stared, the tinted paper still in his hand. 'That's rather irregular, isn't it? You knew I'd taken the specimen. You knew I hadn't completed the post-mortem report. The death certificate should have been held until you'd heard from me.'

The houseman looked at him miserably, cursing his ill-luck at not escaping a few minutes earlier. 'The chief told me to go ahead, sir.'

'Then what did you give as the cause of death?'

'Epilepsy – the original diagnosis.'

'That was Dr Bantrell, was it? He instructed you to do that?'

'I wouldn't have done it on my own responsibility, sir.'

'No, of course not.' Rumbelow put the form back in his pocket. 'Very well, Mr Carten. I'll take the matter up with Dr Bantrell.' The houseman looked relieved. 'Don't lose too much sleep over it. But it might pay you to reflect that any medical man's signature is a powerful instrument. If it's applied lightly, it can land you in trouble. It's not pleasant to be faced with something, perhaps in court, which you've signed without thinking.'

'I'm very sorry, sir.' He was edging away. 'Very sorry indeed.'

'I hope you have an enjoyable afternoon off.'

Rumbelow sat in the Mortlock train, still undecided what to do. The situation was as precise in his mind as a geometrical figure. Under the Births and Deaths Registration Act of 1926, the doctor attending a last illness was obliged to send the death certificate to the registrar forthwith (Rumbelow even remembered that in Scotland it was within seven days). The correct entry for the child should have been, 'Immediate cause of death coma, due to hyperinsulinism, due to nesidiocytoma'. The week's delay was of no significance, the certificates by custom being retained until the post-mortem was performed and the signed pathologist's report in the hands of the physician.

But young Dr Carten had given the cause of death as epilepsy. That was simply an untrue statement. The death certificate was fraudulent. Carten had committed a criminal offence – he was liable to be tried, convicted, punished, and struck from the *Register* into the bargain. That he had acted under instructions from Bantrell was no defence. He might claim it was a matter of convenience in hospital for the housemen to sign death certificates, but that wouldn't get him far with a judge.

Rumbelow had no wish to get the houseman into trouble. With Bantrell himself it was a different matter. He had deliberately caused the lie to be entered on the certificate – through pride, obstinacy and personal dislike of himself. It was he who deserved to be punished. But how could this be brought about?

Rumbelow continued staring from the window as the train steamed through the darkness of the Thames valley towards Reading. Once in Mortlock, he would be too preoccupied with the Jeavons trial to give Bantrell much thought. He must make his decision. He stood up, took his attaché case from the rack, extracted the *Sunday Times* and a sheet of Blackfriars writing-paper, and with newspaper and case as a desk on his knee started to write.

Dear Cramphorn, he began. It was unfortunate that the surgeon must be the recipient, but he was chairman of the hospital committee. The only thing Rumbelow and Bantrell had in common was an opinion of Cramphorn as a crass ignoramus.

It is with much hesitation and distaste that I lay before you a complaint against one of our colleagues on the Blackfriars staff. But it is my duty to do so. In a recent case of Bantrell's I found the cause of death to be an excess of insulin in the blood, due to an adenoma of the islets of Langerhans. Nonetheless, his house-physician, on Bantrell's instructions, gave the cause on the death certificate as epilepsy, the erroneous diagnosis made during life.

This is of course a criminal offence.

I enclose my report on the pathology of the pancreas. The microscope slides are in my laboratory, clearly labelled. Should you wish to verify my statement during my absence from London on official business, Quinley will provide you with them.

I leave it to the medical committee to decide on appropriate action.

Yours,

John Rumbelow.

He posted the letter on arrival at Mortlock Station, though calculating it could hardly reach Blackfriars before first post on the Tuesday. With his attaché case, he walked the short distance to the Red Lion. He found a lively atmosphere inside. Peter Ivors had already arrived by road. He was pleased to be appearing for the Crown – it was said the Attorney-General had relinquished his traditional right in poisoning cases, through some complication involving the politically ambitious Sir Arthur Younghusband, retained by Mrs Jeavons for her defence. Ivors sat in one corner of the small, shabby lounge, which was decorated with the heads of stags and the masks of foxes, brass labels underneath giving the date and details of their extinction. He was with his junior counsel and a man from the public prosecutor's office, laughing over whisky-and-sodas. In another corner was Sixsmith, half-hidden by a spiky-fingered evergreen in a brass pot, enjoying himself with a dozen or so reporters. As Rumbelow appeared in the door, everyone shouted a hearty greeting. The man who had written up the

229

Gretna Green case called out, 'They haven't found the trunk murderer yet, Doctor,' and Rumbelow replied, 'They never will,' for the moment almost forgiving him. He sat down with Ivors, ordering a glass of lager. The disagreeable business of Bantrell went from his mind. The familiar faces, the familiar task ahead, the comradely atmosphere, put him in excellent spirits. It was agreeable to find that for the Jeavons' trial Mortlock was *en fête*.

34

THE SHIRE HALL looked different. The high-ceilinged room which Rumbelow had last seen at the inquest had been repainted in cream picked out with gold, the wooden floor repolished, four new electric chandeliers suspended from the roof. He wondered whether the transformation was a compliment to the assizes, or prompted by the city council's awareness of national interest in the Jeavons case. The furnishing was more splendid than the shabby props afforded the coroner. The Royal Arms had been refurbished, hanging over the dais above a well-polished broadsword and vizored helmet, he supposed symbols from the local mythology. The dais itself was carpeted in red, dominated by an ancient high-backed chair like the coronation throne in Westminster Abbey, itself canopied with tasselled gold and scarlet, facing a massive desk with a green-shaded reading-light and the inevitable carafe of water.

Beside the judge's chair were two less magnificent places for the sheriff and his chaplain. Below to his right was the same witness-box with its wooden umbrella. To his left stood the jury-box. Tables piled with documents tied in pink tape were arranged between for counsel and solicitors. Here Rumbelow took his place as usual, behind Peter Ivors. At his back was the dock, still empty, a plain pen of light oak. Beyond were places for the Press, then three rows of backless uncomfortable benches, under the supervision of a trio of policemen, for the public.

The day was dry and gusty, the sun breaking dazzlingly for seconds at a time through high leaded windows emblazoned with arms in stained glass. Everyone started at a fanfare just outside the building. The judge had arrived, the wasplike Mr Justice Easterbrook. And there would be civic dignitaries in full regalia, Rumbelow thought – the Territorial Army, policemen in their best uniforms, notables of the entire county, all enjoying themselves. A stir in the room made him turn. Mrs Stella Jeavons had appeared in the dock, between two bulky and strikingly ugly wardresses. He saw she had lost weight since their encounter in the street, but she was still pretty and seemed composed. He supposed she had been brought up from the cells by a trap-door. He wondered if the couples who danced across it on Saturday nights gave such usage any thought.

'She's been waiting a long time for this moment, poor thing,' said Peter Ivors.

'That's hardly our fault. It was the defence who insisted on bringing witnesses from Singapore.'

'Did you know a crowd waited half the night to boo when she arrived in a black Maria? Nearly all women, too. That sort of thing sickens me. The whole county seems to have decided already she gave Jeavons the arsenic.'

'Well, someone did.'

They rose, as the judge entered. It was the first time Rumbelow had set eyes on him since the Elgin case. He recalled that Easterbrook was a bachelor, who had no country house and had never ridden a horse nor shot anything in his life. He felt he was not quite a gentleman.

The clerk read the indictment. The jury – eleven men, a solitary woman in a large pink hat – were empanelled and sworn. Peter Ivors rose to start the prosecution's case. Rumbelow leant back, carefully twitching up the creases of his grey striped trousers. He found it all immensely soothing.

He had sat late over his drink in the hotel lounge the night before, while Ivors and Sixsmith went over the case for him. It appeared that Jeavons came from a well-known family in the district – the name was to be seen on a shopfront or two and professional men's brass door-plates. His brother still farmed across the valley on the edge of the Mendip Hills, neither a popular nor likeable person, embittered by the struggle to keep going during the Depression. James Jeavons himself had been a ne'er-do-well, as they said, when he was a young man after the turn of the century. There had been a conviction against him at the same assizes where his widow now stood accused of his murder – for embezzlement, though the sum must have been small, or the judge unusually merciful, or his family influence powerful, because he escaped with a fine. Then he disappeared, to Australia everyone thought. He was renowned at the time as having 'an eye for the girls'.

The Colonial Office had found something of his wanderings. He had turned up in Singapore after the War, then in his thirties, apparently well-off. He took an expensive villa near the Government House Domain in the Cavenagh Road and started a business importing precious stones, buying gold from the mines up-country at Raub and selling to the local Chinese manufacturers of jewellery. He explained he had been in diamonds at Johannesburg, and turned down for war-service through ill-health. He was unmarried, but had a Malayan mistress in his early days. This was a common enough habit, but it helped his association with 'trade' to bar him from the higher levels of society.

Early in 1933, Jeavons decided to sell out. The Singapore police in fact had their eye on him for smuggling, but could prove nothing. The farmer had the first letter from his brother for twenty years. Sixsmith had read it, telling of a longing to end his life where he had begun it, describing the sort of country house he wanted and adding grandly that money was no object. After a shady life he was making a flight into respectability. Perhaps to strengthen this impression, he married the blonde lady some twenty years younger whom he met on the boat coming home.

The steamer had called in at Singapore *en route* from Shanghai and Hong Kong, where Stella Jeavons had been living with her sister, who was married to a Government official, supporting herself by teaching in a British girls' school. In Hong Kong she had the reputation of a bright young thing, flirting with the Naval officers but avoiding any serious entanglement. It was strange, Peter Ivors thought, for her to marry a comparatively elderly man after a shipboard romance. Rumbelow pointed out he had money, and perhaps she was fleeing into respectability as well.

At Blayford, they did not see much of the brother – as among many relatives, he seemed to find the pains of absence more bearable than the abrasions of their presence. Then appeared the man Rumbelow heard of fleetingly at the exhumation. A gardener called Terry Fitt, twenty-two and living alone in a cottage on the far side of the village. Gardening was not his métier. He had appeared from London some months previously giving out that he was a painter, and though the village had seen him occupied/with palette and easel, no one had heard of his work and certainly not of anyone buying it.

Gossip about the young wife and the 'arty' gardener was inevitable, particularly as Jeavons travelled often to London leaving them alone with the maid, a local girl said to be weak in the head. Sixsmith had been sure of a liaison. The pair had been seen often enough inside the house. She had given him money – he said for his paintings. They searched the cottage, but found nothing. Terry Fitt was badly scared, and Sixsmith combined a warning that he might face a murder charge with the assurance that frankness would win the police's benevolence. Fitt admitted making love to Stella Jeavons twice in her bedroom, while her husband was away. He also said he had bought some insecticide to spray the fruit trees, at her urging. He had used only a little of it, as an experiment to test the spray-gun. This was the powder which Rumbelow had analysed as arsenic at Blackfriars.

Much of this story Peter Ivors told in the Shire Hall. He ended, 'It is the contention of the Crown, members of the jury, that on the morning of the second of December last year the prisoner administered a fatal dose of arsenic to her husband in a glass of medicine, a popular "tonic" he was accustomed to take. You are going to hear a great deal during this trial about the drug arsenic, particularly of the various chemical forms it can take. This substance, so lethal in one guise, in another becomes quite the opposite, a healing agent. You will hear that the dead man suffered from a disease for which this sort of arsenic might have been administered, by way of effecting a cure. But you will also hear that the man's death was caused through the other, quite different, form. I shall be calling the greatest forensic medicine expert in the land to guide you in this matter.'

'*One* of the greatest experts, Mr Ivors,' the judge corrected him.

That spitefulness in the newspapers, Rumbelow thought. No one's forgotten it.

The Crown's first witness was the farmer. He was not a success. He told Peter Ivors he was not at all surprised at his brother's reappearance, many businessmen out East coming home once their fortunes were made. He *had* been surprised at the marriage. Stella was unsuitable for him, too young, too flighty. He had his suspicions of Terry Fitt from the start, but kept silent for the sake of his brother's feelings. He had suspected at once that his brother's sudden death was not due to natural causes. His brother had never been seriously ill in his life. He had certainly never undergone treatment for syphilis.

Sir Arthur Younghusband made short work of this. The brother admitted he had disliked Stella from the start. When Sir Arthur suggested he had expectations under the will, and was angered and jealous at being cut out for the new wife, he made answers so ambiguous, so surly, so easily confutable to demolish himself in the eyes of the jury. He admitted his suspicions of Stella and Terry Fitt were based only on hearsay. He admitted he and his brother had met almost as strangers, and that his brother might well have been undergoing treatment for syphilis but kept such an embarrassing condition to himself.

The farmer was followed by the shopkeeper who had sold Terry Fitt the insecticide powder. Rumbelow noticed he managed to give the name and address of his establishment four times in five minutes. Afterwards came Sixsmith, whose evidence-in-chief filled the rest of the day. At four the court rose. There were more fanfares. The judge went back to official isolation in his lodgings, a castle five miles away. The sheriff prepared to chair the annual dinner of the local country gentlemen's association. The chaplain was dining with the bishop, in keen expectation of hearing his preferment to a richer living. Sir Arthur and his junior went back to one hotel,

Ivors and Rumbelow to the other. Mrs Jeavons returned to prison in the next county, which had accommodation for women. Rumbelow calculated that during the trial she would cover a distance of some five hundred miles.

He had the local evening paper brought him in the hotel lounge. Since the preliminary hearings before the magistrates, no evening could pass in a Mortlock public-house without strong opinions being expressed on the case, and the school-children played gruesome games based on the exhumation. Everyone ascribed to Terry Fitt a sexual athleticism outstripping Casanova, and everyone seemed to know a girl or two he had seduced. Rumbelow read the newspaper account carefully, pleased to see it held some flattery of himself. 'Today went pretty well, don't you think?'

Peter Ivors was sitting over a whisky-and-soda before dinner. The unusual state of inactivity, forced to spend days on end in small and generally uncomfortable county-town hotels, spasmodically made him irritable. 'On the contrary, it went badly. I made a mistake calling the brother, to start with. Younghusband scored all along the line.'

'It hadn't a great bearing on the case, surely?'

'Perhaps not. But once a jury see minor witnesses being rattled, they can get suspicious about the star turns.'

'You don't mean me, I hope?'

'No, of course I don't. But you must expect a rough ride from old Easterbrook. You know, he's a contrary old blighter. I've actually heard him with my own ears ask in court, "Who *is* Shirley Temple?" He gave us enough headaches over the Elgin business. Though I suppose that was largely through my own incompetence. Or your over-enthusiasm.'

'Why should you say that?'

'We should never have charged Elgin on a slippery thing like a dying declaration, with no corroboration at all. I know it's easy to look back, but we must have half-taken leave of our senses to start a prosecution like that against a defendant like him. We should have waited our chance. But you wanted to push on with it. You absolutely steamrollered us into it. Well, perhaps the chance will come again.'

Rumbelow thought this criticism unjust. He turned back to the newspaper. Someone had switched on the wireless, the flat voice of the B.B.C. announcer reading the six o'clock news declaring, 'The trial of Mrs Jeavons, who is accused of murdering her husband, opened today at Mortlock Assizes, and is expected to last several days. Among the prosecution witnesses is Dr Rumbelow, the forensic medicine expert.'

'I see I've offended you,' said Ivors. 'I'm sorry, John. I'm in a mood this evening. Oh, we'll come through all right. Like most poisoning cases, this is perfectly simple. I've only to prove that Jeavons couldn't have taken the arsenic himself, and that Mrs Jeavons had one, the chance, two, the motive, and three, the means, to give it him. Convince a jury on all four points, and you get your conviction. Except there's the syphilis thing to mud the issue.'

'But there's no evidence whatever he was having arsenical treatment when he died. No doctor has been found, not even a quack. Even if the defence have something up their sleeve, I can counter it.'

Ivors gave an unexpected hoot of laughter. 'Good God! Something's just occurred to me. The syph's infective, of course? Do you suppose he gave it to the wife? And she passed it on to Fitt? There's an old joke about that, isn't there? Some husband wanting to get his own back on the milkman.'

'It would not be infective at that stage,' said Rumbelow soberly.

'What a pity.' Ivors finished his whisky and looked round hopefully. 'Never a damn waiter in sight. God knows how commercial travellers put up with such places.'

Terry Fitt entered the witness-box during the following morning. It was the middle of the afternoon when Sir Arthur Younghusband rose for his cross-examination.

'Mr Fitt, on the morning of December the second last, were you in love with Mrs Jeavons?'

The artist-gardener hesitated. He was a tall, sallow, skinny young man, Rumbelow wondering at any woman finding him prepossessing. He wore a suit of rough brown tweed and a woven tie. His dark hair was overlong, he had worn a

237

beard but for his own reasons shaved it for the trial. 'I don't think so.'

'Were you in love with her on the afternoon of October the tenth last? And on the afternoon of September the twelfth?'

Another pause. 'No.'

'Yet at both these times you were in her bedroom enjoying sexual intercourse with her?'

'Yes.'

'Without being in love with her?'

'They're two different things.'

Well, thought Rumbelow, *that's* marked him down in the eyes of the jury as an outcast, unbound by the morals cherished by themselves – or at least purported to be.

'You are saying there was no affection between you? You simply took advantage of her husband's absence to persuade Mrs Jeavons to admit you to her bedroom?'

'It was more the other way round.'

'To use a popular phrase, she seduced you?'

'Yes. More or less. She was always after me.'

'Will you tell the jury on what you based that impression?'

'She was always coming out to me at my work. Inviting me in for tea, or a drink.'

Terry Fitt gave his answers in a low voice, staring at the floor of the court. He is really a simple young fellow, thought Rumbelow. He had seen him only once, at Mortlock for the magistrates' court hearings, when he had expected a dashing, raffish sort, a 'Bohemian', as the papers said. Perhaps he was telling the truth after all.

'Wouldn't you think that was the normal behaviour of a considerate employer?'

'No. It worried me. I knew what she wanted.'

'You could have left her employment?'

'Jobs aren't easy to find, sir.'

'But it was only a spare-time job?'

'I needed the money.'

'Will you be more explicit? Tell the jury exactly what Mrs Jeavons said on those two occasions when you claim she invited you to bed.'

'She told me her husband was away for the day. The coast was clear. She suggested I came and made love to her.'

There was a cry from the dock. Everyone jerked round. They had quite forgotten the presence of Mrs Jeavons. 'It's lies, lies! Nothing but lies. Terry, Terry, how could you?'

'Silence!' shouted several voices at once.

'It's not true, not a word of it's true —'

'Mrs Jeavons, I know it is a strain to hear such things,' said the judge quietly. 'But it is necessary for you to bear it in silence. You will have the opportunity in due course to make your reply from the same place. Meanwhile, you must compose yourself, so we may proceed in the proper manner. Please try to remember that others have found themselves in your position, and have similarly been obliged to exercise self-control.'

Her response was to start sobbing. One of the ugly wardresses leant forward with a whisper, but she started to cry louder, then to scream, each one ringing the more grotesquely, the more frighteningly, in that staid room with its pompous furnishings.

The judge rose. 'The court will adjourn for fifteen minutes.'

He was followed out by the sheriff and the chaplain. The wardresses hustled Mrs Jeavons out of sight, still screaming, until the noise suddenly stopped. They've closed the trap-door below the dock, Rumbelow thought. A foretoken of another she would in due course find herself standing upon.

Outside, Ivors lit a cigarette. Rumbelow said, 'That outburst won't help her.'

'It won't hurt her.'

'But the jury know the rules as well as we do. They don't care to see them broken.'

'This isn't a blasted game of cricket, you know.'

When they reassembled, Mrs Jeavons sat chalk-faced but composed between her two guardians. Sir Arthur's questions turned to the tin of powder for spraying the fruit-trees. Terry Fitt described how Mrs Jeavons had asked him to buy it. He agreed, it was the time of year for spraying apples. He had no idea the powder contained arsenic. The tin having already been produced as an exhibit, he was invited to look inside. 'How much powder was there left when you last saw it?'

'It was almost full.'

'How long ago was that?'

'Some time last November.'

'This is a common brand of insecticide in the district. Can you be sure now it's the same tin?'

'Yes.'

'Why?'

'It sort of . . . looks the same, I suppose.'

Sir Arthur switched his attack. 'What were your relations with Mr Jeavons himself?'

'I didn't see much of him, to tell the truth. He wasn't very interested in the garden.'

'Did you once say to Mabel Royce, the maidservant, that you wished him out of the way, preferably for good?'

'That was only a manner of speaking. He'd blown me up about something. Something to do with my work,' he added hastily.

'You said you were not in love with Mrs Jeavons. That did not however prevent your having sexual intercourse with her. Would it have prevented your marrying her after her husband's death?'

'I don't follow.'

'Then I must put it more bluntly. Despite your lack of affection, would you not have found it agreeable continuing to enjoy sexual intercourse with her, and to enjoy in addition the pleasures of her husband's money?'

For the first time he became animated. 'I'd never do a thing like that. I'd never marry someone I didn't love.'

'You would freely have intercourse with someone you didn't love. You don't seem very particular in such matters, do you?'

He gave no reply.

'Mr Fitt, you were not at the house on the day of Mr Jeavons' death?'

'No.'

'You avoided Mrs Jeavons afterwards?'

'Yes.'

'You were frightened?'

He again said nothing.

'You were cunning?'

'Frightened, perhaps.'

'Should you not be sitting in that dock with the prisoner?'

Again no reply.

'Or instead of the prisoner?'

'You should not have asked that, Sir Arthur,' said the judge.

'I apologize, my Lord. No more than anyone else, do I wish to put a witness in the position of incriminating himself. Thank you, Mr Fitt.'

'A sordid business,' murmured Rumbelow to Peter Ivors.

'Oh, it's six of one, half a dozen of the other. He and the wife both enjoying themselves, and now he's scared stiff. We can't blame him, I suppose. But it doesn't make his evidence look any better.' He pushed back his wig. 'There's something wrong with this case. I *know* there's something wrong with this bloody case.'

35

MR CRAMPHORN GENERALLY liked to leave Blackfriars about four in the afternoon, to make his living operating in the fashionable nursing-homes of the West End. He pulled off his gloves as he left the hospital theatre, which was hot and steamy, smelling strongly of ether and antiseptic. It was equipped with a brand-new American device called an air-conditioner, but he always had it switched off, because it made a noise and anyway he thought it only natural for a surgeon to work in such an atmosphere.

Sir George Smallpenny was waiting outside in the cubicle-like surgeons' room, a leather instrument-case in his hand, clearly anxious to be away. 'Sorry to get you up here,' Cramphorn apologized. 'Can you spare a minute?'

'I expect I can persuade my chauffeur to ignore this thirty-mile speed-limit business.'

The surgeon felt for his jacket in one of the narrow green metal lockers. 'Rumbelow.' He handed Sir George the letter. 'Gone potty, as far as I can make out.'

He sat down, filling his pipe, still in his operating vest and white trousers blood-spattered at the ends. Sir George read the letter and the enclosed report-form in silence.

'A bit strong, isn't it, Crampers?'

'Actionable, if you ask me.'

'I suppose Rumbelow feels put out.'

'I wish he hadn't sent it. I dislike all this unpleasantness.'

'Perhaps he's already thought better of it? We all send letters we wish we'd never written.'

Cramphorn struck a match. 'Bantrell will have to see it.'

'Must he?'

'If it were written about yourself, you'd expect me to come out with it.'

'What do you envisage? Pistols for two and coffee for one in the hospital square at dawn?'

'If Rumbelow wants to put it before the committee, to the committee it must go. He's perfectly within his rights.' Cramphorn was a man of flinty propriety.

'I do wish the damn fellow wouldn't make himself so awkward. But I suppose we've no alternative.' He knew as much as Cramphorn that a man with responsibility must often take unpopular or unpleasant action, for the sake of his own self-respect as much as the rights of others. Like most flippant people, it was only a mask for embarrassment at his own deep seriousness. 'Perhaps we'd better see the slides? After all, Rumbelow himself suggests it. We can get Bantrell along. I fancy he lectures this afternoon. Sister can telephone the nursing home to say I'll be late.'

Cramphorn took the coloured report-form, giving a chuckle. 'Nesidiocytoma! That's a very recherché word he's picked up. I certainly wouldn't meddle with one in anybody's belly. I wonder how long it is since Rumbelow examined a *live* patient?'

Cramphorn changed his clothes, and the three met some twenty minutes later in Rumbelow's laboratory. Cramphorn handed Bantrell Rumbelow's letter. They were both prepared for him to be angry, but were unprepared for the violence of his outburst.

'God in heaven, does he expect me to take that lying down? A crime! He's accused me of a crime. He might as well have said I'd been picking his pocket. Does he imagine that I have no honour?' He threw the letter furiously on the workbench. 'To my face he wouldn't say it, no. He's a coward. A contemptible coward. I despise him. He is a person of whom I no longer even wish to speak.'

'I'm sure he'll apologize.' Sir George was desperate to lower the temperature. 'He's not himself, you know. He's been grossly overworking, and his domestic life has gone to pot. One must make allowances.'

243

'The two of us cannot remain colleagues here. That's obvious, surely? He shall have to go.'

'One of you will have to go,' Cramphorn pointed out.

'Do I understand you're taking Rumbelow's side?'

'I'm taking nobody's side. If it comes to the committee, I'll be the chairman. I only want to get the facts straight, without everyone becoming excited.' Bantrell's tirade had upset Cramphorn badly. It was not the manner in which a gentleman behaved. 'Let's start at square one. Here are the slides. We'll shove them under a microscope and have a look.'

'Very well, I agree,' said Bantrell more calmly. He controlled himself, looking a little ashamed.

Cramphorn peered down the instrument first, merely grunting. Bantrell took his place on the high stool. For some minutes he looked through the eyepiece in silence, fiddling busily with the fine-adjustment knob. 'This is ridiculous,' he announced at last. 'It's impossible to make out anything particularly clearly. It was six days after death when these slides were sectioned. The pancreas would have degenerated badly by then. One of my students could tell you as much. *I* certainly can't make an adenoma out of it.'

'Rumbelow might,' said Cramphorn.

'All right, he's a pathologist and I'm not. But I'm no ignoramus with a microscope, you know. There's no adenoma, no trace of one, not in my opinion.'

'Can't say I was impressed myself,' Cramphorn agreed.

Sir George took over the instrument. 'There might possibly be something, you know. Though it would need the eye of faith to see it.'

'Well? What's to be done?' asked Cramphorn.

'Couldn't the pair of you settle it over a cup of coffee?' asked Sir George hopefully. 'Once Rumbelow's back from this sensational murder trial in the West country.'

'I'm afraid that's out of the question. There's more than my personal feelings involved. Even if we dismissed that report as some sort of hysteria brought on by overwork – which I'm not for one moment prepared to do – it says plainly enough that had I treated the child differently she would still be alive. That

244

could land me with a very nasty action for professional negligence. There's no reason why it shouldn't reach the child's parents. Rumbelow might make it his business to provide them with a copy. They're an unpleasant couple. And the working class these days are getting sensitive about their rights. There're plenty of trade unionists and Communists and so on, delighted to make trouble for people like us.'

'You'd be in court on one side, with Rumbelow on the other,' said Sir George.

'You can imagine what an uphill fight that would be. But isn't all this part of a wider issue?' He looked at both men. 'The idea of Rumbelow resigning from the staff is one I've had in my mind for some time, for quite different reasons.' He paused. Sir George, and Cramphorn after a moment, gave a short nod. Bantrell accepted that at some time or another the idea had entered their own heads. 'Does the hospital really want to be associated with all this publicity? With all that public criticism, after Rumbelow sent the poor little motor-mechanic to the gallows? And all the ridicule over that nonsense at Gretna Green?'

'I suppose some rubs off on Blackfriars,' conceded Sir George. Cramphorn said nothing.

Still sitting on the stool, Bantrell folded his arms in the formal black jacket. 'His chasing one of the girls from the library wasn't particularly becoming conduct.'

'Old whiskers sacked her,' said Cramphorn.

'Perhaps he was jealous?' suggested Sir George.

'But you must agree, it really was not to be expected from a colleague. He was behaving like one of the students. And it can well happen again, surely? But I won't labour the point. Much more important is one simple fact – that Rumbelow isn't doing his job here. How can he? Not when he's chasing guineas in mortuaries and coroners' courts all over London. Not when he's appearing in murder investigations all over the country. The trials alone take an enormous amount of his time. Where should he be today? Not giving evidence miles away in the country, but here working in the laboratory.'

'I'll agree to that,' said Cramphorn. 'It takes God knows how long to get a pathological report these days.'

'And then it's generally signed by young Quinley,' added Sir George.

'The routine pathology at Blackfriars is in a deplorable state,' continued Bantrell enthusiastically. For the first time he felt he was making progress with the pair. 'And there's a further matter. I've been going through the pathology pass-lists in the M.B. finals since Rumbelow was appointed. Did you know that only *half* the proportion of candidates from Blackfriars pass, compared with other teaching hospitals? That's quite disgraceful. But apart from his p.m. demonstrations, he takes no interest in teaching whatever. *Those* are the reasons I think his letter should go before the committee. Then his whole existence here can be thrashed out.'

Cramphorn relit his pipe. 'You'd put those views to the committee? With Rumbelow there?'

'Of course I should. Then I'd leave you to make up your own minds. If you ended by asking my own resignation, you would have it at once.' He looked at his wristwatch. 'Now I must go to my lecture, or the students will have cut it. If you want to speak about it further, Crampers, I'm always on the end of a telephone.'

He left quickly. Cramphorn started putting the microscope slides back in their wooden box. 'Can't understand why Bantrell and Rumbelow don't get on. I've put up with some frightful bounders myself.'

'They're two horses out of the same stable, that's why.'

'Pure jealousy, you mean? H'm. I suppose that can lead even to murder.'

'Good heavens, if they get to that stage, Rumbelow really will be in his element.'

Something that had been puzzling Sir George for most of the conversation clarified itself in his mind. Bantrell's angered sentences had a Teutonic ring to them. He remembered his mother, the countess. Perhaps the idea of a duel wasn't so outlandish after all. He understood the accepted way of settling such differences at Heidelburg was with rapiers. It would certainly save them all a good deal of trouble, particularly if they succeeded in cutting each other's throats.

36

AT MORTLOCK, RUMBELOW thought Peter Ivors to be growing more and unnecessarily pessimistic.

'It's all starting to look rather tenuous. It was a mistake to
call that maidservant girl this morning, for a start. She was far
too frightened or too dim-witted to be the slightest use.'

'Her evidence was somewhat contradictory, certainly.'

'God, it was incoherent!' Ivors took a sip of beer. They were
lunching off overdone chops in the dining-room of the Red
Lion, which contained more palms in pots and large sepia prints
of defiant stags and lank-haired Highland cattle. It was the
Wednesday, the third day of the trial. 'I've been through this
experience before. You have a case which seems absolutely cast-
iron, then you come into court and it melts like ice. I don't
know why it happens. I suppose you get into a certain frame of
mind when you read the witnesses' proofs. Once they stand up
in the box, nothing seems to mean quite the same.'

'I hope I pitched my own voice at the right level?' asked
Rumbelow, taking this as a personal slight. He had succeeded
the maid, Ivors completing his examination-in-chief before a
delayed lunch adjournment. As the jury consisted of three fruit-
farmers, two shopkeepers, an accountant, a local government
official, the housewife, and four describing themselves with
serene baldness as 'gentlemen', Rumbelow had assumed them
reasonably intelligent.

'Don't worry, you sounded like a lecture to a Rotarian
luncheon. But I do wish you'd get out of your head, John, that
every murder trial is decided solely on the medical evidence.'

'This one will be.'

'Will it? Well, in another couple of days perhaps we'll find out.'

'Surely you're not really worried the jury's going to acquit her?'

'Frankly, I think there's a perfectly good chance.'

Rumbelow made no comment. Perhaps Ivors had passed his best, he thought, was 'losing his grip', as the Americans said. If they lost the case, it would certainly be Ivors' fault, not his own. He turned the conversation to the quality of the local apples, a topic they self-consciously stuck to until the end of the meal.

When the court reassembled, Rumbelow resumed his place under the wooden umbrella of the witness-box. It was Sir Arthur Younghusband's time to attack.

'Dr Rumbelow, what is the normal content of arsenic in the human body?'

'Nil.'

'You are aware, are you not, that other forensic medicine authorities believe arsenic to be a normal constituent of us all?'

'They are incorrect. They are not responsible authorities.' *That's* a hare shot long ago, Rumbelow thought. But his surprise at Younghusband's trying it on was mingled with wariness of some motive behind the question.

'Would you agree that these authorities maintain that an exhumed body can be contaminated by arsenic? From the soil of the grave, the burial garments, even from the coffin?'

'Yes. But those are other, recognized authorities. I examined the articles you refer to, and found no arsenic. Nor in Mr Jeavons' medicine glass, his tonic medicine, nor in various household articles passed to me by Superintendent Sixsmith.'

'You put the fatal dose of arsenic as two grains. Is that not low?'

'It is low. But Mr Jeavons suffered from a weak heart. Two grains would be fatal.'

'Were you surprised that before death he did not show the classical signs of acute arsenic poisoning?'

'He *did* show the classical signs of acute arsenic poisoning.

These are of two main forms. Jeavons exhibited the form marked by sudden collapse. I would expect as much from the diseased condition of the heart. And from a highly soluble type of arsenic being absorbed rapidly and completely from the stomach.'

'Surely you would not expect it to be absorbed elsewhere than from the stomach?'

Rumbelow decided to counter this sarcasm. 'Fatalities have occurred from its absorption by the rectum, the female vagina, and the lungs – out East there exist "death lamps", their wicks impregnated with arsenic.'

'We are in Mortlock, not Baghdad,' said the judge.

'Yet you found no arsenic whatever in the stomach, only in the liver and kidneys?'

'Yes.'

'In equal or differing amounts?'

'Equal.'

'And none in the "keratin" tissues, the hair and nails?'

'I would expect to only in a person living at least five days after absorbing the poison. Arsenic is stored in these tissues only because they have no blood-supply to remove it, and grow slowly – point-four of a millimetre a day in the case of hair, point-one for the nails.'

Which shows I know what I'm talking about, Rumbelow thought.

'You say you tested chemically for arsenic by the Marsh and Reinsch processes. Will you please describe these to the jury?'

Rumbelow took some time, simplifying the technicalities for the fruit-growers and the gentlemen. Sir Arthur tried to make a point. After five months' burial the organs had so degenerated that the Marsh test – the positive one – was of doubtful value.

'Arsenic is well known to preserve the liver and kidney,' Rumbelow told him.

'You say that Mr Jeavons suffered from syphilis. At the post-mortem, did you examine the meningeal membranes surrounding the brain?'

'I did.'

'Were they normal? Not thickened, with adhesions?'

249

'They were normal.'

'Did the brain itself show atrophy of the convolutions?'

'No.'

'There was not, then, any sign of syphilis affecting the brain and its membranes, as you might expect to accompany its affecting the heart? Had there been, might he have suffered from mental symptoms – depression, a tendency to suicide?'

'Had there been,' Rumbelow repeated.

'Dr Rumbelow, did you examine the brain under the microscope?'

'No.'

'So that syphilis of the brain, with the tendency to suicide I mentioned, might after all have been present?'

'It might.'

That's unfortunate, Rumbelow thought. He's raised the possibility of suicide and dented my reputation in the same breath. I should have sectioned that brain. He searched his mind for someone to blame, and decided it was Dr Halverston's distracting him with quarrelsomeness.

'Mr Jeavons might have been receiving treatment by arsenic for syphilis, might he not?'

Rumbelow was ready for this. The defence must try to get their kite in the air somehow. 'There was no evidence of any medical man treating him. It would in any case be a different sort of arsenic.'

'Let us leave aside your negative assumption about treatment. The drug injected would have been of the "salvarsan" or "606" type, would it not?'

'Yes.'

'Would you explain the difference between "salvarsan" and poisonous arsenic?'

'Therapeutic arsenic is a combination of arsenious acid and aniline. The correct name for salvarsan is dioxydiaminoarsenobenzol dihydrochloride. It is perhaps enough to say that it contains thirty per cent of arsenic, and must be stored in sealed ampoules with an inert gas, to prevent its becoming poisonous under the influence of atmospheric oxygen.'

'Is it completely free of danger?' asked the judge.

'No, my Lord. Even normal doses can have a toxic effect on the heart and liver.'

Sir Arthur resumed. 'Would the "safe" arsenic give the same results in the tests you described as the poisonous sort?'

'No. The safe arsenic is a far more complicated substance.' This had been his object in reciting the long chemical name. 'The tests would react anomalously.'

'Did you perform the Fresenius test, a specific one for this safe arsenic?'

'I did. It was negative.'

'Are you aware that other authorities – other, recognized authorities – regard this test as inconclusive?'

'I am.' He studied Sir Arthur's face. Then he added, 'I also did the Vitali test, on an extract of acidified, dried, minced tissue. Though complicated to perform, it is accepted as reliable. It was negative.'

'What happens to this safe arsenic in the body?'

'It is stored for some days in the same way as ordinary poisonous arsenic. It is excreted in the urine, bile, and faeces.'

'Let us return to the Marsh and Reinsch tests. You say the safe arsenic would give an anomalous result. Could that expression include a positive result – as for poisonous arsenic – with the safe arsenic?'

'That is a possibility.'

'A possibility you had in mind while performing the tests?'

'Yes.'

'So that, while the Marsh and Reinsch tests might not definitely tell you there was safe arsenic present, a positive reaction might *not* indicate the certain presence of poisonous arsenic?'

'Only if the patient had in fact been receiving arsenical treatment.'

'We will continue to leave that question aside. Would you expect to find traces of the safe arsenic in the kidney and the liver?'

'Yes.'

'In which of the two organs would it predominate?'

'In neither.'

'In which organ would you expect poisonous arsenic to predominate?'

'In the liver.'

'Yet in this particular case you found arsenic in kidney and liver in equal amounts?'

'That is so,' Rumbelow admitted.

'Thank you, Dr Rumbelow.'

He made to leave the witness-box, but the judge stopped him. 'One moment, Doctor. Had Mr Jeavons been undergoing treatment with these arsenical preparations, for how long afterwards would arsenic be detectable in his body?'

'Two weeks.'

'You told us a good deal about your analysis. This confirmed a suspicion – you put it to Mr Ivors as no stronger than a suspicion – which came to your mind at the post-mortem examination. But what made you think of arsenic at all?'

'I always think of arsenic, my Lord.'

'Why do you?'

'Despite the Arsenic Act of 1851, it is easy to obtain. It is easy to administer. And it mimics everyday illness. It is the poisoner's friend.'

'So you are telling the court that many poisoners with arsenic go undetected?'

'Yes. But not if I am performing the post-mortem.'

With a small gesture of a skinny hand, the judge dismissed him.

'I wish you hadn't made that last remark,' whispered Peter Ivors as Rumbelow resumed his seat.

Ivors is quite rattled, Rumbelow thought. Yes, he is definitely losing his grip.

37

AFTER SIR ARTHUR YOUNGHUSBAND'S opening speech for the defence the following morning, the first witness was that brought with much trouble and cost from Singapore. Dr McInch was thin, bent and birdlike, with a white cropped moustache; his tanned skin, his not quite correctly cut suit and his air of self-justification marking him as a colonial newly returned 'home'.

'When did you first meet Mr Jeavons?' Sir Arthur asked.

'After the War, sir.' He still had a Scottish accent, and reminded Rumbelow of Urrick. 'When he came to live in the Colony.'

'Your relationship to him was simply that of doctor and patient?'

'Not at all. We enjoyed a considerable intimacy.'

'What was your opinion of him?'

'He was a fine man, sir. In every sense. That's all I need say, isn't it?'

'It is more customary for counsel to ask the questions, not his witness,' murmured the judge.

'Did you ever treat him for a syphilitic infection?'

'I did. It was in 1919. He suffered a primary chancre on the genitals. It was contracted from a native.' His air suggested that in such circumstances the disease was a matter to be expected, and hardly counted against anyone. 'I treated it by injections of salvarsan. With complete success. Syphilis is one of the few diseases we can cure, you know. It is very remarkable. Nobody thinks of that.'

'When was the last injection?'

'Before he sailed for home in 1933. I had thought it wise to continue treatment, an injection every six weeks, as a precaution.' That's ridiculous, thought Rumbelow. Quite unnecessary. Though I suppose he wanted to keep up the fees.

'Did you then give Mr Jeavons advice of a personal rather than medical nature?'

Dr McInch hesitated. 'Do you want me to start at the beginning? I've forgotten what I'm supposed to tell you.'

'Perhaps you might help the witness by rephrasing your question,' suggested the judge.

'Did you discuss his relations with the other sex?'

The doctor looked relieved, picking up the thread. 'After his infection, he swore he would never go again with a native. Or any woman at all. I was very familiar with such a reaction. But with a man like James Jeavons, I felt he meant it. Well, perhaps he did not keep to it – we are human. But before he left for home he said to me, "Jim, you tell me I'm completely cured." I remember it exactly like yesterday, we were sitting on the verandah of my house at sundown. "That is correct," I said. "I'm no danger to anybody?" he asked. Then he asked me outright if it were allowable for him to take a wife. I reassured him, though I was surprised, sir, very surprised. He was not in the first flush of youth, and was regarded in the Colony as a confirmed bachelor.'

'Did he ask your advice specifically on whether he should reveal his medical history to the woman of his eventual choice?'

'He did. I recommended silence. Least said soonest mended.'

'Wasn't that somewhat irresponsible advice?' asked the judge. The doctor looked startled at such wisdom being questioned.

'Of the arsenic you injected, every six weeks until 1933,' Sir Arthur went on, 'would any trace remain in Mr Jeavons' body on the morning of December the second last?'

'It would. That is how the cure is effected, by arsenic remaining in the body. It could remain for several years.'

Rumbelow had been listening with rising irritation. He scribbled a note to Peter Ivors, *This man is an ass. His treatment is wrong. His pharmacology is wrong. He knows nothing.*

With this paper in his hand, Ivors rose for cross-examination. 'Dr McInch, how old are you?'

'Seventy-six.'

'When did you qualify?'

'The date was 1883.'

'When did you go to Singapore?'

'In 1885.'

'Have you returned to your university, or to any medical centre since then?'

'I have never left the Straits Settlements. I am happy there, sir. I shall die there. I didn't want to come home on this occasion, but I had to.'

'How have you kept yourself abreast of medical progress since 1885?'

'I read books,' said the doctor vaguely.

He was followed by Dr Halverston, who gave most of his evidence to Sir Arthur while glaring at Rumbelow. He stuck tightly to a slightly adapted theory – that Jeavons died from heart-failure, caused by high blood-pressure and an old, ill-treated syphilitic infection. When it was Peter Ivors' turn, he asked, 'What is your opinion of the accused, Dr Halverston?'

'I have the greatest admiration for her.'

'Would you do everything in your power to help her in her present predicament?'

'I wouldn't commit perjury, if that's what you mean.'

Ivors sat down. Dr Halverston looked round, staying in the witness-box, unable to believe his contribution to the drama already over. He was replaced by an analytical chemist from Cardiff, the nearest university, to whom Rumbelow had sent specimens of Jeavons' organs. He told Sir Arthur that he found no arsenic at all. Peter Ivors pressed him strongly on his lack of medical qualifications and of experience in investigating cases of suspected arsenic poisoning. The chemist agreed he was more at home analysing water supplies and the atmosphere of Welsh coal-mines than fragments of the human body. The defence were prepared to see their witness discredited. But they had no one better to call. There was only one expert in such things, and that was Rumbelow. There was always Urrick north of the border, of course, but the suggestion had only caused Sir Arthur to shiver.

Then came Stella Jeavons.

She disappeared from the dock, re-entered through a side-door, and took her place under the wooden umbrella. The wardresses had seats almost out of sight. She stood with her hands folded on the edge of the witness-box, looking composed.

'Mrs Jeavons,' began Sir Arthur, 'did you kill your husband?'

'No, no. I did not. It's inconceivable.'

'Will you indicate to us the general early-morning routine of your husband and yourself?'

She seemed relieved to find herself facing familiar innocuous domestic things. 'I would get up about seven. The maid wouldn't have arrived from the village then, so I made the tea in the kitchen and poured out his medicine. He liked to have it every morning, first thing. I would take it up on the tea-tray to our bedroom.'

'You shared the same bed?'

'Yes.'

'What differences were there on the morning of your husband's death?'

'He was asleep when I went downstairs. I knew he wasn't well. He'd been terribly restless during the night, and had got up to be sick. I thought it was something which had upset him at dinner. When I came back with the tray he was awake, and complained he felt very unwell. I could see he wasn't breathing properly, and he was a bad colour. I was very worried.'

'He took the medicine?'

'Yes. He didn't want any tea.'

'What did you do then?'

'I telephoned Dr Halverston.'

'What did you do with the medicine glass?'

'I rinsed it out and put it back in the kitchen cupboard.'

'You always did that?'

'Yes.'

'Mrs Jeavons, you heard Mr Fitt say that on two occasions in that bedroom, during your husband's absence, you had sexual intercourse with him. Is this correct?'

'It is correct.'

Sir Arthur spent some while trying to establish it was at Terry Fitt's urging, that he forced himself upon her. But it was an unconvincing effort. Six of one, half a dozen of the other, as Ivors had said, Rumbelow decided.

'Were you happy with your husband?'

'That's a difficult question to answer.'

'Please do your best.'

'Perhaps I should say it's a complicated question to answer.'

'Would you like to present your witness with specific points?' remarked the judge. 'We all know that human happiness is really a highly complicated affair.'

'What were your sexual relations with your husband?'

'Almost non-existent.'

'Did you foresee the risk of this, when agreeing to marry a man so much older?'

'I didn't think about it. I suppose I assumed everything would be all right.'

'Apart from this, were you normally fond of your husband?'

'Yes, I was.'

'You met on an ocean liner, and married after what I suppose we could term a "shipboard romance". Did these conditions influence your choice?'

'Not in the slightest.' Her voice sounded firmer. 'I was attracted to him because he was older and more experienced. Ready to settle down. That's what I wanted. I'd had plenty of the other.'

'What other?' asked the judge.

'Well . . . gadding about.'

'You asked Mr Fitt to buy some insecticide for the fruit-trees in your garden. What decided you to do this?'

'I met someone in a shop in the village. She said the trees had been neglected for years. She was a farmer's wife, so I supposed she knew what she was talking about.'

Sir Arthur picked up the insecticide tin. He started a delicate line of questioning about the fate of its contents. She had seen it only once before her husband's death, she told him, the morning Terry Fitt bought it. She saw from the label it was

257

poisonous, but she did not know it contained arsenic. After her husband's funeral, when the village was humming with gossip, she remembered it. She found it in the garden shed and threw the powder away, sprinkling it on some garbage in a corner of the garden. She had done it on an impulse, because she was badly frightened. If everyone was saying she'd murdered her husband, it would never do to have poison about the house. She was already terrified the police might call. And when shortly afterwards they did, she could hardly tell of her action without seeming to damn herself. Sir Arthur brought out the story as a chain of perfectly natural acts, prompted by worry and alarm from the wholly undeserved maliciousness of her neighbours, and calling only for the jury's sympathy.

'You didn't even bother to dispose of the tin?'

'I put it back among all the other odds and ends you collect in garden sheds.'

'Why did your husband go regularly to London?'

'On business.'

'What sort of business?'

'He never said exactly. I supposed it was to do with his old business in Singapore.'

'How often did he go?'

'It varied, but I suppose about once every six weeks.'

'How long before his death was his last visit?'

She thought for a moment. 'I'd say about ten days.'

So they're trying to establish he went on with his injections, and arsenic from the last one would still be in his dead body, Rumbelow thought. But who gave him them? The case has had publicity enough, and no doctor's come forward. No, it won't wash, not with Easterbrook.

Stella Jeavons replied to Peter Ivors' opening question, 'Did you not, last December, feel you had made a grave mistake in marrying James Jeavons?' with a spirited, 'Certainly not!'

'We have heard from your paramour, Terry Fitt, that he was never in love with you. What is your opinion of that?'

'He *was* in love with me. He was absolutely infatuated.'

'You liked the idea of that?'

She gave a small shrug. 'It was flattering, I suppose.'

258

'It was all part of the "gadding about" you mentioned in reply to his Lordship?'

'No. That was something in my past.'

'Then you were in love with Terry Fitt?'

'I definitely was not.'

'You let him come to bed with you although you were not in love with him? That is "gadding about", surely?' She said nothing. 'From what you have both said under oath, you enjoyed sexual intercourse though neither of you cared tuppence about the other. That is a little unusual, is it not?'

Ivors waited patiently. 'I *was* in love with him.'

That's good, thought Rumbelow. There's her motive cut and dried. Perhaps Ivors isn't losing his grip, after all.

'On the morning of your husband's death, you could count on being alone in the kitchen until the maid arrived at eight o'clock?'

'It was the same every morning.'

'Why was your husband's medicine kept in the kitchen cupboard?'

'It was more convenient, because I brought it up with the tea.'

'What time did you telephone Dr Halverston?'

'It must have been shortly after seven o'clock.'

'Dr Halverston told my learned friend it was after eight. The maid said she heard you telephoning as she walked into the house.' It was the only concrete evidence Ivors had been able to extract from the girl. 'She was not early that particular day?'

'It was a very confusing morning.'

'I'm sure it was one of great strain. But you waited a good hour until you telephoned? Until the dose had been absorbed? Until you had washed out the medicine glass?'

'I . . . I don't know exactly when I telephoned.'

'When did you first learn your husband had syphilis?'

'Before the inquest. Dr Halverston told me.'

'You mean, in the intimacy of marriage, in the intimacy of the marriage bed, your husband never confessed it to you?'

'Never.'

'Did you ever notice after his visits to London marks on his arms indicating that he had been given an injection?'

'I never looked. Why should I?'

'In the intimacy of marriage, it is unnecessary deliberately to look for such things, surely?'

'I couldn't go over him with a magnifying glass.'

'May I put it to you that you were perfectly aware of your husband's medical history, you were perfectly aware he was having arsenic injections, and you thought it a splendid chance to outwit the doctors who might have to examine his body?'

She shook her head, and abruptly started to sob. *That* scheme wouldn't be past the deviousness of poisoners, Rumbelow thought, particularly female ones. When she recovered, Ivors continued, 'Do you recall accosting Dr Rumbelow outside Blackfriars Hospital in London?'

'That was very stupid of me.'

'Were you afraid that Dr Rumbelow would find arsenic in your husband's body?'

'No, no. . . .'

'Then if you had nothing to fear, why did you take the trouble of travelling to London and bearding him in the street?'

Rumbelow noticed how tightly she was grasping a tiny handkerchief between the fingers of both hands. 'I was afraid that Dr Rumbelow might find something, even if nothing was there.'

'That is rather strange, is it not? You knew that Dr Rumbelow was the leading – one of the leading —' he corrected himself, glancing at the judge, '— forensic medical experts in the country. Would you expect him, of all people, to find something which wasn't there?'

'He always seems to find something.'

'But only if there is something to find?'

The judge intervened. 'Mrs Jeavons, did you wish to protest your innocence to Dr Rumbelow in the same way as to Superintendent Sixsmith? Did you regard him as part of the police force, intent on securing your arrest and conviction?'

'That's what he is, isn't he?'

The judge gave a nod. Ivors went on, 'You would seem to be

a little confused over Dr Rumbelow's official position. But could you possibly believe that any man – particularly a medical man of high reputation, bound by a strict ethical code – would lie under oath simply to see you convicted of a crime you did not commit?'

'I don't know.' Now she sounded helpless.

'Did your husband ever talk of suicide?'

'He got depressed sometimes.'

'But did he talk of suicide?'

'I can't remember.'

Ivors sat down. The judge looked at the clock. 'The court will adjourn. I expect to complete my summing-up, after the closing speeches of counsel, by tomorrow afternoon.'

So early tomorrow evening we shall know, Rumbelow thought. A jury with four gentlemen on it will not go overlong without its dinner.

38

RUMBELOW ARRIVED AT the Shire Hall the following morning
to be greeted by Hugo Kirkpatrick, the American journalist he
remembered meeting at Mrs Mavery's the previous spring.
'Hello there, Doctor! I'm taking bets. Would you like some
money on the verdict?'

'I don't think that would be at all proper.'

'I'm offering six to four on an acquittal.'

'That's favourable to Mrs Jeavons, isn't it?' Rumbelow's
knowledge of such things had not widened since the Derby.

'Very favourable.'

'You've come to cover the trial?' He was flattered at the
international interest.

'I'm taking in the last day of it. It's great value. Any number
of overtones. This Terry Fitt – it's straight out of *Lady Chatterley's
Lover*, very fundamental in understanding the British psychology. I hope you've read the book?' Rumbelow had never
heard of it. 'But there's another big story breaking. About your
King.'

'About the King? What about him? I've certainly heard
nothing.'

The journalist laughed. 'You will! You know Wallis
Simpson's divorce comes up at Ipswich Assizes next Tuesday?'

'I'm afraid the name means nothing to me.'

'She's going to marry the King.'

Rumbelow looked indignant. 'Surely you must be exaggerating? I haven't seen a word in the papers.'

'Of course you haven't. Your Press is muzzled.'

'I can hardly believe that. We're a free country.'

'Oh, sure. So's the United States. Every newspaper publisher's free – to write a headline or put a story on the spike and forget it.'

'I'm very much afraid you're simply wasting your time on a wild goose chase.'

'Would you like to bet on that, too?'

'How do you find Mortlock?'

'It's charming.'

'The local apples are very good.' Rumbelow moved away.

As the court resumed, Ivors rose to apply that Rumbelow might be recalled. The judge agreed, with testy reluctance.

'Dr Rumbelow —' They had rehearsed the exchange the evening before in the Red Lion. 'You heard Dr McInch say that arsenic used for medical treatment might still be found in the body several years afterwards. Do you agree or disagree with this?'

'I emphatically disagree.'

'Are you familiar with this paper by Chalmers Watson, published in the *Lancet* in April, 1922?' With foresight, Rumbelow had brought it among his documents for the trial.

'I am.'

'It says that arsenic may be found in the body fifteen months after such treatment. Do you agree or disagree with that?'

'I disagree. It is an overestimation. The findings have been confirmed neither by myself nor by any other scientific worker.'

Sir Arthur Younghusband offered no cross-examination. His closing speech for Mrs Jeavons relied mainly on the arsenic being injected as a drug, either on Jeavons' last visit to London or lingering from his treatment in Singapore. The alternative defence was of no arsenic being in the body at all. Peter Ivors felt that his opponent should have made more of this. But when Rumbelow said one thing, and another scientist – not even a qualified doctor – said the opposite, the jury knew who to believe.

The judge summed-up half the morning and all afternoon. As Rumbelow had come to expect, he warned the jury to choose impartially between the expert witnesses, not to be influenced over any opinion by its utterer's performance in other murder trials. They must decide if the dead man was secretly having injections of arsenic. 'From what hand?' the judge asked. 'The police, the Press, have all appealed for the doctor, if he exists, to come forward. You may think that a medical man, with a high sense of responsibility towards the community, would most certainly have responded and given evidence in this court.' They must decide, in any case, if there would still be traces of such arsenic in the body. They must rule out poisonous arsenic taken by accident, or for suicide. They must be sure beyond all reasonable doubt that Mrs Jeavons had access to arsenic, had the chance to administer it, and reason enough for doing so. They must think carefully about the timing of her telephone call to Dr Halverston, and about her disposing of the insecticide in the tin. If doubt remained in their minds, they must acquit.

'Pretty fair, I suppose,' said Ivors. He and Rumbelow left the court together as the jury filed out.

'What's the chances?' For the first time, Rumbelow sounded anxious.

'Were we in Scotland, I'd say she'd get away with "Not Proven". Like Madeleine Smith, you know, who gave arsenic to her lover.'

He nodded. 'Yes, she got it from fly-papers.'

'The result's pretty balanced, but . . . yes, I think she'll get off.'

'*Why* should she?' Rumbelow sounded annoyed. Ivors' pessimism had irritated him all week.

'She's pretty.'

'What's that got to do with it in the slightest?'

'Juries don't like hanging pretty girls.'

'They've their duty, haven't they? They've taken their oath.'

'It's just like you, thinking of it that way.'

'Why not? It's the right way. Our whole system of justice would break up if juries went by the prisoners' looks, or manners.'

'I'm sure you're quite right,' said Ivors.

Rumbelow felt a grasp on his shoulder. It was the American journalist again. 'Now I'm offering ten to one against a conviction.'

'I prefer not to bet on human life.'

'Well, you make a pretty steady living out of it,' the journalist told him amiably.

Rumbelow turned and strode down the steps into the street. It was chilly, and almost dark. He paced rapidly along the pavements, not knowing where he was going, taking no notice of his surroundings. The verdict was of enormous importance to him. Every verdict was. His reputation was at stake each time he stepped into a witness-box. Once juries started to disbelieve him, to accept the testimony of lesser men, he saw himself as finished. It was partly by chance, but mainly by desperate effort, he had created the Rumbelow known to the world, and that Rumbelow must not be destroyed. It was good to serve his country, to further the cause of justice. It was magnificent to be above ordinary men, to be the arbiter of their life and death. Only that gave his work, his whole existence, any point.

He found himself walking down a narrow street with blank-faced warehouses on one side, on the other railings enclosing some sort of park, which closer inspection through the darkness revealed as a cemetery. He was lost. He took out his brother's watch. As usual, he had noted precisely when the jury retired. He was surprised that half an hour had passed already. He was alarmed they would return in his absence. In the Armstrong case at Hereford in 1922, another of arsenic poisoning, the jury had been out for only fifty minutes. There was no one to help, only some children squabbling in the lamplit gutter. He tried to retrace his steps, after a while recognizing a landmark or two, hurrying at last, breathless, up the Shire Hall steps. The jury were still deliberating. There was no sign of Peter Ivors, who had probably calmly gone for a drink. Rumbelow stood in front of a board covered with municipal notices, pretending to read them, stuffing his hands in his pockets lest anyone noticed them trembling.

After the best part of half an hour there was a stir in the lobby. Someone said, 'They're coming back.' Another, 'They haven't been long – she's got off.' Rumbelow looked at his watch. Eighty-four minutes. It had no significance, except they had already made up their minds before entering the jury-room.

The court reassembled. Mrs Jeavons reappeared in the dock. The jury found her guilty. Everyone stood up. The judge pronounced the death sentence, one corner of the black cap slipping over his right eye, making him look a shade ridiculous. The sheriff's chaplain said 'Amen' very loudly. Rumbelow hurried from the court-room with hardly a word to Peter Ivors. He collected his bag from the hotel, caught the London express, and was at Paddington before ten. For once he took a taxi. He knew Maria would be at the flat. He hardly greeted her before fumbling with her clothes, pushing her back on the divan, pulling on his contraceptive, driving himself into her. It was a delicious break from tension, a celebration of unexpected triumph, a reward for his labours, for his skilled application of cold scientific knowledge, which had put the strained, blonde widow of Blayford into the condemned cell.

'John, darling,' Maria whispered. 'You were never so wonderful as tonight.'

39

ON THE MONDAY morning, Rumbelow went to Blackfriars. He made first for the committee-room to collect his accumulated letters. He was surprised to find Sir George Smallpenny there, heels on the fender as usual before the glowing coals. It was ten o'clock, when Rumbelow knew the gynaecologist took a ward-round.

'You seem to have cooked that lady's goose in Mortlock,' said Sir George by way of congratulations.

'It was a simple case really. My task was to demolish a lot of unnecessary complications raised by the defence. She should never have got away with it at the time. But the local doctor was incredibly incompetent.'

'I gather you imagined a good many of his patients had been murdered successfully.'

'Doctors never think of poison. Particularly arsenic.'

'Once the news got round, that village might have become a favourite spot to retire with your unwanted wife or rich uncle.' Sir George stared down at his spatted, highly-polished shoes. 'Crampers showed me your letter.'

In his elation over the Jeavons verdict, Rumbelow had almost forgotten it. 'Has he put it to the committee?'

'Not yet. We thought it only right that Bantrell should see it too. Bantrell was very upset, you know.'

'I'm not responsible for his feelings.'

'No, of course you're not.'

'You've seen the slides?'

Sir George nodded. 'So has Bantrell. May I be frank? I must say that we – all three of us – were not terribly convinced.'

Rumbelow put down his handful of letters. 'I'll go over the slides with you, if you like. They struck me as perfectly straightforward sections of adenoma. Surely you noticed the hyalinization? It's remarkably significant.'

'That might be an artefact.'

'It isn't.'

There was a silence. 'Very well, John. Let's leave the slides as an open question. We had a chat about the whole business last night in Crampers' house. The week-end gave us time to reflect, you know, and for Bantrell to calm down. We thought the best course all round would be for you to withdraw the letter. Then we can forget the whole unfortunate episode.'

'And you were deputed to waylay me this morning, to pass on the decision?' Sir George nodded. 'No, I shan't withdraw the letter. Bantrell has committed an offence.'

'Isn't that taking a somewhat legalistic view?'

'And isn't that the only possible one to take, when a man commits a crime of any sort?'

'True, true . . . but John! Aren't you being overzealous? Do try to see things in proportion. The child's dead. She would have died anyway, Crampers is perfectly certain that neither he nor any surgeon living could have excised that pancreatic tumour. If it existed,' Sir George added. 'The parents have dried their tears. To lose a young daughter is sad, but illness is no respecter of human feelings. So what's the odds, whatever diagnosis goes on the death certificate? It might make a minute dent in the Registrar-General's annual returns. But I for one am not particularly reverent about their statistical accuracy. And you must admit that Bantrell's diagnosis from the clinical signs is as admissible as your own from the post-mortem appearances.'

'That's something I won't admit.'

'John, you're being difficult.'

'Anyway, Bantrell should have signed the certificate himself. He's trying to hide behind his house-physician.'

'Now that's downright rubbish.' Sir George for once sounded bad-tempered. 'And you know it.'

'He was the physician in charge of the case.'

'If we all signed our bits of paper, work in the hospital would come to a stop.'

'I always sign mine.'

'I'm not going to argue on such equivocal points. Instead, let me give you a plain warning. Don't let that letter go to the committee. You'd only stir up a hornets' nest for yourself.'

Rumbelow was astounded. 'Why? I've nothing to fear. Nothing but Bantrell's tongue. That's not worth a second thought.'

'Then let me tell you something else. I'm sure you are quite unaware of it – you're always so terribly busy with so many different things outside – but you are not performing the duties for which you were appointed to this hospital.'

'Who has complained of that?' Rumbelow demanded angrily. 'Please tell me, here and now.'

'*I* am complaining, for one. You are supposed to be our medical school pathologist, but you teach no pathology. Our students' record in their exams is unimpressive, to say the least. You *do* little pathology, in the wider sense. You delegate or skimp the routine work from the wards. You do only the p.m.s, which interest you.'

'I should have imagined my work outside – which hardly escapes public notice – and my contribution to forensic medicine in general amply justify my appointment.'

'Your colleagues don't think so.'

'That's pure mean-mindedness.'

It was among the worst few minutes Sir George could remember in his life. And his seat was becoming uncomfortably hot. He moved away towards the window.

'Very well, I shall resign,' said Rumbelow.

'Oh, John! Please don't make the grand gesture. It's so unlike you.'

Rumbelow picked up his letters again. 'I shall resign. I don't need to bother with Blackfriars, if Blackfriars doesn't want me. I could get a consultant post tomorrow at any hospital I cared in London.'

'Why not meet Bantrell half-way? I've seen this sort of thing happen a dozen times. Men have the bitterest squabbles, but in a few years they're forgotten, the pair are the closest of colleagues. Look at old Crampers. He's crossed everyone at Blackfriars in his time, and today no one sits more firmly in our affections. And if you went elsewhere, would you be any the happier?'

'I could hardly be more wretched than you've made me feel this morning.'

'I do wish you would let me help you, rather than turning me into an enemy. Sleep on your decision, at least.'

'That's not necessary. My mind's made up. My resignation will be effective as from the end of this year.'

'It will take us much longer to appoint a successor, you know.'

'Quinley can be my successor. Everyone in the hospital wanted him to have that reader's job – everyone except me, it seems.'

I wonder, thought Sir George, if the fellow is really quite right in the head?

Rumbelow went immediately to his laboratory, to write a letter of resignation to Cramphorn as chairman of the committee. He had been neither impulsive nor dramatic, as Sir George had suspected. The letter was a deliberate act, the only one open to him – that wound from Sir George had been mortal to his self-esteem. Then he began to see it as a stroke of good fortune, a chance to break free of Bantrell and all the unappreciative men at Blackfriars with a few justified and righteous sentences. With his reputation high from the Jeavons case he would easily find another consultancy, to shine even more dazzlingly elsewhere. He left the letter on the committee-room table and walked out of the hospital. He had a word for no-one. He was determined never to set foot there again.

40

NOVEMBER WAS A misty month. On the sixth, the King drove
in State to open Parliament, and promised from the throne that
his Government would do all in its power to further the
appeasement of Europe.

Rumbelow kept his intention of not entering Blackfriars. He
had a handwritten letter of great charm and ingenuity from Sir
George, imploring him to reconsider a sudden decision, but he
ignored it. He made himself busier than ever in the public
mortuaries and coroners' courts. And with his usual energy, he
started angling for another post at once.

He found it a discouraging pastime. Two London hospitals
turned him down flat, if politely. Others were puzzlingly non-
committal. He supposed indignantly that gossip from Blackfriars had spread, that established pathologists had no relish
for an extra colleague who would reward a share of their duties
and laboratories only by eclipsing them. Well, he would bide
his time, Rumbelow decided. He knew two or three London
pathologists nearing retirement, and he would be accepted
more gratefully as a replacement than a supernumerary. He
would be settled all right in the end. The great Rumbelow on
the dole was unthinkable.

His irritations were sharpened by a resounding public outburst over the verdict at Mortlock. He had expected a good
deal of sentimental journalism, but it was galling to see the facts
so twisted almost to make him appear the murderer rather than
Mrs Jeavons. Another petition was organized. Public meetings
were held, one in Trafalgar Square, where he was disgusted to
hear the despised Dr Halverston had made a fiery speech against

him, hardly short of slander. He supposed the doctor was a pawn, moved by Labour politicians and similar agitators, the whole possibly a dark plot to upset the civilized running of the country. He became short-tempered with Maria. She didn't seem to understand what he was enduring, the troubles which had struck so suddenly and mysteriously after the greatest success of his career. She only wanted to go to bed, and to cook his dinner.

One morning while Rumbelow was dressing, a post-office boy knocked at his flat with a telegram saying Rosemary would arrive at St Pancras at noon the following day.

He spent the day in some confusion. He would have to see her. He didn't want her at the flat, that was Maria's territory. For the pair to mix even tangentially was distasteful to him. He had an inquest at twelve, but Carlow could be persuaded to change his cases round. He wondered why Rosemary had decided on the journey. It was plainly a sudden decision, or she would have written rather than telegraphed. It would be a painful meeting. Her presence alone would make him shameful about Maria. But it would have to be faced. He decided against a telegram confirming his meeting the train, as an unnecessary expense.

As Rosemary appeared walking towards the barrier, he was relieved that she carried no suitcase. They greeted each other civilly. He suggested lunch in the station buffet. They sat at a marble-topped table talking about the Jeavons case, which she had followed closely in the newspapers. He thought she was livelier than he remembered. She had put on a little weight, she was less peaky, quite good-looking in fact.

'I'm afraid I've an inquest at two-thirty,' he apologized. 'That had to be rearranged, as it is. I'd have made more time, but it was rather short notice.'

'I'm going back on the four-ten.'

'It's a long way for a short meeting.'

'I'm glad to get out of the house.'

'I suppose it's not very agreeable, living at home?'

'It never was, even before we were married. Perhaps it's worse now. My affairs are the main topic of conversation. My

272

father alternates between the I-told-you-so and the if-I-were-in-your-shoes approach. Both are unbearably irritating. But I'm only a stranger in the family. I always was to some extent, I think.'

Rumbelow was relieved to find her neither hostile nor plaintive. 'I heard you'd got a job.'

'Only temporary. A girl was in the san with TB. Now I'm one of the unemployed again.' He ordered some food. 'How is your flat?' she asked.

'It's convenient. I can look after myself.'

'But you have someone.'

'She doesn't stay all the time.' It sounds as though we're discussing the charwoman, he thought.

'Is she nice?'

'Yes.'

'What is she? Does she have to work?'

'She's an educated woman. She was a librarian at Blackfriars.'

'Well, I could hardly expect you to play the monk. In fairness, I couldn't have expected as much when we were still together. I wasn't any use in that respect. Though I tried. Honestly, I tried.' She might be excusing deficiencies in her cooking, he reflected. 'I always supposed you went with a lot of society women.'

'Only one.' Her expression didn't change. 'Are you annoyed, now you know?'

'Oh, no. Nor had I known at the time. If I didn't know about it, I wouldn't care. I often told myself as much. It's strange how your mind works.' The waitress put two plates of vivid green soup before them. 'I wouldn't mind again, you know. It's done us a lot of good, being apart this six months. There's nothing like distance to reveal the proper landscape of a marriage. If you had someone else, John – just for sexual purposes – I shouldn't be jealous, you know, not in the least. As long as I didn't actually see her.'

So she wants to come back. Rumbelow drank two mouthfuls of soup. He didn't know if he felt frightened, uncertain or quite pleased at the idea. 'I've sold the house.'

273

'We could find another.'

'That takes money.'

'We don't need anything pretentious.'

'But it would be a very . . . well, peculiar arrangement.'

'On the contrary, in my particular circumstances it would be a very natural one.'

'You haven't thought much about Maria – that's the lady's name. What about her feelings?'

'She could see as much of you as ever. Keep on your flat, if you can afford it. Why should I concern myself with her feelings more than that?'

'It's not the thing for a man in my position.'

'But it's going on all the time in society, isn't it?'

'I just don't think it would work.'

'You want to live with the girl?'

'No, not exactly. . . .' He didn't know what he did want. 'You've rather sprung this on me, Rosemary.'

'I certainly wasn't expecting an answer on the spot. Why don't we meet after a pause for reflection?' She took a small diary from her handbag. 'Today's the twelfth. How about December the twelfth? It's a Saturday.'

'All right. Though I may have to change it. I'm very occupied just now. I'm leaving Blackfriars for another hospital.'

She looked surprised. 'Which one?'

'One of two or three. Everything's a bit in the air at the moment.'

Rosemary replaced the diary, with a gesture so familiar to him, pushing back her fair hair. She smiled. It was pleasant being with her, he thought. 'Now we've completed our business, John, we've nothing else to talk about.'

'Talk about anything you like, I don't often enjoy an intelligent conversation with a woman.'

She laughed. 'Well! That's not very gallant towards your girl-friend.'

'Let's say you know me better than anyone else.'

'I do. Far better. But I wonder if that is really very much?'

'Perhaps not. Sometimes I fancy I don't know myself very perfectly.'

274

Suddenly the world looked brighter to Rumbelow. Yes, Rosemary would come back. They would find a house. He would enjoy her company, her cooking and sewing, her intellect. Maria would occupy the same position as at present. If Maria objected, if she ran away . . . well, that would be too bad, but it would save the expense of the flat. He would certainly be invited soon to join the staff of another hospital. A new post, perhaps a professorship, would justify himself in the eyes of the profession. And despite Dr Halverston, despite the speeches and signatures, he would justify himself in the eyes of the public the morning that they hanged Mrs Jeavons.

41

'WHY DO YOU tell me now? Why not before? Long before?'

Rumbelow paced angrily the confined space of his flat.

'I don't know . . . I didn't know . . . oh, I'm so muddled about everything.' In the solitary armchair Maria sat crying.

'Are you sure?' He grabbed her by the shoulders, making her gasp with fright. 'How long is it?'

'I can't remember exactly . . . two months.'

'Two months! Come on, pull yourself together. You must answer my questions. When did you last see anything? Two months ago, was it? About the middle of September? Nothing since? No bleeding at all?'

'No . . . nothing.'

'Have you been sick in the morning?'

'Yes. This last two weeks. I thought it was something I'd eaten.'

'God!' He released his grip, pushing her away from him. Perhaps it's only a trick, he thought, a trick to hold me. She had accused him of being cold and surly often enough since the morning he walked out of Blackfriars. But she sounded damnably genuine about the vomiting.

'I thought you'd taken precautions,' Maria reproached him, still crying.

'Precautions sometimes don't work. It's science, not magic. You should have taken some notice of that side of it, tried to understand the mechanism better. Then perhaps you wouldn't be in this state. It's your fault as much as mine.'

'How can I understand such things?'

'You ought to. You were supposed to be a university student.'

She screwed the handkerchief in her hand. 'I'm not. I never was going to a university. I couldn't have done it. I'm not all that brainy.'

'Then why did you say so?' he asked furiously.

'Oh, I don't know . . . working in the library, I suppose, I wanted to make out I was a bit cleverer.' She looked at him pitifully. 'We all like to do that, John, don't we?'

He turned away in disgust. She was nothing but a common little shopgirl. And she had trapped him. 'I'm not your first lover by a long way, am I?'

'How can you say that? You make me sound awful.'

'If you lied about the university, you probably lied about a hundred things.'

'John, John, why are you so angry with me? I've never done anything to hurt you.'

He stuck his hands in his pockets, staring down at her. 'Anyone else know of this?'

'My mum and dad. I told them this morning. I had to.'

'What did they say?'

'Mum said you must come and see her.'

'That's out of the question.'

'Others will get to know.'

'You're threatening me, are you? Public exposure, the shame of Dr Rumbelow? It's a good line. You'll get some money out of the newspapers.'

'I didn't say that. I didn't say it at all. I meant when I began to swell.'

This vision turned his mind towards the practical side of his troubles. 'Well, we don't even know it's happened. Not definitely. Women miss their periods for all sorts of reasons. Sometimes for no reason at all. You'll have to be examined by a doctor, one who specializes in these things.'

'Will you see my mum?'

He hesitated. 'Very well. Yes, it's only correct. Can she come here?'

'I'd rather you went to our house.'

'Oh, all right, all right. Anything you want.' He decided it would be less painful to get the interview over at once, before the pregnancy was confirmed by a gynaecologist. Then he wouldn't appear fully laden with guilt.

'Am I to have an abortion?'

'What put that idea in your head?'

'Well, what else? Do you want me to have the baby?'

'I told you, I'm not sure that you're having one.'

'*I*'m sure.'

When he took her to the Tube Station, holding her arm tightly, he said as they parted, 'Don't do anything stupid.'

'What do you mean?' She looked at him wide-eyed. 'Suicide, and that?'

'I said, don't do anything stupid.'

He walked away, sick at the idea of her killing herself, leaving a note, then an inquest with everything in the papers. As soon as he reached his flat, he rummaged in a drawer for the roadhouse bill and tore it to pieces.

He had agreed to call on her mother at four the following afternoon. The house was one of the semi-detached villas which had spread over London in the past five years – one gable, pebble-dash front, pocket-handkerchief garden, well-clipped privet hedge. Rumbelow pushed open the gate and strode resolutely up the front path. Maria herself answered the front door. She seemed delighted to see him.

He took off his overcoat. Maria led him into the front room. It had a beige carpet, pink wallpaper with white swans on it, an upright piano with a wireless-set on top, a pair of magenta armchairs and two wooden ones imported for the occasion. Mrs Osgood was fat with glasses, in a red woollen dress. Mr Osgood was small, moustached, nervous, in a blue suit that looked just out of the shop. There was bread-and-butter, a dish of raspberry jam, and an iced cake with walnuts on it. That they were turning it into a social occasion filled Rumbelow with nausea.

The mother beamed at him. 'I'm sure you'd care for a cup of tea while you're here, Dr Rumbelow.'

'I'd prefer not, thank you. But please take tea yourselves.'

'Where did you leave your car?'

'I came by Underground. I have no car.'

She looked disappointed. She's entertaining the most eminent visitor of her life, Rumbelow thought, and hoping for a Rolls-Royce outside the front door for an hour or so. As she went with Maria to fetch the tea-pot, the father said, 'I've read a lot about you in the papers.'

'Thank you.'

'That case you were in last month – that Mrs Jessop. Mind, I don't think she did it.'

'Don't you?'

'Everyone thinks the same, don't they?'

'I would have no idea.'

'I think the other fellow did it. The boy-friend.'

'Do you?'

'You must lead a very interesting life.'

'Not particularly.'

Mr Osgood looked lost, then taking a black briar from his jacket pocket began scraping it noisily with a penknife.

Only when the teacups were full and the first sips swallowed was the subject broached. 'I hear that my daughter's in trouble, Dr Rumbelow,' said the mother.

'She tells me she suspects she is pregnant. Though of course this may not be the case. The symptoms can occur from other causes, or for no physical cause at all. She will have to be examined by a specialist before we can be sure one way or another.'

The mother did not seem to hear this. 'And you're the father,' she said, in a complimentary tone.

Rumbelow winced. For the first time he saw Maria with a bouncy baby, the product not of himself but of them both. A horrible prospect.

'So what do you intend to do about it? As her mother, I'm entitled to ask.'

'You are perfectly entitled to.'

'Well . . . what, then?'

'What would you expect me to do?'

'I should expect you to marry Maria.'

'But I have a wife already. You've known that, haven't you, Maria, all along?'

279

Maria had been sitting in silence, but eating the walnut cake. 'You said you were getting a divorce, John.'

'That takes time.'

'With money you can do anything,' said the father, but nobody took any notice.

'My wife may not wish to divorce me. As the law stands, I could go no further.'

'If you love Maria, I'm sure you'll do everything to persuade her,' said the mother.

'I might add that I've already made my wife aware of Maria's existence.'

'Then we shall have a doctor in the family.' The mother's eyes twinkled. 'The famous Dr Rumbelow! Never did I think of it, when I read about you in the papers. Mind, there's a discrepancy in ages. But the older man often makes the more satisfactory husband, don't you think?'

Rumbelow could endure no more. He stood up. 'I'm afraid this must be a short visit. As you know, I'm an extremely busy man. Can Maria be at my flat by ten tomorrow morning? I'm arranging for the specialist to see her. She will have to make some excuse at her work.'

'She's had to give her job up, of course. Before the other girls could begin to notice.' Something else to lay at my door, Rumbelow thought. 'I know I can rely on you to do the right thing by her. Don't forget, Maria's our only child.'

Rumbelow was already moving towards the door. The father came quickly across the room to cut him off. He halted, for the second alarmed of being kept prisoner, or even of outright assault. He saw a slip of blank paper in the man's hand. 'What's this for?'

'Your autograph.' Rumbelow obliged by scribbling. 'They won't half sit up tonight, when I pass it round the local.'

42

RUMBELOW WAS WAITING in his flat for Maria the following morning when the telephone rang.

'Hello? What's happened?'

The shock of the last two days had upset the precise mechanism of Rumbelow's mind. The enmeshed cogs of fact and logic which drove him were so loosened that he had already embarked on a plan inconceivable in his normal state, horridly repellent. And he had begun to imagine things. The call might have been telling of Maria's suicide, or that her mother forbade her to come – or more happily that she had aborted spontaneously.

'Dr Rumbelow? It's Major Standring here.'

With an effort, Rumbelow made some civil acknowledgement.

'I've persuaded the R.A.F. to lay on another show for us, Doctor. I've completely redesigned those shelters. It was quite wrong having them circular. Lozenge-shaped would be more blast-resistant. There'd be no difficulty over getting our hands on another couple of bodies. I wondered if you'd a day free at the beginning of next month?'

'I'm afraid that's impossible. I'm very busy. I should need at least three months' notice.'

The major sounded sadly disappointed. 'Sorry about that. Of course, the days are short this time of the year, but we could get the job done if we started early enough. I was rather keen to see the structures tested.'

'The war isn't going to start before Christmas.'

'One can't be sure of anything these days.'

Rumbelow promised to telephone in three weeks and rang off.

Maria arrived promptly at ten. He was ready in his fur-collared overcoat and bowler hat. Without inviting her in, he took her elbow and hurried her back towards the lift.

'Where are we going?' She looked at him anxiously as they went down.

'You know. To a specialist.'

'Will I be hurt?'

'Of course you won't.'

She said nothing more until they were walking out of the block. 'You're not going to marry me, are you?'

'That's out of the question. Be reasonable about it, please. It would be a complete failure, right from the start. I don't want to spend the rest of my life in misery, even if you do.'

'What will my mum think?'

'I choose to leave her out of my calculations. It's you and I in this mess, not her.'

'Then if you don't want to stay with me, what about the baby?'

'I'll make all provision for it, all that's right and proper. It's not impossible to have it adopted.'

'You don't think about me, do you? I don't want it. No more than you do.'

'If you're still thinking of an abortion, that's against the law.'

She made a slight expression of contempt. 'Perhaps it is. But lots of girls have them. A girl in the shop had one, while I was there.'

He stopped, giving her a hard look. 'If in some way that could be arranged ... you'd agree to it?'

'Yes. I always thought it would come to that.'

'Do you know what it involves? There are risks.'

'It's better than having a baby.'

'And risks for me, as well. It would be my ruin, were anything to come out.'

'You thought it would come to that, too, didn't you?'

'In this situation, one must think of everything. I'm still

282

worried lest you'd refuse to go through with it, when you were actually faced with the prospect.'

'I'd go through with it. You can rely on that.'

He felt a little easier. He had dominated her. His resolve even to break the law to rid them of this problem had steeled her. He did not see that only her own resolution, her own screwed-up courage, carried along the pair of them.

'What doctor am I seeing?'

'I told you. A specialist.'

'That's only to find if I'm pregnant?'

'Oh, I don't think there's any doubt about that.' He hailed a taxi. It was a desperate morning.

The consulting rooms were as Rumbelow expected, smartly furnished with bowls of flowers everywhere. A woman in a starched white overall opened the door. He said, 'I made an appointment with Dr Elgin over the telephone last night.'

'Oh, yes, Dr Rumbelow.'

Elgin had shown no surprise at his requesting a consultation 'for a friend'. He only implied that Rumbelow was favoured in being granted his appointment at such short notice. Rumbelow had first thought of telephoning Sir George Smallpenny, throwing himself on the gynaecologist's mercy. But he knew that Sir George would never perform an abortion, however much he cared to help Rumbelow out, and it would have ended merely as an embarrassing encounter for both of them. After his call to Elgin, Rumbelow had to make for the bathroom of his flat to be sick.

In the consulting-room, Elgin rose to shake his hand affably. They might have met before only at some social occasion. All three sat down. 'This young lady believes herself to be pregnant,' Rumbelow began.

'How long?'

'Two months.'

'That should be simple to discover clinically. We've no need to resort to this new-fangled business of frogs and toads.' Elgin pressed a button on the desk. 'Perhaps she would step behind the screen in the corner with my nurse.'

Rumbelow returned to the waiting-room. He sat impassively,

K   283

still in his overcoat, bowler hat on his knee. Three other patients arrived, one an elderly woman, two young, all smartly dressed. He wondered if any of them recognized him. He became suddenly overwhelmed at what he was doing, and sweat sprung abruptly from his palms. He was about to break the law. But unthinkable misfortune can push a man into unthinkable acts. It was twenty minutes before the nurse opened the consulting-room door to call his name. Elgin was behind the desk, smiling. Maria sat again in her chair, her back straight.

'Well?'

'Two months gravid, as you suggested.'

'Beyond doubt?'

'I can certainly seek a second opinion, if you wish.'

'I see.' Rumbelow remained standing, clutching his bowler. 'I needn't go into the circumstances. They must be obvious to a man of your experience.' Elgin inclined his head, graciously accepting the compliment. 'My next question must be equally well expected.'

'I don't think so.'

Rumbelow made an impatient gesture. 'We're after an abortion.'

'Really?' Still smiling, Elgin raised his thick eyebrows. 'Well, you're frank about it. I suppose between a pair of medical men that's quite reasonable.'

'Will you do it?'

'My dear fellow! You're inviting me to perform a criminal act.'

'I'm no *agent provocateur*, you know. This is a genuine misfortune. I need your help.'

'Oh, your official position is far too elevated to be turned into such a menial capacity. I've had them here, you know. Policewomen with heart-rending stories. Some of them genuinely pregnant. I don't know if Scotland Yard arranged for the condition deliberately, with its customary zeal.'

'Please stop playing with me, Elgin. You don't imagine, surely, I came here today imagining you'd simply overlook that case at the Old Bailey? In fact, I doubted if you'd even see me. But you must realize – you *do* realize – that prosecution had no connexion with myself personally. I was merely the expert witness for the Crown. I had to perform my duty, just as any other citizen must do his duty to his country. Anyway, you can have few complaints, as you got off.'

'I will ignore that surprising last sentence. It is perhaps understandable from your long association with the mentality of the law. But I don't think you're being very frank, Rumbelow. I know perfectly well you've been after my blood for years. "Gunning for me", as the gangsters say in Chicago. That's the case, isn't it?' Rumbelow saw he was getting nowhere. 'In the first place, I can't understand how you had it in your head that I performed illegal operations.'

'The whole of London knows it.'

'A very imprecise accusation for one so trained in the rules of evidence.'

'Let's not beat about the bush. Listen, Elgin. I'm not rich, but everything I own is at the disposal of this present emergency. I know your fees are high. I'm prepared to offer double.'

'You do seem to think I'm a mercenary sort of chap.'

'Well, if you won't do it, who will?' Rumbelow asked angrily.

'I have no idea. I know no abortionists. I don't move in shady circles. I should have imagined you yourself would have compiled quite a list. But perhaps you don't regard them as at all reliable.' Elgin stood up. 'Rumbelow, long before we faced one another in court I regarded you as conceited, self-centred, ruthless, pushful and unfeeling. Now I know that I was wrong. You are simply an enormous fool. To have come to me like this, with this unfortunate young lady, indicates that quite plainly. Or you have the hide of a rhinoceros, and you're so wrapped up in yourself you don't trouble what other people might think of you. Or you've just gone out of your mind. No, I think it more likely you're a fool.' Rumbelow pulled Maria to her feet. 'My receptionist will show you out. The fee for the consultation will be two guineas. It is customary to pay her before leaving.'

'What are we going to do now?' asked Maria on the pavement.

'I haven't the first idea,' Rumbelow told her.

43

BEFORE THEY STARTED their dinner, Rumbelow had confessed the whole story to Norman Carlow. The coroner listened in silence, his usual jollity leaving him. From the urgency of Rumbelow's voice on the telephone, he had supposed his trouble something to do with Rosemary. A meeting would be inconvenient, he had another appointment, but Rumbelow persuaded him to put this off. Well, he would sting old John for a good meal at the club, at any rate, Carlow decided. No halves of indifferent claret, but something chateau-bottled with liqueur brandy to follow.

'This is a serious matter, John.'

'There's no need to tell me, of all people.'

'When did you see this Elgin fellow?'

'This morning. About ten o'clock.'

'That must have been a terrible experience for you, in itself.'

'It wasn't pleasant. I was prepared for some humiliation. I was not prepared for its having such an agonizing effect on me.'

'No, you'd be something of a stranger to such feelings.' The waiter set a dish of a dozen Whitstable oysters in front of them both. 'But you've no business whatever to be in that *galère.*'

'What option had I? The whole episode – every aspect of it – simply fills me with horror. The thought of that common girl, with her common parents, having a child by *me*. Besides, there's Rosemary.'

'I thought you and she had parted brass-rags for good?'

'I want her back again.' Carlow was unable to stop himself looking half-exasperated and half-resigned. He turned to his

286

oysters. 'Rosemary's willing to come, you know. She suggested it herself. We could set up house again whenever we felt like it. We'd almost fixed a date, when this terrible thing happened. Oh, it's a nasty business. I hate talking about it, I hate even thinking about it. But it's happened to better men than me, hasn't it?' he added, trying to excuse himself.

'True, true. . . .'

'I know it's unfair of me, involving you in it. But who else could I turn to? Honestly, I'm badly rattled.'

'Anyone can see that.' Carlow swallowed two oysters in quick gulps of enjoyment. 'But you can't go breaking the law. Apart from anything else – apart from your own feelings – if it came out, that would be the finish of you.'

'I'm perfectly aware of it. But need anything come out? Hundreds and hundreds of such cases are performed in London every year, and the police never get to hear of them.'

'They'd hear of yours. You're not exactly the criminals' friend.' Rumbelow sat staring at the table. 'You're not eating your oysters.'

'I don't want any. You eat them.'

Carlow reached to remove a shell from Rumbelow's plate. 'You know, the law we live by is an odd instrument. A lot of it's world-wide – kill a man in Lucknow or in London, and you get the same desserts. A lot more is quite parochial. When it's legal to buy a drink or open a draper's shop, that sort of thing. Which includes your little trouble.' Rumbelow looked at him closely. 'Surely, John, you read the society papers? How the Honourable Flossie this-and-that has been over to Switzerland to have her appendix out, or some such twaddle. She always comes home with a great big smile on her face. They take a more tolerant view of a poor girl's plight out there.'

Rumbelow needed some moments adjusting himself to the idea. 'But how do you imagine I'm to get to Switzerland?' he asked shortly.

'It's not you needing the operation. Maria can go herself.'

'No, that's impossible.'

'Is it? She seemed a self-reliant young thing when I met her at the Derby.'

'But it's an enormous journey.'

'Not at all. You can go by the aeroplane now. I knew a fellow who did as much only last week.'

'That's terribly dangerous.'

'Not these days. No more than crossing Piccadilly Circus.'

Rumbelow remembered Graham Trevose, hopping in and out of aeroplanes without a second thought. 'It's enormously expensive.'

'You've got to decide if you think it worth the money or not, haven't you?' Carlow took another of Rumbelow's oysters.

'Who would she go to? I'd have to fix it all from London. I've not even the name of a gynaecologist in a remote place like that.'

'I think I might help you.' For the first time, a watery ray of hope shone on Rumbelow. 'I happen to have an address in Lausanne. One gets to know things, you understand. It's a clinic. Lausanne's only a short train ride from Geneva, where the aeroplane lands.'

There was a silence. Carlow went on eating the oysters.

'Should I do it?'

'I can't see you've any alternative.'

'Very well. Very well, I shall. Give me that address. I'll write straight away.'

'Why not telephone?'

'Someone official might be listening-in.'

'My dear John! Sometimes you're beyond me. This is London, not Rome or Berlin.'

'She may refuse to fly.'

'That's your look-out,' said Carlow, a little wearily.

The next week was one of feverish and alarming activity for Rumbelow. Maria agreed to go, surprisingly readily. She seemed simply excited at the prospect of a trip abroad, particularly by an aeroplane. A week's absence had somehow to be explained to her mother. She had pressed him to perform the duty himself, but he refused point-blank. Maria agreed to lie that they were going away together into the country. Rumbelow didn't imagine the mother would swallow it, but he heard nothing more. Perhaps she had a shrewd idea of what was up, he thought, as she'd had a shrewd idea about the fictitious week-ends in Brighton. She might be glad enough to see her daughter's condition righted, abandoning dreams of a famous son-in-law. If she had ever seriously entertained them, Rumbelow wondered. He could never understand how the minds of others worked. He envisaged human thought as the logical cause of human action, which was ridiculous. He still did not appreciate how Maria had nerved herself to lose the child at all costs. And how his sudden hate of her had engendered a hate against that part of him which was also part of herself. A hate no less revengeful for being beyond her power of expression, even in her own mind.

She was to leave on Friday, November the twenty-seventh. There were tickets to be bought from a bureau in Regent Street. She needed a passport. He signed the declaration of good character himself, as permitted to a medical practitioner, saying he had known her since childhood. He wondered about inoculations and vaccination, but apparently they were not demanded by the cleanly Swiss. The aeroplane was to leave at ten in the morning. It started a clear day. He hired a car to drive the pair of them to Croydon Aerodrome. The expense of the expedition was already staggering, a little more would make no difference.

At the door of the Customs shed, he said, 'Be brave.'

'I'll be glad when it's all over.'

'I'll be waiting with the car when you get back.'

'It's only a week. It hardly seems worth going.'

'Swiss doctors are very good. Everyone knows that. They've a splendid reputation throughout the world.'

She looked through the window pointing excitedly. 'Is that my air liner?'

'I'd presume so.'

'You sit *inside*. I thought I'd have my head in the open, with goggles on, like you see in the pictures.'

'It's quite comfortable. You'll have something to eat. They carry a stewardess, you know, who serves a picnic lunch. You can even have hot coffee.'

'*Hot* coffee!' This amazed her most of all.

'There's no sign of yesterday's fog coming back. You should take off all right.'

'Perhaps I should be getting along?'

He glanced at a clock on the wall. 'Perhaps so.' He kissed her.

'Thank you, John. Thank you for everything.'

All the way back in the hired car he wondered why she had said that.

44

FOR THE NEXT week, every day seemed to dawn in hope and end in black anxiety. Rumbelow heard nothing of Maria whatever. From Croydon Aerodrome he might have dispatched her not to Geneva but to the moon. He had half-expected a card, a letter, even a telephone call. But he kept telling himself she would be kept in bed, in no position to communicate with her distant homeland. He worried that everything had gone well. Death on the table during a therapeutic abortion, for tuberculosis and the like, was far from unknown. And what about her family? They would have expected at least a picture-postcard from the country. They might worry, even talk to the newspapers, or report the pair of them to Scotland Yard. When she got back, she would have to rest in bed for a day or two after the exhaustion of the flight. Then everything would come out. But once the deed was done, he didn't give a damn.

He could console himself only with the internationally acclaimed excellence of Swiss doctors. His work meanwhile went to bits. He had still not been back to Blackfriars. He started turning down coroners' cases, not caring if they were snapped up by others. He spent much of the time in his flat, or idly walking the streets in the fog which seemed to have settled on London permanently. He started marking off days on a calendar, something he had never done before.

While Maria was still away, on Thursday, December the third, he was summoned to the Law Courts in the Strand as expert witness in a long-drawn-out compensation case finally come to trial. As often happened, the unsolvable dispute was settled between opposing counsel with the judge's encouragement after an hour or two. Rumbelow was not called to give evidence. As he walked out through the cathedral-like hall of the courts, filled with hurrying barristers, litigants, blue-uniformed porters, and inevitable hangers-on, he ran into Peter Ivors.

'It's a bad business, isn't it?' Ivors said at once. He was in wig and gown, smoking a cigarette. Rumbelow stared, wondering how he had learnt of Maria. 'About the King. All over this morning's papers. It came as a terrible shock to me. I hadn't heard a word about it.'

'It's been brewing for months, I believe. I met an American reporter down at Mortlock, who hinted something was in the air. I still can't understand why our own Press never breathed a word.'

'I suppose they were entitled to exercise discretion. We can't print anything distasteful about our Monarch, you know.'

'Nor the Germans about Hitler.'

'That's not at all the same thing.'

'Isn't it?'

'Ah, your usual severe view of life, John. Though I admit, all this is bad for the Empire.'

'If it comes to an abdication, we may find ourselves without one.'

'I sometimes think of you as our prime minister of pessimism. I suppose that's unavoidable, with your job. The Empire will stick together, don't worry. It always does. And Baldwin's no fool.'

'By the way, when's the Jeavons appeal coming up?'

'It's down for hearing on the fourteenth. That's Monday week. Their Lordships have a rather severe backlog.'

'How will it go?'

'I can't see how they'll upset Easterbrook. I suppose Younghusband will make something of that Welsh chemist's finding no arsenic in the body. He could claim the trial judge misdirected the jury, by not emphasizing this sufficiently. But it's pretty thin. No, she'll go down, all right.'

'What about the fuss – all those petitions?'

'That's a different kettle of fish.'

'Do you suppose the Home Secretary will order a reprieve?'

'I honestly don't know what Simon will do. Though I doubt it. This country doesn't like poisoners.'

'You also said it didn't like hanging pretty women.'

'She's out of sight now. She's no longer human, only an abstract quantity. Nobody loses their appetite through killing off an idea. I suppose you'll be at the execution?'

'When's it to be?'

'Before Christmas, I suppose. They can hardly expect her to spend a particularly festive time in the condemned cell.'

'At Holloway?'

'I don't fancy the authorities would think that at all right. She'll have to be executed where she is, down near Mortlock. As they'll have her in Holloway during the appeal, it seems a pity they can't save her a journey.' They had reached the plate-glass doors giving on to the Strand. 'John, I heard you were in some sort of personal trouble. I do hope it isn't true?'

Rumbelow felt a sinking inside. 'What kind of trouble?'

Ivors gave a short laugh. 'That you'd committed some crime or other.'

'But how ridiculous! Who told you that?'

'I can't be sure. There's a rumour going round. You know how it is. I think my clerk told me. Yes, that's it, my clerk. They tell you everything.'

'I have done nothing illegal in my life. Nor shall I.'

'Oh, I'm sure you haven't. We're all doing too well out of the law to bite the hand that feeds us, aren't we? But I must say – I didn't want to mention this, John, after all you're the doctor, not me – but you're looking pretty run down. In my eyes, at any rate. I noticed you were overstrung down in Mortlock. Why don't you ease up for a bit, take a holiday?'

'I am having something of a rest at the moment.'

'I'm delighted to hear it. Look – why not come down to us in the country. Say the week-end after next? We could get some golf.'

'I can't play golf. I can't play any games. They've never interested me.'

'I'll teach you. It's terribly simple. Think it over. Give me a ring at my chambers.'

293

'Very well. I'll see if I can fit it in.'

Ivors made towards the barristers' robing-room. Rumbelow stepped into the street. Tomorrow Maria would be home and his anxieties over. He might even think seriously of taking up Ivors' invitation. For the moment, he couldn't see beyond the following afternoon.

He drove in another hired car to Croydon. As soon as he saw her, he was shocked. She was pale, drawn, miserable, shivering, ill. He helped her into the car, the chauffeur tucking the rug round her knees. He noticed her skin was hot.

'What's the matter? Did something go wrong? Wasn't the operation a success?'

'I don't know. I just feel queer.'

'When did all this start? It's important. Try to remember.'

'Only this morning. Perhaps last night.'

'You should have stayed in the clinic. They should never have let you go.'

'I wanted to come home. Anyway, I wasn't too bad till I got on the aeroplane. It was very bumpy.'

'Perhaps it's only airsickness.'

'Yes, perhaps it is.'

'The operation – it achieved its object, did it?'

'Oh, that was all right.'

She fell silent. In a few minutes, he noticed that she was sleeping heavily. He rapped on the glass partition of the Daimler. They were bound for her parents' home in Muswell Hill, but he redirected the man to his block of flats. He had to rouse her as they drew up. When she asked, 'Where am I?' he reassured her it was only a break in the journey.

In the flat, she slumped into the armchair and started to shiver. Rumbelow ransacked the drawers of his desk for a clinical thermometer. He shook down the mercury, and she neither objected nor even seemed surprised when he thrust it under her tongue. For three agonized minutes he waited. She had a temperature of a hundred and four. He was terrified.

'Your temperature – was it up in the clinic?'

'I don't know.' She lay back listlessly, her eyes shut. 'They use different numbers. They didn't seem to worry.'

294

'Which day did you have the operation? Which day exactly?' He shook her. 'Try to remember. It's essential.'

'It would be . . . Saturday. The day after I arrived. In the afternoon. I had to see a lot of doctors first.'

Rumbelow picked up the telephone, looking at his watch. Sir George Smallpenny would still be at his consulting-rooms in Wimpole Street.

Their conversation was brief. Rumbelow turned back to Maria. 'I've just been speaking to another doctor. A gynae-cologist.'

'I know. The one we went to see.' She still had her eyes closed.

'No, you don't know him, though I do myself, very well. He thinks you should go into hospital. Just for a few days, you understand.'

'Aren't I going home?'

'Later, later. We must get you well first.'

'What about mum? She's expecting me.'

'I'll get in touch with her. Come along. The car's still waiting.'

He pulled her from the chair and bundled her through the door, as if every second counted.

'Which hospital?'

'Blackfriars.'

'Oh . . . that'll be nice.'

They put her in a small side-room off the ward, to keep her in isolation – with the added, slim hope of avoiding gossip. Sir George drove back from Wimpole Street. After examining her, he walked with Rumbelow slowly down the corridor.

'There's a secondary infection of the uterus and the Fallopian tubes, I'm afraid, John. It's damned bad luck on the poor girl.'

Rumbelow was unable to say anything. He noticed that Sir George hadn't questioned him about an abortion, nor about his part in the affair at all. He seemed considerately to forget hearing of any connexion between the pair of them.

'I gathered from the patient it was one of the Swiss jobs,' said Sir George.

295

'Yes, in Lausanne. It's perfectly legal there.'

'Oh, of course. Has she parents, relatives, or anyone else in London?'

'Yes, her mother and father live in the suburbs.'

'Do they know of her plight?'

'I was about to tell them. I've hardly had a chance. It's barely three hours since I collected her from the aeroplane.'

'Yes, I think they should know pretty soon. You might ask them to come and see her.'

Rumbelow's terror increased. 'Is she in danger?'

'I can't disguise that, can I?'

'But is there septicaemia?'

'We won't know until we get a blood-culture back from the lab. My house-surgeon's taking a specimen now.'

'You know, don't you? On clinical signs?'

'Well, she's having rigors, and her temperature's pretty high. And there's albumen in a catheter specimen.'

'What're her chances?'

'Some of them recover.'

'Damn few.'

'It depends a lot on the nursing. She can't be better off than here.'

They had reached the end of the corridor. 'I thought that in Switzerland . . . where everything was done properly and above board . . .'

'Infection's always difficult to keep out. The tissues are abnormally vascular, of course, at the time of operation. I'm afraid the fact that the procedure is perfectly legal doesn't automatically exclude bacterial contamination.'

'So we can only wait?'

Sir George nodded. 'It's sad, but there just isn't any remotely effective treatment. I'm sorry, John, but there it is. It's no good my trying to sugar the facts for *you*. I've told my houseman to telephone my home if there's any change. He's a sensible chap, and I can rely on him. I'll be in like a shot, of course.'

He gave Rumbelow a reassuring grip on the arm, and made his way downstairs. Rumbelow wished the gynaecologist had stayed with him – or that someone had, someone friendly in a

296

world which had so suddenly and resolutely turned hostile. He wondered if he should go back to see Maria. Then he remembered her parents. They had no telephone, so he would have to wire. Appearing in person was impossible. He stood in the empty corridor, staring at the floor of polished marble, hands clasped tightly in front of him. 'I'm broken, broken, broken. . . .' He stood repeating it, twenty or thirty times, until someone walked past and stared at him.

He went slowly down to his laboratory. It was exactly as he had left it. He picked up the old-fashioned telephone and dictated a wire. He supposed her parents would be after him, but whatever they said or did was now only a minor irritation. He put the telephone back in its usual place on the windowsill, looking round the familiar little room, unable to believe how disastrously everything outside had changed and how he had changed himself.

Then he remembered Bantrell.

45

RUMBELOW KNEW THAT BANTRELL lived in a large Edwardian block of mansion-flats in the Marylebone Road, not far from Regent's Park. At that hour, he would be at home eating his dinner. Or if he were out, someone would know how to reach him. The heavy, highly-polished oak door on the fifth floor was opened by a girl wearing a black satin dress with lace apron and cap.

'Can I see Dr Bantrell, please?'

'Was the doctor expecting you, sir?'

He heard the noise of cheerful voices inside. The Bantrells were holding a dinner-party. He supposed that a rising fashionable physician had to give a good many. 'I'm not a guest. It's a professional matter.'

'Are you a patient, sir?'

'I've come about a patient. My name's Dr Rumbelow. It's a matter of some urgency.'

'Just a minute, sir.' The maid seemed used to dramatic interruptions of the Bantrells' home-life.

Rumbelow stood in the small hall-way. He shivered. It was a cold night, and until on his way had forgotten that both overcoat and bowler-hat were up at Sir George's ward. He had asked the Blackfriars' gate-porter to find him a taxi. Rumbelow's foibles being better-known than he imagined, the man had looked as amazed as if asked for a sedan chair.

Bantrell appeared almost at once, in a dinner-jacket.

'I'm afraid this is very inconvenient,' Rumbelow apologized.

'No, no, we've almost finished eating.'

'You must be surprised – my bearding you in your den.'

'It's about our lamentable affair at Blackfriars, is it?' Bantrell was perfectly courteous, even affable.

'No, it's not about that at all.'

'Isn't it? I couldn't imagine anything else which would bring you here. You'd better come into my room.'

Bantrell opened the door of a small study. It had shelves of books, a desk with a tidy arrangement of papers and a pile of white-covered *Lancets*, two photographs of a Teutonic-looking castle on the wall. The Countess' family *schloss*, Rumbelow supposed.

'That affair at Blackfriars between us,' said Rumbelow. 'It was trivial, nothing at all, compared with my reason for coming tonight.'

Bantrell glanced at him with concern. 'I say, you don't look too good. Have you had an accident, or something?' Rumbelow shook his head. 'Will you take a scotch? No? Well, sit down, anyway, while I have one myself. I'll have missed the brandy stage in there.'

Bantrell took a heavy cut-glass decanter from the cabinet at his elbow. Rumbelow said, 'I want some sulphanilamide.'

Bantrell raised his ginger eyebrows. 'What, have you cut yourself doing a p.m.?'

'It's not for me. It's for a young woman. You know her. Maria Osgood. She used to be in the library.'

'Yes, I remember.' Bantrell paused. From his expression, Rumbelow knew he had seen that hurtful student's drawing. 'I'm sorry to hear she's ill.'

'She's very ill. She's in Smallpenny's ward with streptococcal septicaemia. It's the result of a septic abortion, performed last week at a clinic in Switzerland. Performed quite legally, you understand.'

'I see.'

'I will save you the embarrassment of asking my interest in the affair. If an embarrassment it would be. I am the man responsible.'

'It *would* have been an embarrassment.' Bantrell looked serious. 'Quite apart from the unfortunate girl, I don't care to see a colleague in such straits.'

'*Former* colleague.'

Bantrell made a small accommodating gesture. 'What's the temperature?'

'A hundred and four. More by now. Oh, all the physical signs are there.'

'Does Smallpenny give much hope?'

'There isn't any to give.'

Bantrell reached for a silver box, heavy and ornate – like everything else in the flat, Rumbelow noticed. As Rumbelow refused a cigar, Bantrell cut one and lit it in silence. 'Look, old man, you've put me in a bit of a fix.'

'You've got some sulphanilamide. You're using it in a trial on septicaemic cases at Blackfriars. I'm only asking you to add Maria Osgood to your series.'

'It couldn't be an addition. It would be a replacement. There's hardly any of the drug in the country, you know. I'm able to use it only with very few patients. Each carefully selected on his clinical merits.'

'You mean, this girl is going to die instead of somebody else?'

'I wish you hadn't put it like that.'

They sat for a moment in silence, Rumbelow looking at the glowing end of Bantrell's cigar.

'Some people are more likely to benefit from sulphanilamide than others, Rumbelow. It's exactly the same with any drug, new or old, isn't it? The condition of each patient needs the most careful study before a decision is made to use it. I'm conducting an investigation, remember. I'm not using sulphanilamide primarily for therapy. Not at all. And I know nothing of this girl's case whatever, apart from what you've just told me.'

'You could go to the hospital and examine her.'

'Quite frankly, it seems already too late. There's a deal of work to be done first – typing organisms, and so on. Anyway, there's another complication. Unless I receive fresh supplies in the next twenty-four hours, I can't even continue treating the patients I have. I'll just have to withdraw it, and they'll possibly die. So I can't risk diverting my precious store to a new case.'

'You're just making excuses.'

'No, I'm not,' Bantrell said calmly.

'You're denying the girl this drug because you don't like me. That's right, isn't it? Because you were angry with me, over that business of the death certificate. Very well, I give in, I concede your point. You were right and I was wrong. Is that good enough for you?'

'That has nothing to do with my present decision whatever.'

'I've resigned from the staff. You've got me out of Blackfriars. Isn't that good enough for you, too?'

Bantrell raised his voice. 'I told you, that quarrel not so much as crossed my mind in deciding whether or not to put the girl on sulphanilamide. It was a decision dictated purely by clinical necessities.'

'You're lying. Ever since you've been on the staff at Blackfriars you've been against me, stirring up trouble for me, spreading gossip like poison, running down my work, trying to break me. I don't know why. I've never troubled myself to find your reasons. I can only suppose it's something in your character.'

Bantrell stood up. 'God! I've never known anyone so stiffnecked. You're right, the rest of the world's wrong. That's your view, isn't it?'

'I've been proved right often enough.'

'Proved right in court. What's that mean, one way or another? That's all artificial, rules, tricks, mumbo-jumbo. It's not the world.'

'So there's no place in your world, is there, for truth and justice?'

'Truth and justice! It's a game, chess, bridge, poker. The cleverest player wins. I'm a realist. I respect those ideals as much as you do, Rumbelow, but I don't let myself become anaesthetized with them.'

Rumbelow stood up too. 'Very well. You will not release any of the drug?'

'No.'

'Then I'll go over your head. To Professor Colebrook at the Middlesex.'

'I'm nothing to do with Colebrook.'

'That's not the truth. He's doing the only official trial in the country. The M.R.C. sends all available supplies to him.'

'I get my supplies direct. Through the Leopoldpalast in Berlin.' Bantrell looked away slightly. 'As you may know, that's the Ministry for Propaganda and Public Enlightenment. Luckily, I have an uncle there. He has eased the way. The Reich Foreign Office quite favours the idea. Oh, it's a great privilege.'

'I see. You're establishing your reputation, by being one of the first to use sulphanilamide in the country. You get it for this purpose from the Nazis.'

'I will ignore your remark about making a name for myself.' Bantrell was speaking calmly again. 'I certainly look to Germany for my supplies. Why not? Why do you blame me? After all, it's a German drug. You know it was invented by Domagk, in Elberfeld last year. As for the Nazis . . . there's a lot of hot air talked in London, of course. But I for one have yet to meet someone unable to admit they've a lot of good ideas.'

'And you talked just now of justice and truth,' said Rumbelow quietly. Then he did something which was never in his mind, and a second later he couldn't explain to himself. He hit Bantrell's cheek with his palm.

Bantrell stood impassively, cigar trailing smoke between his fingers. With his other hand he took a white silk handkerchief from the top pocket of his dinner jacket and slowly wiped the red mark, as though cleansing himself from Rumbelow's contamination. 'You'd better go,' he said quietly.

Rumbelow turned, left the flat, hurried down the stairs and walked into the darkness. Only when the cold of the December night brought him to a stop was he forced again to think. Maria was certainly going to die. Just as certainly as Mrs Jeavons.

46

MARIA LINGERED FOR six more days. Perhaps the excellence of the Blackfriars nursing kept her alive, or perhaps it was her own toughness. Rumbelow never regained any doubt that her finger-tips would slip eventually from the rim of the world. He knew the 'will to live', some force of the mind influencing the diseased body, was only hopeful nonsense. She became anaemic, wore an ugly purplish rash, and developed abscesses in her knee-joint, below her right lung, finally in the sac round her heart. She died just before six in the evening, on Thursday, December the tenth. Rumbelow was in a small room outside the ward, part laboratory and part waiting-room. Her parents came in. The mother was already dressed in black, and weeping. The father wore the same blue suit. During Maria's illness they had acquired a dignity Rumbelow could never have imagined. He no longer thought them laughable. He was frightened of them.

'She's gone,' said the father.

Rumbelow stood, hands folded, staring at the floor. 'I'm sorry.' That was all it seemed possible to say.

'You used her for your pleasure, and you killed her.'

A few days before, the sentence would have struck him as quaint and amusing. Now he accepted it as a simple statement of fact. 'I'm sorry,' he repeated.

'This isn't the end of the matter.'

'I shouldn't wish it to be. There will be an inquest on your daughter. It will be in two or three days' time. I shall be attending as a witness – as an ordinary witness.'

'I hope they send you to jail.'

'I shall suffer disgrace. That's a worse punishment.'

'Perhaps it is. For someone who's always had it soft.'

He took his wife, and led her away. Rumbelow stood in the little room, waiting for them to be well out of sight. Maria's death had not moved him. He had suffered the shock of it when he first took her temperature in his flat, knowing the mercury pronounced the sentence. He felt no grief, and it was not in him to pretend he did. He had never loved her. The father was perfectly right. He had used her and killed her. He felt only guilt and debasement, emotions the more agonizing for being strange, loathed and frightening.

He took out his watch. He started along the corridor and down the stairs to the main courtyard. He wondered which London coroner would conduct the inquest, as he knew them all. He preferred not to speculate on the newspapers afterwards. There was at least no criminal charge they could lay against him. Nothing in the slightest illegal had been done. But he was finished. He tried to see a future not black to eternity, but it was difficult. After all, he was a first-rate pathologist. Even his enemies, even Bantrell, must give him that. There was always need of pathologists while civilized man kept himself alive through studying the death of his fellows – that was the very basis of scientific medicine, ever since the first anatomists broke the thralldom of the Church. Perhaps he could get some minor official post. Perhaps with Major Standring and his Air Raid Precautions. Being Rumbelow, he tried to comfort himself with logic. But he was learning at last that the world continues at all only by remaining perversely irrational.

His steps led automatically to his laboratory. He went inside, sitting again on the familiar high stool, his microscope tilted in position as he had left it. Now Maria was dead, he told himself, he must recover his balance, turn to the everyday business of life. Before his resignation became effective at the end of the month he must clear out the lab, taking away his filing-cabinets. He had started to open a drawer of files, when there was a knock on the door.

He was surprised. No one knew he was in the lab, or even in Blackfriars. 'Come in.'

The visitor was Quinley. It was the first time Rumbelow had

set eyes on him since leaving for the Jeavons trial at Mortlock. He noticed the young man's boils looked rather better.

'Might I have a word with you, sir?'

'How did you find I was here?'

'I knew you were up at Sir George's ward. I waited till you came down and I saw you cross the courtyard.'

Rumbelow drew out a pile of files in manilla folders, laying them neatly on the workbench. 'Anything important?'

Quinley stood in his white coat, arms dangling, looking lost. 'Yes. It is.'

'Well? Can you be brief? I've had a very unhappy day.'

'I've been using this lab in your absence, sir. I've been checking your findings.'

'What do you mean?'

'In the Jeavons case. That zinc you used . . . for the Marsh test. It's contaminated. With arsenic. That's not uncommon, is it? You must have forgotten to test your materials before starting the analysis.'

'How the devil dare you accuse me of something like that?'

'I tested it,' said Quinley simply.

'Why? Why did you go behind my back? I'm still a consultant here, you know. You'd better get that into your head. I can still cause trouble for you, before I finally walk out of the place.'

'I tested it because I suspected there was something wrong with the case. I don't know why, exactly. It just seemed fishy.'

'If you entertained those suspicions you should have told me, to my face. How long have you been sneaking about in my footsteps?'

'Only after you'd left it came into my mind to confirm anything. I admired your work, sir. Quite honestly, I did. I learnt an enormous lot from you.'

'Well, you're wrong about the zinc.' Rumbelow paused. 'You think I dished your chances for the readership job, don't you?'

'I don't think that at all.'

'Yes, you do. You're against me, you and all the others. You're always trying to find a new stick to beat me with.'

'That just isn't true, sir.'

'Well, none of you need bother any more. I've done your job myself. I'm disgraced, finished, broken. You know the story. Nobody will have wasted time putting it round the hospital. Now get out and leave me in peace.'

Quinley went on, 'It isn't only the Jeavons case. Once I could look round this lab without being stopped like a thief. . . .' He stared at Rumbelow, frightened by what he was saying. But Rumbelow was leaning against the workbench, arms folded, his face now expressionless.

'Then there was that homosexual who shot his friend. The Tilling case. Tilling said it was suicide, didn't he? I've been through your case notes, in the cabinet there. I found a key which would open it, don't ask me how. You got Tilling hanged on the direction the bullet took. You got your facts from firing at a skeleton. One strung up for the anatomists, the ribs held together by wire. In the living human it's not the same at all. The muscles pull the ribs into different positions entirely. I tested it in the p.m. room, running wires into the bodies then compressing the chests. I got one of the house-surgeons to put a long spinal needle into the wall of my own chest, and had it X-rayed. The bullet may have come from the angle you said it did, across the room. But . . . well, there could be doubt, sir, you must admit. I've the X-ray picture up in my room, if you want to see it —'

'I'm indebted to you for your observations,' said Rumbelow quietly. Quinley seemed to have exhausted himself. 'It's a pity you didn't make them earlier. Then we could have checked my own work and your experiments on it together. The needle in your own chest-wall was an extremely bright idea.'

Quinley slowly stroked his cheek, disfigured by the puckered skin of past boils. 'Have you nothing else to say to me, sir?'

'No.'

'I'm afraid you must be very angry.'

'No scientist is angry at another contradicting his results. On the contrary, he welcomes it. That is the only way to approach perfection.'

'You don't take me seriously?'

306

'I do. In this context, at least.'

'Then what's to be done about the Jeavons case?'

'You've no more to add? No more than that the zinc was contaminated with arsenic in the first place?'

'Nothing more, sir.'

Rumbelow remained silent, arms still folded. Slowly, looking more miserable than ever, Quinley left the laboratory. As the door shut, Rumbelow opened the glass-fronted cupboard where he kept his chemical apparatus. His movements again precise and quick, he set up the flask with its thistle-shaped funnel and long, angled tube for the Marsh test. Into the flask he tipped a little metallic zinc, from the same bottle used when testing organs from Jeavons' exhumed body. He ran in the dilute sulphuric acid, watching as the mixture bubbled with hydrogen. He lit a Bunsen burner, placing it in the middle of the angled tube. He took out his watch. There was half an hour to wait.

He sat on the high stool, hands clasped in his lap, staring blankly at the frosted glass of the window. He did not turn his eyes until the full thirty minutes were up. Then he looked at the tube beyond the flame. A faint deposit, brownish-coloured against the flame, then passing through steely grey to jet black. Arsenic.

Rumbelow turned off the Bunsen.

'I didn't test this zinc.' He spoke aloud. 'I didn't forget. I didn't want to test it. I wanted to find arsenic. That's what it is. I wanted to.'

Suddenly a load rolled from his brain and the whole of life became brilliantly crystal-clear.

47

RUMBELOW HAD THREE letters to write on the Flying Scotsman from King's Cross to Edinburgh the following morning. The first was to Peter Ivors.

Dear Peter,
    You will have heard by now of the letter I left at the Home Office last night. I thought that the correct manner in which to make my move. Whether it will simply be admitted as fresh evidence at Mrs Jeavons' appeal, or whether she is released immediately, strikes me as a matter for the Home Secretary.
    Mrs Jeavons would seem to have a case for compensation by the Crown. It will be of interest whether her claim is limited from the moment of her conviction, or from her arrest. There will doubtless be not only considerable legal but political repercussions. But I think Sir John Simon will ride the storm. Anyway, Mrs Jeavons will certainly do handsomely selling her life-story to the newspapers.
    I made a mistake. I am sorry, when you yourself put so much work into the case. I may have made mistakes in the past. That is more than possible. But at least this one can be rectified.
    I am also sorry that I'm not able to play golf with you.
                    Yours,
                      John.

The second was to Major Standring, at the Air Raid Precautions Department of the Home Office.

Dear Major Standring,
    The air-raid shelters should be of metal, preferably of corrugated steel, which can be assembled from sections and sunk in people's gardens. They

*would be cheap, and most valuable if war comes. Please put this idea up
to your people.*

*You might also mention in the proper quarters that I have decided
from a study of my notes the drop should be increased by one inch in all
cases. This will make hanging more humane.*

Yours sincerely,

John Rumbelow.

He started the third one to his wife.

Dearest Rosemary,
I have always loved you. . . .

He stopped. It was so difficult, conveying such concepts on
paper with any exactitude. The words meant different things to
different people, and at different times. If they had any meaning
at all. Would she expect him to write that? Did it really matter
or not, her knowing he loved her? Did he know himself? Once
he believed he knew what love meant. But like much else in his
life, that was an expression of his own over-confidence. He
crumpled the paper, let down the leather strap, and threw it out
of the window.

Rumbelow settled back with the morning's paper. King
Edward was abdicating. He would be broadcasting that night
to the Empire as a private individual, Mr Edward Windsor, and
was expected to leave the country afterwards for an unknown
destination. He was succeeded by his brother, who nobody
seemed to know much about but had a lovely wife and two
pretty little daughters, pictured playing in the garden. Were
Mrs Jeavons immediately released, Rumbelow wondered if she
would get much space after all. A dining-car attendant put his
head in the compartment to announce lunch. Rumbelow was
going first-class, even if he wasn't on official business.

In Edinburgh that evening, he carried his attaché case from
Waverley station to the small hotel where he had reserved a
room by telegram. It was the one he had stayed at before, and
the staff remembered him. He was shown to a pleasant single
room on the first floor. 'We're still serving tea, sir,' said the
porter.

'I've a good deal of work to do. I'll step out and find a meal somewhere later.'

'Very good, sir. Sad about the King, sir, isn't it?'

'Yes. Very sad.'

It was chilly. Rumbelow lit the gas-fire. He left his case unopened, sitting with arms folded on the bed, still in his overcoat. It was all part of a process, he thought, perfectly logical when looked at sensibly. It had started that night in Diana Flavell's flat and ended with Maria's death and the contaminated zinc. Things which had seemed unrelated, or even passing irritations – his wife's leaving, her brief return to London, Dr Halverston's tantrums, Evan Greensmith's pen – they were all meaningful parts of it. It was like the manifestation in various organs of a single, generalized disease. Like the abscesses and the fever which killed Maria.

After some fifteen minutes Rumbelow stood up abruptly and took his overcoat off. He started to undress, removing jacket, shoes, collar and tie. He stopped, collar in hand, wondering exactly why. He picked up the eiderdown and laid it along the bottom of the door. He lifted the curtain and turned the catch on the closed window. He switched off the gas-fire, waited a minute for the mantles to cool so they would not re-light, then turned on the gas again and lay on the bed. He laid his brother's watch on the table beside him. Ten minutes would be enough. Well, he would never have to admit publicly he was wrong. And through a legal quirk, in Scotland suicide was not a crime. When there was ringing in his ears and his head was bursting, his last thought was that he had never in his life broken the law.

48

DR URRICK HAD a different system than followed at Blackfriars. At noon he came into his post-mortem room, brisk as usual, bibbed red rubber apron tied round his waist, pulling on yellow rubber gloves. He was accompanied only by one young assistant in a white coat, report-form clipped to a board, fountain-pen in hand, ready to take notes as Urrick went along.

'Oh, the fellow was really a bit of a fool. The public's right, in its heart. It always is. The greatest experts are the crassest blunderers in life. Never trust an expert. Though he did the right thing in the end for the Jeavons woman, we must allow him that much.' Urrick started arranging his instruments. 'Do you know what his real trouble was? He never understood people. He never saw they were human entities, who ate and drank and frolicked with their girls, and had passion running in their veins. He thought we were all the theoretical concepts of a lot of lawyers. That's a depressing idea, isn't it?'

He picked up his long scalpel.

'But God knows how many poor folk went to the gallows because of his ignorance and pig-headedness. Maybe he's been introduced to a few of them up there by now?' Urrick gave the laugh which had always so irritated Rumbelow. 'Though mind you, it wasn't all *his* fault. The law let him get away with it. Well, if there can be worse, prejudiced, blind fools in the world than some of us doctors, it's the whole lot of the lawyers.'

Urrick adjusted the tip of one glove-finger. 'Do you know his greatest virtue? He was an enormous snob. That was his only human frailty, and alone it raised him to what he became. It's a powerful thing, snobbery. More than love or money any day of the week.'

Urrick made the sweep from chin to pubis, through skin bright pink from the coal-gas, exposing the organs which God distributes with impartial exactitude among the two fundamental divisions of His creatures, the judges and the judged.